J

By Fate's Design

Delia Parr

St. Martin's Paperbacks

BY FATE'S DESIGN

Copyright © 1996 by Mary Lechleidner.

ISBN: 0-312-95926-5

Printed in the United States of America

St. Martin's Paperbacks edition / September 1996

10 9 8 7 6 5 4 3 2 1

Dedicated to

Jennifer Enderlin

An uncommon editor
whose heart overflows with
joy for the craft of writing,
enthusiasm for the romance genre,
and encouragement for her authors.

We are all truly blessed.

Prologue

S truggling with an oversized travel bag cradled in both arms, seven-year-old JoHannah Sims suddenly lurched and froze in place. Monstrous shadows leaped into the dormitory-styled sleeping room and lunged at her feet. Her heart thumping, a scream caught in her throat and her bottom lip began to quiver. She fought the swell of tears that flooded her eyes and blurred her vision as two grotesque, silhouetted figures with capped heads and baggy gowns blocked the doorway, momentarily cutting off most of the light filtering into the room from the outer hall.

JoHannah hugged the travel bag to her chest and backed up against her assigned cot, the first in a row of four that hugged the wall opposite the only door to the room. As the women walked toward her, she closed her eyes. Tears rolled down her cheeks as she braced for the blows the women would deliver to punish her for trying to run away.

Mama! Papa! I need you!

When a cold hand cupped her cheek, she flinched, her eyes snapped open, and she gasped. Distorted eyes behind

thick spectacles stared at her, and she tried to stop her knees
from knocking together as she pulled her face out of reach.
Blinking hard, she recognized Sister Regina, caretaker for
all the girls who shared the room with JoHannah, crouching
down low in front of her. Shuddering, too afraid to breathe
or cry out, she bit her lower lip.

"What are you doing, child?"

JoHannah gulped, fearing that a lie would only add to
her punishment. "I'm . . . I'm going home."

"Your home is with us now."

The clipped reprimand did not sway her, and she shook
her head. "I want to go home."

"The child isn't deliberately trying to be contrary. She's
just too young to understand all that's happened," the other
woman counseled as she took a step closer.

JoHannah looked up, recognized Sister Lucy, and took a
step back, watching apprehensively as Sister Regina stood
up and the two women bent their heads together. She
strained to hear their whispered conversation, wondering
what sort of punishment they were planning for her; instead, she heard words that only added to her confusion.

"It's only been a week since her parents died and her
guardian brought her to us. Give her time, Sister Regina.
She's as confused by the sudden loss of her parents as she
is by the strangeness of our ways."

"That's no excuse to run off and frighten us all half to
death. We've been searching for her for nearly an hour.
The other children will be tempted—"

"The other girls are busy helping Sister Claire in the
kitchen," Sister Lucy noted gravely. "They probably
haven't even noticed JoHannah isn't with them, and they
certainly don't need to know what happened." She pursed
her lips and shook her head. "If adults find death very
difficult to comprehend, let alone accept, how can we expect a child as young as JoHannah to understand it?"

Taking a deep breath, Sister Regina glanced down at

JoHannah. "I know you want to go home," she cautioned, "but your guardian wants you to stay here with us."

Guardian? Is that the wicked man with the scary face who took me away from home and brought me here to live with the Shakers?

JoHannah's shoulders stiffened. "I want to go home. I want to be with my mama and papa."

Bending down, Sister Regina put her hand on Jo-Hannah's shoulder. "I know you miss your parents, but they've gone to heaven to be with the Heavenly Father and all His angels."

The sister's explanation sounded familiar. Hadn't the freckle-faced man in the black suit told her the same thing just before the man sister called her "guardian" took her away?

Her head began to ache, and her nose started to run.

There had to be some kind of terrible mistake. Even if her parents had gone to heaven, they would never have wanted that wicked man to bring her to this strange place.

She yawned, suddenly tired and wanting very much to curl up in her papa's lap and go to sleep. Her arms tingled and ached, and she dropped her travel bag to the floor. Sniffling, she wiped her nose on the sleeve of her gown. Didn't anyone understand how much she wanted and needed to live in her own home?

Her eyes welled with tears, and she tried not to cry. "Please. Will you take me home?"

Sister Lucy knelt down beside Sister Regina and tilted JoHannah's face up. "It's growing late and it's very dark outside. It would be hard to find our way tonight. Maybe you should stay . . . just for tonight."

When JoHannah started to shake her head, Sister Regina added, "Tomorrow isn't very far away, is it?"

JoHannah looked back and forth from the night-darkened, curtainless window to the faces of the two women in front of her. While the sisters no longer frightened her, she still was not certain she could trust them. ''Are you sure you'll take me home tomorrow?''

Sister Lucy smiled. ''Why don't you put your travel bag under your bed? Just for tonight. We'll have some hot cocoa, and then we'll pray about this together before you get a good night's sleep.''

''Perhaps tomorrow,'' Sister Regina interjected, ''we should take a break from our normal routine. After school and chores, we could plant your tree. Every child has one. We even put your name on it. Would you like to do that?''

JoHannah took a deep breath. Maybe if she did what the sisters asked, they would keep their promise to take her home tomorrow. Reluctantly, she slid her travel bag under her cot and turned to face them.

Sister Regina took one of JoHannah's hands while Sister Lucy grasped the other as they led her from the room. ''You must learn to be obedient, child,'' Sister Regina admonished, her voice as firm as Mama's when JoHannah needed a scolding. ''Your guardian has full authority over you now, and he sent you to us. We have rules that must be followed, and you must never run off like you did tonight.''

Hanging her head as they walked down the hall past numbered sleeping rooms and walls lined with peg boards holding sisters' capes and brethren's hats, JoHannah vowed to find a way to convince the sisters that her guardian was a mean and nasty man who had forced her to leave her home.

Her terror abated now, the echo of the footsteps of the sisters at her side brought back a happy memory. One night, not so very long ago, she had had a nightmare. She could almost feel her papa's strong arms around her, holding her, while Mama had gone down to the kitchen. And in the afterglow of a terrifying dream, she had heard footsteps mount the stairs as her mama carried a tray to JoHannah's room.

She wrinkled her nose and sniffed the air, and she could almost smell the delicious aroma of cocoa and cinnamon and taste the swirl of fresh cream in her cup. . . . A huge knot in her chest made it hard for her to breathe. *Mama.*

"Sister Regina?"

"What is it, little one?"

"Is there cream for my hot cocoa? My mama . . . my mama always put cream and cinnamon on top."

"Sister Lucy, do you think you could make that for JoHannah?"

"I suppose. Do you think you could show me how to make it, JoHannah?"

Her head bobbing up and down, JoHannah agreed.

"Don't you see?" Sister Regina said gently. "We truly do need you here to teach us new things. Maybe you can think about staying with us a bit longer."

Longing for her parents and her home where she had had her very own room with a ruffled canopied bed brought a new wave of tears that stung JoHannah's eyes. "Just till tomorrow," she whispered. "Then you can take me home."

Chapter 1

With an impish grin, JoHannah popped a small chunk of chocolate into her mouth, closed her eyes, and sighed as her favorite treat melted into pure pleasure. "Sumptuous and precious," she pronounced, licking her lips. She glanced at the patient seated next to her at a window overlooking a stand of trees that lined the road to the Shaker village and smiled.

Sister Evelyn, confined to the second floor infirmary that she usually supervised as the community's physician, stared at the two remaining slivers of candy nestled together in the brown paper wrapper that sat on her lap. "Where did you ever get the idea that chocolate was the proper remedy for lung congestion?"

JoHannah laughed and tucked a blanket around her mentor's shoulders. "Not from you, dear Sister. You have far too much devotion to the herbs in your cherished garden to give thought to anything else. It was a gift. A divinely inspired—"

"A false gift, more than likely, and I suspect it's just a clever way to indulge your sweet tooth. Or is it yet another ploy to keep me from getting back to my duties? I've trained you too well," she suggested, raising one brow. "I truly feel much bet—"

A series of chest-rattling coughs interrupted Sister Evelyn's latest protest and echoed ominously in the room. JoHannah quickly secured a draft of honeyed water which she raised to Sister Evelyn's lips as soon as the coughing subsided. "You can't even sit by the window for more than a few hours a day. Perhaps tomorrow..."

The physician shook her head and smiled. "That's what you said yesterday. And the day before. And still the day before that." Her eyes narrowed into glistening slits of gentle censure. "You've made the same promise now for nearly a week."

JoHannah laid her hand atop her mentor's folded hands, her pale skin a sharp contrast to the ebony, thick-veined hands of her beloved sister in faith—hands that once had been chained in slavery. She hugged their hands together, a bond of love and fellowship erasing all the boundaries that separated many World persons of different races.

She smiled. "Years ago, Sister Lucy and Eldress Regina convinced a very frightened little girl to stay here at Collier by stretching one tomorrow into nearly fourteen years."

Poignant memories of her first harrowing days at the Shaker community, softened by the patient wisdom of these two gentle Shaker sisters, brought tears to JoHannah's eyes. She swallowed hard, grateful for the tender love and life of faith she had found at Collier, a community that had once been so alien to her.

"And now you are nearly ready to sign the covenant." Sister Evelyn turned toward JoHannah. "Are you very sure that you are called to join us? On your next birthday in August, your indenture expires. You could... you could go home."

Muted recollections of a home not so very distant in

miles from where she sat flooded JoHannah's mind. She shook them away. "Collier is my home now," she responded, mindful that this joyful oasis of faith protected her from the outside World—a World that was full of temptation, pain, and sorrow.

"Unless your guardian thinks otherwise."

JoHannah smiled confidently. "He hasn't been to visit for several years. Even the Trustees haven't had any contact with him. I'm sure he's quite unconcerned about me." She chuckled. "But I haven't forgotten how you kept me talking for so long yesterday afternoon that you missed your nap. If I'm going to be a good assistant to you, I can't neglect my duties. I'll help you back to bed."

Sister Evelyn held up her hand. "Let me stay by the window. Just a while longer. I can't believe how dramatically the weather has changed. Two days ago, we had a frigid blast of sleet and heavy snow. Today, the sun is out, and it's as warm as springtime. It feels good to these old bones, and I enjoy watching nature's tricks. The snow is melting right before my eyes."

She paused and nodded toward the door. "Sister Lucy has been downstairs in the dispensary all morning. I shudder to think . . ." Shaking her head, she frowned, her large obsidian eyes misty. "Sister Lucy has such good intentions, but she does get befuddled rather easily when she's tired. Would you relieve her for a spell and send her upstairs?"

JoHannah's brows furrowed with mock sternness. "If I do, will you let her settle you into bed for a nap?"

"Of course," the physician said innocently.

Laughing out loud, JoHannah hesitated just long enough to make her reluctant acquiescence seem convincing. As she made her way down the sisters' staircase on the east side of the building, the kindness Sister Lucy had shown to JoHannah that eventful night so long ago washed over her. With sweet and gentle ways, and a bit of cocoa, Sister

Lucy had reached out and calmed JoHannah's desperate confusion. Now nearly ninety, she was the oldest Shaker sister at Collier, and for JoHannah, the most beloved of all.

When she reached the bottom stair, she adjusted the delicate lace cap that covered her hair and straightened the crisp, white shoulder kerchief that demurely hid most of the bodice of her aproned, lavender gingham gown. Visitors to Collier had rooms on the first floor near the dispensary, and she was even more determined to maintain a proper appearance when the World's people were nearby.

Humming softly, she proceeded down a long corridor to enter the dispensary which faced the main walkway in the village. Greeted by a pungent banquet of medicinal aromas that lay heavy in the air, her gaze skimmed the familiar room. Symmetrical wooden shelves filled with a rainbow assortment of bottles and jars of remedies lined the far wall. On a narrow counter, a small package lay waiting to be picked up. Sister Lucy, however, was not in the room. Making her way behind the counter through a storage area, JoHannah found her in a small workroom, totally absorbed in preparing a batch of witch hazel bark to be distilled.

It took little effort to convince the elderly sister to exchange places for the afternoon, and JoHannah quickly settled into her new task, but remained alert to her responsibilities should anyone come to the dispensary for medicine—yet another reason why the elderly sister would be better assigned to the infirmary. It was not unusual for the dispensary to be unattended for short periods of time, but JoHannah welcomed this unexpected opportunity to see sisters and brethren after being confined in the infirmary for several days.

Warm sunshine poured through the bare windows and splashed onto her work table, and she yearned for a breath of the fresh air that hinted at spring in a world whitened by snow. Unable to reach the windows without disturbing the pile of bark, she cracked open the rear door before resuming her work.

Thoroughly content now, she broke the bark into smaller fragments and realized that the Shakers had lovingly taken the terrifying and painful memories of her past and broken them into pieces small enough for a grieving child to handle—one day at a time. Like the bark of the witch hazel, which would be distilled to create a healing lotion, her life had been redeemed and transformed by the Shakers. Their strange customs had gradually become cherished traditions, and the gift of true faith a source of never-ending joy.

Community living had created a wider network of kin than would ever be possible in the World for JoHannah, and there was great comfort in knowing she would never again suffer the loss of her entire family in a single, tragic incident. Shaker traditions remained constant, surviving and growing stronger with the passage of both time and Believers. And unlike the nebulous character of the World, life at Collier was safe.

The echo of voices in the dispensary caught her attention, interrupting her work. Wiping her hands on her apron, she turned away from the table to walk back to the dispensary. As she entered the storage area, a nettled, frustrated male voice sounded a warning that shattered her tranquil world and slowed her steps: A World person was in the dispensary.

A gentler voice, which she recognized as Brother Avery's, calmed her racing heartbeat. A convert who just recently had signed the covenant, Brother Avery and the visitor were still out of her view, and she stopped, feeling awkward and very uncertain about overhearing their conversation which continued to argue tension between the two men.

When they suddenly came into her line of vision, she backed up against the wall in the storage room, reluctant to embarrass Brother Avery by making her presence known. Too late to retreat to the workroom without being noticed, she closed her eyes just long enough to say a quick silent prayer for peace between the two men.

To her dismay, the World man persisted. "I saw Abigail and Jane on their way to school this morning, even if I couldn't speak to them. How *are* your daughters, Avery? Or have you forsaken them, too?"

Like a blast of frigid air, the man's words chilled her body, and his harsh accusation pierced her heart. Eyes downcast, she stared at the planked floor, certain now that neither of the men was aware of her presence.

"I haven't forgotten my girls, Michael," Brother Avery countered softly. "I've given them new life. God's will is greater than mine. Or yours."

Michael. She had a name for this World person, but who was this man and why was he being so unkind to Brother Avery?

"God didn't claim Martha in childbirth to convince you to turn your back on your obligations so you could live . . . live like this!" Michael argued, so forcibly she could almost reach out and touch his chagrin.

"Three stillborn sons in four years. The last took half a day to die before he joined his mother in the grave." Brother Avery's voice cracked. "The flesh. Sins of the flesh," he murmured, almost too softly for JoHannah to hear him.

"Their deaths were not God's punishment! Abigail and Jane need their father's love, not some strange caretaker's. Come home. Give yourself more time to heal. With people who love you—"

"I have brothers and sisters now—"

"*I'm* your brother. Abigail and Jane are your own flesh and blood. They deserve to grow up at Lawne Haven where we did, just like every Lawne since 1645! As the first-born son, you have a responsibility to continue family tradition. And you can't move with some of these people to Kentucky. The idea is preposterous!"

Michael was Brother Avery's World brother? She sucked in her breath, suddenly very frightened that he would convince Brother Avery to return to the World. Almost too afraid to breathe, she held very still and prayed that Brother Avery would be true to his faith.

"I haven't turned my back on my family or tradition, Michael. Don't you understand anything I've said? I've opened my heart to the will of the Lord and embraced other Believers as my sisters and brothers in faith."

A sigh. A long stretch of painful silence. JoHannah's heart pounded in her chest. *Please, Heavenly Father, help this World man to accept Your will.*

"Come home, Avery. Lawne Haven is your birthright, not mine." Michael's voice had softened into a plea that touched the core of her soul, and she realized how very hard it must be for Michael, a non-Believer, to accept his brother's calling.

"My faith is my soul-right, dear brother. I'm sound of mind and joyful of heart, and I want you to turn your energies to continuing the traditions at Lawne Haven instead of trying to force me to return to a life I no longer want. Perhaps you're less concerned about me than you are about settling down and meeting your own responsibilities."

A harsh intake of breath told her Michael was offended. "I'll do what has to be done," he gritted. "I'll keep Lawne Haven and make it prosper. When you come to your senses, someday, I'll deed it back to you."

The sharp wind of Michael's voice had gratefully tapered into the gentler breeze of reluctant capitulation, and JoHannah's heartbeat slipped back to normal as she silently mouthed a prayer of thanksgiving.

Brother Avery, however, did not let the matter drop without a plea of his own. "Free your heart and mind from false hopes. You're not my guardian or my father. You're my *brother*, Michael. Let me live my life as I'm led."

Risking a quick glance, she saw Brother Avery walk toward the counter, pick up the package, and hand it to his brother, who had his back to her. "Take this medicine back home for Nora to help her rheumatism." He sighed. "She was like a second mother to me. Give her my love. Tell her . . . tell her the girls miss her, too."

Silence, long and painful, stretched for several tense minutes. The sound of an embrace as the two men obviously reconciled just before they took their leave of the dispensary allowed JoHannah the luxury of a soft sigh.

Realization that her presence had gone undetected washed added relief through JoHannah's body. Visibly shaking, she made her way back to the workroom. Too upset to resume her work, she slipped outside.

Shadows from the building, cold and penetrating, forced her out to the shoveled walkway where she lifted her face to feel the incredible warmth of the sun. She wrapped her arms around her waist and stared through snow-capped tree limbs at the dusty blue sky. The sound of snow melting to the earth and an icicle plopping to the ground broke through the silence of winter. Brother Avery's conversation with his World brother had shattered her confidence that she was safe from the World at Collier. What would happen if her guardian ever came to see her? Would he accept her decision to become a formal Believer as Brother Avery's brother had done? Or would he force her to leave?

Gratitude that Michael eventually had acquiesced to his brother's decision filled her spirit with joy, and she tried to chase away troubling thoughts about her guardian. Guilt for eavesdropping, even unintentionally, tugged at her conscience. Was it a sin? As grievous as opening her heart to fear and doubt that the Heavenly Father would protect her and keep her within His fold?

"I must pray," she murmured to herself. She began to shiver and turned to go back inside when a sudden movement and flash of brown against the white landscape caught her attention. A man. *A World man.* He had turned the corner of the clapboard building and was walking directly toward her. Was it Michael, or yet another visitor who approached?

Fear and surprise nailed her in place, and she dropped her gaze as a rumbling sound, very much a distant echo compared to the thundering of her own heartbeat, vaguely registered in her mind.

Before she could marshal her thoughts, strong arms grabbed her, pulled her against the hard planes of a man's body, and swirled her about. A sheet of ice-glazed snow, apparently launched from the roof of the dispensary, fell with the suddenness of an avalanche. Fortunately, only one edge broke against the man's back and sprayed her face with iced crystals of water. The bulk of the snow lay heaped just behind them.

Nearly shoulder to shoulder with the man, she gasped out loud as the force of the roof slide jolted them both. The danger, however, had not passed. The collar of his opened coat rubbed against her neck, and he held her so firmly against his lean, powerful frame that the bottle of medicine stored in his coat pocket pressed against her hip. Aghast, she could find no voice to express the horror that her breasts were crushed against his chest. Barely able to take a breath without having their embrace become even more intimate, she grew dizzy as her body tingled with a strange, shocking rush of pleasure. A blush heated her cheeks, and her pulse raced out of control. Reeling with confusion from the faith-threatening reaction to being held in a man's embrace for the first time in her life, she struggled to free herself.

"Are you all right?"

She recognized his voice immediately. Michael's question startled her, and all conscious thought fled as luminous gray eyes met and trapped her gaze, holding her far more captive than his powerful arms which were wrapped around her. He was undeniably more handsome than any man she had ever seen, and she drew a sharp breath. Silver at his temples streaked through ebony hair like lightning in a storm-darkened sky. Pulled back into an old-fashioned queue at the nape of his neck, dark hair framed compelling features. Firm lips above a strong, square jawline pursed with half a smile as his commanding gaze bore through all her defenses and immediately proved the wisdom behind the rule that a sister should never meet a man's gaze with her own.

His eyes simmered with such intense emotion that she quivered. Captured in their gray depths, the glazed image of the physical pleasure that coursed through her body stared back at her. Desire—a World evil that was so strong it left her trembling with fear—flashed like quicksilver in the depths of his eyes.

Beyond the startling evidence of intense physical attraction that filled his gaze, she saw the essence of his character. Michael was a man who rarely accepted defeat. He was a man of strong will who lived life on his own terms. Although she had overheard his conversation with Brother Avery, she could see for herself he was a man as devoted to tradition as she was to her faith.

"Are you all right?" he repeated.

Nearly overpowered by sensations she did not completely understand, she dropped her gaze. "F-fine. I'm fine," she lied as she dropped her gaze and her body went slightly limp. "I—I . . ."

Chuckling, he smoothed a lock of hair from her cheek. "You almost got buried in snow, but I wonder if Fate was being kind to you or to me. I'm glad I happened to make a wrong turn after I told my brother I'd have no trouble finding the stables,'' he admitted as he looked up at the meeting house on the crest of the hill.

Mercy!

His touch sent shivers dancing across her face and down her spine. Totally distraught, she stepped back as he released his hold with a reluctance that was only too clear in the way his hand lingered overlong on her elbow. She smoothed her skirts and readjusted her shoulder kerchief with shaking fingers as she tried to find her voice. ''I didn't realize how quickly the snow was melting or that it might be dangerous. Thank you.''

His laugh was easy and good-natured as he dusted the glistening snow and ice crystals from his coat. ''It would be an understatement to admit it was my pleasure.'' He paused, his gaze as hot and burning as a roaring fire. ''Perhaps you'd be kind enough to walk with me to the stables. So I don't get lost,'' he suggested quickly in a voice laced with more than just a glimmer of hope. ''I'm Michael Lawne. I was here visiting my brother. And you are . . . ?''

Frightened by the prospect of spending a single minute longer in his presence for fear her soul would be forever lost to sin, she answered instinctively as she backed away from him with her gaze locked to the ground. ''JoHannah Sims.''

She flinched. Why, oh why, had she used her World name? Was his influence powerful enough to resurrect her past and make her forget who she was? Or did her mind choose to deny that, as Sister JoHannah, she couldn't possibly have yielded to the temptations of the flesh?

''JoHannah.''

Unabashed interest and open admiration resounded in his voice and unleashed another wave of sensations that raced through her body and challenged her will to resist him. She cupped one hand and shook it to the ground to force away the World evils that threatened her.

"You've lost your cap," he said gently as he bent down and retrieved her lace cap from the mound of fallen snow.

Her hands flew to her head, and the moment her fingers felt her hair, her lips began to tremble. The abject horror of having her hair exposed to this man's view eclipsed the ignominy of allowing him to mold her body to his and incite one of the World's greatest vices in her heart—lust.

Tears sprang to her eyes, and she blinked them away. She took the cap out of his hand and clutched it to her chest as shame painted her soul black. Heart pounding, she spun around and raced back into the workroom, thoroughly convinced that her world at Collier, unfortunately, was far more unpredictable than she had ever imagined it could be.

Nor was it safe. Not when this man, Michael Lawne, was near. The only redeeming thought that charged through her mind as she closed the door behind her and collapsed against it was the knowledge that Michael Lawne had no reason left to visit Collier now that he and Brother Avery had reached an understanding.

She would never have to see Michael Lawne again.

And in the months that remained before her birthday when she would sign the covenant that would bind her to her faith forever, she would pray for forgiveness for her impious thoughts about the sinful pleasures of the flesh and find a way to forget they had ever met.

Or the amazing, soul-wrenching experience of being held in his arms.

Chapter 2

Michael stared straight ahead as a blur of lavender skirts disappeared behind the door that closed behind her like a shell snapping closed on an oyster to protect it from a predator. Certain that JoHannah Sims had either collapsed against the door or fallen to her knees in prayer to beg for forgiveness, he rubbed his cheek where her soft, auburn hair had touched him ever so briefly.

Thoroughly befuddled by his own reaction to her, he remained immobile, a prisoner of his own thoughts. For a woman whose faith declared the pleasures of the flesh a sin, but whose face and form contradicted that tenet as aberrant and contrary to every law in nature, she had been clearly unable to hide her feminine reaction to him or to disguise the shame that had dusted her cheeks a delightful shade of red when the reality of the powerful attraction between them shook her virtuous world.

Why had she allowed him to hold her in his arms long after the danger had passed? Had she merely been satisfying her curiosity about a World man in the aftershock of nearly being hit by a snowslide, or had she discovered a cruel truth: Shaker-mandated, platonic relationships between men and women violated the very nature of human existence?

Further surprised by the tender emotions she had unleashed in his heart when he gazed into her face, his body had complicated matters and literally ached with unsatisfied desire. Not that his entire being hadn't jumped to immediate alert the moment he pulled her out of harm's way and into his protective embrace.

Beneath the Shaker-style, baggy gown with its deep, concealing shoulder kerchief, her long, slender limbs had pressed against his legs. His hands had discovered her narrow waist, but when her full, soft bosom had pressed into his chest, he had barely been able to breathe for want of knowing her better. Far better.

It was only then that he had gazed deep into her eyes and saw the abject fear that had turned them a deep shade of violet. Those glorious eyes. They haunted him even now, and he realized that their unusual color had been made even more distinctive by her lavender gingham gown. The rosy blush on her cheeks had accentuated her pale, unblemished skin and gifted her heart-shaped face with an innocence far too uncommon in his experience with women, but her chin was slightly too pointed and her lips too full for her to be considered beautiful.

Just fascinating enough to capture his undivided attention and stir his imagination.

To his credit, he would never have had the opportunity to discover her many physical charms save for his timely rescue. The fact that she was as tall as most men left him more intrigued than threatened, and he longed to hold her in his arms again. And again.

"JoHannah."

He whispered her name, thoroughly confused by the sense of loss he felt now that she had slipped away. When he had gazed into her face, he recognized a woman of great worth, a woman who had strength of character, a woman who . . .

"Damn!" He turned and strode down the walkway, putting distance between himself and this beguiling but unattainable woman.

Choking back his gnawing sense of frustration and failure from a day marked by unsettling events not only with his brother but also a gentle Shaker sister, Michael found his way to the stables, saddled his mount, and spurred his way down the village lane to the main road. Turning north, he headed for Lawne Haven beneath a late afternoon sky that had been invaded by a sea of clouds. A burst of brisk, cold wind lashed against his face and he slowed his horse to button his coat. He cursed the sudden return to winter weather as an omen that there were difficult days ahead.

He was returning home to Lawne Haven without Avery. A hollow feeling in the pit of his stomach told him that Avery was never coming home. He was going to spend the rest of his life as a Shaker. Why? Why would Avery turn from his duties to his family?

Brain sick.

He was brain sick. Just like every single man, woman, and child in the blasted community.

That was the only answer that made sense. How else could Michael explain the joyful harmony he found every time he visited Collier and tried to convince Avery to break away from these strange people and come home?

Reflecting back on his conversation with his brother, he faced the truth: Avery could not be swayed from his decision, and within several weeks, he would be traveling with a band of religious fanatics to Kentucky.

Shivering in the cold, Michael pulled up the collar of his lamb-skin coat and urged the horse into a gallop. Maybe *he* was brain sick to have wasted so much time trying to change Avery's mind. No, he admitted ruefully. Not brain

sick. Just determined. He had to be sure Avery was satisfied
with his decision to join the Shakers and would not change
his mind about deeding Lawne Haven over to Michael.

Easing the horse back into a spirited canter as he approached a fork in the road, he told himself that he had
more than enough problems to contend with. If Avery was
unwilling to meet his obligations, Michael was not. Title to
Lawne Haven required more than dedication to family tradition and land their forefathers had claimed from the wilderness. It required a son to inherit and guard the priceless
legacy of hopes and dreams that continued, unbroken, from
one generation to the next.

For that he needed a wife, and the idea of marriage,
surprisingly, appealed to him. Would he be able to find a
woman who shared the same commitment to family and
tradition that he did? A woman who would find joy and
pleasure in the marriage bed and fulfillment in birthing an
heir to centuries of devotion to land?

JoHannah's face and form flashed through his mind, and
he shook his head. He needed a wife, not a religious fanatic.
Not a woman wedded to celibacy.

And definitely not a woman like JoHannah, who pre-
ferred the unnatural order of life in a community of fools
to a home with a husband and children of her own.

Leave the violet-eyed little saint to her own fate!

Let Avery chase whatever wild and lunatic faith he
chose.

Michael's mind began to race with the possibilities that
now loomed in his immediate future. He slowed the horse
down to a walk and shifted in the saddle to stretch his
frozen limbs. Heir to responsibility that now bore heavily
on his shoulders instead of Avery's, he followed the road
under the muted light of a winter moon that broke through
the cloud cover.

He was only twenty-eight. Strong enough to meet the

challenges of the land. Young enough to fill Lawne Haven
with children to continue the family line. And absolutely
determined that once his responsibilities to his family's
traditions were met, he would return to the adventurous life
he loved and had had to abandon to return to Lawne Haven:
life at sea. He simply could not fathom living the rest of
his life on land, and the call of the sea flowed in his veins
as surely as life itself. Neither Avery nor the housekeeper,
Nora, knew Michael planned to return to sea one day, and
the burden of his secret lay close to his heart.

JoHannah.

Thoughts of the gentle Shaker sister came unbidden to
his mind, and he laughed softly. Life, it seemed, had a
perverted nature. Was it fate or just coincidence that he had
met a woman who fascinated him more than any other in
the past, a woman who would make an ideal wife for him,
and she had no interest in ever marrying anyone?

And if by some odd quirk of fate, she did? He snorted.
God help the man who had to unravel her notions of marriage. Lord knew Michael was not interested, but he was
man enough to admit that finding a woman who could in-
trigue him as much as the virtuous JoHannah might be the
most difficult challenge of all.

That task, however, was only slightly more problematic
than the ones that loomed before him—when he returned
to Lawne Haven.

''Are you daydreaming . . . or praying as you work?''

Startled, JoHannah dropped the witch hazel bark in her
hands and swirled around from the table in the workroom
in the rear of the dispensary where she had fled after her
calamitous meeting with Michael Lawne. Wiping her hands
on her apron, she felt a blush warm her cheeks. ''Eldress
Regina,'' she murmured, horrified to think someone might
have witnessed her encounter with a World person and mis-

construed what had actually happened. *Or guessed what was in her heart?* "Forgive me. I didn't hear you come in."

The Eldress smiled and glanced nervously about the workroom. "Has Sister Lucy been exiled to the infirmary?"

Sighing with relief at the Eldress's innocent question, JoHannah approached the older woman and remembered a time when she had had to look up to meet Eldress Regina's gaze. The Heavenly Father, however, had gifted her with a height normally reserved for most men—which only reminded her of how sinfully well she had fit into Michael's embrace. She looked down to find the Eldress's eyes twinkling behind thick spectacles, a dark glass medicine bottle in her outstretched hand.

"Sister Emily stopped by the dispensary earlier for my medicine, but there wasn't anyone here. Sweet child. I nearly had the spoon in my mouth before I thought to check the label on the bottle. Would you be a dear and get the right medicine for me?"

Ignoring the Eldress's comment which clearly confirmed JoHannah's absence, she studied the neatly scribed lettering on the label pasted to the bottle and nearly choked. "This is for horses!"

"An honest mistake." The Eldress sighed. "Unless Sister Lucy thinks my hair should be as thick as a mare's winter coat."

Unable to hold back the giggles that erupted and covered the release of her nervous tension, JoHannah led the Eldress back into the dispensary, put the bottle back on its proper place on one of the shelves, and secured the correct medicine Sister Evelyn had prescribed for the Eldress's arthritic knees.

She handed it to the Eldress who checked the label and smiled as she slipped the bottle beneath the warm woolen folds of her Dorothy Cape. "Thank you, Sister. You'll keep this between us, won't you? I'll speak to Sister Lucy tomorrow. Perhaps it's time she took a turn in the laundry."

JoHannah's eyes widened. "I don't think the brethren have quite forgotten—"

"Yes. Yes. You're right. Then it's back to the kitchen." She wrinkled her nose, her wireless spectacles bobbing precariously. "I'll ask Sister Mercy to pay close watch."

"And put larger labels on the herbs?"

The Eldress actually blushed. "That, too."

Guilt, however, lay heavy on JoHannah's heart, and her cheerful conversation with her Eldress only accented the depth of grief that hugged her soul. How should she even begin to tell her Eldress of her sins? "I was contrary to order," she blurted, choosing to confess to one of her lesser sins—meeting a man's gaze—first.

Too unsteady to speak further, her eyes misted with tears as she cupped one hand and shook it downward as though able to erase her sinfulness.

The Eldress moved to JoHannah's side and led her back to the workroom. "You're trembling," she murmured.

"I'm sorry . . . I'm so sorry," she cried as she told her Eldress about meeting Michael Lawne and looking into his eyes. Troubled by her amazingly sinful reaction to this man, she was unable to describe the horror of having her body touch his so intimately or losing her cap and having her hair exposed to his view. "I never . . . I mean . . ."

"You're still young and innocent, Sister. In years and in faith. I saw Michael Lawne when he visited Brother Avery last week. It's only human to venture a direct look at such a young, strapping visitor. But remember: 'If you open your heart to a small vice, a greater one may enter.' "

Chastised effectively by the long familiar proverb her Eldress quoted, JoHannah realized that she finally had an understanding of the sacrifice that the life of celibacy required by her faith would entail. Taking a deep breath, she wiped a tear from her eye. Her hands shook as she picked up a large chunk of witch hazel bark and cracked it in half.

Eldress Regina laid her hand on top of JoHannah's and squeezed gently. "Pray, dear Sister. In union with your brothers and sisters in faith, the cross of obedience will be easier to bear."

Relieved that her Eldress had no hint of what was really racing through JoHannah's mind and body, JoHannah nodded, unable to speak. As her heartbeat slowed to a gentler cadence, her commitment to living a life of faith returned, stronger than before. "I'm sorry," she whispered, wondering if she would ever be able to confess the true depth of her shame or the shocking nature of her deeper sins. Convinced that she must try to find forgiveness on her own before revealing her transgressions to her Eldress, lest she risk her opportunity to sign the covenant and become a formal Believer, JoHannah remained silent.

After pulling the cape tighter around her shoulders, Eldress Regina gave JoHannah's hands a quick, final squeeze. "You must be obedient and never look at a man directly. We have rules that must be followed—"

"And I must never run off again," JoHannah reminisced, echoing the Eldress's warning when JoHannah had tried to run away so long ago. She sniffled and pulled out a handkerchief from the pocket of her apron to wipe her nose. "Do you think you have time for a cup of hot cocoa?"

The Eldress smiled. "With cream and cinnamon on top." She stretched and reached up to put her arms around JoHannah's shoulders. "Come along, Sister. We'll join some of your other sisters, have a cup of hot cocoa, and pray about this together."

As JoHannah walked toward the door, lingering memories of the man's Worldly temptation sent her heart into a nervous skip. A simple cup of hot cocoa—an uncommon remedy—had calmed her frightened heart so long ago. She prayed as she walked, hoping that the remedy would help to close the tiny hole in her heart that her disobedience had opened before a greater vice slipped through.

Again.

Chapter 3

A month later, JoHannah bleakly admitted that not even prayer had worked. Images of Michael Lawne had filled every free waking moment, and he had barged his way into her dreams at night. Even now, in the dining hall surrounded by her sisters and brothers, just the thought of him triggered an implosion of physical reactions that frightened her with its intensity.

And just as Eldress Regina had forewarned, a greater vice had slipped into JoHannah's heart: the cross of the flesh.

No mere metaphor, the cross was real, it was heavy, and whenever she thought about this man, her shoulders literally ached from trying to bear the weight of it.

The crushing reality of her own carnal nature, ever present in the spiritual travail of many other Believers, had surprised her. Caught her off guard. And sent her back to the Sacred Hill to cleanse the sin from her soul in frenzied, solitary worship.

Near panic at her inability to wash him from her thoughts again, she began to tremble. Bowing her head, she took a deep breath and prayed frantically for the gift of peace of mind. She inhaled the warm and tempting aromas of the evening supper that chased away the bitter February cold, but did little to ease her distress.

In contrast to the frenzied hammering of her heart, only the gently ordered sounds of spoons dipping into bowls of steaming vegetable soup or knives spreading pale creamy butter on still-warm bread broke through the monastic silence in the dining hall. According to custom, her sisters in faith occupied benches alongside identical wooden trestle tables that lined the north side of the hall; on the opposite wall, the brethren grouped together at smaller tables of four.

Eyes downcast, she wiped a small smudge of buttery grease from her knife onto the slice of bread on the table next to her soup bowl relegated for that purpose and took a serving of plum sauce which she spread on a heel of crusty pumpernickel bread. Raising the bread to her lips, she nibbled halfheartedly on the chewy crust, but her heart still fluttered with need and her cheeks still burned with hot shame.

She closed her eyes briefly and prayed, "Hands to work. Hearts to God." A simple refrain, she repeated it silently over and over, but she was discovering, once again, that the words were far easier to say than to put into practice. Eventually, her heartbeat dropped back to a normal rhythm. As deliberately as a butterfly that gently opened and closed its wings for balance as it feasted on the nectar of a late summer blossom, JoHannah's spirit latched onto the simple tenets of her faith. She fought to regain her spiritual equilibrium and to rally against her sinful thoughts about the man.

Why was this happening to her?

Was she too weak in faith to carry the cross of the flesh? When apostates occasionally left the faith to marry, she had found it disillusioning and alarming. Had she also been terribly wicked, enjoying an alarming sense of self-gratification in the others' failure by voicing harsh judgment? Never once had she felt the stirrings of physical desire for any of her Shaker brethren or occasional visitors from the World, but this man, Michael Lawne, was different from any of the others.

He was the epitome of the World's temptation, the creator of doubt, and the harbinger of doom and disaster for the joyful life she led here.

A loud pounding sound followed by the harsher echo of wood slamming against plaster walls scattered JoHannah's miseries like a flock of birds startled into flight. Her head snapped up, and she almost expected to see the spirit of Mother Ann Lee, foundress of her community, resurrected for the sole purpose of condemning JoHannah as an apostate. Eldress Regina gripped one of JoHannah's arms, and JoHannah watched with searing anxiety as the leader of their community of faith bolted out of his seat and approached two World men who stormed their way into the center of the room.

Fueled by tales of World persons who invaded peaceful Shaker communities to snatch away uncovenanted children and return them unwillingly to their families, wails of fright and horror from her sisters in faith drowned out the echo of the men's bootfalls on the bare, planked floor. Several small children, no older than six or seven, clung to their caretakers at a nearby table. Stoic Eldress Regina never flinched; neither did she relinquish her hold on JoHannah. Most of her brethren, their backs straight against spindled chairs, kept to their seats except for several who rose and secured the doors while Elder Calvin and the intruders argued over a piece of paper that looked like a document of some sort. Two young girls who sat opposite JoHannah started to cry as the other sisters began to weep louder. The Eldress's lips moved in silent prayer as she strengthened her hold when the men started to cross the room and headed directly for their table.

Staring hard, JoHannah recognized one of the men as the local sheriff, Peter Lunden. She froze in place the instant the shortest of the three men turned and looked in her direction.

Eleazer Bathrick.

My guardian.

Eyes wide, she locked her knees together to keep them from shaking and watched him guardedly beneath downcast eyes. Of average height and weight, he was slightly less than nondescript except when he was surrounded by men who dressed far simpler as a matter of faith than he did. His only distinguishing feature was a small brown mole that clung to his face just below his left cheekbone, a defect that had scared her when she had looked at him when she was a child. Looking past him, she noticed that his wife, Leila, was standing just inside the doorway with an expression of disdain covering her face.

A storm of fears and rationalizations for Bathrick's surprising and dramatic appearance, rooted in fearful, childhood memories, pelted JoHannah like huge hailstones, further undermining her already shaky composure. With time and maturity, she had come to realize that Bathrick was not an evil man. But at this precise moment, her stomach knotted with fear exactly as it had when she was seven years old.

Heart pounding, she remained seated on the bench and stared at the bowl of soup set before her. Her appetite gone, the chunks of purple-laced turnip and unskinned potatoes grew hazy, and she tried to suppress the horrid memory of the day he had ripped her from her home—and the impossible notion that he was about to do it again.

The sheriff stepped away from the other men and walked toward her, stopping a few feet from the table, now abandoned by the other sisters except for the Eldress and JoHannah. "JoHannah Sims? I've come to see you're escorted home," he announced in a deep, gravelly voice.

She gulped twice, staring at the table to avoid meeting his gaze. "Collier is my home. These are my sisters and brethren," she responded, far too softly to give much strength to her statement. "I'm indentured to the Shakers until I'm twenty-one this August."

Close enough to her now that even with downcast eyes she could almost count the wiry hairs that protruded like spider's legs from the mole on his cheek, Bathrick shoved the paper into her line of vision. "The court has revoked your indenture."

"At whose request?" She tilted her chin up. She was an adult now, not a child, and she refused to let him intimidate her. "I made no such plea to any court, especially a World court. I'm happy here. This is my home now. I—I don't want to leave."

The sheriff leaned toward her. "Your guardian had every legal right to petition the court on your behalf. Judge Weldon ruled that your indenture is invalid. I'm sorry, but you'll have to leave with your guardian," he prompted gently.

Bolting to her feet, JoHannah's hands gripped the edge of the table, and she forced herself not to look directly at either man. "My guardian had no just cause—"

Bathrick grunted. "The judge ruled differently. Come along, my dear. It's futile to argue the point. The judge signed the order, and you must honor it." He bent closer and his breath fanned her cheeks. "Just as you must obey my wishes. My wife and I have made an arduous journey on your behalf. I won't take it lightly if you create a scene that forces the sheriff to carry you bodily to my coach."

"But why? Why are you making me leave?" JoHannah cried, too upset to care that she continued to defy Shaker order and challenge a superior. "You haven't even come to see me—"

"I'm here now. As for why you're leaving," he grum-bled, as he gazed around the room, "the answer would be fairly obvious if you weren't surrounded by fanatics and social misfits. You're leaving because you've reached the age to marry."

"No!" she blurted, blushing at her impertinence, but keeping her head bowed. "It's forbidden—"

"Forbidden?" He laughed. " 'Tis expected, my dear. Your father left you a vast fortune, and you have a respon-sibility to marry and continue the family line. He willed it, and as your guardian and executor of his estate—"

"No!" she cried out for the second time, noting that Leila now stood next to her husband, a man clearly twenty years her senior. "My faith forbids marriage. The tempta-tions of the flesh distract the spirit from serving God."

"What pious, saintly nonsense!" Leila mocked, her voice shrill.

JoHannah cringed, sinking back onto the seat of the bench and shaking a cupped hand to the floor.

"Look at me," Leila ordered.

Raising her eyes, JoHannah met and held Leila's cen-suring gaze.

"You'll do what you're told. Is that clear? I'll tolerate no babbling, religious prattle about joining these sacrile-gious fools. You're duty bound to obey your guardian."

Standing, JoHannah squared her shoulders. Although her legs were quivering beneath her skirts, her voice was calm and sure. "My duty is to a higher authority, and my elders will not stand idly by and let you take me back into the World against my will."

Leila snickered. "No court would dare interfere with Judge Weldon's ruling, especially since your father left spe-cific instructions in his will. Mr. Bathrick has spent most of his life studying the law. He's researched the matter thoroughly, and the law says—"

"The Lord's law—"

"Silence! Both of you." Bathrick cleared his throat. "No matter what your friends try to do, the courts will eventually rule in my favor. You can save everyone a lot of unnecessary expense by simply accepting your fate. Whether you wish to marry or not is of little consequence, my dear. On the day you reach your majority, you will be married."

JoHannah swallowed hard. "I wish to stay here. This is my home. Please," she whispered.

Bathrick reached out and touched her shoulder. "After you've had a good rest, you'll think better of turning your back on everything your father worked so hard to provide for you."

Eyes brimming with tears that escaped slowly, one at a time, JoHannah took a deep breath. Where was her faith? Didn't she trust her Heavenly Father to protect her against His enemies? Or was He giving her one final test of faith because she had opened her heart to the temptations of the flesh?

Michael Lawne suddenly seemed less dangerous to her than either of the men who stood at her side. Michael Lawne may have been the serpent of temptation for her, but at least he had had the decency not to force Brother Avery to leave Collier.

Terror sliced through the last vestige of her bravery, and she swayed on her feet. Casting aside her shield of false bravado, she turned and embraced the Eldress who rested her head on JoHannah's shoulders. "Please. Don't let them force me to leave and take me away," she pleaded. The thought of marriage and reentering the World with all its inherent sinfulness and vice frightened her no more than leaving everyone she held dear to her heart. Bone-chilling tremors wracked her body.

She had lost her family once before.

She could not bear to lose her family again.

The Eldress hugged JoHannah close and patted her back, but the tremors solidified into rigid fear. Warm fingers wiped away JoHannah's tears, and the Eldress smiled up at JoHannah with deep brown eyes that were shimmering behind misted spectacles. "Trust in the Heavenly Father. He will care for you. Pray to Holy Mother Wisdom that the court will reconsider." The Eldress looked over to the Elder. "Elder Calvin?"

"We'll do all we can," he promised, "but World courts are not swift to act against one of their own."

JoHannah bit her lower lip and frowned, desperate for hope that she would be reunited with her sisters and brethren. "Please. You'll try, won't you?"

"Of course we will, but for now, I'm afraid we have no choice but to honor the court's order."

When Bathrick took her arm, JoHannah flinched. His grip tightened painfully as he ushered her past tables of disapproving brethren, and her forearm and fingers tingled. Mustering the remnants of her dignity, she wrapped herself in the comforting fabric of her faith and tried not to recoil when Leila Bathrick placed a luxurious fur cape around JoHannah's shoulders. Punishment for her sinful nature and weak faith had been swift and sure, and her heartbeat quivered in her chest as slow, steady steps carried her toward the portal.

Did she have to leave because this was God's plan to strengthen her weak spirit and make her worthy of the calling to become a formal Believer? Was Michael Lawne the Lord's instrument? What about Eleazer Bathrick and his wife? JoHannah had no way of knowing for sure, but she vowed to pray fervently and remain true to her faith while the Shaker community fought for her in the courts.

If her heart was sincere and her faith rock steady, Holy Mother Wisdom would guide the conscience of the judge and convince him to let JoHannah stay to continue her spiritual travel as a Believer. Like a Christian martyr being led to the Coliseum, she dutifully followed her guardian out the door and stormed the heavens with prayers for the courage to face the terrifying beasts in the World . . . and the lions that lay in wait for her unfaithful heart.

Chapter 4

Midmorning, after three days of travel, JoHannah welcomed the feel of solid earth beneath her feet, even if it was cold enough to freeze her toes. She stepped away from the coach and glanced up the steps that led to a plantation-styled mansion that was oddly out of place in the eastern mountains of New Hampshire. She tilted her head back, her gaze following the two-story columns that rose the full height of the redbrick building and joined scalloped bric-a-brac that laced the roof line.

And she knew without being able to see it that there was an observatory perched on the roof that was fully encased with walls of glass. The knowledge startled her and she lowered her eyes, her gaze focusing on the heavy drapes that hung inside tall, wide windows on the first and second floors and hid the interior from view. The thick fabric no doubt protected the inside rooms from the blustering cold wind that swirled around the house and sent chills down her spine despite the heavy fur cape draped over her shoulders.

Huddling beneath the cape, she mounted the stairs ahead of her guardian and his wife to reach the veranda, blinking back a whole host of memories that rushed helter-skelter into her consciousness and reassured her that this house had been her home.

She paused, letting vague recollections of the house sharpen and bring back the oft-told story of how her father had had a house built for his wife in a style that would remind her of her home in Georgia. As JoHannah scanned the barren, snow-dusted veranda, she remembered a wicker settee where she had sat side by side with her mother learning how to embroider, a rocking chair where her father had held her, drying her tears when her puppy had died, and a serving table overflowing with still-warm sugar cookies and glasses of chilled lemonade.

"Go on inside. What are you waiting for?"

Bathrick's harsh voice chased away the bittersweet memories and rekindled the terror of being sent away by her guardian and his wife as soon as JoHannah's parents had been buried in the family cemetery just beyond the woods that surrounded the estate.

Bathrick ushered his wife past JoHannah and headed for the front door. It opened before they reached it, and a large, round-faced woman met them with a worried expression that reached her eyes. "I'm sorry, sir. I didn't hear the coach." Her high-pitched apology hung in the air as Bathrick and his wife entered the house and walked straight past the servant. He turned and motioned for JoHannah to follow, and she stepped inside with more disturbing feelings of familiarity wrapping around her senses. She followed her guardian into a parlor where Leila stood warming her hands in front of a sputtering fire.

"Never mind your usual apology for not minding your duties, Anne," Leila chastised. "We're half frozen to death. Bring a pot of tea upstairs to my room and send Ralph in to rekindle the fire you've no doubt forgotten to feed. Where's Cassandra?" she demanded as she let her cape drop to the floor.

Her arms already laden with Bathrick's overcoat and JoHannah's fur cape, Anne scooped up her mistress's wrap with an awkward gesture. Lips quivering, she backed toward the door. "Miss Cassie has taken to her bed with a headache."

"Oh, my poor dear!" Leila whined, casting a shrinking glance at her husband as she hurried from the room. "I told you I shouldn't have gone off with you to get JoHannah. Cassandra's health is too fragile for her to be left alone."

Leila's parting remark echoed in the silence that followed her departure, and JoHannah searched her memory bank. She vaguely recalled a young, dark-haired child who had accompanied her parents when JoHannah's father invited his solicitor, Bathrick, and his family for weekend visits. Was JoHannah's memory more than fair, or was her mind playing tricks on her? Before she had a chance to mull over the confusion of her past as it collided with the present, Bathrick raised his hand and motioned for her to take a seat next to him in front of the fire.

"I'd prefer to stand," she croaked, her gaze locked on the painting that hung over a dark green marble mantel. Taking small, unsteady steps, she approached the images of the man and woman who stared down at her, even though her faith forbid viewing portraits.

On the left, a fully bearded gentleman with wide, blond side whiskers smiled gently. Standing tall, his shoulders were even with the mantel in the portrait that caught the unusual color of the actual mantel just below the gilt-framed portrait. Piercing, pale blue eyes met her curious gaze, and JoHannah looked away quickly.

Startled, her one hand gripped a chair back for support as she studied the brunette woman seated next to the man in the portrait. Dressed in an elegant burgundy velvet gown, she sat in a chair that looked very much like the dainty Queen Anne chair beneath JoHannah's fingertips. The woman's posture seemed unnaturally stiff, but there was a hint of humor in her expression that brought a smile to JoHannah's face that slipped almost the instant it formed.

And on the woman's lap sat a girl child, possibly two or three years old, with auburn curls and startling lavender eyes.

Feeling slightly faint as she gazed at the images of her birth family, JoHannah turned away. She slipped down into the softly upholstered chair and closed her eyes to hold back her tears.

"Your parents loved you very much. I should think you'd respect their wishes."

The coldness in her guardian's voice jolted her, and her eyes snapped open. She stared at him, quickly reconciling the childhood image of the brash, unsympathetic man who had taken her away from her home with the stern, dictatorial man who sat across from her now. Ashamed to have acted contrary to order by meeting a man's gaze with her own, she lowered her eyes. Encouraged by what she had seen, however, she smiled shyly and toyed with her hands. "I still don't understand why I had to leave Collier," she began, hoping that he would be willing to reconsider and allow her to go back.

Eyes downcast, her gaze caught sight of the lavish, ostentatious furnishings that surrounded her and screamed the excesses of the World at her simple spirit. She clasped her hands together and stared at her lap. "We . . . we haven't talked for several years," she suggested, realizing that her guardian could have no idea how important her faith was to her. Perhaps if he knew how much she wanted to stay at Collier, he might allow her to return. "I'm very happy doing the Lord's work. I planned to sign the covenant on my birthday."

He waved a hand in the air. "The idea is fanatical lunacy!" When she shuddered, he sighed, as though he considered his words too brash. He lowered his voice. "I thought it best to place you far away from the unhappy memories here in this house. Perhaps I was wrong. Forgive me, my dear. But I can't put aside my obligations to your father. You needn't worry. I'll handle all the details, just as he would have done for you."

JoHannah chewed on her lower lip, unable to speak.

Bathrick leaned forward in his seat. "You've grown into an attractive young woman. A bit over tall, perhaps, but that's neither here nor there. You've fortune enough to attract a man in spite of it."

"But I don't want—"

"What you *should* want to do is to fulfill your destiny. Marriage and motherhood are preordained for women. To live as a maiden woman all of your life is . . . well, it's . . . it's unnatural!"

"It's perfectly natural," she responded, her voice shrill, "to serve the Heavenly Father. I've trained with many sisters. I've taught school. I've been a caretaker for the children. I've—"

"Orphans and castoffs, not your own flesh and blood. Now, enough of this nonsense, child. You'll have a good and proper life here with a home of your own, a husband to care for you, and children of your own flesh, God's grace be given. First, I have a few legal papers for you to sign," he suggested, taking her hand and helping her to her feet. He led her to the library where she signed a stack of legal documents, too numb to care what they contained.

When they were finished, he ushered her up the stairs to the second floor. "A seamstress is coming for you tomorrow. For tonight, just try to think about the wonderful future you'll have, now that you're back home where you belong."

Too choked up to chance a response, JoHannah clenched her teeth together. The future? How could she dare to embrace a future in the World? She mounted the highly polished steps, her heart heavy with the grief that her guardian had no intention of listening to any plea she might make. She refused, however, to give up hope.

She had to be patient and wait for the court to reconsider its decision.

Until then, she accepted her situation for what it was: one final test of her faith that she would not fail.

Michael evaded the inevitable—telling Nora the truth—for several days. When the housekeeper, who had celebrated her seventy-third birthday the previous fall, announced plans to redecorate Avery's bedroom and asked Michael to store the furniture in the attic so the room could be repapered, he did what he had been dreading every moment since he had returned from Collier.

Forcing the pint-sized woman into a rocking chair perched next to the hearth in the kitchen, he pulled a bench in front of her and rested his hands on her shoulders.

Her dark eyes, the color of ground pepper, crackled with impatience. "There'll be no getting around it, Michael. Avery will be back by spring. When he finally comes to his senses and returns home, I want no aching memories to hit him square between the eyes when he wakes up every morning in his old room. You've been dawdling around this place for days. Time to stretch those muscles of yours and move that furniture."

Cracking a sad smile, Michael shook his head. "You've been telling me what to do all my life. This time you need to listen to me."

Pursing her lips, which deepened the crevices in her wrinkled flesh, the old woman shook her head. "Always did like to argue with me. Your poor mother—"

"Mother's gone now. It's just you and me."

Disbelief flashed through her eyes. "No. There's Avery

and my little Abigail and Jane.'' Sniffling back tears, the woman's shoulders began to shake. ''I thought for sure you'd be able to convince Avery to come home this time.''

Facing his own failure was difficult enough, but disappointing this fragile woman filled Michael with shame. ''He's not coming back, Nora. He's on his way to Kentucky with his new family to join another community of faith. Abigail and Jane—''

''No!'' she insisted, sitting forward in the rocker, her shoulders stiffening. ''Avery wouldn't turn his back on Lawne Haven and leave New Hampshire. I can't believe it.''

Sliding off the bench, Michael bent down on one knee and clasped Nora's hands between his own. ''He's on his way to Kentucky, Nora. I tried, but I couldn't change his mind.''

Her eyes widened, darkening with an agony that reached out and tugged at Michael's soul before they filled with disbelief. Once again, the apparent lack of interest he had shown in Lawne Haven before he had left to wander the seas came back to haunt him. Still, he was not quite sure if Nora really believed that Lawne Haven would fascinate him to the extent he would commit his life to it. He wondered if she knew him so well that she guessed he intended to remain at Lawne Haven only long enough to set his affairs in order by marrying and providing an heir. With the right mistress for his estate, he would be able to return to adventures at sea, satisfied that during his absences, Lawne Haven would be run well.

Grief, however, overshadowed her surprise, and he knew that she mourned the loss of Avery's daughters whom she had tended with the same love and devotion she had showered on Avery and Michael when they were little.

''I'm so sorry,'' he murmured as he pulled her close. ''I really tried to convince him to come home, but he's not the same man we both love. He hasn't been the same since . . .''

Unnerved by the tears that wet his shirt, Michael left the rest of his words unsaid. He did not have to convince Nora of anything she had not seen with her own eyes. Finding it an odd reversal of roles to be the comforter instead of the comforted, he let Nora spend the last of her tears before he reached into his pocket for a handkerchief and handed it to her.

She dabbed at her red-rimmed eyes and blew her nose. "Do you think someday he'll change his mind? Will I ever see my little ones again?''

Michael wanted to lie, to placate Nora's fears with assurances, but she deserved the truth. "Not for a long time, if ever. I—I promised to have a home for Abigail and Jane if they decide to come home when they reach their majority. As for Avery, Lawne Haven is his birthright. If he ever changes his mind—''

"Once Avery sets his mind to something, he's as obstinate as you are unpredictable,'' she interrupted. Moistening her lips, she gazed up at him. "Have you really washed the lust to wander from the soles of your shoes? Will you really stay home now for good?''

He smiled, avoiding yet another lie. "I promised Avery that I would make Lawne Haven prosper.''

"You can't run Lawne Haven by yourself,'' she sniffed. "If you intend to stay, you'll need—''

Laughing, he squeezed her shoulders. "I'm not alone. You're here. Dolan and Genevieve are good neighbors, and they live close enough to help if we need them. In the spring—''

"That's not what I meant.''

"I know exactly what you meant,'' he teased. Getting back to his feet, he held out both hands and helped her to stand. "Looks like you win the battle you've been waging for the past few years after all.''

Poking his stomach, she got him to back up against the bench. ''And what war might that be, you young rakehell?''

Laughing, he held up his hands. ''You know perfectly well that you tried to get me to marry any number of the available young women living within fifty miles.''

''Not that you paid any heed,'' she argued. ''Now that you've a mind to take a wife, most of them are already taken. And despite what you think, it won't be easy. Choosing a *suitable* wife isn't going to be like going to a shipyard and picking your favorite from the ships along the dock.''

His eyes glistening with devilment, he baited her further to help keep her mind off of losing Avery and the girls and focus, instead, on their closest neighbor who had courted and married his wife before the moon completed a single phase. ''Why not? Dolan did.''

''Out!''

She shooed him to the door of the kitchen and handed him his coat. ''Chop enough wood to jar your senses into place. My bones tell me there's another snowfall coming.''

Grinning sheepishly, he grabbed a pair of gloves and gave her a quick peck on her cheek before opening the kitchen door. ''Half a cord should do it. Not a log more. Unless you're making pot roast for dinner. Then I'll—''

''You'll freeze an old woman's bones,'' she fumed and shut the door in his face.

As he walked toward the toolshed for an ax, Michael knew that it would take a long time for Nora to grow accustomed to the idea that Avery and his girls were not returning to Lawne Haven, and even longer for her to accept that Michael's promise to stay as the master of Lawne Haven was more than a whim.

She would grieve the loss of Avery and his girls like they were her own flesh and blood, but he also knew that Nora was as tough and resilient as the field stones that his ancestors had used to build the two-story home on land that had housed every Lawne for ten generations. Loyal to the core, Nora would help him assume his new duties and whether he liked it or not, she would have a great deal to say about the choice of the future mistress of Lawne Haven.

Lost in thought, he selected the first ax he saw, hacked at a few scraggly branches of the overgrown lilac bushes on either side of the shed, and started chopping a stack of wood. Overhead, thick heavy clouds churned in the sky, and thoughts of one woman with amazing violet eyes haunted him. The air was cold and damp but strangely quiet and still, except for the rhythmic echo of metal splintering wood as he raised the ax over his head time and time again to swing it in a wide, powerful arc. With strong, steady motions, he exorcised the last vestiges of his failure to bring Avery home, but he could not extinguish his memories of the gentle Shaker sister.

As he continued to work, he forced himself to think about the future—his future—and gradually found a new excitement building in his heart.

His responsibilities. *His* land. *His* heirs.

Pausing to rest and wipe his brow, he realized he was more than a little reluctant to accept the gauntlet his brother had tossed to him, despite the fact that he had always been envious of Avery's position as the first-born son. Michael could not remember a time when he was growing up that he did not dream about being the master of Lawne Haven. Fiercely competitive as a child, he had tried to outwork and outshine his brother, only to be stymied time and time again by the irreversible and fateful timing of his birth which, according to family tradition, precluded any future role for him at Lawne Haven. Angry and resentful as an adolescent, yet intensely loyal to Lawne Haven, he had hidden his true feelings from his family by playing the sometimes reckless and always carefree second son. Finding it increasingly difficult to play the role, he had escaped at seventeen and forged a life for himself at sea. A veritable bird of passage, he had migrated to wherever the winds of chance had carried him.

Fate eventually claimed him as a favored son and gifted him with a new love: life at sea. Distance, time, and a number of lucrative ventures had erased the deep-seated longing in his soul to be master of Lawne Haven—as well as the guilt he felt for coveting his brother's birthright.

And now, under circumstances he never would have imagined, his long-abandoned dream had turned into a reality he no longer wanted, but was willing to embrace—as long as he knew he could someday return to sea. He could not turn his back on his responsibility to continue family traditions and dedication to the land. He would marry, beget heirs to continue that tradition, and then he would find a way to return to sea with a clear conscience.

Exhilarated by the thought that he would be free to live his life as he truly wanted, he raised the ax over his head and swung hard, metaphorically seeing the log as any possible obstacles that might stand between him and the sea— obstacles he could now split and burn into ashes.

Inexplicably, he misjudged the edge of the log and the blade of the ax swooshed through the air. Thrown off balance, his eyes widened in horrified disbelief as the steel blade embedded itself in the flesh of his lower leg. Pain exploded throughout his body and sucked the air out of his lungs. The sickening crunch of metal against bone split the air. Staggering backwards, he lost his balance and landed full-bodied against the frozen turf with a thud. Dazed, he managed to turn his head and, through blurred vision, he was mesmerized by the sight of his blood as it pooled on the ground.

Blackness descended, extinguishing the colorful display of fireworks bursting in front of his eyes. Mercifully, all semblance of pain and conscious thought faded into oblivion.

Yet he carried with him the grief that he had had too little time to settle his affairs at Lawne Haven so he could return to sea and the regret that he might never see the gentle, violet-eyed Shaker sister again.

And the ultimate, dream-shattering fear that the sins of the past had leaped forward into the present to wreak their final vengeance. Fate had designed a cruel destiny for him, indeed.

Chapter 5

One of the most fearsome beasts in the World, Jo-Hannah discovered, was humiliation. Its fangs were fearsome and relentless, ripping away her dignity and plunging deep to the very essence of her soul.

The abject horror of having her breasts exposed in the shocking, low-cut gown she had been forced to wear surpassed the shame of having her hair deliberately uncovered for the first time in her adult life. Ruffled lace that edged the bodice of her lavender gown reminded her of the iced trim on a tempting, mouth-watering sweetcake. It was demeaning and degrading to her as a woman of faith to have her body decorated so sinfully, but it was no more than she expected, living now in a world distracted by physical pleasures, lust, and idleness.

Still, she had obeyed her guardian's order to wear the gown and closed her heart to the sin of disobedience, lest any greater one slip through. During the last four portrait sessions, JoHannah had found solace in prayer as well as the strength to bear her humiliation, chanting silently and incessantly while she held her pose.

Today, an unusually brilliant winter sun warmed the glass-walled observatory where she sat and brightened her hopes that she would someday return to her community of faith. Even after nearly three weeks with no word from the court. And even though Leila had tossed JoHannah's lace cap into the fire and ordered her high-necked, long-sleeved gown destroyed.

Blisters on JoHannah's fingertips, the painful price she had paid for disobeying her guardian's wife by pulling her cap from the fire, had healed. But that sin of disobedience, compounded by hiding the charred remnants and bribing one of the maids to smuggle her gown back to her, had left JoHannah in an all-too-familiar crisis of conscience that she had finally resolved once and for all.

Eldress Regina's challenge to trust in the Heavenly Father and pray for Holy Mother Wisdom to convince the court to reconsider its ruling sustained JoHannah. She no longer questioned her guardian; she meekly obeyed him and placed herself in the palm of God's hand. He would protect her, accept her humble obedience to His laws, and ultimately, reward her faithful heart by restoring her to her proper home.

The minutes dragged into stiff, merciless hours during this last portrait sitting, and she tried to find some way to escape the degradation, the boredom, and the utter sense of uselessness that consumed her—in spite of her prayers. Her guardian had been able to force her to sit here, but he could not, she discovered, control her thoughts or contain her spirit.

Focusing her gaze on a distant, snow-covered hill, her soul took flight, soaring beyond the observatory and winging its way back to Collier where it joined with other souls devoted to the Lord's work. Peace filled her spirit. Joy filled her soul, but not for long.

The artist stopped working, walked over to her, and still clutching his brush, used his free hand to lower the lace ruffle to expose more of her breasts. She flinched back to reality, shocked by his intimate touch.

"Still so shy," Richard murmured, his fingertips brushing her throat as he lifted a long curl of her auburn hair and positioned it provocatively over her collar bone. He smelled of sweet wine and stale tobacco—sinful, indulgent vices that made her nostrils flare and shake one cupped hand toward the floor.

She pressed her lips together, relieved when he stepped away and picked up his brush again. No man had ever handled her hair, and if he had, it would never have been such an elaborate cascade of curls which had taken the maid several hours to style. Such a frivolous waste of time and energy when a simple knot would have sufficed!

A fleeting memory flashed through her mind, challenged her, and tugged at her heart until she clearly remembered a treasured tradition from her childhood. Sitting up in her bed at night after prayers, her mama had brushed her hair and curled the ends around each of her fingers. Warm and comforting, the memory of her soft voice and gentle touch flowed through her.

Richard's touch made her skin crawl.

She had expected the artist to react to her decadent costume in typical World fashion by trying to seduce her. He had not. The only time he actually touched her or even talked to her was when he was arranging and rearranging her like he was creating an exquisite display. Why hadn't he touched her more intimately? Was he afraid of angering her guardian, or had she somehow misjudged Richard?

His detached demeanor, instead of inspiring relief, created a dizzying whirlwind of self-doubt. While she had found the courage to tolerate the portrait sittings, she also had become thoroughly confused about World men, their reaction to her, and more importantly, perhaps, her reaction to them.

Neither Richard nor her guardian posed any more threat

to her virtue than had any of her brethren at Collier. Neither did their presence or their touch evoke any sinful physical response from her, for which she was grateful. But she remained unconvinced that it was because of her strong convictions.

Not when the mere thought of one man, Michael Lawne, sent her pulse skipping straight down the path of sin.

He had stripped her to her soul the only time they had met—and she had been dressed as a simple sister, although she still remembered the horror of losing her cap. If he saw her now and she gazed into his eyes, she knew she would see pure, unadulterated, physical desire, a desire that she knew, God's blessings notwithstanding, she would feel coursing through her body. Her eyes misted with remorse.

Carnal lust.

It had slipped into her heart, just as Eldress Regina had predicted, the first day she had seen him at Collier. Even now, when JoHannah seemed to have tamed the world's beasts, she had yet to slay the lion nipping at her heart.

"Just tilt your head a bit," Richard urged, snapping her back to reality. "Perfect. Now try to relax. Just a few more minutes and we'll be finished." Humming softly, he began to paint again. He nodded when Leila emerged at the top of the winding staircase that led upward from a second floor sitting room that adjoined JoHannah's bedroom. She walked toward him, virtually ignoring JoHannah's presence.

"Stunning. Absolutely stunning," she remarked as she approached the canvas. "You were quite right to pose her here."

Grinning, he bowed and pointed to the canvas. "But of course I was right. You see how the sunlight creates highlights in her hair? With a backdrop of sky, her height is not so apparent. Her gown was an excellent choice, Mrs. Bathrick. It accents the . . . the unusual color of her eyes."

He coughed, his face reddening.

Leila stepped alongside the artist as she studied the canvas closely and nodded. "We have done well. Both of us," she murmured, her eyes gleaming with self-satisfaction. "My husband will be pleased. When can the portrait be displayed?"

He shook his head. "Not for several weeks, at least. I still need to add a few details, but I'm quite finished with Miss Sims. I'm sure she's found this whole experience a bit tedious."

Tedious?

JoHannah's eyelids fluttered. Tedious did not come close to describing the sinful vanity, the frivolous expense—

"Tradition has a price every woman must bear. JoHannah will appreciate this portrait in her later years," Leila snapped, her hand fluttering at her neck where tiny flaps of aging skin had started to form. "Every young woman of social standing must have her portrait painted."

And her shame captured for all time?

Thoroughly caught betwixt and between worlds, JoHannah felt like she was balanced precipitously on a tightrope. One misstep and she would plunge headlong into decadence and soulful disaster. Unshed tears blurred her vision. She had to be strong. She had to believe that she could maintain her balance long enough to return to the safe haven at Collier.

"Come along, JoHannah. Richard is through with you. Mr. Bathrick has a coach waiting for you outside."

Sighing, JoHannah's gaze settled on Leila's face. Her shoulders slumped, but when she saw how low her bodice dipped, she inhaled sharply and straightened her back. Stretching her tight neck muscles, she moistened her lips. "May I change first?" she whispered.

"Sally is waiting for you in your chamber. Be quick about it. Mr. Bathrick doesn't like to be kept waiting."

How odd, JoHannah thought, to refer to one's husband so formally. She did not dare ask Leila the reason, any more than she could discuss the Shaker rule against secular titles or question her destination this afternoon. Lessons for survival, learned in her childhood, were quick to surface, and she slipped a mask of indifference on her face.

Deliberately ignoring Leila and Richard, more to avoid a chance glimpse of the portrait than anything else, JoHannah made her way to the staircase, turned, and started descending backwards. Once she reached the sewing room, she paused to pull the bodice as high as it would go before proceeding. After being in the observatory for most of the morning, she had to blink several times until her eyes adjusted to the dim light. Walking quickly, she entered her bedroom and stifled her surprise at finding Cassandra, not Sally, waiting for her.

The Bathricks' only child lay sprawled on a chaise lounge set at an angle beneath the windows. Petite and slender, she was the image of World femininity—decorative, but helpless. With her dark black hair sleekly coiffed away from her face, her lips dimpled the flesh between full, round cheeks. Her brown eyes, however, were dull and listless, and JoHannah saw firsthand the direct consequences of a life of idleness and self-indulgence.

Rather than let Cassandra know that Sally's absence had been noted, JoHannah proceeded into the room and pretended Cassandra's presence was not out of the ordinary. "Are you coming with us?" she asked as she stepped behind a dressing screen to change her gown.

"I begged Papa to let me come," the girl whined, sounding more like seven than seventeen, "but he refused, just like he did the last time. Why must I miss all the fun?"

JoHannah paused before stepping out of her lavender gown, wondering what occasion that might have been. As near as she could recall, Cassandra had accompanied her parents and JoHannah every time they had left the estate in the past several weeks. Their excursions, however, had been limited to rides in the country or visits to Reverend Whiting. His freckles now enfolded in large jowls, the minister had spent hours trying to rehabilitate JoHannah's Christian faith. All of the Bathricks as well as the minister's wife had witnessed these debacles. It was hard to understand how any decent soul would describe them as entertaining, JoHannah mused, especially when she had been subjected to one attack after another until she found it easier to acquiesce, mouth the words they all expected to hear, and keep her true faith safe within her own mind and heart.

If Cassandra considered watching someone's faith being peeled away, layer by layer, an amusement, then the girl had a twisted sense of humor in addition to her unconcealed bad temper.

As JoHannah buttoned the bodice of the modest fawn gown Sally must have left for her behind the screen, JoHannah grew curious. Why wasn't her guardian permitting Cassandra to accompany them to the parsonage today?

Unless they were not going to see the minister.

A premonition of impending doom made her shiver as she slipped on her fur cape, but she refused to take Cassandra's bait and ask her to divulge their destination.

"You're not going to see Reverend Whiting," Cassandra pronounced, obviously anxious to continue the topic, with or without JoHannah's cooperation.

JoHannah's hand suspended in midair as she reached for the matching fur muff that sat on top of her dresser. Her gaze locked with Cassandra's, and JoHannah held her breath.

Swinging her feet to the floor, Cassandra stood up and arranged the flounces in her gown. Hips swaying, she glided to the door and paused beneath the door frame, turning as slowly as a revolving statue in a music box on its last pirouette. "Frozen silent, JoHannah? Still hoping your sacrilegious friends are coming for you?" Her lips formed a pout, and she shook her head. "Stubborn, willful Shaker. Despite what you tell the minister and my parents, you're never going to give up your odd faith, are you? Well, after today, you won't have any choice . . . not unless you enjoy martyrdom."

JoHannah's arm dropped to her side, and her heart started to pound. "Where . . . where am I going?" she whispered.

Cassandra grinned. "To court. Judge Weldon is presiding at your hearing again, and Papa said that by the time dinner is on the table, your friends will be mourning for sweet Sister JoHannah—lost to the World forever."

Momentarily stunned, JoHannah watched as Cassandra swept into the hall. One word—*home*—ricocheted in JoHannah's mind and eclipsed the others. Impulsively, she retrieved her lace cap and gown from their hiding places. She stuffed the cap into her muff, hid the folded gown beneath her cape, and rushed downstairs to the waiting coach.

"Oh, Heavenly Father, I thank you," she whispered as she descended the veranda steps. Her heart filled with joy. Regardless of what Cassandra thought, JoHannah instinctively knew that God was sending her home to Collier where she would be safe. In union with other Believers, she would be given God's grace to carry the cross against the flesh. "I'm going home to Zion," she murmured before she stepped into the coach.

"Amputation. It's the only answer." Dr. Carson repeated his diagnosis so loudly that Michael's ears rang.

"I'm . . . not . . . deaf," Michael gritted, clinging to lucidity by sheer effort. Burning with fever and weakened by the physician's aggressive attempts to save his leg, Michael found strength in outrage. "No! No amputation."

"You have no other choice," Carson responded sternly. "The infection is spreading. Within days, you'll be dead. There. I can't make it any clearer than that. Forgive me, son, but you're being obstinate, and your pride will cost you much more than your leg."

Michael squinted his eyes and gripped the physician's hand. "No," he ordered again, rankled as much by the weakness in his voice as the fate the physician decreed. Michael could not lose his leg. He refused to even consider it. A weak, cane-dependent cripple would not be a strong, competent master for Lawne Haven.

Or a captain capable of commanding a ship?

"Nora," he rasped, too weary to lift his head from the pillow.

The physician loosened Michael's hold and set the patient's arm beneath the coverlet. "Nora is resting," he murmured before pulling a chair alongside the makeshift sickbed that had been set in front of the fireplace in the parlor. "She's as exhausted as you are."

Michael swallowed hard, recalling every horrid detail of the accident that had put him flat on his back. Literally. After he had regained consciousness and dragged himself back to the house, Nora had nursed him through days and nights that had blurred into a never ending cycle of pain so intense, so piercing that he had welcomed the proffered draughts of laudanum as eagerly as a sailor who had been swept overboard clung to a life rope. Eventually, her nursing skill had him well on his way to a full recovery.

Then Fate, obviously feeling cheated, had intervened.

Determined to get back to the business of running Lawne Haven, he had fashioned a pair of crutches and, despite Nora's warnings, attempted a few chores. Two weeks after the accident, he was flat on his back again after losing his balance, falling, and ripping open the stitches that Nora had used to close his wound.

Within twenty-four hours, infection had set in and after Nora's efforts to draw the infection out with hot compresses had failed, he had sent her for Dr. Carson.

That had been . . . what? Hours ago? Several days? His mind had lost track of all time, just as his body apparently had not responded to the three-pronged approach the physician employed to save Michael's leg. Emetics and purge medications had not expelled the poison from his system. Blood-letting had not cleansed his blood, and blistering had failed as well. Michael grew weaker with each passing hour, and he did not need Dr. Carson's diagnosis to confirm what his body told him with every labored breath he took. Without a miracle, Michael would either die or spend the rest of his life as a one-legged cripple.

And in either event, what would happen to Lawne Haven? Avery would never agree to return to Lawne Haven simply because Michael had lost half his leg. Breathing shallow breaths of air, he knew that Avery would simply pray for him and expect him to rise to the occasion.

The unintended pun resulted in a sardonic laugh that caught in his throat and set off a series of coughs that sent the physician scurrying to get a glass of water. As Michael sipped the drink, he realized that the only way to get Avery home was to choose death. Then and only then would there be a chance that Avery would feel guilty enough to abandon his friends in faith and come home where he belonged.

When Michael thought about his brother and how adamant he had been about joining the Shakers, Michael resisted the urge to laugh at the absurdity of his situation: He had finally found a way to bring his brother home.

Yet as much as Michael's death might accomplish what he had failed to do while he was alive, there was only one problem as Michael saw the whole damned situation.

He was not ready to die.

He finished drinking and turned his head toward the physician. "A week," he said, trying to forestall the inevitable. "Try the treatments for another week."

Dr. Carson shook his head. "You won't live that long."

"How . . . how much longer can you wait?"

The physician scowled. "Two days. Three at the most."

Michael's jaw tightened. He nodded. "Give me two days. I need to see Nora."

"I'm here now, Michael."

As Nora bent over him, Dr. Carson stood up and moved out of the way. "I'll be back in the morning. You know what to do," he said resignedly. "And while you're at it, see if you can't talk some sense into the boy. By all rights, the surgery should be done today." With a snap of his bag, he walked out of the room.

Michael waited until he heard the doctor's buggy pull away before he spoke to Nora. "You heard?"

She kissed his forehead. "You mustn't be afraid. Dr. Carson is a good physician. You're young and stubborn enough to recover from the surgery."

Michael used the last vestige of his strength to speak before the laudanum-laced tonic Dr. Carson had slipped into Michael's drink took effect. "Go to Uncle George. Tell him—"

"I won't leave you alone!"

Fighting the drug that was slowly pulling a blanket of sleep over him, he clutched her hand. "Send Dolan with a note," he urged, hoping that Nora would be able to convince their neighbor to leave his wife, who was only two months away from delivering their first child, and carry a message to Michael's uncle. "Tell Uncle George to send someone . . . someone to help you after the surgery." Beneath half-closed lids, he saw relief flicker through Nora's eyes before they filled with guilt.

"You're delaying the surgery because of me? Michael, don't be foolish. I know I'm not as strong as I should be, but I'm rested now. Please. Let Dr. Carson operate in the morning.''

"No. No surgery. Not until help arrives for you," he insisted as he gazed at her beloved face. Thin translucent skin, accented by deep wrinkles, lined her face, and dark circles etched the underside of her red-streaked eyes. She looked wearied to the point that Michael feared she might suffer a stroke, and he would rather die than have Nora's health threatened any further because she had to nurse him. He loved her too dearly. "Promise me. . . ." Too weak to finish his plea, he closed his eyes as his voice trailed off.

"You're stubborn and willful . . . and I love you, too. I'll send Dolan to your uncle while you rest. That's right, my boy. Sleep. Build your strength."

Michael's eyelids fluttered closed, and as he let sleep overtake him, he prayed that help would arrive in time. He drifted into a world without pain and suffering where all his hopes for the future lay as bright and shining with promise as they had before his accident. And much to his relief, the same dream that greeted him when he slept throughout this illness embraced him once again.

The summer sun hung high in the heavens, and when it occasionally broke through the canopy of trees, it warmed the top of his head. His sleeves were rolled up to his elbows, and his arms were tanned from working outdoors. Throat parched, he walked toward the house through the woods surrounding Lawne Haven, satisfied with the number of trees he had notched for felling.

As he approached the rear of the house, he heard the rumbling laughter of children inside. The kitchen door opened, and a woman raced out to greet him. Tall and lithe, she glided toward him, her arms open wide. They embraced, and he tilted her head back for a kiss. His breath caught in his throat when he gazed into her beautiful eyes.

Soft violet eyes that were filled with love.

For him.

The woman turned, a teasing smile on her face, and started to run from him. He gave chase. His heart began to pound. He was breathing hard. Running faster and faster . . .

The dream faded out of focus and swirled into a maze of muted images. He stirred, moaning softly until the dream resumed, hoping that this time, it would have a different ending. This time he would be able to catch the elusive minx.

Chapter 6

"*S*ilence!"

The judge banged his gavel angrily, effectively ending a vitriolic argument that had erupted between the two lawyers. Again. "I'll see Miss Sims in my chambers. Now," he announced, repeating the order that had precipitated the latest fray. He rose, spoke briefly to the bailiff, and left the courtroom.

JoHannah's naive optimism had drained into numbing bewilderment as the court hearing had dragged on for several hours. It resurged into hope as she dutifully followed the bailiff into a small room, too emotionally exhausted to pray or to be unduly afraid.

A cozy-covered teapot in his hands, Judge Weldon looked up as she entered. "Take a seat," he suggested gently, all anger expunged from his demeanor.

As the door closed behind her, she slid into one of two wooden chairs in front of the judge's desk and settled her cape and muff on the seat of the other chair.

He handed JoHannah a cup of tea and took his own seat behind an uncluttered desk. Her cup rattled on its saucer, and she steadied it with her other hand, frowning as she inhaled the strong-scented liquid.

"Would you like cream and sugar?" he asked as he added a generous amount of each to his own tea.

"Thank you, no." She blushed, wondering how to tell him that she did not want the tea, either. She was not sure if he would understand that her faith forbid its use, but in any event, she could not risk offending his hospitality. Maybe she could just hold on to the cup and saucer for a while, and he would not notice that she was not drinking the beverage.

Her hands wrapped around the cup for warmth as her gaze slipped to the seat of the chair next to hers. Her forbidden gown was well hidden in the folds of her cape, but the edges of her burned cap peeked out of her muff. She looked away quickly, and with downcast eyes, chanced a peek at the judge as he sipped his tea. Wisps of unruly gray hair curled about his ears. Twin overhanging cliffs of wiry hairs, peppered with gray, hung over his deep-set, troubled eyes. He appeared to be as preoccupied now as he had during the hearing when he frequently had asked the lawyers to repeat themselves or restated his own, already-answered questions.

He leaned forward, put the empty cup on his desk and sighed. "Waste of good money and the court's time," he complained as he shook his head. "No matter how I rule, the losing party will appeal and demand a higher judicial ruling, and the cycle will continue until one of two things happens: Either one side will see this as an expensive exercise in futility and give up, or these ridiculous appeals will stretch until August when you turn twenty-one and the issue becomes moot."

More curious than afraid, JoHannah turned her head slightly to hear him better. Was it possible that Cassandra had been wrong and Eleazer Bathrick did not have undue influence with Judge Weldon? Unsure if she would upset him by making a comment, JoHannah held silent.

He looked directly at her, and she quickly averted her gaze.

"Tell me about your life at Collier."

"It's my home," she answered quietly. "I was very happy there."

"I'm more interested in knowing what you *did* while you were there."

His gentle reprimand sent a shiver of apprehension down her spine. What impact would her answer have on his decision? What if she said the wrong thing? She took a deep breath and said a hurried prayer before she answered. "I used to teach, and I've worked in the kitchen and the laundry. I helped with the planting or harvesting, if my brethren needed an extra hand. Lately, I worked with Sister Margaret, then Sister Evelyn. . . ."

"This Sister Margaret. What does she do?" he asked, his brow furrowing.

JoHannah moistened her lips. She still was not sure why the jurist was so interested in the specific details of the work she did at Collier, but she was encouraged by his question. Obviously, he had not decided what to do with her, and optimism flared back to life as she answered him. "Sister Margaret is in charge of drying and packaging seeds."

He smiled, obviously familiar with the successful business venture pioneered by the Shakers. "And Sister Evelyn?"

JoHannah stared at the rim of the tea cup to avoid seeing her own reflection. "She is our physician."

"A female?"

The surprise in his voice deepened her smile. "And a freed slave," she remarked. Dead silence filled the room, and she wondered if she had made a mistake by exploding yet another ridiculous World view of women and their proper roles by mentioning the issue of Sister Evelyn's race and status.

The squeak of a chair preceded his deep intake of breath. "A Negress physician. Mercy sakes!"

Silence filled the room again, broken only by the sound of their breathing that stretched her nerves taut and tempted her to chance another furtive glance in his direction.

"You're offended," she remarked, surprised by her boldness.

"On the contrary. I'm intrigued. You've been trained by Sister Evelyn?"

"As her assistant. I help to care for the patients she treats." When he looked over at her, she dismissed the order never to look directly at a man. Mesmerized by the worry that clouded his eyes, her heart filled with compassion. A man who had served on the bench for as long as he had, judging by his age, would have been able to set his own problems aside while hearing a case. Instead, he had lost his concentration often in the courtroom, and she felt his distraction could only have been caused by serious concerns. Such as worry for a friend or relative who was ill? "Have you need of a physician or a nurse?" she ventured, giving voice to her sense that his interest was much more than mere banter or idle curiosity.

Startled, he blinked repeatedly before he answered and assumed a stern posture as though forcing himself away from concerns that troubled his heart. "What I need to do is to settle this dispute between your guardian and the Shakers instead of focusing on my own worries."

She dropped her gaze, afraid she had annoyed him with her question.

He cleared his throat. "I assume you have a preference on how I rule," he said firmly as he redirected their conversation back to the matter which had brought her to court.

Nodding, she gripped the curved edge of the saucer.

"And?"

"I wish to go home. To Collier."

He sighed. "I didn't think you'd make this any easier for me. You realize, of course, that if I send you back to the Shakers, your guardian will eventually find a judge on a higher court to order you back under Bathrick's authority. At the same time," he continued as he stood and started to pace about the room, "it seems unfair to raise your hopes by finding for the Shakers and sending you back to them. Quite a dilemma, I'd say."

Or a divinely inspired test of faith?

"I would gladly wait on the higher court's ruling wherever Holy Mother Wisdom guides you to place me," she offered in a last-ditch attempt to spare herself the grief of being sent back to live with her guardian and his family which was apparently what the judge seemed inclined to do. Strangely at peace as a sudden gift of inspiration and courage infused her spirit, she held his gaze. "Perhaps . . . perhaps you are overlooking another option, one that might help both of us. I don't mean to be forward or to intrude on your private concerns, but I sense that you know someone who might have need for my skills as a nurse."

He rocked back on his heels and turned around to face her. He paused as though struck by thoughts that collided with hers. Sadness filled his eyes and shadowed his face. "My nephew. He's very ill and faces a long and difficult recovery. I'm very worried about him. His housekeeper is elderly, but I'm at a loss to find someone to help her nurse him. I'm sorry. I should be able to set aside—"

"It's only natural to be worried about a loved one. If you think I'd be able to help, I'd be glad to assist his housekeeper with his care."

His eyes widened. "Do you really want to avoid going back home with your guardian that much?"

Her smile was gentle.

"What are you suggesting? That I place you in a position as a nurse because you'd be in a setting that favors neither side?"

When she nodded her assent, he cocked his head. "Rather unusual," he mused as he rubbed his chin, and the worry that had dogged his expression earlier began to fade. "Even providential," he murmured as his eyes clouded with unspoken thoughts before glistening with resolve. "Your guardian has an overinflated sense of his own importance, and it galls me to see him ride roughshod over your desire to remain with your community. Since there's little doubt the court will eventually rule in his favor against you and your community, there probably isn't much I can do to prevent his ultimate victory. But I can forestall it—especially since you so kindly offered to help. More than likely, he'll file another suit charging that I decided against him to serve my own interests, but I can deal with that."

The judge smiled at her before walking straight back to his desk where he sat down and started to write. The scratch of pen on paper echoed the pounding of her heart as she waited for him to explain exactly what he had decided to do with her.

After several intense moments, he paused to look up at her. "You would have to pledge your word that you would obey the court's order and promise that you would not go back to Collier unless and until you are so ordered by the court."

"Of course," she replied, more relieved to be spared being sentenced to Bathrick's authority again than disappointed at not being sent directly back to Collier or frightened at the prospect of serving as a nurse in the World.

"Members of your community of faith would be forbidden to visit you."

Her brows lifted. "And my guardian?"

"So enjoined."

She smiled.

His eyes twinkled.

He dipped his head and started to write again. When he finished, he held the pen out to her. She put her now cold cup of tea on his desk and signed her name on several documents.

"For the next several months," he explained, "you'll be placed where you can be free from the influence of either side so that *if* the appeals last until your birthday, you'll have had the opportunity to come to your own decision about your future."

He paused, his voice choking with emotion, and she held her breath and clutched at a copy of the order the judge handed to her.

"I trust you have no second thoughts about assuming the duties of a nurse for my nephew. If so, tell me now. As much as my nephew needs your services—"

JoHannah stiffened her back and stood to her full height. "No second thoughts," she responded, overwhelmed with gratitude for being given a task that would be meaningful. The judge's smile warmed her heart.

"Thank you," he murmured before clearing the emotion from his voice. "Now, young lady, we can go back into court together, or you can set out while I make my ruling. I leave that up to you."

JoHannah hesitated, unsure if she could withstand her guardian's wrath or the disappointment of her brethren when each side found out they had both lost. At least for now. "How far must I travel? The sky is overcast, and the air is heavy. If a storm should break—"

"Two full days at least," he admitted.

"Then I think it best if I leave now," she answered solemnly. "My brethren have a trunk with my . . . my possessions which were left behind at Collier. May I take it with me?"

''No harm in that. Wait here while I secure a ticket for the stagecoach.''

JoHannah nodded absently, and the judge left her alone with her thoughts. Being sent to act as a nurse for some poor unknown soul was not exactly the ruling she had hoped for, but it was a far sight better than being sent back with her guardian. Apparently Holy Mother Wisdom did not want JoHannah to return to Collier immediately, but had found a way to give her the time to come to terms with her sinful nature so that when she finally did return to Collier, she would be worthy of becoming a formal Believer.

Curiosity eventually led her to look at the order signed by Judge Weldon. As she read his bold script, her eyes widened and filled with tears. Her hands began to shake, and the room began to spin.

Icy fingers of doubt and fear gripped her soul, and she swayed on her feet as one name leaped off the page and clawed at her heart: Michael Lawne.

She had been sent straight to the lion's den.

JoHannah had endured a two-day journey to Lawne Haven. She had passed the intense scrutiny of the housekeeper who guarded Michael. But would she survive coming face-to-face with the one man who stood between her and the life of faith she longed to claim?

At the entrance to the sickroom, JoHannah rocked to a sudden halt. Her nostrils flared at the overpowering stench of human misery that filled the air. With a quick glance about the first-floor room, obviously converted from a parlor to a sickroom, she swallowed hard, and her training as a healer took precedence over her own concerns. Everything she saw chafed at what she had been taught by Sister Evelyn.

Almost completely hidden from view beneath a mound of covers, the patient rested on a bed placed too close to the fireplace. Dust-catching velvet drapes on either side of the mantel closed off light and fresh air. Her gaze settled on the table set at a right angle next to the headboard. Drawn into the room, she inspected the array of instruments and bottles of medication. By the light of a single kerosene lamp that spewed its own distinctive odor, she read the contents of the bottles: calomel, a purgative; mustard, an emetic. Light glittered on a lancet, and she shivered at the thought that the physician also had bled the patient.

She closed her eyes and took a deep breath. The physician who had been treating Michael Lawne was obviously a devotee of Dr. Benjamin Rush, once a leader in effective treatments and recognized countrywide for his medical expertise. Unfortunately, Michael's physician also had failed to update his medical knowledge and clung to old-fashioned treatments that had failed to cure his patient. In fact, his treatments had put Michael dangerously at risk of surviving his injury, let alone the planned surgery.

Heart pounding, she turned away from the table and approached the patient as he slept. Nora sat on a chair by his side, bathing his flushed face with a cool cloth. Steeling herself against the demons that would send her pulse racing and paint a blush on her cheeks, JoHannah gazed at his face. Shock, however, numbed all of her senses.

On wooden legs, she moved closer to him, and Nora paused in her work as JoHannah studied his features. Several days' stubble covered his face, but even in the shadows, she could see the physical strain of his injury. His features were now gaunt and sharpened by a drastic loss of weight. Flushed cheeks indicated fever, an outward sign that the infection in his leg threatened his life and also reaffirmed that the physician's outdated and overly aggressive treatments had been ineffective. "When is the surgery?" she croaked, desperately overwhelmed with guilt for only thinking about herself. Michael Lawne was not a lion that lay in wait for the lamb of her unfaithful heart; he was a desperately ill man who needed her help.

"In the morning," Nora answered softly, her voice laced with sorrow and resignation. "Michael was recovering so well until he fell and reinjured his leg. I tried to tell him. . . . If only he hadn't . . ." Her voice slipped into a whisper, but the unspoken guilt she carried was abundantly clear.

"I'm sure you did everything you could to help Michael," JoHannah offered, using Michael's given name comfortably since her faith did not recognize World titles such as mister. She moved closer to Nora, who looked almost as gaunt and weary as the patient. "You must be exhausted," JoHannah said quietly. She pulled another chair alongside the patient. "Come. Sit here and rest while I take over your duties."

Nora sighed and rested her hand on Michael's cheek. "He's still burning with fever. I can't understand it. Dr. Carson has tried everything."

JoHannah changed places with Nora, dipped the cloth into a bowl of water, wrung it out, and placed it on Michael's forehead. Before JoHannah voiced any judgment at all about the physician's treatment, she had to be sure that her suspicions were correct. She chose her words carefully. "Has the doctor been practicing very long?"

Nora chuckled softly. "Longer than Methuselah, but the man has the stamina of a horse and the stubborn nature of a mule."

JoHannah nodded. "He seems to have left no path unexplored. Has he actually used all those medications?" she asked, pointing to the row of bottles on the table.

"He wrote down an hourly schedule," Nora responded, reaching into the pocket of her apron. She handed a small paper to JoHannah who held it out to the light to be able to read it. She caught her breath and let it out slowly. "How many times has he bled Michael?"

Nora winced. "Usually twice a day. It seems to drain Michael's strength, but who am I to judge?"

Clutching at Nora's good common sense, JoHannah shook her head. "Most physicians have abandoned the practice."

Eyes wide, Nora looked at her askance, and JoHannah wondered if she had been wrong to tell Nora about Sister Evelyn and her work at Collier. Or was Nora's reticence more likely caused by the fact that JoHannah was a Shaker sister from the very same community that had, in Nora's opinion, lured away Avery and his two daughters?

"Dr. Carson is a fine physician," Nora insisted, but her voice wavered.

"I'm sure he is." JoHannah reached out and grasped Nora's hands. "If the surgery is tomorrow morning, you should get some rest. I'll . . . I'll stay with Michael."

Nora's eyes filled with tears. "I should be here with him."

"And you will be. Tomorrow when he needs you most," JoHannah insisted as she urged Nora to her feet. "If I need you, or if Michael asks for you, I'll come wake you."

Nora trembled as she walked, and JoHannah stayed by the woman's side until they reached the staircase. "I'll be fine. Really." Nora looked up at JoHannah, her lips quivering. "Go on back. Stay with Michael. If he needs me—"

"I'll come for you."

Nodding, Nora's lips twitched with the hint of a smile. "Mine is the last room at the end of the hall. Bless you, child."

JoHannah stayed and watched Nora as she ascended the stairs, turned and finally disappeared into the darkened hallway.

Once back inside the sickroom, JoHannah knelt at the foot of Michael's bed and bowed her head. Every healing instinct in her body told her that Dr. Carson's course of treatment was wrong, but she held no place in Michael's world that would give her the right to question—let alone alter—the physician's orders. Judge Weldon had sent her to Lawne Haven to nurse Michael back to health after tomorrow's surgery. Nothing more.

If only she had arrived earlier, before the infection had become too dangerous to risk trying different treatments. If only she had the medicines Sister Evelyn used.

Tomorrow.

Anticipating the operation, she looked around the room and decided that if she could not forestall the inevitable, she could give Michael the benefit of a more sterile environment for his surgery and recovery.

She checked to make sure Michael was still asleep before setting to her task. Working as quietly and as efficiently as possible, she removed the velvet drapes and carried them out into the hall. She rolled up the carpet and pushed all extraneous furniture back against the walls. She scrubbed the floor, wiped down the bed and bed table, and washed the windows before cracking them open.

With one task left just before dawn, she surveyed the state of her gown and decided to change into one of her Shaker gowns before Michael awoke. Her trunk was still sitting just inside the front door, and she lifted the lid. Everything she had once owned lay neatly stacked inside: several gowns, starched white shoulder kerchief, undergarments . . . and a tin of her precious cocoa.

Out of the corner of her eye, she spied a small oval box. Heart racing, she lifted it up with trembling hands to open it. She gasped and covered her mouth with one hand. Sister Evelyn had packed a sampling of her remedies! Was this a sign from God that JoHannah had been meant to come here? Joy was fleeting, and her heart sank with the realization that she had come too late to save Michael from the surgery. Dejected, she set the box aside.

After quickly changing gowns and donning the familiar white shoulder kerchiefs, she set the trunk back to order. Disappointed that there was no lace cap to cover her hair, she rescued her burnt cap from its hiding place in her muff, folded the charred edges inward and placed it on her head. Even though the hair that framed her face still lay exposed, the comforting feel of the cap on the back of her head satisfied her. For now.

Returning to the sickroom, she prayed harder than she had ever done before. She moved the bed table several feet away, took hold of the bed's footboard and moved it in an arc as far away from the low-burning hearth as she could. Panting from the exertion, she never took her eyes off Michael's face. He stirred briefly as if in pain before falling still. She repeated her actions at the headboard and moved back and forth from one end of the bed to the other until it was centered in the middle of the room. After dousing the obnoxious kerosene lamp, shadows enveloped her, and she worked by the muted winter light that filtered through the uncovered windows and the soft glow from the hearth to reposition the bed table and a single chair.

She turned away and walked over to the window to rest her forehead against the frosted panes of glass. She had done all she could for Michael without overstepping her bounds. In the morning, the well-intentioned physician would remove the lower half of Michael's leg, and she wondered if Dr. Carson would ever realize that with different treatment, Michael might have avoided that fate— treatment she had no right to begin even if it was not too late to try.

She closed her eyes, breathing in cold, fresh air, still troubled by the image of the proud and confident Michael Lawne, now condemned to spend the rest of his life as a cripple. Unless she intervened. "I can't discern Your will," she whispered in prayer. "Not unless You give me the gift to know what to do. Fill me with Your spirit," she prayed. "Use me as Your instrument, and I will serve You."

Chapter 7

"Oh, what are we to do? The whole world has been dipped in ice. Look over there! Even the roadway is as slick as a frozen pond. God help us, there isn't a coach or horse that could travel today." Nora's voice dropped to a pained whisper. "Dr. Carson won't be able to get here to do the surgery."

"Maybe it's a sign that we should try to save Michael's leg while we wait for a thaw. The medicines I told you about are in my trunk. Dr. Carson's treatments didn't work, but if you're willing to help me . . ."

Roused by the sound of female voices, Michael opened his eyes and blinked back the flood of light that poured into the room through uncovered floor-to-ceiling windows. He raised his head and stared through the window. He saw a strange, translucent world where pale argentine sunlight glistened on glass-limbed trees with thick, cracked ceramic trunks and delicate crystal shrubbery. A mirrored roadway reflected muted images of a natural world turned surreal.

He sucked in his breath, alarmed by the fever-induced hallucination that turned the outside world into porcelain. He looked over to the other window. Shadowed, two figures stood side by side in hushed conversation, their bodies pressed close to the ice-covered panes of glass. He recognized Nora, even from behind. Dwarfed by a taller woman, the housekeeper's shoulders were slumped and her head was bowed. The other woman, however, stood erect, seemingly self-possessed with an inner calm. He shook his head to clear the impossible notion that this might be the gentle Shaker sister from Collier, although when he squinted his eyes, he could almost swear a white lace cap rested on her head. He sighed, convinced that he was too ill or too drugged even to see clearly.

But if it was not JoHannah, who was this woman? Far too slender to be Genevieve, his neighbor's wife, there was only one other woman she could be: Nora's helper.

He closed his eyes and laid his head back against the pillow. With no idea of how long it had been since Dr. Carson had issued the verdict that sealed Michael's fate, the arrival of this woman meant that the surgery would be soon. He cracked his eyes open, surveyed the room, and slammed them shut again. The room had been stripped and rearranged in anticipation of the surgery.

He gritted his teeth and clenched his jaw. There would be no reprieve. No miracle. *No dream.* He took a deep breath and braced himself for the inevitable. He was not afraid of the pain that lay ahead—it had been his constant companion for too long. Admittedly, he was daunted by the prospect of living as a cripple for the rest of his life. His sense of responsibility as the master of Lawne Haven was strong enough that he was now willing to crawl rather than relinquish that right, and he was equally adamant in his determination to return to sea.

No. Oddly, that grief that hugged his soul was for his dream, that tempting glimpse of idyllic life where he was joined in body, spirit, and heart with JoHannah. That was the hardest to give up. He had lived the dream for nearly a week, yet it was not nearly long enough. He wanted a lifetime of weeks, but he might be willing to sell his soul to live the dream . . . for just a few more days.

He dug his right heel into the mattress to shift position. Excruciating pain bolted through his injured leg, and he groaned. His hands balled into fists until the pain gradually ebbed into a series of pounding throbs. His senses alert, he heard the rustle of skirts as the women approached his bed.

Damn!

He did not want to let Nora know how much he hurt, and he sure as sin did not want to see the pity in her eyes now that reckoning day had arrived—pity that would no doubt also fill the expression of the other woman who could be nameless and faceless for eternity for all he cared at this particular moment.

"Michael, are you in pain?" Stitched with worry, Nora's voice cracked.

He nodded, his eyes sealed shut as he felt her touch his brow.

"Still fevered," she whispered.

"Sorry. To be so much trouble," he gritted, waiting for the second woman to make her presence known.

"Hush. You need your strength," Nora admonished gently.

He sighed. "How much longer before Dr. Carson—"

Nora silenced him with a squeeze of her hand. "Not today. There's been an ice storm."

Despite his determination to remain hidden in darkness of his own making, Michael glanced over to the windows. "An ice storm," he repeated, relieved that his surreal vision of the outside world was not a bizarre figment of his fevered state. He heard footsteps leave the room and stared at the sheet that covered his legs. He closed his eyes again. "You have someone to help you."

"She arrived last night before the storm, thank goodness.

She's a physician's assistant, Michael, and she's treated wounds like yours before.''

He snorted, unable to hide his bitterness. "Experienced in amputations? Uncle George always did have the most amazing knack for—''

"I'm trained to heal.''

From directly behind him came a vaguely familiar voice, firm but steady, to chastise him. Struggling to sharpen his hazy, drugged senses, he stiffened, wondering how the woman had gotten back into the room without making a sound. "It's too late for that now. Bad timing, either on your part or mine.''

"God's timing prevails in the end,'' she insisted gently.

Frowning, he refused to open his eyes while battling wits with her as he concentrated, instead, on blocking out the tempting aroma wafting in the air. His stomach growled and rumbled in the room like a prolonged clap of thunder.

"Will you take some broth?''

"Why bother?'' he grumbled, ravenously hungry after days without food. "The medicines purge whatever I eat or drink.''

"They leave you too weak to battle the infection in your leg. You won't be needing any of Dr. Carson's medicines between now and the surgery, whenever that will be, especially the laudanum. It's too powerful a drug to use for so long.''

His eyes flashed open. He stared at Nora. "Where's Dr. Carson?''

Nora moistened her lips. "We can't contact him.''

"Whose idea is it to challenge his orders? Yours or hers?''

"Mine,'' answered the new voice that was growing more irritatingly familiar by the moment.

"No. Ours,'' Nora insisted, her eyes narrowing into slits of determination. "Unless you . . . Michael, listen to me.

There's a chance we can use this time to try another way to save your leg—''

''If Dr. Carson couldn't do it, what makes you think she can? She's not a physician. Only an assistant, a nurse at best.'' Even as he spoke, hope wrapped around the thick base of his disdain. He fought against it, angry words his only defense against the sweet yearning that would only sour into despair when the new treatment failed—as he feared it would.

''You're determined to lose your leg. Without a fight,'' the stranger said quietly.

''Cowardice is not one of my vices,'' he spat, tossing a harsh retort over his shoulder.

''Nor mine.''

That voice! No, it was impossible. . . .

He turned his head sharply around to face her, this nameless, faceless adversary who dared to challenge him and offer him false hope. He opened his mouth to speak, but the words died on his lips. He blinked several times to clear the image of the woman who had haunted his dreams. To no avail—she was real . . . she was here, standing only inches away from his bed. Eyes downcast, her lips set in a firm line, she clutched a wooden tray in her hands. ''You?'' he rasped. ''Uncle George sent *you*?''

She nodded.

The corner of her lips twitched almost imperceptibly, and he understood in that one small movement that she acknowledged the incredible irony of her presence in his home. Without saying a word, she admitted, albeit with blushed cheeks, that even though they had barely spoken to one another before now, the attraction he had felt for her had been mutual.

''Do you know JoHannah?'' Nora asked.

Only too well . . . in my dreams.

But this was no dream. This was reality, and Michael

found it hard to reconcile his emotions to that harsh fact of life. He cleared his throat and stared at JoHannah. "She's from Collier. I met her once when I visited Avery. I had no idea the Shakers left their community—"

"We usually don't. My guardian had my indenture revoked and forced me to leave," JoHannah interrupted.

Michael cocked his head. "Now he's set you out to work?"

"No."

Nora fussed with his sheets. "Your uncle sent her here."

Thoroughly confused, Michael looked from JoHannah to Nora and back again. "He *sentenced* you to be here?"

"N-no," she stammered as she stared at the tray. "It's a very long tale. One I'll share with you while you eat." She put the tray on the bedside table, now devoid of Dr. Carson's prescribed medications, and handed Michael a napkin. His mind raced with possibilities that might explain JoHannah's presence, and he leaned forward while Nora fixed several pillows behind his back.

"I'll leave you two to get better acquainted while I get the bandages to change your dressing," she whispered before she slipped from the room.

He stared straight ahead, his thoughts still ajumble as images of his dream danced in the flames that flickered in the fireplace. *JoHannah.* More intriguing and more alluring than a woman had a right to be. And now she stood beside him when he was an invalid, a soon-to-be cripple.

He slammed his fist against the bed. He had to think of a way to get her to leave, or he would spend the next few months in a hell more viciously designed than the one he was already in.

JoHannah gratefully claimed victory as she laid the spoon next to the empty bowl. Michael had polished off every last bit of beef broth. It was still premature, however, to gauge the success of the battle raging in her mind and body. The brush of her hand against his stubbled chin, and the feel of his breath on her fingertips as she fed him, left her trembling. Forbidden sensations made her heart beat erratically, and she steeled herself, willed herself, to face them and find the strength to defeat them once and for all. She shook a cupped hand to the floor.

"This treatment of yours. Will it work?"

His deep-timbred question allowed her to focus on a topic much less unsettling than the discussion they had had about her training under Sister Evelyn, the revocation of her indenture, and Judge Weldon's order which had sent her to Lawne Haven. "I don't know."

He snorted. "At least you're honest."

"I'll try my best to help you. With God's grace, the leeches—"

"Leeches? Did you say leeches?" Michael bolted upright, groaned with pain and grabbed her arm. "Woman, are you properly trained in medicine or in sorcery? You intend to put leeches on my leg?"

She gulped hard and stared at the dark hairs on the back of his hand. She noted that a few of them were silver, just like the hair at his temples. "They'll suck the poison from the wound."

"They'll drain my lifeblood! What kind of medicine do you fanatics practice? Of all the preposterous, ludicrous, idiotic—"

She twisted his wrist to expose the inner flesh of his arm and pointed to several rows of stitched cuts. "Dr. Carson bled you several times a day, and when he did, your lifeblood drained from you. I fail to see the difference between his treatment and mine, except—"

He pulled away from her and folded his arms across his chest. "Dr. Carson used accepted medical procedures."

"It's outdated and dangerous medicine, especially when

combined with purgatives and emetics," she countered without raising her voice.

He snorted. "According to the Gospel of Sister Evelyn, I presume."

She flinched. Even though she had expected him to criticize her mentor, she was not prepared for the venom in his voice. "Blasphemy is a sin," she informed him. "God created his creatures to help man. Each has his purpose, if we are open to His wisdom."

"Leeches," he muttered, shaking his head.

Beneath downcast eyes, she watched as he laid back against the pillows and closed his eyes. His chest expanded rhythmically as he took measured breaths of air. Was he trying to control his pain or his disgust and anger?

An eerie quiet filled the room and stretched into awkwardness. She watched him openly, and just as she was about to voice yet another argument in her favor, he opened his eyes and caught her staring at him. Blushing, she dropped her gaze again, her heart pounding at the intensity of pain and hope that churned in eyes of murky gray.

"Do it. Do whatever you have to do."

She took a deep breath and met his gaze, mesmerized for just a moment as understanding of his desperate need filled her spirit and overwhelmed her own misgivings about her skill and the dangerous attraction he had for her. "I'll need to cleanse the wound first. Nora will help me, but it will be painful."

He nodded once. Stiffly.

Without saying another word, she cleared away the tray and secured the oval box from her trunk while Nora boiled water and gathered fresh linen for the bed. After moving the table to the foot of the bed, JoHannah set out her meager array of instruments and remedies while Nora folded back the sheet that covered Michael's wounded leg and removed the bandages that held a splint in place.

Braced for the worse, JoHannah's breath caught in her throat as she inspected the exposed limb. From knee to ankle, swollen angry flesh stretched along his shin bone and looked almost ready to explode. Red lines snaked through bruised, purpled flesh and infection oozed from the gaping horizontal wound that extended midway across the lower half of his leg.

She did not blame Dr. Carson for his decision to operate, not after seeing that Michael's wound was indeed grievous and life-threatening. In the same heartbeat, she gave unmeasured glory to God's power and acknowledged her role as His instrument. She handed Michael a flavorful root. "Place this between your teeth."

"For pain? What drug is this?"

She smiled. " 'Tis only a pleasant-tasting root to ease your pain. Nothing more."

Turning back to his leg, she gripped Nora's hand, bowed her head, and prayed silently. *Guide my hands and fill me with Your wisdom.*

Dozing in a chair near the hearth, JoHannah bolted awake and pitched forward as a log broke and the fire crackled and hissed. Her lace cap flew from her head and landed on the floor, dangerously close to the flames. Heart racing, she grabbed at the already charred edges and pulled it away. Holding it up to the muted light of late afternoon, she sighed with relief when she realized it had not caught fire again.

"What happened . . . to your cap?"

She spun around, clutching the bit of lace in both hands at her waist. Wide-eyed, she stood speechless.

"Did you get close to the fire once too often?"

She moistened her lips, wondering if he had any idea at all that he was far more dangerous to her than an inferno. "I didn't know you were awake. How are you feeling?"

"Like I've been mauled, covered with honey, and set out as a feast for parasites, which is to say that I feel as well as you should expect me to. What happened to your cap?"

She gulped and twisted the cap in her hands. "My guardian's wife said it wasn't fashionable. She tossed it into the fire."

He squinted and stared at her hands. "Obviously you salvaged it."

She nodded and proceeded to fold back the burnt edges again so she could put it back on. Her hands trembled as she bowed her head and set the cap in place.

"I like it."

Her head snapped up.

"I do. It's quaint, but very feminine. Especially now that it's not quite as severe as before."

If blushes could cover one's entire body, JoHannah was certain she was scarlet from the top of her head to the tips of her toes. Her pulse quickened, and she drew short, jerky breaths of air. "When I return to Collier," she said quietly as she moved closer to the bed to inspect his wound, "I'll have a proper cap."

"You mean if. *If* you return."

She paused and held very still. "I will return," she reiterated, unwilling to give quarter on the issue. She could not believe that God would send her here to face Michael Lawne if He did not intend for her to one day return to His flock.

Leaning closer to the bed, she cautiously studied every nuance of Michael's wound, noted the ashen color to his foot and the still-dangerous swelling in his leg. Crestfallen that there seemed to be no improvement in his wound, her heartbeat sunk into a rhythm that pounded in sync with the devastation she felt at seeing evidence that her treatment had apparently come too late.

"Well, Doctor, what's the verdict? Did the treatment work?"

"I'm not a doctor," she insisted without looking up at him for fear he would see her failure reflected in her eyes.

"You avoid answering questions just as adeptly."

"There's little if any improvement. I'd hoped there would be more evidence of a change for the better."

"Which means you failed?"

"I'm not sure," she whispered, "but I think we should continue the treatments."

"But will they save my leg?"

His hand pulled on her sleeve, but his question tugged at her heart. The fate of this once strong and vibrant man, humbled by his injury, lay in her hands, and she could not bear to think she had raised his hopes only to be met by failure. "It's too soon to tell," she murmured, praying there was yet time for her remedies to prove effective.

"But you—"

"I don't know yet. It's been less than twelve hours." She straightened, reached over, and checked his pulse by wrapping her fingers about his wrist. "Steady, but weak," she murmured softly, glad that he would never know how fast her own pulse raced at that moment. Discouraged by all the signs indicating her treatment was not working, she laid her hand across his brow. He had the decency to close his eyes, although she noted before he did that they were still glazed with fever. "Slightly cooler than before, but still too warm to be considered normal," she announced before he could question her.

"Where's Nora?"

JoHannah pulled her hand away. "She's making supper. Are you hungry?"

He shook his head.

"You should have more broth."

"Only if you feed it to me."

She blushed again and wondered if her skin would be permanently stained the color of overripe raspberries. "Nora—"

"Nora wasn't sent here to be my nurse. You were." He opened his eyes, reached out, and with one finger, pressed down on the tip of her chin. "Look at me."

"I mustn't," she argued, jerking back and closing her eyes.

"Why not? You did earlier."

She clenched her jaw. "I was contrary to order."

"Meaning?"

She took a deep breath. "My faith forbids looking directly into a man's eyes."

He chuckled. "Does it now? I seem to recall another time. At Collier. Just after . . . ."

Her eyes flashed open, and spewed sparks at him she could feel herself.

"What other rules do you break?" he whispered, deflecting her outrage with a shield of experience and determination she could not penetrate. When he trailed the back of his fingers along one of her cheeks, she trembled, and all thoughts of her apparent failure to cure the infection in his leg scattered. His soft, admiring gaze held her immobile as silken sensations flowed through her entire body. Her eyes filled with tears, and she blinked them away as she stumbled back to escape his gentle teasing and seductive touch.

To her horror, she found she enjoyed them.

The Eldress's warning not to open her heart to a small vice, lest more serious ones enter, echoed in her mind. She sped through the doorway from the sickroom to the outer hall, turned, and pressed her shaking body against the wall for support. She gulped in deep breaths of air and yanked the cap from her head.

She stared at the charred, ragged edges of her cap, and it became a glaring visual image of the state of her once-pure soul. Michael's words replayed in her mind. Oh, how he had baited her and flattered her until she had been cornered in his lair. Lord, he was handsome and so . . . so seductive!

Tears filled her eyes as she gazed at her beloved cap. She was weak. Too weak in flesh and spirit to resist Michael's charming flattery, and what had once been an integral part of her identity as a woman of faith had become a frivolous World adornment.

Why? She should be able to resist him.

She had been trained from an early age to expect, even welcome, the World's scorn and contempt. When Leila Bathrick and Cassandra had mocked her for wearing her cap, JoHannah had stoically turned the other cheek, absorbing each wicked taunt with faithful dignity until Leila had ended the cruel game by tossing JoHannah's cap into the fire.

Overconfident, JoHannah had been totally unprepared for Michael's more subtle approach and her wicked reaction. Warm delight filtered through her body when Michael confessed he found her attractive, and without warning, yet another vice—vanity—had slipped into her heart.

She folded and refolded the cap until it was small enough to clench in her fist. She should never have worn this cap! It did not cover her head the way it was supposed to do. Eyeing her trunk, she opened it and searched through the contents until she found one of her white cotton shoulder kerchiefs, vowing to make a new cap to cover every hair on her head, wishing it would be as easy to stitch up the hole in her heart.

And for the first time since she had left Collier, she knew beyond any shadow of doubt that the lion who had been lying in wait for her unfaithful heart was a far gentler beast than she had expected.

Her soul trembled.

Chapter 8

Final Judgment Day, when Michael would be held accountable for taunting and teasing JoHannah, loomed in the very distant future. The moment of reckoning, when his worldly fate would be sealed, arrived just before midnight.

Surrounded on all sides by Nora, JoHannah, and Dr. Carson, Michael had an uncommon sense of relief. Now it would end, once and for all: the waves of hope that crested and crashed into despair with rhythmic certainty, the never-ending, excruciating pain that robbed him of his self-control. Without the laudanum, he had slept fitfully at best, and without the calming relief of his dream or the numbing of his senses, he felt like an animal caught in a trap. Bewildered and nearly crazed, he almost prayed for death to release him from life's painful stranglehold.

Still prone, he stared down at his injured leg. Despite the bright glow from the kerosene lamp which had been set back in its place, the mass of wrappings that held the splint obscured any view of his wound. Dr. Carson's probing examination had opened the floodgates of such hellacious pain that Michael was tempted to be done with it, even if he had to cut off the offending limb himself. Muscles rigid, teeth clamped together, he was grateful when Nora moved closer to the bed and took his hand.

"Well, Dr. Carson?" he gritted, too ill to trust his own judgment about JoHannah's treatment—judgment that was based on irrational hope instead of sound reason.

The physician grimaced. "I'm sorry, Michael. I see no reason to forestall the amputation."

Michael's heart pounded immediate denial. "There's no improvement? None at all?"

"On the contrary. With the bone cracked open, the infection may have spread there as well. Miss Sims's treatment was well intentioned, but highly unorthodox. Discontinuing the medications I left for you was more than ill-advised. It was—"

"But it's been less than twenty-four hours," JoHannah interceded, speaking quietly and gently, her head bowed slightly. "Treatments take time."

Dr. Carson ignored her and spoke directly to Michael. "Time is not a luxury you can afford, son. By this time tomorrow, you'll be on the verge of delirium," the physician argued sternly. "Unless I amputate."

"Look at Michael's eyes," Nora pleaded as she left Michael's side to stand beside JoHannah. "They're still clouded with fever and pain." She paused and took a deep breath. "I'm sorry. I know you were trying your best to treat Michael's injury, but he's getting worse, not better. Perhaps Dr. Carson is right. Amputation is the only way to save Michael's life."

"I've been treating patients for forty years." Dr. Carson turned to JoHannah, his face suffused with anguish. "Unless I amputate, the infection will spread through his entire body. There's nothing more that you or I can do to prevent that."

Michael stared at JoHannah who was remarkably silent during this latest exchange, but whose face was nearly hidden by the folds of the absurd, ill-fitting cap she had made for herself. "And what do you say?" he murmured softly, studying her intently and waiting to see the subtle habit that would indicate she was nervous.

True to form, she dropped one arm and shook a cupped hand to the floor. "Dr. Carson is a physician with many years of experience."

"Then you agree with him."

"I didn't say that."

Michael pounded the bed, grimacing when pain shot through his leg. "Speak your mind, woman!" Irritated by her natural inclination to avoid confrontation of any kind, especially with anyone she considered to be her superior, he waited for her answer. Would she remain stoically silent like she did every time he tried to flatter her? Or would she finally speak her mind?

Her hands trembled but she stood erect, her shoulders set and her backbone straight. "I believe the infection can be cured. With another few days of treatment, your leg should begin to heal properly."

"I disagree!"

Michael glared at the physician, almost as distraught by Dr. Carson's denial as he was shocked by her boldness, particularly in light of the seeming failure of her treatments. "When would you amputate? In the morning?" Dr. Carson's nod nearly stopped Michael's heartbeat. "And if I wait?"

"You'll be dead in less than a week." He paused and ran his hand through his hair. "You can't wait, Michael. You can't put your trust in treatments that quite obviously do not work and put your very life at risk. That's one risk I would strongly advise you *not* to take."

Michael exhaled slowly. "And if it were your leg? Your future at stake?"

The doctor's eyes filled with sorrow, his answer caught in the depths of his own soul.

Nora squeezed Michael's hand. "I'll be here with you, and so will JoHannah. Dr. Carson is, after all, a competent physician."

"That he is," Michael murmured as he closed his eyes and tried to block out the physician's recommendation. He wanted to save his leg. He wanted to be healthy again and strong enough to be master of Lawne Haven. He wanted to believe in JoHannah and her treatments, but was her strong conviction that he would keep his leg *and* his life based more on her odd brand of faith than on her elementary, questionable medical treatment? Or was she luring him into a false sense of security and blinding him to life's brutal realities, just as her fellow Believers had done to Avery?

He opened his eyes and stared at her. Arms at her sides, both hands were now hidden in the folds of the lavender gingham gown he remembered only too well. The valleys of the shoulder kerchief deepened ever so slightly as she took small, even breaths of air. Her face was serene, and he wanted desperately to look into her eyes, but as usual, she kept her gaze to the floor.

He glanced away to look at the others. Eyes brimming with tears, Nora's lips trembled as she moved back to his side. Dr. Carson met Michael's gaze and held it with stern authority.

Confidence. Uncertainty. Authority. Each attitude personified in the people standing over him, pulling him in different directions, teasing his hopes and dreams or destroying them.

Risk.

Just one more calculated risk, he realized. For victory or defeat, with victory evoking far sweeter memories.

Reflecting back on his life at sea, he remembered taking chances—on the sea, on the weather, on his crew. The pounding sense of adventure, the quickening alarm, the surge of triumph in the end. Man against nature: the never-ending battle he raged and won time and time again.

His one near failure had been swift and devastating, and the memory of it chilled his glowing memories of success. One failure to listen to his own instincts had nearly led to disaster . . . and he had been forced to take unnecessary risks to save his ship and his crew.

Lawne Haven. Nourished by centuries of dedication, the land had been kept in the family only because his forefathers had taken risks with their lives and with their fortunes. Here Michael envisioned a future where he would survive or fail from one season to the next because Nature was a bit more forgiving, offering her cycle of birth and rebirth as a constant incentive to maintain family traditions.

As heir to those traditions, Michael had only one choice, a choice that recognized that a one-legged cripple could not plow the fields or harvest the timber to keep Lawne Haven alive. Neither could a maimed man have any hope of courting and winning the hand of a woman who would carry his name and bear his sons—the eldest of whom would continue those traditions, freeing him to return to sea knowing that he had met all his responsibilities.

All of which meant, for Michael, there was really no choice at all.

"We'll wait . . . and continue her treatments," he gritted, placing all of his hopes and dreams in the hands of the gentle Shaker sister who already had custody of his dreams.

After five exhausting, bewildering days battling a tug of war between hope and despair, JoHannah stood at the foot of Michael's bed. She watched Dr. Carson as he once again inspected Michael's leg, witness to the melange of heavy emotions that anguished his face. They shredded her pride and gripped her spirit.

His long, gentle fingers shook ever so slightly as they probed Michael's limb, and the corners of his lips trembled with soundless words he spoke only to himself. When he completed his examination, he covered the limb with a sheet and took a step back.

"Well? Is the infection cured?" Michael's agitated voice broke through the tense cloud of silence that hung in the room.

"Gone. It's completely gone. I've never seen anything like it, not in a case this advanced. I really thought . . ." Shoulders slumped, the physician mopped his brow.

"JoHannah was right!" Michael whooped and slapped the mattress, seemingly oblivious to the pain he must have caused himself. "Wait till Nora hears this! I was hoping she'd be back from visiting Dolan and Genevieve by now. She's not going to believe it! You were right, JoHannah. Your treatment worked!"

"Nora won't be home for a few hours yet," JoHannah said quietly, wishing she could find a way to soften Michael's praise and contain his exuberant joy. The change in Michael was nothing short of miraculous. Completely fever free, Michael had gained strength. The once-angry flesh in the wound had turned healthy pink against puckered black stitches, and the leeches that he detested had been abandoned. Relief that Dr. Carson agreed that her treatments had worked and Michael's life and leg would be spared filled her heart.

Her sense of accomplishment, however, quickly and surprisingly evolved into yet another vice: pride. When had her prayers for Michael changed from a humble request to serve God's will to heartfelt pleas to spare Michael's life and leg . . . so that her confidence in her treatment and her ultimate success after a disastrous beginning would be assured?

Exhausted as much from constant nursing duties as by untold hours of prayer that left her vulnerable to the sin of pride, JoHannah longed to return to the tranquil, faith-filled life she had led at Collier . . . before the World ripped apart her heart and completely stripped away her faith.

Pale and shaking visibly, Dr. Carson reached for his worn medical bag, obviously devastated to have been so wrong. His pain was so deep, it reached out to her and begged for kindness, for some assurance that he was not too old or too old-fashioned to be considered competent in his life's work.

"Dr. Carson?" She used his title willingly, as if acknowledging his profession might soften his failure.

The physician turned toward her. His shoulders stiffened, as though preparing to carry the added burden of guilt she was about to heap at him for being wrong. At that moment, she realized that the sin of pride that had filled her spirit would be strong enough to destroy both of them . . . unless she reached out right now and replaced it with compassion.

"Thank you," she began, searching for the words that would soften his pain without having to resort to an outright lie that he would reject the minute she uttered it. The simple, humble truth, straight from her heart, tumbled out. "The aggressive treatments you started kept Michael alive until I arrived most unexpectedly. My treatments have failed as often in the past as they have succeeded. I—I don't think we'll ever know for certain why they worked so well for Michael, but I do know we both served God's will, and He alone should be praised for the wonder of His mercy."

"You're very kind," he whispered. His eyes misted with the gratitude his voice apparently could not find the courage to say. "See that Michael rests that broken bone for a few weeks before he takes to crutches. In the meantime, you'll need to exercise the muscles in his ankle and foot." He paused and turned toward Michael with one hand extended. "Son, you've got a second chance. Use it wisely. Maybe someday you can forgive an old man. . . ."

Michael shook the physician's hand. "No apology necessary, sir. JoHannah is right. You kept me alive. I'm very grateful."

"I'm off to see Mrs. Tucker now. Should I save your good news, or may I tell Nora—if she's still there."

Michael laughed. "Shout it along the way! While you're at it, see if you can't convince Dolan and Genevieve to come by for a visit."

"It had best be soon." The physician smiled. "There's only another six weeks or so before Mrs. Tucker's confinement ends, and I think the last few weeks are best spent at home."

JoHannah slipped out of the room as Michael detained Dr. Carson in animated conversation that seemed to brighten the physician's spirits and restore his confidence. Certain that she had only slightly redeemed her own sin of pride, she made her way to the kitchen, her shoulders sagging beneath the weight of a greater cross—one that would be harder to carry now that Michael was on the straight and narrow road to recovery: the cross of the flesh.

Chapter 9

The end of another March day brought yet another challenge to JoHannah's faith. The last waning rays of twilight filtered through the kitchen window. A healthy fire crackled in the hearth. Seated at a round oak table, JoHannah stared at a small parcel wrapped in printed pink cotton and tied together with twine.

"Open your gift, dear," Nora urged as she nudged the package closer to JoHannah.

Hands cupped on her lap, JoHannah's chest tightened. She dropped her gaze, wondering how to decline Nora's present without hurting the woman's feelings. "I—I don't know what to say," she stammered as wondrous childhood memories of the presents her parents had given to her clashed with the stronger taboo her faith placed on presents—of any kind.

"A simple 'thank you' is enough," Nora insisted. "It's only a little token of my gratitude for . . . for what you've done for Michael. Even if you still insist that Dr. Carson's round of treatments might have set the stage for Michael's recovery, I truly believe you worked a miracle. I'm sorry I . . . I doubted you."

Blushing, JoHannah folded her hands together. "I was

only God's instrument. Glory and thanksgiving should be given to Him.''

''I've been prayin' so hard that He would find a way to spare Michael, and when Dr. Carson told me today that Michael's leg was free from infection, I . . . I . . .'' She paused to dab at her eyes. ''The Good Lord knows my heart is full of thankfulness for His mercy. I just wanted you to know. . . . Here!'' She pushed the parcel so hard JoHannah had to grab it before it slid past her on the waxy surface of the table and landed on the floor. The older woman's eyes startled wide open like a window sash thrown up to let in fresh air after a storm. ''Oh, dear! It isn't much, but I didn't mean to shove it at you!''

''It's all right,'' JoHannah responded, her heart and voice softened by Nora's good intentions. Without hurting Nora's feelings, she could find no way to refuse Nora's gift. She hushed the nagging voice of her conscience and listened to her heart, untied the twine and peeled away the thin fabric.

In the next heartbeat, tears blurred her vision, and she ran trembling fingers over the finely knitted cap that nestled before her on a bed of pink fabric roses. Unable to swallow enough air to give sound to her voice, she closed her eyes, a single tear trickling slowly down her cheek.

''Oh, oh dear! It's not all that grand,'' Nora insisted. ''I—I don't pretend to understand your faith, and I feel bad that Michael teases you so. I know your faith is important to you as sure as I know that your heart is kind and sweet and generous. A new cap was the only thing I could think to make for you. . . .''

JoHannah gazed across the table and reached out to clasp one of Nora's hands. ''Thank you. It's beautiful.''

Nora's eager smile reached her eyes. ''Put it on. Let's see if it fits.''

Just as anxious to try it on, JoHannah eased the makeshift cotton cap off her head and replaced it with the gift Nora had so lovingly created for her. JoHannah felt along the hairline that framed her face and followed the edge of the cap that covered her ears and accommodated the thick coil of hair at the nape of her neck. "It's perfect," she exclaimed, "but much more than I deserve. I really didn't—"

"Yes. Yes, you did, young lady. Now . . . before Michael wakes up and bellows for you, why don't we share a pot of tea?" Blushing instantly, her hands fluttered in the air. "Oh, I've done it again! I'm so sorry. You must have told me a dozen times in the past week—"

"It's not a problem. Really." JoHannah rose, folded her old cotton cap and wrapped it up in the pink rose fabric before tying it closed with the twine. "Do you . . . do you suppose there's enough milk to fill two mugs?" she ventured, praying Nora would not think her too bold.

A puzzled look flashed across Nora's face. "Yes, of course."

"Good. Warm some milk. I'll be right back." Hurrying from the kitchen, JoHannah slipped past her now-empty trunk, pausing just long enough to make sure Michael was still asleep before she mounted the stairs to get to her room. Moments later, she reentered the kitchen and handed a tin of cocoa to Nora who was stirring a pan of milk on the stove.

A grin slowly worked its way into a smile, and Nora pointed to a cupboard on the wall to her left. "Check the third shelf. If I'm not mistaken, there's a single stick of cinnamon left in a blue jar with a white lid."

Excitement gripped JoHannah's heart as she found the cinnamon and secured two heavy pewter mugs from the cupboard. The budding affection between herself and Nora gently eased JoHannah's crushing loneliness for her sisters in faith. Accepting Nora's friendship as a far greater gift than the cap, she put two heaping spoonfuls of cocoa into each mug, vowing to return Nora's kindness by finding the words to soften the pain that Brother Avery's conversion to the Shaker way had caused the housekeeper.

As Nora poured the warm milk into the mugs, JoHannah stirred the cocoa up from the bottom. A whirlpool of rich brown cocoa swirled and blended into the creamy milk, and a sudden gift of inspiration made her wonder if God's plan for her was a bit more complex than she had originally thought. Consumed with worry about the state of her own soul, she had failed to comprehend the full range and magnitude of His abiding love and concern for all His human creations. Maybe He designed her exile into the World not just as a test to strengthen her own weak faith, but also as an opportunity for her to bear witness to the Shaker way and ease Nora's troubled spirit.

Hadn't He lifted JoHannah away from the Bathricks, whose World excesses tore at her spirit? Hadn't He delivered her to a home where love abounded in a simpler style of living much closer to the one she cherished?

As the aroma of rich cocoa filled the air, a measure of peace filled her spirit for the first time since she had arrived at Lawne Haven.

"JoHannah!"

Michael's powerful voice rumbled into the kitchen like a freight train powering its way through a sleepy town, rattling the windows of her soul and shaking the foundation of her newfound peace.

With an apologetic grin and a shrug of her shoulders, she set her mug of cocoa aside and walked out of the kitchen, wondering if Michael might be in greater need of a train engineer rather than a nurse. At least then she would have some hope that he would stay on his own tracks . . . and off of hers.

Propped up in bed, his back cushioned by a mound of pillows, Michael drummed his fingertips on the bed. Buoyed by Dr. Carson's pronouncement, he had taken a good hard look at his treatment of JoHannah. He did not like what he saw, especially when he knew that, despite her kind words to the physician, she deserved the credit for saving his leg. It was not her fault that Michael found her overly attractive or as irresistible in the flesh as she was in his dreams. He could not alter his past behavior, but he could try to change and make amends, which is precisely why he had called out for her.

Growing impatient, he held very still and listened hard. He could have sworn he had heard JoHannah's footsteps come running just moments after he called for her. That seemed to him to be a good five minutes ago!

Accustomed to having his orders obeyed immediately, he clenched his fist and took another deep breath. "Jo-Hann—"

She stepped into the room, cutting him off before he could finish hollering her name. "What is it?"

One long, burning look at her, fueled by a whirlwind of surprise and disappointment, charred his planned apology and scattered the ashes of his good intentions. He scowled. "Where did you get the new cap?"

"Nora made it for me," she informed him as she made her way to the fireplace, stoked the logs, and added a new one.

Golden light from the fire leaped through the scalloped openings in her cap and turned her auburn hair into a shimmering sunset. His pulse quickened to double time. "I think I prefer this cap over the one you made for yourself," he rasped, shooting a compliment at her that would penetrate through her armor of stoicism and convince her to wear the hideous cotton cap again. Maybe then he could rein in his growing desire to burn every cap she possessed, unpin the thick knot of hair at the nape of her neck, and run his fingers through each brown, spun-with-copper strand.

Her smile was innocent, but his compliment boomeranged right back at him. "Nora is very skilled with the knitting needle. With her rheumatism, I know it took great pain to finish this so quickly. I'm . . . I'm glad you like it. Nora will be pleased."

Instinctively, Michael levied another compliment that would hit its mark and stick. "You should smile more often," he purred.

"Why is that?" she tossed back offhandedly as she tucked in the bedclothes at the foot of the bed.

"Because when you smile, you look . . . well . . . as beautiful as an angel."

Perfect strike!

She froze, perfectly still, and he watched as a crimson tide washed over her cheeks. True to form, she shook one hand toward the floor and took a deep breath before fumbling with the edge of the blanket and tucking it under the mattress.

"W-why did you call for me? Is there something you need?" she croaked, twisting her hands in front of her skirts as she stared at the floor.

You. Only you.

Her misery, however, renewed and intensified his guilt. Reminded of his purpose for calling her, his chest tightened. The distress in her face, the curve of her slumped shoulders, and the stain on her cheeks touched his soul, and the subtle game he had played with her for the past two weeks revealed itself as nothing less than a selfish, tawdry ploy.

Fully ashamed of himself, he could not find an iota of justification for his behavior that would redeem this unforgivable flaw in his character. Determined to make amends, he cleared his throat. "I thought we might talk," he suggested, wondering if she would trust him not to tease her again, not that he had given her any reason to think otherwise.

She sighed. "It's growing late. You should turn in for the night. Dr. Carson suggested you start using your crutches tomorrow, and you'll need all the strength—"

"Are you too tired?"

Her backbone stiffened so quickly he almost expected to hear it snap.

"No. Of course not."

He sniffed the air. "Is that cocoa I smell?"

She nodded. "Nora and I were just sitting down—"

"Bring yours in here. Is there enough for another cup? I haven't had hot cocoa since I was a little boy."

The blush on her cheeks darkened, but she nodded stiffly and hurried from the room. While he waited for her to return, he had an opportunity, once again, to mentally compile a list of his sins against her. Despite her kind words to Dr. Carson, Michael was convinced that her unorthodox treatment ultimately had saved his leg. Even so, he had teased her unmercifully and enjoyed her discomfort. At times, he had feigned helplessness just to keep her by his side. He *wanted* her, perhaps the most grievous of his transgressions, yet he could not fathom a single, rational reason why he should not.

She was as beautiful in spirit as she was to him in the flesh. Soft-spoken but courageous, she was ever patient, ever selfless and gentle. Quite literally, she was the woman of his dreams, and in every waking moment he had shared with her, she had endeared herself to him forever—with her uncommon heart.

The rattle of mugs on a tray announced her return, and he swallowed hard, searching for the right words to use to apologize for his behavior and to thank her for making it possible for him to spend the rest of his days as a competent master for Lawne Haven.

He leaned over to clear a space on the bed table, and she sat the tray down, reaching up to douse the kerosene lamp. His eyes adjusted quickly to the dark cast to the room, and he groaned. If she had hoped the darkness would shield her from his teasing, she had either overlooked or underestimated the cozy effect of firelight in an otherwise darkened room.

The flames' shadows leaped into the corners of the room and cast a golden aura around his bed . . . and her face. "Where's Nora?" he asked quietly, wondering why Jo-Hannah had failed to bring along her recent ally.

"She's gone to bed."

He lifted a steaming mug from the tray, held it aloft in a silent toast and sipped eagerly. Tears sprang to his eyes as the burning liquid scalded his tongue and the roof of his mouth. He swallowed, too late to undo the damage, and tried a weak grin to cover his embarrassment. "T-t-too h-hot," he stammered, his mouth throbbing with pain.

Did she really giggle? *Giggle?*

He glared at her.

Eyes dancing, she immediately dropped her gaze and continued to stir her own mug of cocoa with a stick of cinnamon. Blowing softly at the rim, she took several small, careful sips before setting the mug back on the tray. "Still a trifle too warm to drink," she noted and rose to leave briefly, returning with a thick book in her grasp.

"Wh-what are you doing?" he groaned. His attempt to talk sent pain ricocheting into every corner of his mouth.

Ignoring him, she settled back into the chair and laid the book open to the light on her lap. She flipped through the pages, found the one she had obviously been looking for, and tilted the book up at an angle to better catch the light. "While we wait for the cocoa to cool a bit, I thought I'd read to you."

"From the Bible?"

"I'm not permitted to read World books, but I think this one might be all right, especially if I choose something from the Old Testament."

He groaned, fell back against the pillows and closed his eyes. He had the uncanny desire to cover his ears, but managed to resist the urge, fearing he would appear to be a total child.

"I think I have a passage you'd like, unless you have one you'd like to request."

He shook his head, wondering if she had deliberately heated the cocoa to the boiling point to scald his flattering tongue into a blistered mass to insure his silence.

"Here it is. Genesis, chapter three, verse one." She took a deep breath and paused dramatically. " 'Now the serpent was more subtle than any of the beasts which the Lord God had made. And he said to the woman . . .' "

Michael slithered further down under the covers, his skin suddenly feeling impossibly cool and scaly.

After she had washed the mugs clean, dried them, and put them back into the cupboard, JoHannah made her way in the dark up the staircase with heavy steps. Her spirits buoyed by her successful efforts to shame Michael into silence mitigated the guilt she carried for accidentally overheating the cocoa. It wasn't her fault, it was his, she mused as she neared the top step. He had gushed one compliment after another until her head was spinning, and he had drowned every well-intentioned vow she had made to resist him with silken words that appealed to her base, sinful nature. Was it any wonder she could not even heat a pan of milk properly?

At the head of the stairs, she turned halfway to her left to go to her room. She paused and turned the other way, her curiosity piqued by a light coming from the room on her right. Furrowing her brow, she walked toward the door, noting that Nora's door at the end of the hall was also ajar. As she got closer, a whisper of a soft melody reached her ears. Peeking into the room, she saw Nora, dressed in her nightclothes as she dusted a small chest of drawers.

"Nora?"

The tiny woman stopped humming and looked up, her dark eyes sad. "Rather foolish, aren't I?" she murmured. "Come in. This is . . . this was Abigail's room," she explained as JoHannah slipped inside and glanced around the small chamber.

Unlike the thick woolen carpet in JoHannah's room, an oval rag rug hugged the wide, planked floor between the chest of drawers and a bed that resembled a sleigh which was covered with a dainty, lace-trimmed, patchwork quilt. Walls washed with pale blue were unadorned, but a ruffled, blue gingham curtain matched the drawer scarf in Nora's hand and dressed the single window directly behind Nora.

She watched as Nora put the scarf back in its place, opened the top drawer and sat four small wooden figures on top of the chest. Nora bowed her head for a moment and walked over to the bed where she ran a trembling hand across the quilt.

"It's a lovely room," JoHannah murmured, feeling as though she had intruded on a very private moment. She walked over to the chest of drawers. A family of roughly hewn bears—mother, father, and two little cubs—nestled together on top.

When JoHannah turned around, Nora was sitting on the bed, her hand caressing a cream, heart-shaped section in the quilt. "This is a piece of her mama's wedding dress." Her hand moved to another square, this one mint green. "This is mine," she continued, explaining the family's history by pointing to different patches in the quilt.

Nora's insistence that this room, and the room across the hall which must have been Jane's, was too small for Jo-

Hannah finally made sense. Overwhelmed by the emptiness in Nora's voice, JoHannah sat down beside her. "You must miss Brother Avery and his children very much," she whispered as she put her arm around Nora's shoulders.

Sniffling back tears, the woman leaned against Jo-Hannah. "I try not to judge Avery. He's a man full-grown, entitled to make his own decisions, but the girls . . ."

"They were happy at Collier," JoHannah said quietly.

Nora sat up and looked at JoHannah. "You knew them? You've seen Abigail and Jane?"

JoHannah smiled. "They were darling, well-behaved children. Abigail was very quick with her figures which pleased her teacher to no end, and Jane . . . well, little Jane figured out very quickly that the way to Sister Claire's heart was to be the first in line to help dry the dishes."

Nora smiled through her tears. "Did you notice the little white stool in the kitchen? Jane pulled that over to the sink almost the day she took her first steps. 'My little helper.' That's what I called her. Were they . . . were they truly happy? Did they have enough to eat and warm covers on their beds?"

JoHannah hugged Nora. "It was an adjustment for both of them, but they were very fortunate to have their father with them, especially when they moved to Kentucky." JoHannah continued to hold Nora, answering all of her questions and sharing memories of those first days at Collier when loving, gentle Shaker sisters had welcomed her into a new life.

After a particularly long yawn, Nora reluctantly agreed to take to her bed, and JoHannah found her way back to her room, the one Brother Avery had shared with his wife.

By candlelight, rich flowered wallpaper, which had screamed *frivolous* at her the first time she had seen it two weeks ago, surrounded her now with the lifelike beauty of a spring garden that almost chased away the chill in the room. Shivering, she realized that she had quite forgotten to feed the fire. Dying embers gasped for life, and she added a log thick enough to burn until morning.

Mesmerized by the flames that licked at the log, fighting for life, she thought about the world she had found at Lawne Haven. Michael's dedication to family traditions, rooted in honest toil, and his willingness to risk his life to be able to continue those traditions as master of Lawne Haven surprised her. The depth of love Nora shared with Avery's family and the grief Nora felt at their loss tugged at JoHannah's heartstrings. As a little girl, JoHannah had experienced that terrible, gnawing grief; it was as profound as the grief that gripped her spirit when she had been forced to leave Collier.

The difference between life at Lawne Haven and her birth home where her guardian and his family now lived was amazing. The superficial bond that held the Bathricks together, based on the adulation of physical beauty and the perverse accumulation of material possessions, more closely matched the sinful image of the World JoHannah had been taught to expect.

Two very different families.

Two diametrically different worlds.

And she belonged to neither.

"I want to be in God's world, not either of these," she whispered out loud. But she could not quite dismiss Lawne Haven as an oasis of sin . . . not when she compared it to her birth home, now occupied by her guardian and his family. She rose and walked over to stand before a long dresser, its beveled mirror covered with a sheet to guard against a forbidden glance. She reached out and ran her fingers the length of a silver hand mirror that lay face down on the polished mahogany wood. A lady's silver comb and brush set rested alongside the hand mirror—as if waiting for Avery's deceased wife, Martha, to return.

Was this a morbid little shrine, or was it testimony to a love between Brother Avery and his wife . . . a love so deep that he could not part with something that had belonged to her?

JoHannah turned around and leaned the small of her back against the dresser. Inconsistencies in her understanding of the World, especially marriage, seemed to be multiplying. Was the bond between a husband and wife a sinful creation designed to give men and women free rein to indulge in carnal lust, or was love between a man and a woman who pledged to join their hearts and bodies as one a natural expression of God's love for His children?

She dropped to her knees and bowed her head in prayer, longing for the companionship of her sisters and brethren. She needed the wisdom of Eldress Regina and Sister Lucy who would be able to help JoHannah confront and answer the gnawing questions that assailed her spirit.

When she could pray no more, she undressed and pulled the covers from the bed, ready to fashion a sleeping place for herself in front of the fire just as she had done every night because she had been unwilling to sleep on the same mattress where Brother Avery and his wife had yielded to the sinful pleasures of the flesh.

She stared at the mattress, decided after two heartbeats that sin was no more contagious than grace, climbed into bed, and blew out the candle. She pulled the covers up to her chin, gave praise for a comfortable mattress, closed her eyes and fell promptly to sleep.

Once the patter of footsteps overhead stopped, Michael would know that JoHannah finally had taken herself to bed. Not that she would be likely to find her rest in the bed Avery and Martha had shared as husband and wife.

Poor little saint.

JoHannah did not have the courage to ask for another

room, not after Nora had rambled on and on about how hard she had worked to bring life and sparkle to it. The housekeeper had no idea that JoHannah would rather sleep on iced porcupine quills rather than lay on anyone's marriage bed. But Michael knew, and every night, he waited to hear the creak of the bed.

It hadn't happened.

He tensed when the footsteps overhead stopped, then relaxed when they resumed. His eyes grew heavy, and he exhaled slowly. *Wasn't she ever going to go to bed?* Better put, wasn't he ever going to stop this silly game and go to sleep before she did?

Creak!

His heart nearly jumped out of his chest.

Squeak!

Holding deathly still, he listened hard, but the pounding of his heart made it impossible to hear if the telltale creak of the bed overhead continued. By the time his pulse beat normally, there was not a sound to be heard, except for the crackle of wet wood hissing in the fireplace in his room.

She must have fallen asleep. His own sleep, however, would be a long time in coming, he realized, as new questions replaced the old ones that had plagued his mind. Now that she had finally given in and decided to actually sleep in the bed, what did it mean? Was she perhaps finding the outside world she had left behind as a child more appealing to her now than the cloistered life she had led in the Shaker village? Had his flattery finally worn a hole in the fabric of her faith? Or more likely, had she rewoven the weakened fibers, making her faith strong enough to sustain her existence here until she was able to go home to Collier as she believed she would?

He sat up and stared into the fire. The flames flickered and danced, creating images of her heart-shaped face and gentle violet eyes, and the memory of her well-chosen Bible verse echoed in his mind. Trying to undermine her faith by appealing to her female vanity in hopes of forcing her to leave had obviously not worked.

He swallowed hard. How much longer could he have her so near, inciting his desires with her very presence, and yet know with every beat of his heart she was the one woman he could not have?

Unlike the other women in his past who had eventually succumbed to his charms, JoHannah resisted him. She was quite a singular woman. She was . . . simply and uniquely JoHannah, and he realized his approach would have to be just as different as she was.

He laid his head back on the pillow and stared up at the ceiling. In the quiet stillness that surrounded him, an astounding realization made his pulse begin to race, almost as quickly as the thoughts that ripped through his mind.

JoHannah.

Why had he tried to force her to go back to her world? All of his reasons, including his daily teasing, now seemed either irrelevant or easily conquered, the court's ruling notwithstanding. His leg would heal completely, guaranteeing a strong future for himself and breathing new life into his ultimate goal: to return to sea. To achieve that goal, he needed a wife so he could meet his responsibilities to Lawne Haven. The sooner the better.

JoHannah.

With her Shaker training, she had all the skills to make her an exceptional mistress for Lawne Haven. He found her distractingly attractive, and the very idea that she might one day warm his bed made him tremble with desire. She would be the perfect wife and mother for his children who would be the heirs to his family's traditions. The only obstacle that prevented her from filling that role was the peculiar ban on marriage her faith prescribed.

Juxtaposed, a second question sent his blood rushing to

his head. Could he somehow convince her to be his wife? Was there any chance . . . any chance at all . . . that if given the opportunity, she would choose life beyond Collier?

Bitter memories of being the second son resurfaced, sliced through thick scars, and opened old wounds. He wanted JoHannah as the mistress of Lawne Haven, and he would brook no notion of failing to win her hand.

The fierce competitiveness forged in his childhood, the stratagem for survival from his adolescence, and the strength born in adversity during his adulthood coalesced into bold determination.

Dawn was still hours away, but he knew he would never find any rest tonight . . . or any other . . . until he had learned enough about her world and had shown her the goodness in his to be able to convince JoHannah that she belonged in only one world: his.

Chapter 10

The distinctive aroma of rich, hearty oatmeal and oven-warm bread announced breakfast just as JoHannah put the finishing stitch on a leg of Michael's trousers. After snipping it, she inspected twin rows of thread-bound holes, one on each side of the opened seam than ran from mid-thigh to ankle and hoped she had judged correctly.

She started at the top row and carefully laced a long piece of twine halfway down the length before she realized she had cut the rope too short. After carefully measuring out a new piece, twice as long as the first, she laced the entire seam together and tied it shut at the bottom with just enough excess twine left to take into consideration the added width the splint would require.

Used to Shaker perfection in all her tasks, she crinkled her nose at the sight of twice-laid twine, pale against the heavy black wool. Fortunately, Michael would not need to wear altered trousers for much more than a month. By mid-April, the splint could be removed, and his regular trousers would fit. Satisfied that she had confined her handiwork to the inner fabric of the seam, she took solace in knowing that once the seam had been restitched, his trousers would be none the worse for wear.

She put the scissors and sewing notions back into the basket, looped it over her arm, and carried the trousers with her as she made her way from her room and down the stairs. Hoping Michael had not forgotten her thinly shadowed message last night, she entered the sickroom with no small twinge of apprehension.

"Good morning."

Her heart still fluttered, even though the seductive tone that usually laced Michael's voice was oddly absent. "It's a blessed day for you," she responded and laid the trousers on the empty pillow next to his head after she set the sewing basket on a table against the wall. Although she was able to resist the urge to look at him directly, she could tell he was anxious to get out of bed for the first time in weeks.

A shaving brush, soap still lathered on the bristles, rested next to a single-edged razor mottled with fine whiskers. A film of soap covered the water in the wash basin, and several strands of black and silver hair glistened on his hairbrush. His nightclothes lay strewn on the floor. As she stooped to pick them up, a blur of dove gray fabric that covered his broad chest swirled into her line of vision. "Are you hungry? Would you like—"

"These are ingenious! I was wondering how . . . let's see if this works," he exclaimed as he inspected the trousers.

She barely had time to turn her back before he shoved off the bedclothes covering his lower body and struggled to get into his altered trousers.

Heavy breathing, followed by whispered expletives. The pound of his fist on the bed. Silence, heavy with failure.

"May I help?" she ventured, mindful that this everproud man was still unable to completely dress himself.

A deep sigh. "Please."

She bowed her head. "Are you . . . that is, do the covers . . ."

A swish of sheets. "There! I'm fully covered in all the

right places, but there's an unholy disaster at my feet," he blustered.

She bit her lower lip to snip the grin that threatened to blossom into a smile. After depositing his bedclothes on the chair, she made her way to the foot of the bed. Both trouser legs were twisted together like a tangled hank of worsted yarn, and a belt loop had caught on the end of the splint.

She eased the belt loop free, separated the trouser legs and frowned. "Socks first. Then your trousers." After slipping a thick woolen sock onto each foot, she began by working the waistband of the trousers up his good leg to the knee, stopped and bunched the rest of the trouser leg until the hem reached his ankle. She paused to wipe away a thin line of perspiration along her upper lip. "That was the easy part," she murmured. "Are you sure—"

"Just be done with it."

She gulped once. Maneuvering his injured leg through the trouser leg was not going to be a simple matter. She hesitated, fearful of causing him pain. *Heavenly Father, guide me.*

Although the splint made for awkward work, the trousers were baggy enough at the unbuttoned waist and seat to accommodate the splint easily, and the opened seam at the point she had judged to be midthigh allowed her to work the trousers well above the knee of his injured leg.

He only groaned once.

Several tense moments later, Michael's trousers hugged the lower part of his thigh just above his knee. Stymied, she paused, the sound of her own heartbeat pulsing in her ears.

"I have an idea, but I'm not sure it will work." He sighed. "Never mind."

"Tell me your idea."

"No. It was a bad idea. I don't want you to hurt your back."

"My . . . back?" She lifted her gaze carefully, stared at his chest and caught sight of the low headboard. "How on earth . . . ? Oh, I see." Without hesitating, she walked behind the headboard, braced her feet, and from the waist, bent forward. Reaching behind him, she leaned her chin over his shoulder and wrapped her arms around his chest, and before he could utter a single word of argument, she lifted his torso up from the mattress. "Pull. Quickly!" she gritted as she slammed her eyes shut.

As he tilted his head back, his face brushed against her cheek and nudged her cap askew. Damp tendrils of his hair caressed her naked temple. The taut muscles in his body drained her waning strength, but his scent—fresh and clean and terribly male—overpowered her senses.

"Done!"

She yanked away and opened her eyes while she righted her cap. Heart stammering, she took heaving gulps of air and shook both hands to the floor.

"Are you all right? You didn't hurt yourself, did you?"

"I-I'm fine. Just out of breath," she panted as she rubbed the strained muscles in her arms. *I'm so wicked. Forgive me, Father.*

"Are you sure? You're trembling."

Her eyes flew open. He had turned onto his side and looked at her over the headboard, catching her gaze with gray orbs of sincere worry. Her lips quivered with a hint of doubt. "Are you ready to try the crutches?"

His smile was gentle. "Not until I thank you. For everything. I don't know what I would have done without you."

"I'm only God's instrument," she whispered, noting for the first time that a rim of deep black circled each gray iris like a dam holding back the deep waters of a mountain river fed by melting snow. Thick, long lashes shadowed the hollows of his cheeks. Shivering, she closed her eyes before she was tempted to rest her gaze on his lips.

"I'm sorry."

Her heart slammed against the wall of her chest.

"I'm sorry for teasing you."

She shook her head to clear her hearing.

He chuckled. "It's customary, even considered polite to accept an apology."

She stared at the floor and twisted her hands together. "It's not necessary to apologize." Her voice shook, and her heart flip-flopped.

"I think it is, and I wanted you to know that I respect your right to—"

"Michael! You're dressed!"

Nora's arrival shifted the kettle of confusion boiling in JoHannah's mind and heart onto a back burner. While Nora fussed over Michael and praised JoHannah's skill with the needle, Michael managed to get a boot on his good foot. JoHannah fetched Michael's crutches from the corner where they had been stored and leaned them against the footboard.

Nora picked up the wash basin. "I'll set another place at the table for breakfast. JoHannah, would you make sure Michael doesn't fall between here and the kitchen?"

A cheerful melody accompanied the sound of Nora's footsteps as she walked back to the kitchen. JoHannah waited as Michael swung his legs over the side of the bed and tested his strength by putting some weight on his right leg. She put a crutch into each of his outstretched hands and moved to the side.

Michael leaned on his crutches, apparently waited until the dizziness passed, and took his first tentative steps. His whitened knuckles caught her attention. And held it. As he slowly made his way to the doorway, a knot in her chest formed and tightened. Would prayer alone be a strong enough crutch for her weakened faith, or had the serpent turned into a fox whose cunning and guile would be far more difficult to avoid?

Midway through his meal, which he barely enjoyed because his tongue was still scalded, Michael leaned back in the spindle-back chair. His left leg was stretched out straight and his foot rested on Jane's little white stool. More exhausted than he expected to be from simply walking from the parlor to the kitchen, his underarms ached and his fingers were stiff from gripping the hand rest on the crutches. The next four weeks dimmed into twenty-eight interminable long days that would continue to challenge and frustrate him, even as he pursued his plan to court and win JoHannah's hand.

Nora jumped up to answer a soft rap at the kitchen door, and he took special notice of JoHannah's reaction. Using the excuse that she was not hungry, she had not taken a seat at the table. She backed up out of sight against the cupboard, her dark brown skirts rustling as gently as the wings of a sparrow ready to take flight.

"Dolan!" Michael grinned as his neighbor lumbered inside.

A giant sequoia of a man with unruly brown hair the color of faded autumn leaves, his chest was broad and ample. The muscles in each burly arm were strong enough to support an eagle's nest, and tree-trunk legs moved him with a heavy gait. He pumped Michael's hand. "Good to see you up and about."

"Well, I'm up, but that's about it. It'll be a while before I can wield an ax again, but one thing is for sure. The first cord of wood I chop will be stacked in your woodpile. I really appreciate—"

"Good neighbors help one another." Dolan blushed, his ruddy complexion deepening to scarlet. The chair groaned as he settled himself at the curve of the oak table opposite Michael's outstretched leg. "Didn't want to bother you and Nora before, but Doc Carson told Genny this morning you were healing up good. Thought I'd check up on you."

Michael laughed. "Did she lock you out again?"

Grinning, Dolan plowed a spoon into the bowl of hot oatmeal Nora had set in front of him. "I'm getting real good at repairing splintered door fames and busted locks."

Nora poured coffee into Dolan's mug. "With tempers like that, you two are bound to birth a tornado next month instead of a babe." She glanced up. "JoHannah, dear, please sit down and meet Dolan. He's always calm . . . after the storm."

Wide-eyed, the blood drained from JoHannah's face when Dolan turned and looked at her. "I'm not really hungry. I think I'll strip the sheets from Michael's bed while he has a visitor." She swirled around and bolted from the room.

Dolan gaped at the now-empty doorway. "Who was that?"

Michael handed him a jar of honey to dribble on his oatmeal. "JoHannah Sims. Uncle George sent her here to help Nora when it looked like Dr. Carson was going to amputate my leg."

"She's . . . she's some kind of nun?"

Laughing as he poured cream into his coffee, Michael splashed some onto the table. He wiped at it with a napkin. "She's a Shaker sister from Collier," he began, detailing JoHannah's predicament while they both finished breakfast and Nora excused herself to help JoHannah.

Dolan listened attentively. "What about Avery? When is he coming home?"

"He's moved to Kentucky with some kind of Third Family from Collier."

"Did Abigail and Jane go with him?"

Nodding, Michael's eyes narrowed. "Avery deeded Lawne Haven over to me before he left." Michael patted the thigh of his injured leg. "Notching trees won't be much of a problem, but I'll need help to fell the timber, Dolan, if you've a mind to it. There's not much in the way of coin—"

"Tell me when and where you need me. I'll be there as long as it doesn't interfere with my crops."

"Not unless you first agree to share the profit."

"That's not necessary."

"I think it is."

Dolan leaned both elbows on the table. "Then I'll tell you what I want."

Michael nodded, anxious for Dolan's help.

"Give me enough lumber to add a porch to the house. Genny's been pretty lonesome for home. Thought I might build her a fine wide porch like her stepmother's, but with the late frost last season, I barely made enough to make ends meet. I'd sure appreciate the chance to get Genny her porch."

Michael extended his hand. "Done and fair."

Dolan squeezed hard. "I'm obliged. Now tell me more about this Shaker lady. Is it true . . . ?"

Still flustered by the earlier, unexpected visit from Michael's neighbor, JoHannah trembled, but she knew her uneasiness could not be explained away quite as easily by blaming it on the presence of a strange World man.

In the shadow of late afternoon, JoHannah knelt down at the side of the bed, sat back on the heels of her feet, and propped Michael's foot on her lap. Flesh pressed against flesh, their bodies once again radiated the magnetism that brought a quiver to JoHannah's voice, making her mind hopscotch from duty to pleasure and her spirit ache.

Using her left hand to hold either side of the splint to

make his leg stationary, she cupped the heel of his foot in the palm of her hand. "Rotating your ankle is important. The joint is stiff, and before you put any weight on your injured leg, it's best to exercise the muscles and loosen the kinks."

Head bowed, she applied enough pressure to the heel of his foot to rotate his ankle without disturbing the splint and tried to concentrate on her task. His sharp intake of breath yanked her selfish and wicked thoughts away and replaced them with compassion. "I'm sorry." She paused until his breathing became regular and rotated the ankle once more before she wrapped her hand around the ball of his foot. She urged his foot toward his shin and back again.

He tensed. "How . . . often . . . did . . . you . . . say . . . you had to do this?"

"Several times a day. In a week you can try to put some pressure on your leg."

"I can hardly wait."

She smiled and repeated the exercise once more before putting his foot to rest gently on the floor. "Finished for now," she said quietly as she got to her feet. "Unless you need something else, I should help Nora with supper."

"Will you sit down with us to eat tonight?"

She stared at the hem of her gown. "I'm not permitted to—"

"This isn't Collier, and unfortunately, there's only room for one table in the kitchen. After all you've done for me, it seems inhospitable to treat you like a servant and have you taking your meals separately. For mercy's sake, Nora is my housekeeper, but she—"

"My faith doesn't allow women to take meals with men at the same table."

"Is that why you bolted when Dolan arrived and sat down to breakfast?"

Blushing, she nodded, unable to shake the fear that had

filled her entire body when Dolan had ambled into the kitchen. More massive than any man she had ever seen in her entire life, he obviously possessed a wicked temper—despite his seemingly gentle nature with Michael and Nora.

Although Dolan did not incite any of the spontaneous sensations that washed over her whenever Michael was near, he was a World man and thus dangerous.

"Dolan is a good man. He would never bring you harm," Michael assured her as though reading her thoughts.

Somehow, she believed him, but that did not alter the fact that even without Dolan present, she would have found another reason to avoid sharing a meal with Michael; something she was loath to tell him without risking a battle of wills sparked by yet another difference in their worlds.

Michael leaned forward, and she felt his gaze on her. "Do I frighten you?" he whispered so softly she had to struggle to hear him.

"No," she lied. "My faith—"

"Doesn't stress men and women are equal?"

Why was his voice low and sincere—without any hint of sarcasm or guile? Why the sudden interest in trying to understand her beliefs instead of taunting her about them? Shaken by his apparent sincerity and the very real notion that he might actually keep his word not to tease her, she took a deep breath. "Of course we're equal . . . before the Lord."

"Then why do the women always serve the men first and sit at separate tables?" he asked, reminding her that he had eaten in the dining hall when visiting his brother.

"Because . . . because it is our custom. A sign of respect for our separate roles. Men grow and harvest the food; women prepare and serve it to them. We sit at separate tables to prevent any . . . any undo contact between the sexes. It's no different from our custom of using separate entrances or staircases for the sisters and brethren."

She heard him take a deep breath as he leaned back in his chair.

"Our custom at Lawne Haven is to share meals together as a family," he explained calmly. "When my parents were alive, my mother cooked and served the meals with Nora's help. After my father led us all in a blessing, he dished the food out onto our plates. Nora and I take our meals together now because we are still a family. If you joined us, you and Nora could sit together, and I would sit on the other side of the table where there would be room for the stool to prop my leg. Would that be difficult for you to do . . . to follow the custom here?"

She bowed her head and closed her eyes. Scenes still recent enough to be vivid soured the taste in her mouth. Dining with her guardian and his family, oddly enough, had not been as difficult as she had first thought it would be, although the elegant extravagance in the formal dining room nearly took away what little appetite she had had. Conversation, if any, centered around Cassandra, and JoHannah usually was ignored, except when Leila decided to mock JoHannah's ignorance of formal table manners. Accustomed to ordinary flatware and wooden dishes, JoHannah had been as frightened by the chance of a sinful vision of her own reflection in the nearly translucent china as she had been by the vast number of gleaming silver utensils on either side of her plate.

Thinking about the meals she had shared with Nora at the nicked oak kitchen table while Michael had been confined to bed sweetened the taste in JoHannah's mouth. Although she found conversation with Nora awkward at first, those moments together now had become as special as the indescribable pleasure she took in sharing time with Nora at the end of the day . . . over a cup of hot cocoa.

Adding Michael to the recipe for meals was like adding a cup of salt to her cocoa. Unsettled by his very presence, she found it difficult to think clearly. She also found his new attitude more than slightly suspect.

He shifted his position and leaned forward again. "Have you made up your mind? What is it to be? Meals shared together in the round, or . . . are you going to force a crippled man to build a small table-for-one that would fit by the hearth?" He chuckled. "It wouldn't be easy, but I think I could manage it. Unless I slip and fall in the process. Might crack my head open this time or break an arm."

Blushing, she almost let a giggle escape. "You're not even well enough to attempt building a stool."

"But I'm stubborn enough to try," he countered.

"Yes, I believe you are," she acknowledged. Any man stubborn enough to survive Dr. Carson's early treatment and risk his life to save his leg was certainly bullheaded enough to try to build a table while he was propped on crutches. If he got hurt again trying to accommodate her faith, she would never forgive herself. "I'll take my meals at the round table."

"And you'll spare me any more fateful accidents. You're sure? You'll share meals with me . . . with my family?"

The delight in his voice was a dangerous melody that strummed at her heartstrings. She nodded slowly, worried that by saving him from his alleged fate, she might have sealed her own.

Chapter 11

". . . and bless and keep us all. Amen." Michael hesitated and added an afterthought. "If you have a spare moment, Lord, keep a watchful eye on Dolan and Genevieve so they don't have another battle today. We're looking forward to their company at supper. Amen." Grinning at Nora, he heaped a pile of griddle cakes on two plates. He passed them to Nora and JoHannah before stacking a mound next to a thick slab of ham, still sizzling in its own juices, on the plate in front of him.

"Well, ladies, there's a busy day ahead of us. Dolan and Genevieve should be here by midafternoon. I've got a schedule of chores for each of us. JoHannah, you can handle baking the bread. I set the flour out on the counter for you. Nora, why don't you fix something simple for dinner? There's enough ham left from last night's supper to make cold platters. Maybe you can check the root cellar to see if there's anything there you can use. I'll start peeling more apples." He paused, confused by their twin expressions of exasperation. "Unless you want me to start with the potatoes," he added. He took a bite of ham and let the brown sugar crust on the edge melt in his mouth while he waited for an answer.

Nora shrugged her shoulders and nodded to JoHannah. "Did you notice how he barks orders at us like he was still captain of his ship and we're part of his crew?"

JoHannah's eyes widened even as she stared at her plate. "You were a sea captain?"

"For the past four years," he said quietly. His chest tightened as memories of his life at sea struggled against the anchor of responsibilities that kept him at Lawne Haven.

"He spent years at sea before he got his own ship. Finally harnessed his thirst for command and gave it up to come home where he belonged. Or so I thought," Nora grumbled.

He furrowed his brow. "Do I detect a hint of sarcasm this morning?"

"Sarcasm? Why bless my soul! Did you hear that, JoHannah? Captain Lawne wants to know if I have reason to be distressed." She picked up her fork and toyed with the food on her plate.

He leaned forward, his heart beginning to beat a little faster. "You're upset. What's wrong?"

Nora put her fork down and stared at him. "*What's wrong?* Do you really need to ask? Try listening to yourself. Ever since you started wobbling around on those crutches of yours, you've staked out the kitchen and taken it over like it was your captain's quarters. You organize our chores for the day and issue orders left and right." She narrowed her eyes and pinned him to his seat. "Lawne Haven is not your ship, and neither JoHannah nor I are members of your crew."

Nora's less than gentle diatribe shocked Michael back into boyhood. "I—I was only trying to help. My—my only intention—"

"You're banished from the kitchen," Nora announced. "Effective today."

He gulped, and a mouthful of food lodged for a moment in his throat. He coughed until tears sprang to his eyes. "By whose order?"

"Mine. And JoHannah's."

He looked up and found JoHannah's eyes dancing with Nora's. "Are you joining in this . . . this mutiny?"

Nora snorted. "Of course she is. You may be lord of the manor now, but I still command the kitchen." Her voice softened, but her gaze never left his. "I've been able to set out good meals and take care of this house for more years than you've been alive. Find something else to occupy your time. Just stay out of my kitchen."

Crestfallen, Michael sat back, absorbed Nora's words, and realized she was right. Now that he was almost back on his feet, boredom had set in quickly. Still unable to resume his heavy chores, however, he had invaded Nora's domain and usurped her authority. Her feisty stand now reminded him of the banter that had always marked their relationship, and he accepted her reprimand as a sure sign that he was getting better and she was back in form after hovering over him during his ordeal. Holding out his hands, he displayed the small nicks and cuts on his fingers he had earned peeling fruits and vegetables. "What about my battle scars? Don't these entitle me to mercy?"

In unison, Nora and JoHannah chimed, "No," before mutual grins burst into a waterfall of giggles that cascaded easily between them.

Satisfied that he had been somewhat forgiven, he sat back in his chair and studied both women. Nora, who had been old for as long as he could remember, looked rested and happy, in spite of her attempt to shame him back into his own realm and out of hers. JoHannah looked . . . ? Radiant was the only word that came to mind.

Captivated, he studied her openly, confident that she was too preoccupied to notice. Laughter added luster and a hint of peach to her creamy skin. Her full lips teased a smile across even white teeth beneath the gay blush that painted her cheeks. Her eyes. *Mercy.* Her eyes glistened like rain-kissed lilacs dancing in the wind.

His heart lurched in his chest.

The transformation took his breath away and breathed new hope into his determination to win her hand.

Gone was the pale, nervous woman who had sat stiff and silent during those first awkward meals they had all shared together. Day by day, meal by meal, he had watched her gradually relax, although he knew better than to engage her in one-to-one conversation for too long. Only then did he notice the subtle stiffening of her upper lip or see one of her hands slip from the table to shake nervously at the floor.

Feeling confident, even playful, and unwilling to let Nora have the last word, he grabbed hold of his crutches. He eased out of his seat and fought to find and hold his balance.

A quickly-sobered Nora cocked her head. "Where are you headed?"

"Since I've been stripped of my power here, I'm going to take asylum in the parlor. I thought I'd write to Uncle George and ask Dolan to post it for me. Unless you've reconsidered . . ."

"Scoot! JoHannah and I have a lot to do, especially if Dolan and Genevieve are coming early so he can take down your bed in the parlor and help us set the room to right."

A shadow crossed JoHannah's face. "You're moving back to your room?"

He held out his left crutch and still maintained perfect balance. "See? I'm strong enough to handle the steps now so there's no sense bothering the first floor with a sick-room."

"What if you slip and fall on the steps?"

He flashed her a smile. "I won't fall. But if you're worried about me, you can give me your shoulder to lean on.''

The moment he saw the worry in her expression fade into fear, he wanted to bite back his words. He had tried so hard to keep to the boundaries he had set for himself, but the jocular atmosphere this morning had relaxed his guard. He had stepped over the line separating his old approach from his new one, and he knew he had to retreat quickly.

The misery on JoHannah's face and the frown on Nora's lips only added to his own feelings of guilt. Struggling to restore the good cheer that had marked their conversation before his critical error in judgment, he lifted his crutch in a mock salute. ''I accept my fateful exile, but you'll regret your mutiny, mates. Mark my word. You'll wish you hadn't sent me away when you need to peel half a sack of potatoes. And that's just enough to feed Dolan.''

Nora playfully tossed a napkin at his head, just like she used to do when he was little.

Laughing, he ducked and watched the napkin sail through the air and land in a heap on the floor.

''Say one more word,'' Nora cautioned, ''and I'll sit you down and force you to eat your way through all four apple pies sitting in the pie safe.''

''Only four? I remember a time when you dared me to—''

Another napkin sailed through the air and bounced harmlessly off his head. ''All right. I'm going. I'm going!'' He leaned on his crutches and threw his weight forward, getting out of the kitchen as fast as he could.

Cool morning breezes gave way to afternoon gusts of warm wind that blew in the window over the sink that Nora had opened. JoHannah worked at a countertop on the other side of the room kneading bread. When Nora's hand suddenly gripped her own, JoHannah flinched. She blinked and looked down at Nora who had an odd smile on her face.

"I think you have enough flour now, don't you?"

Puzzled, JoHannah glanced down at the counter. Piles of flour, like small mountains, formed a range around the bread dough. She sucked in her breath and quickly scooped one pile back into the flour sack. "I'm sorry. I didn't mean to make such a mess!"

Nora helped her to clear the countertop. "Martha used to say that there wasn't a better way to find a solution to a problem than by kneading bread. Lets you work out the lumps in your life."

JoHannah's throat constricted. "I'm not usually so . . . so distracted." *Or disappointed.* Sharing meals with Nora and Michael had become an enjoyable World ritual. But when the conversation had sidetracked today and Michael had openly suggested he would relish leaning against JoHannah if she helped him to mount the stairs, disturbing thoughts about having his body touching hers and sinful sensations about the pleasure that might bring had swirled through her mind and body.

Thoughts are the parents of actions.

How many times had Eldress Regina and Sister Lucy issued that warning? And how many times would JoHannah think she had closed her heart to the temptations of the flesh only to have it ripped open again?

"There! All cleaned up." Gently clapping her hands together to remove the excess flour, Nora wiped them clean on her apron. "There's no need to worry or to be nervous about supper. It's just Dolan and Genevieve. They're good, God-fearing people. You'll like them . . . and I know they'll like you."

Her lips dry, JoHannah moistened them to remove a fine coating of flour. Relieved that Nora had misread the cause of her distress, JoHannah thought it safer to let that misassumption prevail. "Do they really argue . . . I mean . . .

does she really lock him out of their house?"

Nora chuckled. "Genevieve did that the second time Dolan came to call. At her father's house, that is. To hear Dolan tell the story, he was so smitten, he practically crashed in the door to propose. Genevieve, of course, found the whole episode terribly romantic and accepted him on the spot, although she broke their betrothal several times before they finally married . . . a few weeks later."

Horrified, JoHannah's hand flew to her cheek. "What did her mother and father do?"

Nora separated the bread dough into two pieces, handed one to JoHannah, and started kneading the other. One gnarled fist dove into the dough. "Genevieve's mother passed away years ago. Her father remarried, so it was her father and stepmother who had to handle Genevieve."

Her hands idle, JoHannah started shaping and reshaping the bread dough. "Didn't they try to protect Genevieve?"

Nora laughed out loud. "In their own way they did. It's hard to explain, but when you meet Genevieve, you'll understand." Putting her half of the dough into a pan to rise, Nora looked up at JoHannah. "For better or worse, I'm not one to hold my tongue for too long. Not when folks I care about seem troubled. I don't think you're just upset about meeting Dolan and Genevieve. I think it's something far more serious than that."

JoHannah's body tingled with apprehension. "There isn't anything else—"

"I might be old, and my eyes certainly don't see as clearly as yours, but only a blind fool would be able to miss the sparks that fly between you and Michael. They're hot enough to set fire to the kindling wood in the fireplace."

Exhaling slowly, JoHannah felt her shoulders sag beneath the heavy weight of the cross of the flesh. Weary in spirit, she ached for a friend. Someone who would help her to untangle the knots of confusion and undo the twisted strings of doubt that were strangling her faith. Someone she could trust as deeply as Eldress Regina or Sister Lucy. But a World person? How could a non-Believer possibly guide her back to the path of righteousness? JoHannah was convinced, however, that Nora was no ordinary World person. JoHannah had learned enough about the housekeeper during their late evening cocoa rituals to recognize Nora as a good and caring woman, one whose wisdom often reminded JoHannah of Sister Lucy.

Nora put her arms around JoHannah's waist and gave her a hug. "Do you want me to post a letter to Michael's uncle and tell him to find another place for you? Maybe if you were away from Lawne Haven, you might be able to sort through your feelings."

"No," JoHannah whispered. "I shouldn't run away. Judge Weldon sent me here because you and Michael needed someone to help. It wouldn't be right to leave. Even though Michael isn't far from total recovery, he still needs care, and you have work enough with keeping the household in order."

She paused to take a deep breath. Over the course of the past few weeks, her respect for Nora had grown into deep affection. Accustomed to confessing her sins to her Eldress, she opened her heart to reveal her sins to Nora. "The Heavenly Father sent me here because . . . because my faith is weak. I have opened my heart to the temptations of the flesh, and I must conquer them . . . if I am to be chosen to become a formal Believer."

"I see." Nora cocked her head, her gaze soft. "Your faith does not permit marriage. Ever?"

"No, it's considered a sin. The pleasures of the flesh distract a soul from serving God."

"The pleasures of the flesh within marriage are not an evil." A faraway look glazed Nora's eyes. "My Simon.

Oh, he was a handsome rogue. I used to shudder just think-ing about that man. I could scarcely breathe, my heart used to race, and my whole body would just tingle. And when he was near . . .'' She looked up at JoHannah, tears misting her eyes. ''He was the dearest, sweetest soul God ever made.''

JoHannah felt her throat constrict, and she eased out of Nora's embrace. Bewildered that Nora could so closely de-scribe how JoHannah felt when she thought about Michael or was near him, she started to tremble.

''Your feelings are perfectly natural, my dear,'' Nora murmured, ''not sinful. Love is a wondrous gift, but it takes wisdom to know the difference between true love and or-dinary physical attraction.''

JoHannah sighed. ''It's so confusing. I understand love for my Heavenly Father and Holy Mother Wisdom. I love my sisters and brethren in faith. But this . . .''

''Love between a man and a woman is different, Jo-Hannah.''

''And sinful.''

Nora took hold of JoHannah's hand. ''No. Anything the Good Lord creates must be good. He created those feelings to bind a man and a woman together forever—in marriage. It's man who destroys the beauty of love. To share the pleasures of the flesh with any man who is not your hus-band is wrong. That is evil, and that is a sin.''

Nora paused, her expression more serious. ''Let me ask you this. If you truly believe, as you've been taught, that a life of faith requires the commitment of celibacy, isn't that faith or that commitment even stronger when you choose it freely instead of blindly?''

''I—I suppose.''

Nora walked over to the cupboard, took out the tin of cocoa JoHannah had stored there, and put it in the palm of JoHannah's hand.

Puzzled, JoHannah looked at Nora askance. "What are you doing?"

"Just answer a few questions for me. Will you do that?"

"Of course, but I don't see how cocoa—"

"We both know you enjoy hot cocoa."

Smiling, JoHannah nodded.

"And if your faith forbid the use of cocoa, what would you do?"

"Why . . . I would give it up."

"Are you sure?"

"Certainly."

Smiling, Nora folded JoHannah's fingers around the tin. "And you would miss it, wouldn't you? Tell me what you would miss."

JoHannah's mouth began to water. "I would miss the flavor and the aroma—"

"And what else?"

"I guess I would think about all the times when I was hurt or lonely or confused when my mother or my sisters would sit with me and share a cup of cocoa. I would miss that. I would miss sharing it with you, too," she added shyly.

"So if you gave up cocoa, it would be a sacrifice, one you would willingly make because your faith required it."

"Yes, but—"

"Now let's assume," Nora said as she took the tin of cocoa away from JoHannah, "let's assume your faith also forbid the use of something else. Let's see. . . ." She led JoHannah over to a row of spice tins. "Look at these. Is there any spice here you haven't tried?"

Intrigued by trying to follow Nora's logic, JoHannah read the labels on each of the tins. She picked up the last one. "This one. Cumin."

Grinning, Nora took the tin away from JoHannah. "You've probably eaten gingerbread spiced with cumin, you just didn't know it. Anyhow, suppose you're told that cumin is forbidden. Would you ever use it?''

''No.''

''Would that be a great sacrifice?''

JoHannah laughed. ''Of course not.'' A glimmer of understanding began to flicker in her mind, but it seemed so preposterous to compare an edict against the pleasures of the flesh with one against cocoa or cumin, she thought she might have misunderstood Nora's point. She gazed at Nora who was smiling ever so gently.

''Sacrifice is truly meaningful only if you feel the loss of what you're giving up. Don't be afraid to be human, dear child. Don't be afraid to find out if what you're feeling for Michael is love . . . or even infatuation. At the end of your time in the outside world, if the court decides you may return to Collier, you must search your heart for the right thing to do. If you still choose to follow the Shaker way, your faith will be ever stronger . . . and the joy you would have found in the married love you deny yourself will be multiplied many times over in the love God will return to you for your sacrifice. There is more than one path to Heaven, but you are the only one who can know which path is yours.''

''But I couldn't possibly . . . our rules are very strict. Eldress Regina says—''

''It's time for you to make up your own mind, JoHannah. Search your heart. Pray for guidance. And trust God to protect one of His own and guide you to the path He has chosen for you.''

Michael ran faster, his eyes searching the woods for a telltale swish of color breaking through the muted earthtones. There! A flash of purple. He changed directions and cut through a low stand of shrubbery. Heart pounding, he charged forward. He had to catch up with her. He had to find her. He had to hold her in his arms and tell her he was sorry.

"Michael! Michael! Wake up. Dolan and Genevieve are here."

Startled awake, Michael shook his head. The vivid images of his dream faded quickly, but his heart pounded in his chest. He looked about the room, stared at Nora, and smiled weakly. "What? Oh, I guess I must have dozed off."

"Dolan just pulled his wagon into the barn."

Perspiration covered his forehead, and he wiped it away. "I'll be along in a moment."

"Are you all right? Do you feel ill?"

He held up his hand. "I'm fine. I was just dreaming, I guess." He grabbed the crutches leaning against his chair, convinced that the dream was just a reflection of his inner turmoil. Had he frightened JoHannah this morning and ruined the tenuous trust that had developed between them?

He started to make his way toward the kitchen, painfully aware that he might have precious few opportunities left to win her hand.

If ever.

By the time he struggled down the hall, slipping twice on the way, the back door was already open. Nora greeted Genevieve who, in turn, threw her arms around Nora.

Wide eyed, JoHannah stood to the side, and Michael took one look at her and started maneuvering his crutches faster, hoping to reach JoHannah's side before Genevieve did.

Chapter 12

Not quite sure if she could believe her own eyes, JoHannah gaped at Genevieve, a mammoth, she-bear of a woman draped in a pink and orange striped tent that served as a gown. Almost as tall as her husband, but twice as round, it was impossible to discern that she was with child, let alone near the end of her confinement. Honey-colored hair framed her moon-flat face and curled halfway down her back, a singular touch of feminine beauty on an otherwise imposing and almost masculine figure.

JoHannah backed away, watching in horrified fascination as Genevieve's huge arms wrapped around Nora in a bear hug that lifted the housekeeper off her feet. "You've been a stranger lately. I've missed you."

"Easy," Michael warned with a soft whisper, startling JoHannah out of her fascination. She dropped her gaze, praying that Michael was the only one who had witnessed her sorry behavior.

By the time Nora was back on her feet, Dolan had ambled into the kitchen and closed the door. He lifted his nose in the air and sniffed. "*Mmm*. Smells good, Nora. Roast lamb? Or could that be goat?"

"Goat!" Nora put both hands on her hips and glared at

him, a rather ridiculous stance for a woman who was standing in the shadow of a man four times her size. "Do you think for one minute I'd let anyone slaughter my goats?"

Genevieve turned and swatted Dolan on the arm. "Don't you dare start teasing Nora about her goats, and mind your manners! We're not sittin' down to supper till our chores are done, and we're not startin' chores till I've met the Shaker lady." She looked over Nora's head and smiled at JoHannah. "Doc Carson tells me you're a mighty fair nurse. I'm Dolan's wife, Genevieve. We're real thankful for what you've done for Michael."

The sound of the woman's soft, melodious voice seemed incongruous with her physical image, surprising JoHannah as much as the reputed words of praise from the physician. "I'm JoHannah, but I only—"

"How come you're allowed out of your village? I heard tell—"

"Now Genny, don't be meddling into the lady's affairs." Dolan put his arm around his wife's shoulders.

She shrugged free. "I'm not meddlin'. Just curious is all. What if Doc Carson isn't there when I need him? Besides, when my time comes, I'd like to have a woman with me. The midwife up and left with the tin peddler, Nora's too fragile to lift half my weight, and my stepmother—"

To JoHannah's profound relief, Michael swung one of his crutches in the air to interrupt Genevieve. "Hey! What about me? Don't I get a proper greeting?"

A huge, raspberry blush mottled Genevieve's cheeks. "Oh, Michael, I'm plumb sorry! You're lookin' good. Too skinny, of course, but you never were much more than a wisp of a man. I'm just all aflutter now that my time's almost here."

Michael laughed. "You're forgiven."

Nora took Genevieve's arm and led her away from the others. "Of course you are," she murmured. "This is a trying time for you, and I want you to rest up a bit while we help Dolan set that parlor to right. I'm gonna take you in and get you a good comfortable chair so you can watch, but you're not lifting a finger to help. Not in your delicate condition.''

Delicate? JoHannah had the distinct impression that Genevieve could dismantle the sickbed with one hand and with two solid breaths of air, blow every stick of furniture back into place. Relieved that Michael had steered the conversation away from Genevieve's thinly shadowed request for JoHannah to be her nurse, she dutifully followed Michael and Dolan as they made their way down the hall to the parlor.

Nora's tale about Dolan's unorthodox courting behavior rang in her ears, and she understood completely why Genevieve did not need the protection of her parents. A small grin played on JoHannah's lips. If anyone needed protection, it was probably Dolan, and JoHannah wondered if the World was quite prepared for the arrival of their soon-to-be-born progeny.

Standing just inside the door to Michael's bedroom, JoHannah tightened her grip on the stack of bed linen in her arms. Why did fear suddenly grip her heart? She was no stranger to a man's sleeping quarters. As a sister, she used to sweep and freshen the brethren's rooms every morning after breakfast. Neither did the fact that Michael's room was directly across the hall from her own seem odd since sisters and brethren lived together as a family in the same dwelling house, with brethren's rooms alternately assigned with the sisters' on the same floor.

Her heart pounded and her body trembled because this was Michael's room. Her first impression was of him as the king of all the World's beasts who waited to attack her. That impression roared back to life. His room became his lair, and she became his prey.

Tossing back her shoulders, she dismissed any immediate danger since Michael was still downstairs. She walked over to the bed that Dolan had carried back upstairs from the sick room. Centered between two windows that overlooked the northern expanse of Lawne Haven and provided a sweeping view of the White Mountains, the single bed took up little room in the chamber that was every bit as large as the bedroom where JoHannah slept.

She closed her eyes and pressed her face into the bed linens to inhale the sweet smell of fresh air and sunshine captured in the sheets. Grounded again, she quickly made up the bed and chose a fresh blanket and quilt from the linen chest in the hall to drape on top.

Her task completed, she stepped back and glanced around the room. Unlike the space-saving built-in drawers that marked Shaker sleeping rooms, Michael's room was furnished in typical World order with free-standing furniture: a single chest of drawers, a chair, a shaving stand, and a writing desk. His room, however, was almost spartan. No curtains covered the windows, no rugs hugged the highly polished floor, and no wallpaper decorated the walls which had been painted pale almond. The walnut woodwork and floor were warm, earth brown, and the only splash of color came from the green and beige striped quilt JoHannah had placed on the bed.

Except for the seascape hanging on the wall over the bed.

Recalling that Michael had once been a sea captain, JoHannah approached the painting and studied it up close. A full-sailed schooner strained against strong winds and rode high on the crest of a huge wave in an angry sea. The painting was so realistic, she could almost feel cold sea mist on her cheeks and had the urge to grab on to the headboard for support. The powerful image of the ship unleashed a desperate longing to dodge the court battle being raged on her behalf, to cut the tightrope she walked between her world of faith and the World, and to escape from the ever-present confusion in her soul.

At sea, she would be free, and she could let the winds blow her where they may. On land, where there had once been only one life path stretching before her, a multitude of paths had emerged, placing her at a crossroads. Which one would she choose? Which one *should* she choose?

"Beautiful, isn't she?"

Startled, JoHannah spun around and found Michael leaning against the door jamb. In a crisp, white linen shirt with long billowing sleeves, forbidding black wool trousers, and ebony hair sleeked back and held by the customary leather thong, he exuded all the strength and power a captain would require to command the ship in the painting.

He smiled, and she noted a wistful look in his eyes as he gazed over her shoulder to stare at the painting. In that instant, she knew without even asking that the ship she had been admiring had been his. "What did you call her?"

"*Illusion.*" He hobbled toward her and pointed straight ahead. "Look closely at the bow. Her name is painted there."

Turning around, JoHannah edged closer until she was standing next to Michael. Just as he had said, pale gray letters, almost obliterated by sea foam, were painted on the ship: ILLUSION. "Do you miss her? Do you miss the sea?" she asked, as curious about Michael's past as she was about his life at Lawne Haven.

"Every minute of the day. Life at sea is the ultimate challenge."

Intrigued, she looked at him, deliberately seeking out his eyes. She had tried in vain to follow the Shaker order not to look directly into a man's eyes, but with her height nearly matching his, she found eye-to-eye contact almost impossible to avoid. "I should think it would be an exciting life, one that gives you great freedom.''

The color of his eyes deepened to charcoal slate. ''It was all of that and more. There's nothing quite like the thrill and the power at the helm. Nature constantly tests you with a sudden squall or a doldrum, and when you beat her, the victory is sweeter than spun sugar.''

''Nature is but the hand of God,'' she whispered, her gaze locked with his. When his eyes grew troubled and churned with emotions too raw for her to handle, she dropped her gaze. ''If you love the sea, why did you leave?''

He exhaled slowly. ''Avery needed me.'' He paused and shifted on his crutches. ''When I came home, I discovered that the demons that had driven me away from Lawne Haven were still here.''

Caught off-guard by his honesty and the incredible notion that this proud, confident man had ever been driven by anything other than his own strong will, she swallowed hard. ''What demons could ever have possessed you?''

He never flinched, although she knew she had invaded the privacy of his past. ''Frustration. Envy. Even bitterness and rage.''

When she raised a brow in disbelief, out of the corner of her eye she caught him frowning. ''I coveted my brother's birthright. All my life, for as long as I can remember, I wanted to be master of Lawne Haven. After my father died, as the second son I had to stand back and see everything I ever wanted handed over to Avery. I tried . . . I tried staying here, but time only deepened my disappointment. Rather than spend my life in my brother's shadow, I left. I forged a new world at sea and found my life's true calling. I was finally convinced that fate had not been cruel to me after all.''

''But you came back.''

''A year ago.'' He looked at her, his eyes gentle. ''My

life at sea was more fulfilling than I ever dreamed it would be, but I could never turn my back on my family, tradition, and land that my ancestors claimed from the wilderness more than two hundred years ago. When Avery sent for me, I returned for what I thought would be a short visit. Instead, I found that my old dreams to become the master of Lawne Haven had finally come true. I never told Avery that I had replaced those dreams with new ones—ones I found at sea.''

Mesmerized by the pain that pervaded Michael's words, the events at Collier surrounding Avery's conversion and Michael's attempts to lure him back into the World did not seem to make sense. ''Is that why you tried so hard to convince Brother Avery to come back? So you could return to sea?''

He shrugged his shoulders, but she sensed that his casual attitude was an attempt to mask feelings far too troubling to reveal to her. ''I had to be sure, very sure, that the new life he claimed for himself was something he truly wanted instead of something he chose because he could not come to terms with burying three sons and losing his wife, not because some brain-sick, fanatical—'' His eyes widened. ''I'm sorry. I didn't mean to . . .''

She touched his arm. ''The World always condemns what it does not understand.''

''I'm trying to understand. The last time I saw Avery, he seemed happier than he'd been in years. I came back to Lawne Haven convinced I had to accept his decision and willing to meet my responsibilities here at Lawne Haven. Until . . .'' He dropped his gaze and stared at his splinted leg. When he looked back up at her, he penetrated the essence of her spirit. ''You gave me back my place in this world, and I will never, ever forget what you've done for me.''

''I only—''

"You gave me back my world," he repeated, "and all I've done for you is to challenge yours."

"That's not true. You—"

He placed a finger on her lips. "Let me have my say."

Nodding, it was all she could do to keep her fluttering heart from taking wing. His touch, ever gentle, sent tingling waves of pleasure through her body and paralyzed her lips.

"I owe you an apology. Several, it seems. I'm truly sorry for—"

"Michael! JoHannah! Supper's on the table." Dolan's voice bellowed up the stairs.

JoHannah turned to leave, but Michael reached out and put his hand on her shoulder, bringing her to an abrupt halt. "We'll be right there. Meet us in the kitchen. We'll use the back stairs," he hollered back.

"Don't be too long. I'm powerfully hungry after moving all that furniture."

"Five minutes. I'm still slow as a turtle on these contraptions."

Dolan's rumbling laughter died out as he apparently made his way back to the kitchen. JoHannah's heart began fluttering madly like the sails on his ship struggling against strong winds, but she held perfectly still, anchored by shimmering gray eyes that pleaded for her to stay. "Everyone is waiting," she whispered, desperate to flee from him before she was so confused she lost sight of who and what he was—her nemesis.

"The last time I tried to apologize the same thing happened. This time, I won't be interrupted, and I mean to finish. You need to hear what I have to say."

Gulping hard, she shook one hand to the floor.

He took hold of her hand and turned her back to face him. "Do I always make you nervous?"

"I—I'm not nervous," she countered, only too aware of the pulse beating in his fingertips.

"That's impossible for me to believe," he said quietly as he shook his head. "It's not easy to miss that little habit of yours."

Puzzled, she glanced up at him. "Habit? What habit?"

"You shake your hand to the floor. I've seen you do it often enough almost to predict when you'll do it."

Cheeks burning, she pressed her lips together and moistened them. Encouraged by his own honesty, she took a deep breath and tried to smile. "It's true. That is a custom of mine, but it's not because I'm nervous. It's . . . it's . . . here, let me show you."

His grip loosened, and she pulled her hand free. Cupping her fingers, she held her hand palm up. "When we pray, we hold our hands like this to . . . to show that we have opened our hearts to receive God's love." With a twist of her wrist, she turned her palm to the floor and shook gently. "When we face evil or are confronted by sin, we shake it away." She dropped her arm against her side, waiting for him to respond by mocking her customs or accepting them.

"Which am I, JoHannah? Evil or sin?"

Pain, deep and mournful, echoed in his words and tugged at her heart. She stiffened, and the gift of true inspiration graced her spirit. "You are neither," she murmured as she absorbed full responsibility for her own sinful nature. How remarkable, she thought, that all this time the beasts of the World and the lion nipping at her heart were merely illusions. The real enemy lay within herself, with her own frail and sinful nature.

"If I am neither, then why do you shake your hand when we are together? I've never seen you do it when you talk with Nora." His brows furrowed. "There were a few times with Dr. Carson that I saw you do it. Is it him, too, or just me?"

"No. Not Dr. Carson and not you," she gushed, mentally

stumbling through a maze of explanations and trying to find one to give to Michael that might make sense without revealing her wicked nature. "With Dr. Carson, I . . . I had to face my sins, not his . . . and not him."

Aghast, Michael tugged on her arm. "Your *sin?* If it hadn't been for you—"

"Pride. I was so proud my treatments had worked, I almost let my conceit hurt Dr. Carson. He's a good man, and even though—"

"What sin do you think you've committed while you nursed me back to health?" he asked, dismissing her account about the physician so quickly she wondered if Michael had paid any attention to her explanation.

She bowed her head. Remembering the night she bared her soul to Nora, she chafed at revealing her deep, dark sins to Michael. On deeper thought, he deserved to know the truth as it had just been revealed to her. Maybe if he understood . . .

Dolan's yell shattered her thoughts. "Michael? Jo-Hannah? Nora said to tell you we're not waiting another minute. Genny's eaten half a dozen biscuits, and if you don't hurry along, there won't be any left."

Laughing, Michael grabbed the hand rest on his crutches. "We're on our way." He edged closer to Johannah and nodded toward the door. "Come on, little saint. The crew is getting restless."

Relief rained over her body, but froze in the next blink of an eye.

"After Genevieve and Dolan leave and Nora is tucked in for the night, you and I are going to sit down at the kitchen table, share a kettle's worth of hot cocoa, and talk this through."

"There isn't anything more to discuss," she argued to his back as she followed him down the hall. "I've told you that it isn't you. It's me. There's nothing to talk about."

He turned his head and grinned at her over his shoulder. "Oh, yes there is. There's quite a bit we have to discuss, except for one very important thing."

She stared at him, her puzzlement teased into utter frustration by the twinkle in his eye. "What might that be?"

"Who gets to heat the milk." He laughed. "And it won't be you."

Her sides ached. Her eyes were swollen from shedding too many tears. Exhausted, she leaned back against her chair and realized that she had never laughed so hard or so often in her entire life.

Comparing Dolan and Genevieve's hilarious antics during supper to the monastic silence during meals at Collier was like comparing boiling water to a stack of snowballs. Dolan and Genevieve had bickered and had eaten enough food in between barbs to feed the multitudes gathered at the hill which prompted the miracle of the loaves and fishes.

During the entire comedy, however, never once did the love light in their eyes dim below magnificent. It simply dazzled her, just like it did now as they polished off the last pie. The fourth apple pie, JoHannah realized as she glanced at the empty pie tins that formed a circle in the middle of the table.

Observing this unaffected, mutual display of affection, however bizarre, opened yet another window in JoHannah's understanding of married love. She wondered how it could be sinful or evil to share such devotion. Could it be that the sin might be that such devotion should be given to God alone?

Neither Genevieve nor Dolan could possibly have room in their hearts for anyone else, although they each seemed overjoyed by the prospect of their impending parenthood. Was it possible that the human heart could actually expand with love? Was there room in everyone's heart for all the love needed for a spouse and children, as well as for God?

Midponder, a sharp knock at the door brought silence to the table, and JoHannah watched with interest as Nora went to the door. Several more impatient poundings rendered the silence again before Nora reached out and opened the door. Cool twilight air swept into the room ahead of a young boy of eight or nine years. Pale and scrawny, his eyes glazed with urgency as he burst into the room. Nora grabbed his arms as he lurched past her. "Hold it right there, young man. Just who might you be?"

"Jeremy. Jeremy O'Neal," he stated, trying to squirm away.

Nora held fast. "Where are you from?"

Gulping for air, his answer came in spurts. "We're livin' at the old Dudley farm. Doc Carson sent me. Wants the Shaker lady to come help." Tears streamed down his face. "Leah was just tryin' to help Ma make soap, but . . . but the pot tipped over and . . . and . . . her screamin' was somethin' awful."

Nora hugged the boy and looked over to JoHannah, who had already risen from her seat. "The Dudley farm is a few miles east. Do you think you could go?"

"I'll take you in the wagon," Michael offered. "It will be dark soon."

JoHannah's hands gripped the edge of the table. "I can walk with Jeremy. You shouldn't be driving a wagon."

Dolan rose and walked past Nora and the boy. "I'll hitch the horses. Genny, help Nora to pack up something for the boy to eat on the way home."

Surrounded by a flutter of activity, JoHannah bowed her head and said a quick prayer. She went up the back staircase to get her remedies from her room, wondering why the boundaries of the World kept stretching and pulling her further away from Collier. The image of a suffering child flashed before her mind's eye, and she hurried her steps.

Chapter 13

The smell of charred, damp wood filled the night air. Tugging on her hand, Jeremy pulled JoHannah toward the ramshackle, single-room cabin. She stepped through the open portal clutching her box of remedies close to her. With a quick, visual sweep of the room, her soul understood the depth of dire poverty.

A single hearth on the wall directly in front of her provided the only heat and light which cast weak shadows on the earth-packed floor. A rough-hewn table, benches, and a row of shelves for storing tableware and cookware were obviously handmade by a man who could not claim any talent for woodworking. One piece, however, caught Jo-Hannah's eye. A beautifully carved rocking chair sat near the hearth, as out of place in this cabin as she felt in the World.

To her left, burlap sacks advertising grain hung clumped together on a rope that stretched across the room to create a separate corner for sleeping. Her gaze rested on three small children huddled together on a corn husk mattress that had been thrown on the floor. Eyes wide with terror, their tear-stained, sallow faces looked pinched with hunger.

They stared at the physician who knelt on the floor tending his little patient.

JoHannah had taken two steps toward him when she noticed a woman, obviously the child's mother, pressed against the wall and trembling in the shadows. At the sound of approaching footsteps, Dr. Carson looked up and relief flashed through his eyes. "Come quickly," he urged, and as JoHannah went to him, Jeremy joined his brothers and sisters in the corner.

She knelt down, and without bothering to remove her cape, set her box of remedies down and peered at the injured child. JoHannah's heart nearly stopped beating. She closed her eyes briefly to concentrate on quelling the uneasiness in her stomach.

"Can you help? Is there something you can do? Frankly, there seems to be little hope."

JoHannah shook her head. "The child's been burned too badly. There's barely a patch of skin unscathed, except for her face and head." She stared at the child, avoiding another glance at the blackened flesh on her mutilated body. Even with smudged cheeks and eyes swollen shut from crying, this was a beautiful little cherub probably not even two years old. A cloud of tight black curls, singed at the ends, cradled her face. Her breathing ragged, the child lay still, her body gratefully shocked beyond pain now.

Dr. Carson pulled a yellowed sheet up over the tiny body and tucked it around the girl's shoulders. "She hasn't much time, I knew there was nothing I could do, but I was hoping—"

JoHannah put her hand on the physician's arm. "I can't work miracles. Only God. . . ."

He bowed his head.

JoHannah could scarcely breathe. The lump in her throat was too large. "I'm sorry. I wish I could do something to help."

Inhaling deeply, the physician nodded toward the mother. "Perhaps you can take Tess and the children outside or nearer the hearth. I'll close the curtains. There's no sense—"

"No!" Tess bolted forward, her eyes frantic. "I'll stay with my Leah."

Dr. Carson got to his feet, took hold of her arms and held her back. "Mrs. O'Neal. The child's near death. Her burns . . ." He shook his head, his voice cracking. "Just remember her as she was. Your other children need you."

Sobbing uncontrollably, the mother fought against the physician's hold. "Let me hold her. Let me—"

JoHannah rose and put her arms around Tess's shoulders and used all of her strength to hold the grief-stricken woman still. "Sit in the rocking chair, and I'll bring Leah to you. Where's your husband? He should be here with you."

Tess O'Neal blinked and stared at JoHannah. "He's . . . he's takin' a walk. This is too hard for him. He's a softhearted man—"

Gently cajoling the mother away from her child, JoHannah led Tess to the rocking chair and eased her into the seat. "I'll bring Leah to you, and then I'll see to the other children till your husband comes back."

Eyes wide, Tess nodded, but her body was stiff, as though she was ready to bolt out of the rocking chair if JoHannah broke her promise. JoHannah held her gaze for a few moments, trying to understand the depth of the woman's despair before turning back to get the child. Dr. Carson shook his head as JoHannah approached. "The child is horribly burned. It'll do no good to let the mother see her like that."

JoHannah slipped out of her cape. "Her face is unscathed. It's important to the mother to hold her little one, and I can't help but hope it will ease the child's last few hours."

He stepped aside, and JoHannah knelt down to wipe the little girl's face with a damp cloth and wrap her in the cape. Small whimpers brought tears to JoHannah's eyes as she carried the dying child to her mother.

Tess' outstretched arms reached frantically for her child, and JoHannah laid the tot in the crook of her mother's arms. Tears blurred JoHannah's vision, but she did not miss the beatific smile on Tess' face. The chair began to rock, and a haunting lullaby, half melody, half sob, echoed in the room.

JoHannah turned away, her chest tight and her chin quivering. When she saw Michael leaning on his crutches just inside the door, she realized that she had forgotten all about him. She had rushed into the cabin with Jeremy as soon as the wagon had rolled to a stop, and the grief and heartbreak that greeted her had dominated all of her thoughts.

His face was solemn, and one look into his eyes told her that he did not know little Leah was dying. Reluctant to speak the inevitable out loud, she simply shook her head and started back to the other children.

Before she had taken more than a step, a slurred voice rang out, and she heard the sound of footsteps stumbling into the room. "Whas . . . whas all this? You're . . . you're one of them Shaker harlots!"

Cringing, she half turned toward the voice, but a strong grip on her arm swirled her about. Spun off balance, the room whirled before her eyes. She totally lost focus as she fell to the floor. Her skirts tangled about her legs, and pain exploded in her face as her cheek scraped the ground, stinging like it had been set afire. The momentum of her fall to the floor knocked the wind out of her lungs, and she braced herself up with the palms of her hands, watching as her cap went flying in the air. Heart pounding, she gulped for breath and tried to unscramble her thoughts.

"Get out! Get out of my house! Before I—"

A scuffle ended the man's bitter command, and when JoHannah finally had the wherewithal to look around, she saw a man lying next to her, pinned to the floor with the end of Michael's crutch at the base of his throat. Eyes bulging and saliva drooling from his mouth, the man who could only be Leah's father looked like a rabid animal.

On hands and knees, JoHannah kept her eyes on Michael as she edged away from her attacker, as anxious to be away from him as she was to flee the stench of whiskey that soured the air with every deep, heaving breath he took.

Rage contorted Michael's features, and she cowered, frightened by the very real threat that the murder in his eyes was a forewarning that violence would soon erupt. Desperate to prevent that, she scrambled to her feet, pushed her hair out of her face and put her hand on Michael's crutch. "I'm not hurt. Please don't do this," she pleaded, her eyes begging him to listen to her.

Michael took a deep breath. "He has no right to attack you."

"He's addled. He's out of his mind with grief!" she argued. She dropped her voice to a whisper. "His little girl is dying." When the muscles in Michael's arm slowly relaxed and he eased the crutch away, she bent down and helped the man to his feet. O'Neal backed away from her, contempt blazing in his eyes. Shaking, he wiped his mouth and stumbled back a few more steps. He glared at Michael. "Get her outta here. I won't have one of those . . . those Shaker harlots near my wife and children. I heard stories about the goin's on in them villages, men and women livin' together in the same house, whorin' in the name of—"

Michael fairly leaped forward on his crutches, but JoHannah stepped in front of him and gripped both of his arms. "There's nothing more for me to do here. Dr. Carson will see to the other children and . . . and this man should be with his wife."

Michael stared at her like she had risen from the dead. "O'Neal should be keelhauled for abandoning his family when they needed him. What kind of man—"

"Please. Take me home. If I stay, it will only make matters worse." He held her gaze, and she could feel his eyes caress the bruise apparently already evident on her cheek.

He turned and poked the edge of his crutch into O'Neal's chest. "I'm taking every bottle of whiskey in this cabin with me, and if you ever take as much as a swig of anything harder than sweet cider, I'll be back. Now wash the stink off your breath and share what little time your child has left with her and your wife."

Fumbling with her hair, JoHannah searched the floor for her cap. When a glint of white, shadowed by flames, caught her eye, she fought back tears. This time, however, she did not try to pull her cap from the fire. She simply turned and walked past Dr. Carson, paused to accept a hasty, whispered apology, and stepped through the doorway. Her heart felt heavy, her steps were weary, and her hair tumbled shamefully down her back.

Shivering, Michael pulled on the hand brake and stopped the wagon alongside a small stream. Filtering through the trees that lined the path, moonlight glistened on JoHannah's head, but bathed her face with shadows. With his leather coat wrapped around her slumped shoulders, most of her hair was hidden, except for a few wisps of auburn curls near her bruised cheek. Stone silent, she stared straight ahead, apparently oblivious to his presence or the fact that the wagon had stopped.

Mentally cursing his broken leg for making it nearly impossible for him to have protected her from O'Neal's attack, he wanted to take her in his arms and hold her.

Promise her that he would never let anyone ever hurt her again. Instead, he gripped the front of the driver's box and swung to the ground. From beneath the driver's seat, he grabbed the two bottles of whiskey he had confiscated from O'Neal. Ignoring his crutches, he hopped less than a yard to the gurgling stream and emptied the whiskey into the water before tossing the empty bottles behind a bush. He saturated his handkerchief with crystal cold water and returned to the wagon.

Leaning back against the wagon wheel a moment to catch his breath, he hauled himself back into the seat, ignoring the shooting pains in his lower leg. He turned to her and tilted her face toward him and out of the shadows. She tried valiantly to blink back the tears that streamed down her face. To no avail. Trying to be gentle, he wiped the dirt from her face and held the cold handkerchief gently against her swollen cheek. "I'm so very sorry," he whispered, his chest tightening.

His heartbeat quickened when her shoulders began to tremble. Quite to his surprise, she leaned toward him and pressed her forehead to his chest. Soft sobs broke almost instantly, and he instinctively cradled her against him. "Shh. It's all over now. He can't hurt you anymore. It's all right."

She burrowed closer, and he wrapped her tighter in his embrace. He felt her tears hot against his neck, and her lips warm against his flesh. She clung to him, as though fighting for a safe place to be in a world that continued to be cruel to her.

How often he had dreamed of touching her and holding her close to him, letting the flames of passion engulf them both, but he had never expected to feel the sensual energy that pulsed through his body when he held her simply to comfort her. Transcending ordinary physical desire into a mystical need, his senses reeled. He pressed his face against the top of her head and held her until she quieted. And in the lingering aura of his attraction, he knew he would never be content until she agreed to marry him.

He waited, counting every heartbeat as the last, and blessing the next, before she realized she had gone willingly into his embrace. Even now, when the worst of her terror had seemed to pass, she lay against him, unearthly still and oh so very warm. He hoped it was because she was reluctant to pull away from the comfort he offered her, but he was half afraid to move and break the spell that kept her in his arms. He was just as afraid to take advantage of her distress and cause her even more when she realized that her breasts were crushed against his chest and her lips were pressing against the base of his throat.

Poor little saint.

Once she came to her senses, she was likely to spend the next month with stones in her shoes as penance.

He brushed her hair from her face and gazed down at her face. Expecting to see her eyes filled with doubt or shame, he leaned closer. Disbelief pounded in his heart. Above lips slightly parted and tear-stained cheeks, her eyes were closed. Her breathing was deep. She was asleep.

Asleep?

Chuckling to himself, he leaned back, propped his splint on the front of the driver's box and cuddled her while she slept, enjoying this unexpected gift a few precious moments longer.

Crickets chirped. Frogs croaked. A heart beat against her cheek. Warmth. Comfort. *Michael!*

Stirring awake, JoHannah felt too weak to move. Every muscle in her body had turned to melted wax. It was too great an effort to lift her head, and her mind refused to function beyond the present moment.

"Feeling better?"

Like velvet, Michael's voice wrapped around her troubled heart. She nodded, unwilling to speak or break the gentle spell that bound her to him. Battle weary, she closed her eyes again and hoped Michael would continue to hold her—just a little longer. When she felt his muscles tense, her heart started to race. When she realized that he had only shifted in his seat, she sighed contentedly.

"Would you like to talk about what happened?"

A tingling sensation ran down her spine as he toyed with a wisp of her hair and caressed the tender flesh at her temple. He entwined his fingers with hers and squeezed them reassuringly.

"I just want to go home," she whispered as tears sprang to her eyes.

"I know," he murmured. "You want to go home to Collier."

She bit her lower lip, overwhelmed to think that he knew her heart so well.

"Even if I wanted to take you there, I couldn't. You have to wait for the court's ruling."

She shook her head. "I can't. I can't wait. I have to go home."

"Where you're safe."

"The World . . . the World is too hard," she explained and eased from his arms. Deeply troubled, she sat up next to him, their shoulders touching, their hands still entwined.

"Tell me what you're thinking," he urged.

She was too numb to argue. "Tonight . . . tonight with Tess O'Neal and little Leah I saw such anguish and pain. I saw helplessness crush Dr. Carson's spirit. I saw the other children, hungry and frightened, and their father . . . too weak to protect them. All the evil that can be thrust at man was there in that cabin."

"You saw life, JoHannah," he argued. "Sometimes it's very harsh, but it can be filled with hope and blessed with great joy. I have the sense that your life at Collier was too ordered and isolated. The life you lived there wasn't real. It was just an illusion of real life. Despite the fact that you were forced to leave your community and were then sent to Lawne Haven, you now have the opportunity to learn that for yourself.''

The insinuation that she should return to the World she had left behind so long ago, just as he had returned to Lawne Haven, was abundantly clear. She shook her head and tried to sort out her thoughts. By breaking them down into smaller pieces she could handle one at a time, perhaps she could find a way to make him understand her turmoil and help her through it by telling him exactly what she had been experiencing from the moment she had left Collier. ''I was so frightened when my guardian forced me to go to my birth home. When I got there, every warning about the World sprang to life. It was nearly unbearable, but with constant prayer, I managed to endure. I—I wasn't sure how much more . . .''

He exhaled slowly. ''And then you were sent here to Lawne Haven.''

''The lion's den,'' she whispered, shivering as the terror of being led from the dining hall at Collier back into the World flashed back into this moment.

''The what?''

She repeated what she had said, opening her heart fully to him, hoping he would understand that her troubles were not his fault, but hers. ''When I was cast out into the World, I felt like I was one of the early Christians sent to entertain the Roman mobs.'' She blinked back tears, and he tightened his hold on her hand.

''Why would you think that?'' he murmured while caressing her fingers with the side of his thumb.

''Because . . . because I had sinned and opened my heart to the temptations of the flesh. I thought I was being pun-ished because I was too weak to carry the cross of the flesh because I found you . . .'' Too embarrassed to put her sins into words for fear he would think her foolish, she bowed her head.

His handhold tightened. ''Did you know I felt that way about you?''

Impossibly amazed, she looked up at him. Their gazes met and locked, and the emotion that simmered in his eyes turned them into sparkling silver pools so deep she felt like she was drowning.

He leaned his face closer to her, and his breath fanned her cheek. ''Did you know, sweet Shaker sister, that I haven't been able to get you out of my mind since the first day I met you at the village?''

Her eyes widened until her lashes touched her brow. Was it true? Could he possibly feel the same magnetism drawing her to him as she felt whenever he was near? Had the attraction been there for both of them from the moment their eyes first met? She shook her head, but he caught the tip of her chin with his finger.

''It's true,'' he murmured. ''I thought you were the most intriguing woman I had ever seen, but I never, ever considered you would give me a moment's thought.''

Totally astounded by his open admission, JoHannah moistened her lips. Even more compelling was the honest and from-the-heart nature of their conversation that reminded her of nightly meetings with her sisters and brethren, although the topic was certainly not one that would be sanctioned by the elders! ''You haunted my dreams,'' she admitted, hoping they could discuss their mutual attraction and disarm it before it destroyed both of their lives.

''As you did mine.''

She closed her eyes, haunted by the memory of those long nights when dreams of Michael robbed her sleep and blackened her soul. To know that he had similar dreams about her made her tremble at the full and unforgiving nature of sin. She tried to slow her racing heartbeat, but the very thought that he had dreamt about her only heightened her own guilt. Somehow, in a way she could not imagine, she must have done something sinful to attract his attention. Woefully ashamed, she needed to convince him that she did not intentionally try to lure his interest . . . then or now. "I tried so hard not to think about you. And then when I came here . . ."

He sighed. "You walked right out of my dreams and straight into my world."

Michael traced her jawline with his fingertip and alarming sensations tingled across her flesh. "Is my world so very unbearable?" he asked, his voice low and husky.

Her chest tightened, and she found it hard to breathe. "Lawne Haven is not like what I expected, which only confuses me more. I never had a single moment when I thought to leave Collier, but now . . ." She took a deep breath. "Nora has become my friend, and she's tried to convince me that my confusion is natural, that there is more than one path to salvation, but . . . but I'm torn between two worlds, and I'm afraid I don't have the strength to be faithful to mine."

"Because of me," he whispered, so softly she wanted to cry.

"No," she answered. The lie caught in her throat. "Yes," she admitted, her voice cracking. "Yes."

He pressed her hand against his lips. "I want you. More than I've ever wanted any woman."

Startled by the husky emotion in his declaration and the gentle leap of her heart, she tried to pull away. Just as she had feared, the sin of lust had overtaken him, too. Would he take advantage of her confusion and carry her with him into a realm so replete with sensual pleasures that she would never find her way home? What would happen when he tired of her? Would he simply send her away, his sensual appetites satisfied?

He held her fast, and when he looked at her, he mesmerized her with his silver-gray eyes. "I want you, sweet JoHannah. As my bedmate and my wife."

The metaphorical wooden cross upon her shoulder suddenly turned to stone, and she nearly cried out in physical pain. His proposal should have brought her joy since he obviously did not intend to lure her into the pleasures of the flesh only to discard her when he grew bored. His offer of marriage, however, frightened her to such an extreme that she physically trembled. Her hand started to shake to the ground. What he suggested was certainly honorable by World standards, but for her, marriage was a sin. The least sin, according to her faith, but sin nevertheless. She tried to pull away from him, to distance herself from the temptation of his touch, but Michael refused to let her go.

"Please don't pull away from me. I know that what I am saying frightens you, but you have to try to understand that I don't simply want you to warm my bed. I want to share my world with you honorably. Marry me," he whispered.

"I . . . I can't," she cried. "I can't . . . and if you care for me, you'll try to understand—"

He pulled her closer. "Just give me a chance to give you a glimmer of the good life we could share together."

Dazed and nearly overpowered by the way his heart pounded against her cheek, JoHannah felt the tears begin to well in her eyes. "Why are you doing this to me?"

He pulled his coat tighter around her shoulders and pressed a kiss against her forehead that she felt clear down to the tips of her toes before he released her. "I thought it was obvious. I'm doing this because I believe you belong at Lawne Haven, and I intend to court you most properly until you agree to be my wife."

"Why would you do this? Why—"

"Because we belong together." His gaze hardened. "When I became master of Lawne Haven, I knew I needed a special woman who would be my helpmate. From the first time we met, the attraction between us has been very strong. Even though you deny it as sinful, I know it is real and it is right. So, my precious little saint, you have little say in the matter. You're simply going to have to give in and agree to be my wife."

"That's . . . that's ridiculous!" she sputtered. "You can't just . . ."

He grinned as he released the hand brake. "Watch me."

She grabbed hold of the seat as the wagon lurched forward. "This can't work. It *won't* work. There are a million reasons why it won't happen. It would take a miracle—"

He laughed and flexed his injured leg. "Is there any rule that says a man can't have more than one miracle in his life?"

She blushed. "You can't just decide to make me your wife and expect me—"

"Yes I can."

His confidence slipped into arrogance she found annoying. "What about Nora?"

"Nora adores you."

"What about the court?" she argued. Did he honestly think he could control the entire legal system?

"I have Uncle George on my side."

"But what if my guardian prevails? He's already told me he was arranging my marriage."

He grinned. "Good."

"Good?"

He grinned again. "Of course it's good. You'll simply have to marry me, and if he seems reluctant to agree, I have two very influential friends who will set him straight."

She glared at him, frustrated by the twinkle in his eyes.

"Oh really? Who might that be?"

He started laughing. "Dolan and Genevieve, of course. Between the two of them, your guardian doesn't stand a chance."

"You are overly confident," she whispered, all banter aside. "What makes you so certain that I'll choose your world instead of mine?"

He reined the horses to a halt and tilted her face toward him. His eyes turned from playful to serious. "Never underestimate the power of prayer."

"Prayer?" That was the last answer she ever expected to hear from him.

"You don't hold an exclusive claim on saying prayers, JoHannah. Some of mine have already been answered, although I wish one answer hadn't been given quite the way it was," he murmured, his eyes caressing every inch of her face. A small frown graced his lips as he lifted a wisp of hair off her cheek and pressed it back in place against her head.

She raised a brow. "You prayed for me . . . to lose my cap?"

He turned away, clicked the reins, and started to whistle instead of answering her as he drove toward home.

She stiffened her spine and refused to ask him again, certain that God would not have answered Michael's prayer and sent her cap flying into the fire.

And then again . . .

Chapter 14

While watching JoHannah unhitch the horses and get them settled into their stalls after returning from the O'Neals', Michael gripped the hand rest on his crutches. Feelings of inadequacy whitened his knuckles as simple frustration grew into downright chagrin. Her matter-of-fact attitude about assuming this task chafed at his manly pride. How was he supposed to court her when he could not even perform the simplest chore for her?

When she finished, he hobbled along beside her as they made their way back to the house without speaking. His crutches poked into thawed earth, and a hint of the promise of spring scented the air. Light streamed from the kitchen window to guide their way, and when she reached out to open the door, he saw the dirt smeared on her hand and stained into her gown.

The kernel of an idea popped into his head. Heated by his desire to do something special for her, it burst wide open into a plan of action that would give her no time to question his intentions or his ability to keep his promise to make her agree to be his wife. He followed her into the house and hit the door closed with his crutch.

A well-fed fire blazed contentedly in the hearth and

warmed away the chill in his body. The rocking chair was empty, and apparently, Nora had taken to her bed. As he tried to rearrange the stumbling blocks that threatened to keep his idea to just a wistful thought, JoHannah walked over to the hand pump at the sink to wash her face and hands.

Quickly deciding that time and cunning would override the obvious disadvantage of maneuvering about on crutches, he plopped into a chair at the kitchen table and slid his crutches to the floor. If he could only figure out a way to keep JoHannah busy for an hour . . .

But how? Telling her precisely what he had in mind defeated the whole purpose behind his scheme to surprise and delight her, and he dismissed it immediately. Hope sank into a quagmire of possibilities, all of them eventually rejected, and he did not realize she was standing next to him until she touched his arm. Startled, he turned in his seat.

JoHannah slipped off his borrowed coat, and he noticed she had recoiled the rope of hair at the nape of her neck. She moistened her lips, a shy look in her eyes. "Thank you for letting me use your coat. Would you like me to take it to your room, or do you want it hung by the door?"

"Just . . ." A flash of brilliance rendered him momentarily speechless. "Just hang it on the peg," he drawled, planning his next move carefully. As she turned and walked toward the pegs on the wall near the door, he shifted in his seat to follow her with his eyes. "I'll try to get Dolan to stop by the O'Neals' to get your cape back for you."

Her shoulders stiffened briefly. "Please don't send him anytime soon. They have enough to worry about—"

"It's only March and cold still bites the air. You can't very well go outside without a coat or a cape of some sort."

She reached up and hung his coat on the peg. "I'll manage without it for a while. I don't think I'll be going out again, at least not anytime soon." She sighed and turned around. "Please don't bother yourself or Dolan about it."

He searched for her gaze, found it, and deliberately held it. "I was thinking more about Nora."

JoHannah's brows furrowed, and her lips turned down into a frown that accented the heart shape of her face. "Nora?"

He nodded, never breaking eye contact, even when she seemed to struggle against it. "Now that I don't need much more than my daily routine of exercises, I was going to ask you to help Nora. She's not as strong as she used to be, although if she ever heard me say so, she'd be bound to throw something at me a lot heavier than a napkin."

Her frown turned upside down, and her smile dazzled him.

Before he lost his advantage, he plunged straight ahead. "Nora's rheumatism seems to act up more when the weather changes unpredictably in the spring. Would you mind terribly if I asked you to assume most of the outside chores? I doubt if she'll let you near her precious goats, but if you could bring in firewood, gather eggs, and feed the chickens—"

"Of course. I should have thought of that." Her cheeks turned pink. "I'll start in the morning."

"Then you need your cape." He grinned. "Isn't this where our conversation started? I'd just as soon stay clear of Brady O'Neal for a while. I'm sure Dolan won't mind."

Panic turned her soft violet eyes into pools of deep purple anguish. "No. Please. Don't send Dolan over there tomorrow. I'll just use Nora's coat for the time being."

He laughed, and for a moment her eyes dimmed with hurt until the absolutely ludicrous idea that she could wear a coat several times too small must have occurred to her, too. She laughed with him, and he realized it was only the second time he had heard the sound of her laughter.

He did not intend for it to be the last.

"If you're not too tired, I do have a suggestion that might satisfy both of us," he offered. "Unless you're not feeling up to it, or you're truly exhausted."

"No, of course not."

She took the bait so quickly and so completely, he almost felt guilty. "Do you remember when I told you that my family has lived here for almost two hundred years?"

She nodded.

"Depending on your point of view, we have an attic that is lined with trunks and filled with either useless mementos or family treasures. If I recall correctly, one of my ancestors was just about your size. If I didn't have this blame leg, I'd try to make it up the attic stairs and find something warm for you. Do you mind rummaging through the trunks by yourself? Otherwise, I'll ask Nora to help you in the morning."

"No. I'll do it."

She started toward the hall, and he waited until she had taken several steps before calling out. "JoHannah?"

She stopped and turned around.

"While you have the trunks open, would you see if there are some trousers you could alter for me so I don't ruin the few I have left?"

"All right. Anything else?"

"No. No, that's all I need. Don't be too long. It's been an eventful night. You need your rest." He was out of his chair before she reached the stairway to the second floor, racing against time and determined to bring a smile to her heart—for him.

JoHannah carried a lit candle in one hand and lifted her skirts with the other as she mounted the steep, narrow steps that led to the attic. The palms of her hands still smarted, and her knees ached from her fall. Her cheek felt stiff and sore. All she wanted to do was climb into her bed and put thinking about what happened tonight to rest. Tomorrow would be soon enough to sort out the dizzying implications of her heart-to-heart conversation with Michael that he quickly turned to his advantage.

Instead, she was climbing up into a dusty attic in the middle of the night to search for a coat she did not want and trousers Michael only yesterday had said he did not need. And the only reason she had agreed to do it was to prevent Michael from sending Dolan into a situation that might explode into more violence and hatred when Brady O'Neal realized that his child had died . . . wrapped in a *harlot's cape*.

She shivered, still overawed by the malicious World lies that tainted the splendid innocence of life in Shaker communities like Collier. When she reached the top stair, she shivered again as cool drafts of air greeted her arrival in the attic.

She held the candle aloft and cupped one hand around the top to steady the flame. The flame flickered its light about the room. Low eaves meant she would have to work from the center, and there was barely an aisle to give her access. Michael was right. The attic was literally stuffed with enough family heirlooms to fill a museum—or a trash pit. A spinning jenny like the one Sister Agatha used, albeit draped with a layer of spider webs, rested on top of an odd assortment of wooden farm implements splintered beyond repair. She moved the candle to her right, illuminating a rocking chair, minus one rocker, and an old barrel with strappings rusted into thin wires that seemed destined to snap if caught in a single burst of wind.

Forging ahead cautiously, she ducked her head and made her way to a wall of trunks stacked four high on top of one another that blocked off the rest of the attic. Praying that she would find what she needed in a top trunk, she set the candle on a high, three-legged table perched atop a crate and pried open one of the lids. Hinges creaked in protest as she raised the lid and peered inside.

A quick perusal of its contents, however, sent hope flying into the past century. Old military uniforms, official documents yellowed with age, and an array of rusted weaponry testified to the family's patriotism. Pacifist by faith and inclination, she closed the lid abruptly and turned to the adjoining trunk.

By the time she had rummaged through the top trunk in each stack, her hands were covered with dust and grime, her mouth felt like it was stuffed with cotton, and her eyes were weary from straining in the dim light. She still had no coat for herself or trousers for Michael, but she probably had learned as much about Michael's family as he knew himself. His people had never known great wealth, apparently, but it was clear they valued family and tradition.

Crude samplers captured a young girl's first awkward attempts at stitchery, patchwork quilts chronicled life events long past, and bits of velvet or lace cradled gnawed children's teething beads like precious jewels. They were items all lovingly and carefully stored away, their deepest meaning lost to all but those who shared them, but the essence of Michael's ancestors' love and devotion to one another almost crowded the room with its presence.

She paused to rest and closed her eyes, wondering what it might have been like to grow up in a home with parents who passed down family traditions from one generation to the next. Would it be so very different from life at Collier where Shaker traditions passed down from one family of Believers to another?

She rubbed her fingers against her eyes, shook her mind free of all but her task, and went back to work. Six trunks later, she had a brown woolen jacket in hand that fit like it had been tailored for her, although it was obvious that it had been made for one of Michael's male ancestors, a detail he had kindly neglected to mention. She was about to admit defeat when it came to finding trousers for Michael when she uncovered two pair of homespun breeches, their knee lacings in remarkably good condition.

Too tired to think beyond relief that she would not have to do any alterations, she grabbed both pair, eased the trunk closed, and backed down the stairs with barely an inch of candle left.

As she made her way to the staircase that led to the first floor, she gazed longingly at the door to her room. On the other side of that door was a bed and on that bed was a soft mattress. . . . She took a deep breath to give her the willpower to resist. The sweet scent of spring lilacs teased her imagination. Lilacs? In March? She shook her head, deciding that she was so exhausted she was hallucinating.

She scurried down the steps, fully intending to thrust the breeches into Michael's arms, hang her coat on a peg next to Michael's, and take to her bed before he came up with another idea as brilliant as his first.

The closer she got to the kitchen, the stronger the scent of lilacs grew. Convinced that she was indeed on the verge of physical and mental collapse, she took one step into the kitchen, braced to a sudden halt, and dropped her attic treasures to the floor. She blinked her eyes, certain she had stepped into a dream. A wonderful, miraculous dream.

At least a dozen or more candles, arranged in a circle on the oak table, glowed gentle light on a copper tub set before the hearth. Nearby, Jane's little white stool held a stack of thick towels, a cake of soap, and her brush.

Tentative steps carried her into the room. To rinse her hair, a bucket held fresh water that was tepid, but the water in the tub was ever so warm to the touch. She trailed her fingers along the surface and watched the delicate flower-ettes of dried lilacs swirl in a hypnotic water dance.

She glanced around the room again, looking for Michael

as she tried to imagine how he had managed to do all this while on crutches. Instead, she saw the white shirt he had worn the first time she had seen him draped across the back of a chair, a touching gesture for after her bath. Directly above it was a note propped at the base of one of the wooden candlesticks. Her fingers trembled so hard she had to read it twice:

JoHannah—
I hope you like lilacs.
Their color reminds me of your eyes.
Michael

Tears fell as suddenly and gently as a spring shower when she read the postscript and his promise to act honorably echoed in her mind:

I'll come downstairs in the morning
to empty the tub.

She tucked the note into the pocket of her apron and moving nearer the hearth, she undressed and folded her wrinkled shoulder kerchief and stained gown and hid her undergarments beneath them on the seat of the chair. She eased beneath the warm, sweet-scented water and laid her head back to let her hair trail over the rim and skirt the floor. Waves of heat from the fire bathed her face, and she sighed as the bathwater almost instantly soothed away the stiffness in her limbs.

Decadent.

The thought stunned her, but there was no other way to describe the pleasure that invaded all of her senses. Cupping her hand, she caught a delicate purple petal and lifted it out of the water, mesmerized as it floated in a miniature pond in the palm of her hand. The color fascinated her.

Was Michael right? Were her eyes truly the same hue? The light was too dim to find out, even if she defied order to try to see the color of her eyes in her reflection in the water.

To occupy her thoughts more properly, she washed her hair, rinsed it twice, and lathered her body until her skin tingled and all visible traces of tonight's dramatic and tragic events were gone. Reluctant to end her bath, she granted herself five more minutes to lean back against the rim and simply soak.

Her gaze settled on Michael's shirt as her eyelids started to droop. *Michael.* A man of amazing depth, he was as compassionate as he was single-minded about his dedication to family and tradition. *Michael.* His handsome features were made even more attractive by his giving spirit.

She shifted in the tub, only too aware that her talk with Michael tonight marked a turning point of immense importance to her. Despite his shocking proposal and almost arrogant confidence in his ability to claim her hand in marriage, he had helped to clear the paths at the crossroads of her life, making them more distinct so she could make her choice freely about whether to remain in the World or to return to Collier, unless the court ruled otherwise.

Even then, she knew she would find a way to return to her community of faith—if that was her heart's desire. Faced with a monumental decision, once made she knew it would be a lifelong commitment, and she would pledge her body, her spirit, and her soul to it.

It was not the Shaker way, but as Nora suggested, it would be JoHannah's way.

More relieved than afraid, she knew in her heart that Heavenly Father and Holy Mother Wisdom would not abandon her. She would continue to pray for guidance as she continued her life at Lawne Haven with Michael and Nora while waiting for the court's ruling, although it would be much more difficult now that JoHannah knew Michael's intentions.

Distracted by her thoughts, she did not realize the water had cooled until she shivered. Water lapped against her breasts and teased her nipples into hardness. Several flower petals clung to the tips of her breasts, and the curious sensations made them tingle. She bit her lower lip, trying to block out the image of Michael's hands caressing her breasts and brushing his lips against her nipples. Would the sensations that flowed through her body be the same? Or stronger?

Horrified by how naturally her body and mind had weakened and yielded to lust, she escaped from the bath like she was leaping out of a hot skillet. She toweled herself dry and pulled Michael's shirt over her head to cover her nakedness, and her body caught fire. Barely covering her buttocks, the end of his shirt trailed seductively against her skin and made her tremble. She folded the cuffs on the sleeves back once over and laced the neck opening closed, and the soft fabric caressed her sensitive nipples. A longing tightened her abdomen, and his male scent seduced every breath she took, deepening the mysteries of physical desire.

Michael.

Did he truly care for her, or was he simply driven to have her as his wife so he could meet his responsibilities at Lawne Haven? Did she return his growing affection, or had sin simply changed cloaks to tempt her away from her faith? How would she know?

Michael was a strong-willed, confident man, but she would match him with her own strength and determination. She squared her shoulders, and her cross slipped ever so slightly. She paused for a moment, then gathered it lovingly in the arms of her soul and placed it in her heart where it would stay . . . until she was ready—someday perhaps—to carry it back with her to Collier.

*   *   *

Gallantry had its limits.

Down on one knee with his injured leg stretched out straight, Michael groaned as he stuffed a towel into the blasted inch of space between the bottom of the door and the floor. There! If that did not block the heavy scent of lilacs that turned his chaste intentions to surprise JoHannah into visions of lust and seduction, he might have to sleep in the barn.

Not that he could manage to find the strength to crawl an inch beyond his room. After positioning the copper tub, a not-too-difficult task since it was stored in the dining room since his accident, hauling near twenty buckets of water from the hand pump to the tub and heating water on the cookstove for her bath, he was plumb exhausted. He had abandoned one crutch and used his free hand to carry the buckets and spilled more on himself than he probably got into the tub. More times than he cared to remember, he had inadvertently put his injured leg to the floor only to recoil instantly when pain shot through his leg.

The ache in his loins was almost as severe and increased with every aroma-filled breath of air he took into his lungs. He leaned back against the wall and closed his eyes. A faint breeze wafting in through the windows cracked open on either side of his bed carried the lilac scent straight back to him. Like angry seas dashing against a reef and pummeling it into submission, new waves of desire crashed against his promise to remain upstairs as visions of Jo-Hannah, her porcelain body flushed from her bath and seductive in its innocent beauty, flashed in his imagination.

His eyes snapped open, and he crawled to his bed. *Another wrong move.* As he sank onto the moonlit mattress, he imagined the first time he would take JoHannah to his bed. He could almost feel her body next to his and could envision kissing her full, sensuous lips and teasing them open to explore the sweet recesses of her mouth. His lips literally tingled.

He slammed his eyes shut, but the bulge beneath his trousers hardened, transcending pulsing need and pounding with desperate desire. Hauling himself to his feet, he hopped to either side of the room, opened both windows wide and pulled the green and beige quilt from the bed, cursing the moonlight that filtered into the room for the tenth time.

He wrapped the quilt around his shoulders and settled himself into the chair facing the windows. Glowering at the painting over his bed, he swallowed hard, barely able to make out the outline of his ship. A sardonic laugh bubbled past his lips when he read the name on the bow.

Illusion.

Gallantry, indeed, was an illusion, and he was hard pressed to imagine the next several months courting Jo-Hannah without bedding her as anything less than pure, living hell.

And he himself had opened the gates.

•

Chapter 15

Sensual dreams of Michael, interspersed with nightmare visions of little Leah, a mother's grief, and a father's drunken fit of anger clawed at JoHannah's sleep. For relief, she simply had given up her bed and spent the hours just before dawn on her knees. The solace she found in prayer added to her resolve to use her time in the World as a proving ground and inspired her to find some way to ease the O'Neals' plight.

At the first streak of daylight, JoHannah tiptoed out of her room and down the hall to the stairs. She made her way to the kitchen, bound and determined to set it straight either before Nora came downstairs and asked more questions than JoHannah cared to answer at the moment or Michael had to dissemble her bath. One glance around the light-bathed kitchen, however, sent her heart flying straight up into her throat where it caught and pulsed madly. Grainy eyed, she blinked, but all trace of her decadent bath had disappeared—except for the gentle scent of lilac that still lingered in the air.

Dazed, she walked around the room. The tub was gone. Jane's little white stool was back near the sink and all the candles had been removed from the round oak table. She found a small dollop of spilled wax left behind and spotted puddles of water on the floor, the only visible evidence that JoHannah did not dream the entire episode.

When had Michael cleared the kitchen? She was sure that it was well past midnight by the time she had slipped into bed. It was barely six o'clock in the morning now, and since she had been awake for the past few hours, it seemed unlikely that Michael had left his room without her hearing him—not the way he banged about on his crutches. The only other way for Michael to have been able to empty the tub and restore the room . . .

A sudden chill gripped her heart. Gooseflesh dimpled her skin. Had Michael planted his note to lull her into trusting him and then stayed downstairs . . . to watch her bathe and clear the room as soon as she took to her bed? It was hard to imagine any other explanation, and his betrayal shattered his promise to act honorably into a wicked ploy to lull her into trusting him. Shudders wracked her frame, and she wrapped her arms around her waist. She turned to leave, but was unable to take a step as the World she was now in seemed much more dangerous than she had thought.

"Sorry. Forgot to close the door. Didn't realize there was such a strong draft coming from the dining room. You're up awfully early."

Near a dead faint, she spun on her heels and stared at Michael—World temptation in the flesh. Damp against his muscled chest, his shirt clung to him like plaster in a mold. Broad shoulders tapered to a trim waist, and just below, a cluster of purple petals caught in the top lacings of the damp wool pants that hugged his thighs.

Relief quickly evaporated into shame for doubting his honorable intentions and dismissing his promise as shallow. "I—I thought I'd empty the tub before Nora got up," she stammered as she noticed the water stains on his crutches.

His smile nearly dazzled her out of her wits. "Just finished. Didn't you see my note? I couldn't find it this morning, so I thought you knew I'd take care of everything for you."

He started toward her, but the bottom of one of his crutches slipped in a puddle he obviously did not see or expect. As he toppled sideways, his crutches crashed to the floor. She lurched forward and caught him around the waist. Breathing hard, she braced her feet to hold his weight until he regained his balance. Nearly overpowered by the scent of lilacs that saturated his clothing, she shivered as the horrible consequences of the fall that had reinjured his leg flashed before her eyes.

Her one shoulder pressed against his, and their bodies hugged together from thigh to chest. His hands gripped her shoulders for support, and he moaned as his strong fingers dug into her flesh. She held him tight. "Are you all right?" she questioned, the urgency in her voice as taut as the muscles beneath her fingertips.

"Fine. I'm fine," he gritted. The veins on his neck bulged and the flesh reddened as he took several deep breaths of air.

The crisis had passed, but her pulse refused to stop pounding in her ears. His chest pressed against her with each breath she took, and his strong grip changed into a caress along the upper curve of her shoulders.

"Did I hurt you?" His voice was husky and low. Very low . . . and seductive.

"No," she whispered. She eased from his grasp, tugged at the makeshift cap that had been pardoned from its exile into use again, and straightened her shoulder kerchief. Eyes lowered, she almost shook her hand to the floor, but chose to grip her skirts instead.

"Thank you. Again. That's twice you've saved me, you know," he remarked as she handed the crutches back to him.

Her head snapped up, and she met his gaze. Soft clouds of gray jolted denial ahead of words of gratitude for his consideration last night. "You wouldn't have needed rescuing if you hadn't . . . I mean . . . it's—it's not your fault. It's mine." Her heart skipped a beat as her mind hopscotched into so many thoughts she grew dizzy.

He chuckled softly, his lips opening just far enough to give her a glimpse of even white teeth that had looked so dazzling last night in the moonlight. "*I* spilled the water. *I* slipped on it. How is that *your* fault?"

She moistened her lips. "I should have emptied the tub last night and tidied the room. You . . . you were very kind and thoughtful to have set up a bath for me. I thank you for it now, but the least I could have done—"

He reached out and put his finger under her chin. "It gave me pleasure to do something for you after all you've done for me."

Sweet sensations skirted across her face, and she took a step back, too unnerved to think clearly. "That's not necessary. I was sent here to be your nurse."

"That doesn't change what happened. The first time you rescued me, you saved my leg as well as my life. That puts me in your debt, at least until I can do something as important for you."

How could he turn one event inspired by faithful devotion to help others into one requiring some kind of payment in kind? "That's . . . that's ridiculous," she sputtered.

"No. Just an old proverb or truism. I remember hearing something like that from my father."

She toyed with her hands, hoping it would not occur to him that she owed him a debt of her own since he had rescued her from the snowslide at Collier. Last night's events, however, were much more troubling. What would have happened to her if Michael had not been there last night to stop Brady O'Neal? "Your debt was paid last evening," she whispered.

He stiffened, and his hands tightened around the hand rest on his crutches. "I couldn't move fast enough to keep O'Neal from grabbing you. I'm sorry. Are you really all right?" he asked as his gaze scanned her face.

She touched her cheek and smiled. "Just a little stiff. Does it look . . ."

"The barest hint of a bruise, that's all," he assured her, his voice catching just slightly.

"Then it will be fine in a day or two." Her heart simmered with emotions that quickly boiled over into the desire to feel his arms around her again. "I'll wipe the floor," she said quietly. To put distance between them, she walked over to the drawer in the cupboard to look for a rag.

"I suppose my first debt to you has been paid, but I'll still be waiting."

She spun around and put her hands behind her to grab the edge of the cupboard. "Waiting?"

He shrugged his shoulders. "To come twice to the rescue. You just helped me avoid another bad fall. I'll just have to stay close to you and wait for that one shining moment when I can return the favor and save you from some horrid fate. Might take a lifetime," he mused as he worked his way carefully past the puddle that had just been his undoing.

A teasing gleam in his eye kept her pinned to her spot, and as he got closer, her heart began to flutter like a baby bird trying its wings for the first time. When he stopped and leaned over to whisper into her ear, she closed her eyes. The gentle breeze of his breath against her skin made her tremble. "I'm a very, very patient man. If you think I'm exaggerating, ask Nora. She'll explain what I mean."

There was no doubt in her mind that he was referring to the fact that JoHannah would eventually accept his proposal

and decide to live in his world. Seizing the chance to prove
that she was just as determined to make up her own mind
and still considered returning to Collier as her most likely
decision, she took a deep breath and tilted her head just
enough to be able to meet his gaze. "I will ask her," she
promised. "As long as you don't ask me to explain anything about last night to her."

The dark circle around his dove-gray irises hardened into
a rim of iron. "About O'Neal?"

Innocently, she shook her head. "No. Your proposal."

Before she could say another word, Nora swept down
the back staircase into the kitchen, took one look at her
floor and marched straight to Michael and JoHannah. Hands
on hips, she stared up at each of them. "Who's been track-
ing water all over the floor?" She sniffed and glared at
Michael. "You . . . you smell like you fell into a lilac bush!
What's going on here?"

Giggling, JoHannah put up her hands, grabbed a basket
to gather eggs, and headed toward the door.

"Where do you think you're going, young lady?" Her
eyes squinted tight. "And where's the new cap I made for
you?"

Guilt bubbled into nervous laughter that escaped from
JoHannah's lips. "Ask Michael," she managed before she
slipped her attic coat from its peg and hurried out the
kitchen door with no intention of trying to rescue Michael
from the housekeeper's temper when she found out he had
been doing chores again. As for the details surrounding the
specific chore that puddled water all over Nora's kitchen
floor, she thought it rather appropriate that Michael would
be humbled once again.

Half a dozen warm eggs nestled in JoHannah's basket after
she had fed the chickens. The horses had fresh water and
grain, and she had raked the stalls. A day's worth of fire-

wood lay stacked by the kitchen door. Biding for more time before she had to go back into the house and face Nora and Michael, JoHannah searched for another chore. Overheated from her work, she removed her coat and looked around. Not even tempted to get an ax from the tool shed to chop wood, she followed the sound of goats bleating their hunger.

She wanted to give Michael enough time to explain to Nora what had happened last night at the O'Neals' cabin— after he tried to explain away JoHannah's bath. She also needed to be alone and out of Michael's presence to erase the fevered memory of finding herself wrapped in his embrace for the second time in less than a full day.

She wandered toward the barn feeling guilty for leaving the chore of mopping up the floor to the housekeeper and wishing for something to do that would excuse her selfishness. Despite Nora's overprotective, even possessive, attitude toward the goats that supplied Lawne Haven with milk as well as butter and cheese, JoHannah decided to milk them to save Nora the trouble. She made her way to their pen, stopping at the barn along the way to get some feed, the milking stool, and a pail.

She had milked enough cows at Collier to be fairly hopeful that milking goats would not be very different. If anything, goats were assuredly smaller and less dangerous than cows. She passed the back corner of the barn and approached the rear of a lean-to. As she got closer, the sound of hooves scratching against rock and high-pitched bleats grew louder. Smiling to herself, she turned the corner and found four goats lined up along the wire pen. She kept her voice low and reassuring. "Good morning, little friends," she cooed. "Ready to share your milk?"

In the next breath, JoHannah stumbled over a rock and lost her footing. The milk stool and pail went crashing into the wire fence while the feed bucket flew over it and smashed into the ground with a thud. Instantly, the dainty little goats exploded into a frenzied herd. They raced around frantically, knocked into one another, bleated like they were being beaten . . . then silence. Thick, heavy silence.

JoHannah caught her breath and got to her feet. When she looked into the pen, four bodies littered the ground, their stiff legs pointing skyward. The goats were all dead.

Dead? Had she literally frightened them to death?

Her hand flew to her mouth as she backed away. Nora. Maybe Nora could do something, anything, to help bring them back to life. Heart pounding, JoHannah raced back to the house, wiping away her tears to clear her vision. Her cap flew off her head. The knot in her shoulder kerchief came undone. She grabbed the end of the kerchief, but let the cap go. Faster. Run faster! She practically crashed through the kitchen door and rocked to a sudden halt. Three people, not just Nora and Michael, were gathered around the table. Michael and a male visitor had their backs to her, but Nora looked at her directly.

"I killed them," she wailed, too distressed to care who the visitor might be. "Oh, Nora, I didn't mean to hurt your goats!" She battled for air, and the rest of her words gushed out in gasped phrases. "I—I was only trying to help . . . I fell . . . the milk stool went flying . . . the bucket . . . and all of a sudden . . . they were . . . they were all dead! Help," she urged, "you have to come . . . you have to try to help."

While Michael struggled to get to his feet, Nora bolted out of her seat and took JoHannah's arm. "Calm down. Calm down. Take a deep breath. That's it. One at a time. Everything is all right. Really."

Nora wrapped her arms around JoHannah's waist and held her close. Chest still heaving, JoHannah closed her eyes and tried to follow Nora's directives. When she could finally breathe normally again, she opened her eyes, looked down, and found an odd twinkle in Nora's eyes. "You're not . . . you're not angry with me?"

Michael chuckled as he made his way toward her, and JoHannah's head snapped up. "If there's any humor to be found, I daresay it's rather cruel and heartless to laugh now. Nora loved her goats."

He sobered immediately. "They're not dead."

"Of course they are," she spat. "I know what I saw."

Nora patted her arm. "They just fainted dead away, poor dears, but by now they're probably scampering about the pen. None the worse for what happened, except that today's milk is probably spoiled. There's little harm done," she insisted, "except to you."

"Fainted?" JoHannah's eyes widened. "Fainted?" she repeated. "Like . . . like people?"

"Stupid critters. I forgot to warn you. They're as nervous as a herd of vir—" Michael caught himself, but his cheeks turned scarlet. "Nervous as a cat," he offered weakly. "Happens all the time."

"But I never heard tell . . ." JoHannah stared down at her dirty skirt and realized she had her kerchief in her hand. Her hair tumbled around her face. If her blunder reddened her cheeks, her mortification at the state of her dress painted the blush to the tips of her ears. She caught a glimpse of the cupboard and wondered if there was room enough inside for her to crawl in and shut the door. Her hands shook as she donned the shoulder kerchief and smoothed her hair into a knot.

"Consider yourself a real part of the family now," Nora suggested as she led JoHannah to the sink while Michael returned to his seat. "There isn't a one of them who didn't assume the worst when the same thing happened to them . . . including our visitor."

JoHannah began to wash her face and hands, trying to get at the dirt under her nails. Her hands froze in place when Michael and the visitor began to reminisce.

"Remember when Ma got her first two goats? Pa had pink ribbons tied around their necks. He took Ma, blindfolded, to the pen and let us watch. Remember?"

A deep voice laughed. "To this day, I can hear your mother cry out for joy. The next minute, she was sobbing, blaming your father for killing the goats by tying the ribbons too tight."

"What about the time . . ."

One story followed another. Chuckles crumbled into fits of laughter. Howling, riotous, belly-aching laughter. Jo-Hannah was almost tempted to laugh herself, but she was too busy trying to place the visitor's voice. Eventually, the conversation waned, and she heard Michael come up behind her. "I'm sorry. We weren't laughing at you. I should have told you about the goats."

She dried her hands and turned around slowly. One hand trembled as she touched the back of her hair. "I—I lost my cap."

He smiled gently, and his gaze softened. "We'll get you another, but right now, we have a visitor who wants to talk to you."

Eyes downcast, she followed him back to the table. His large frame blocked most of her view, but when he stepped aside, a man's trousers came into sight. Her gaze slowly worked its way upward, stopping when she recognized the curve of his mouth and the wisps of gray curls that framed his ears.

"I see you're still adapting to the outside world," he said gently.

Her bottom lip quivered, and she twisted the end of her kerchief in her hands. A hot blush climbed up her neck to her cheeks. "Judge Weldon," she croaked, wondering if it would be too ironic for her to faint.

* * *

"Shame on you both," Nora grumbled, apparently still fuming as she led them all back to the house without letting go of JoHannah's arm.

Properly contrite when he apologized to JoHannah earlier, Michael walked next to her. He exchanged winks with his uncle and looked away before he started to laugh again. "We're both sorry," he managed to say before a new round of chuckles erupted.

Uncle George tried coughing to cover his own rumble of laughter. He failed miserably.

"Never you mind those two," Nora counseled. "They'll get their own wickedness back twofold." She patted JoHannah's arm. "Now that you've seen the goats are back to normal, do you feel better?"

JoHannah nodded, still dazed by Judge Weldon's surprise visit and Nora's insistence that their visit together would have to wait. Had there been a new ruling? Would she be allowed to go back to Collier, or would she be forced to return to her guardian? Now that she had finally come to terms with remaining in the World as she tried to find her life's path, neither ruling appealed to her, an irony that was not lost among her other thoughts.

Once inside the kitchen, Nora led JoHannah up the back staircase and ushered her away before Michael could apologize. Again. He followed Uncle George into the parlor and took a seat near the door so he could see when JoHannah was approaching. The judge pulled a chair over by the window, cracked it open, and sat down to light his pipe.

Michael smiled. "Old habits die hard, don't they?"

Uncle George nodded as tobacco smoke caught in the draft and wafted out the window. "Your mother never did approve, but she didn't have the heart to make me sit outside." He chuckled. "Remember when I left my pipe behind when I went upstairs to get a book, and she caught you trying a puff? Thought I'd get sent to the barn along with you.''

The memory tugged at Michael's heart. "First and last time I ever tried tobacco, but it wasn't my last trip to the barn.''

His uncle smiled sadly. "I can still see the way your parents looked on the day they were married. I miss them both, even more as I get older.''

Michael scanned the room filled with a lifetime of happy memories, many of them shared with his mother's bachelor brother who had raised her after their parents died. "You should take the time to visit more often.''

"Tell that to the blame folks who keep clogging the courts with frivolous lawsuits. Which reminds me where we left off when we were interrupted.'' He sat forward, his head haloed by a ring of smoke. "To answer your earlier question, Judge Lambert issued a stay on my order so Miss Sims is to remain here—for the time being. He asked to meet with me to discuss the matter, and I thought I'd stop here on my way to talk to her again.''

Michael exhaled slowly and tried to keep his expression calm. "How long do you think the stay will hold before another court gets to rule on it?''

His uncle shrugged. "Can't be sure. Sometimes the docket is jammed for months in advance. Occasionally,'' he mused, stopping to relight his pipe, "occasionally, files are lost. It can take a good two to three months to find them.''

Hope surged in Michael's heart. "Two to three months?'' He calculated ahead. He needed four months, if he was going to have all the time between now and Jo-Hannah's birthday to press his suit. "Bathrick will be none too happy.''

"You do know I stretched the law a bit to send Miss Sims here to help you. I'm too ornery to care and too stubborn to back down to the likes of Eleazar Bathrick, but I am interested in knowing your intentions toward Miss Sims.''

Startled, Michael swallowed hard. "Is it that apparent?"

Uncle George laughed. "Your father asked me the same question once when I cornered him about his intentions toward my sister."

Certain that his feelings for JoHannah were based only on physical attraction and honest respect for her many skills, Michael dismissed his uncle's suggestion that he loved her with the same intensity that his father had loved his mother. Anxious to have his uncle's approval, however, Michael started at the beginning by describing how he had first met JoHannah and watched his uncle's expression change from mild interest to concern when he concluded with a complete chronicle of events from the previous evening.

"Do you love her, Michael?"

Michael took a deep breath and his chest tightened. Images of JoHannah filled his mind and tugged at his reluctant heart with the same mystical power as an enchanting sea maiden who tempted him, lured him into dangerous, uncharted waters. He shook his head to clear his thoughts. Love for any woman was an emotion far too costly for him to consider because love meant total, unequivocal commitment and giving up his dream of returning to sea. No. He did not love JoHannah, but he was attracted to her and supposed he cared for her well-being. He would be able to provide a good life for her at Lawne Haven; in return, she would bear him strong sons to continue his family's landed traditions. She was more than competent at running a household, and in time, he would return to the sea for voyages knowing that while he was gone, she would run his estate well. Her life would be no different than those that other wives of sea captains led, except that she would not be living near the coast. "JoHannah and I are well suited, and I'm prepared to do almost anything to keep her guardian from forcing her to go through with a marriage she doesn't want," he answered calmly.

His uncle shook his head. "What if she decides to return to Collier, assuming her guardian loses his suit?"

Michael squared his shoulders, unwilling to even consider placing second to a faith that would deny him this woman. "She won't. Right now, she's . . . well, she's considering my proposal of marriage. All I need is a little time to convince her to accept me. Can you get me the time I need?"

Michael swallowed hard and waited for his uncle to decide whether or not to help his cause. Eventually, his uncle's expression changed from somber to agreeable. "I'll see Judge Lambert this afternoon and see if we can't manage to bury the files for a few months."

Relieved, Michael was about to express his gratitude when the sound of approaching footsteps forewarned him that JoHannah was coming. When she stepped into the room, he rose and used a single crutch to make his way to stand next to her. "Uncle George would like a moment to speak with you. I'll wait—"

"No. I'd like you to stay. If . . . if that's all right," she asked, looking to his uncle for permission.

"Certainly. You two take a seat. What I need to say won't take long."

Michael waited until she had taken a seat on the sofa before finding his own right next to her. She sat rigid, her hands folded on her lap and her gaze cast to the floor. Her makeshift cap covered her head.

Her thigh pressed against his leg, and her shoulder touched his. His heart began to beat a little faster when he detected the delicate lavender scent that clung to her hair. His brow began to perspire as images from last night flashed through his mind. He loosened the lacings on his shirt. Did she deliberately press against him, immune to his presence, or was she trying to inflame his desires and make him suffer again for his proposal?

Fortunately, Uncle George started to speak and distracted Michael's thoughts away from the dangerous path they had taken.

"The last time we talked, you seemed content to come to Lawne Haven while each side pressed their suits in the courts," Uncle George began, addressing JoHannah directly. "You should know that one additional suit has already been filed, and Judge Lambert has agreed to let my ruling stand, at least until we get to discuss the case. I was on my way to see him when I decided to stop here first."

She nodded.

Michael inched away as discreetly as he could.

"What I need to know is whether you want to continue here or go back to live with your guardian."

She inhaled deeply. "I want to stay here. For now," she said firmly.

"Then it's settled, as far as I'm concerned."

"Settled?" She looked up at him, her eyes wide with surprise.

Uncle George rose from his seat and walked toward her. "I think Michael can explain the rest. If I don't leave now, I'll never get to Lambert's before dark.

Michael started to get to his feet, but his uncle waved him back into his seat. "I know the way out, young man. You tend to this young lady and tell her what we've discussed. I'll stop to say my good-bye to Nora on my way."

Michael turned to JoHannah, took a deep breath, and started to recount Uncle George's less than honorable plan to keep her at Lawne Haven. Reminded of the legal chicanery that had allowed his creditors to rob him of his fortune after he had lost his ship, Michael found the workings of the legal system just a little less slanted against justice than he had thought and a whole lot more to his liking.

The only thing that ultimately surprised him after he had told JoHannah what his uncle planned to do was that the little saint did not consider deliberately manipulating the legal system a cardinal sin.

Chapter 16

Rain. Three straight days of cold, miserable rain.

JoHannah peered out one of the parlor windows. Gray skies and dark clouds swirled overhead. Tree limbs bent beneath a gust of heavy wind, dipping budded branches low to the earth. A shallow stream flowed in the main roadway past shrubbery tinted with the first green of spring. The threat of another cloudburst was undeniable, and she sighed, greeting a fourth dreary day with disappointment.

She moved to the hearth and bent down to stoke the fire. After spending two days in bed with her rheumatism, Nora was upstairs cleaning Abigail's room. Michael was in his room poring over account books—for the third straight day. JoHannah, however, literally had nothing to do—except to watch the sky and wait for the rains to begin again. Save for the dining room which was still closed off, every room in the house had been cleaned and polished to Shaker perfection, although the upholstered furniture and carpeted floors doubled the work she would have had at Collier. A pot of stew bubbled on the cook stove and fresh bread was cooling.

Moments like these evoked memories of her life at the

Shaker village where she rarely had been bored, even in the worst weather. She had almost always had the company of several sisters and recognized her main complaint here at Lawne Haven the past few days as simple loneliness. She missed Nora's company. She even missed being with Michael, despite the tension his proposal of marriage caused between them. Was he deliberately avoiding her or just giving her time to consider his proposal?

A sound from outside caught her attention. After peeking out the window, she ran to the door and opened it before the familiar buggy rolled to a stop. "Dr. Carson!" She greeted his unexpected arrival with enthusiasm, particularly pleased that he had not let what had happened at the O'Neal farm keep him away. "Come in," she urged.

He smiled, his thin frame bent against the wind. "Good morning. Finally got a break in the weather, and I thought I'd stop here on my way to check up on Mrs. Tucker." He climbed down from the buggy, lifted out a bulky wicker basket topped with oilcloth and carried it with him as he made his way around a series of puddles.

"I'm afraid the rain isn't done yet," she remarked as he cleaned the mud from the bottom of his shoes on the boot scraper just outside the door.

"That's why I can't stay too long."

He stepped into the house, and she ushered him into the parlor, amazed at how quickly she had adopted some World customs and not only greeted a male visitor, but also looked forward to sharing his company. "I'll tell Michael you're here. Would you like a hot drink?"

"No, thank you. I really can't stay, and I didn't come to see Michael," he said as he put the basket on the floor. "I came to deliver something to you." He moved aside the oilcloth and lifted a dark blue garment out of the basket. He handed it to her and pressed her fingers around it. His eyes began to twinkle. "Someone once told me your faith forbids presents . . . so I didn't wrap it.''

JoHannah stared at the hooded wool cape. Its fiber was much finer and softer to the touch than her old garment, but it was his thoughtfulness that moved her more. The World was such a very strange place. Three nights ago the World's intolerance had hurt her; today, she was touched by its kindness. Accustomed to a steady rhythm in life, it was this constant shift from one extreme to another that unsettled her most about the World and the people who lived in it. ''I don't know what to say. It's . . . I can't let you. . . .''

''Of course you can. It's the least I should do after what happened. I didn't think you'd want to wear the other one again. Not after . . .'' He took a deep breath and sighed when she tried to hand it back to him. ''Please. It's not a gift. It's just a replacement.''

Touched by his caring spirit, she swallowed the polite refusal she knew she should have given and slipped the cape around her shoulders. ''It's lovely. Thank you,'' she murmured as she tied it closed at the neck. His face lit up with pleasure, yet another gift to her, although she wondered if he realized it.

''You're very welcome.'' He picked up his basket and nodded toward the door. The light of pleasure in his eyes dimmed into regret. ''I'd best be on my way, but before I go I wanted to apologize again. I'm truly sorry. I never would have sent Jeremy for you if I had known what his father would do to you.''

She reached out and touched his arm. ''It wasn't your fault. I only wish I could have helped his little girl.''

''You helped her mother . . .'' He paused to take a deep breath. ''You were right to let Leah spend her last moment in her mother's arms. She died more peacefully, I think. I just . . . I wanted you to know that.''

She smiled. ''Thank you. Again.''

His lips started to move as though he wanted to say more but thought better of it. As he took his leave, she walked with him, reluctant to part with his company. When they reached the buggy, she realized that the wind had died down. Although the skies still looked troubled, the threat of rain seemed less likely. After being cooped up inside for three straight days, the thought of a buggy ride made her heart skip a beat.

He put his basket back into the buggy and climbed to his seat. He picked up the reins and held them still as he looked toward the main road. "I don't suppose . . . no, never mind. I'm sure you have more important things to do with your time than—"

"I'm not busy," she blurted, wondering if her longing for a buggy ride was too apparent.

"I thought you might want to know more about the O'Neals. Not that anything I've learned would excuse Brady's behavior, but it might help shed some light on what happened."

The troubled look on his face reminded her of Elder Calvin when he knew he had to try to convince a Believer that his gift to go sledding instead of chopping wood was a false gift.

"Maybe things are best left alone. And I really don't trust this weather," he suggested, apparently thinking better of his offer.

"I'd like to listen," she admitted. Curious to know what life circumstances might explain O'Neal's outburst and thrilled by the prospect of an outing, she did not want to wait for another opportunity. "I don't have to ride the whole way, and I could walk back. I've been so busy with Michael's care and helping Nora with the housework that I haven't really seen much of Lawne Haven."

His brows furrowed. "Maybe we should ask Michael to come along," he hedged. "That way I wouldn't have to worry about you walking home alone.''

"He's shoulder deep in account books. Unfortunately, figures weren't exactly Avery's strong suit. I'll be back before he even realizes I'm gone." She climbed onto the seat next to him and arranged the cape to cover her skirts. She looked at him and smiled. "This is a good opportunity to see how warm my cape is, don't you think?"

Although refreshed by her outing and a new understanding of Brady O'Neal that softened her frightening experience, JoHannah was still leery about traveling back alone on the main road where she might encounter someone she did not know. She tried a shortcut back to Lawne Haven that Nora had mentioned Dolan used when he came for visits without Genevieve.

Enjoying a bit of freedom after being confined by her duties for so long, she wandered through the tall-treed forest along a narrow path. The smell of recent rain and damp earth mixed with the stronger scent of cedar trees that must have been as tall as the masts of ships. She drew in deep breaths of the musky air as she walked and searched the shrubs and bushes that lined the path with an eye for remedies she could make from the abundance in the forest.

Halfway home, the skies rumbled overhead and literally opened, unleashing a downpour that was so sudden and intense it left her gasping for breath. Her cape flew open, and she held it closed as she started to run. The soft garment had indeed proven to be warm during her outing so far, but she prayed it would keep her close to dry. She huddled under the cape and kept her head down, trying in vain to keep the hood in place with her other hand while the wind and pelting rain mocked her frantic efforts.

As quickly as it had begun, the torrential rain stopped, the clouds opened, and a patch of brilliant blue painted the sky. Sunshine! Glorious and warm, it bathed the path, and the lush foliage surrounding her glistened like it had been sprayed with liquid crystals.

Nature's shift to a better mood buoyed her spirits again. She removed her sodden cape and squeezed out the excess water, amazed to find her kerchief and gown only slightly damp. Her poor makeshift cap, however, was soaked through, and she tucked it into her apron pocket for safe-keeping.

She skirted an overlarge puddle and slowed her pace to savor the husky sweet smell of spring. Wildlife emerged from cover. A chipmunk scampered across her path, and birds announced their presence with gusto as a family of rabbits dashed into the brush. Out of the corner of her eye, an odd shape caught her attention.

She walked over to the side of the path and found an antler that must have been molted last fall. It was too thick to belong to anything other than a moose, and she picked it up, trying to imagine the strength and power of the ani-mal who would carry two of these on his head. She lifted it over her head and held it up high, her muscles straining with her effort.

Clearly out of sync with the rest of the forest's sounds, a strange rustle in the undergrowth to her left sent chills racing up and down her spine. She paused and slowly turned around, her arms frozen above her head.

Huge brown eyes bored into her, and she forgot to breathe or blink an eyelash. Heart pounding, she swallowed hard and stared at a massive bull moose—only half a dozen yards away. Too terrified to run or cry out, she observed him with almost detached interest, as though she were watching this happen from afar . . . to someone else.

When he lowered his head, she braced for an immediate attack, but to her surprise, he merely scraped velvet-covered spring antlers against the undergrowth, raised his head, and stared at her again. Nostrils flaring, he bellowed.

She nearly jumped out of her skin.

"Drop the antler and hold still. He won't charge unless you start to run."

Her heart leaped again, but she nodded very, very slowly. She dropped the antler and attempted to take a measured breath, grateful for the man's unexpected presence and advice. She would have been more than curious to find out the identity of the man behind the voice, but at the moment, a pair of brown eyes set in a massive head atop a mammoth body garnered all of her attention.

The stand-off continued for a good twenty minutes. The moose repeatedly performed his odd behavior, almost as though he was issuing a challenge—one he dared her to accept. The man's whispered voice, however, continued to keep her calm. To her immense surprise and even greater relief, the animal eventually turned, lumbered away, and disappeared into the forest, seemingly bored by the whole encounter.

Disbelief held her immobile for endless moments as her terror faded. Relief made her knees weak and turned her bones into quivering mush. But when she turned around to face her ever-faithful rescuer, her mind instantly revolted, denying the identity of the man with wide-set black eyes and scruffy beard who had saved her life—even as his name came to her lips.

"Brady O'Neal," she whispered. Her knees buckled, and she realized what Dr. Carson had told her about the man must have been true. Why else would he have helped her?

He steadied her until she regained her tenuous hold on reality before he stepped back and removed his hat. "You . . . you sure you're not still gonna faint?"

She shook her head. "Not now. Maybe before when . . . thank you. I—I never really came upon a moose before."

He shrugged his shoulders. "Dumb beast, he is. Saw the rack of antler and thought you were another bull tryin' to move into his range. That's why he raked those antlers of his against the brush. Wanted to warn you off. Finally decided you got his message, I reckon.''

She shuddered. ''Oh, I did. I consider myself properly warned. I won't take this shortcut again.'' Her gaze dropped to the ground. ''I—I didn't expect to meet anyone else along the path.''

He cleared his throat. ''I'm not trespassin', if that's what you're thinkin'.''

''No. I didn't mean that. I'm just surprised—''

''On my way to . . . to apologize,'' he said softly. ''For what I did to you the other night. Not that there's any excuse for manhandlin' a female. I was just crazed outta my mind. My little girl hurtin' so bad, her mama cryin'. I just took off, got good and juiced till it didn't hurt no more. Loosened my tongue and . . . well, Tess told me later what you done, and I'm beholden to you. I . . . I hope you can find a way to accept my apology.''

She moistened her lips. ''Of course I do. I . . . I wish I had been able to do more.''

He shifted from one foot to the other. ''Guess I'll be headin' back now. Told Tess I'd be quick.''

JoHannah nodded. ''I have to get back home, too, but I'd like to come for a visit soon. If . . . if that's all right.''

''We're leavin' as soon as I get back. Tess . . . Tess wants to go back to her folks to visit for a bit,'' he answered, his voice cracking. He disappeared down the path and cut through the woods.

She stood there and watched him until the forest seemingly swallowed him up. Awed by the double blessing of Brady's rescue and apology, she was reluctant to expect a third. She hurried on her way back to the house, all the while hoping that Michael and Nora were still too preoccupied to have noticed her absence.

The path finally opened in a clearing just beyond the goat

pen. She slowed her pace and watched her step for fear of startling them again, but as she passed, they paid no attention to her. She hung her drenched cape and wet cap on the clothesline, grabbed an armload of firewood to set by the hearth to dry, and carried it inside.

The pot of stew still bubbled on the wood-burning cookstove and filled the air with mouth-watering aromas. One loaf of fresh bread and a crock of butter sat on the table which already had been set for three. Feeling guilty for being too late to set the table herself, she went in search of Nora. They nearly collided in the doorway.

"Goodness, child, you scared me!" Nora chuckled and looked at JoHannah closely. "Where's your cap?"

JoHannah's eyes widened as she felt her hair. "Oh, I . . . it's hanging on the line."

"Well, dinner is just about ready, and I just told Michael to knock on your door on his way down. I thought you might be resting."

JoHannah stepped aside to let Nora pass. "I'm sorry. I didn't mean to be so long."

The housekeeper stirred the stew and moved the pot to a cooler section. "Where did you say you went?"

"I—I didn't." Knowing a double reprimand was coming for leaving without telling anyone and getting caught in the cloudburst, JoHannah hedged for time to think how best to tell Nora about her morning adventure. "Dr. Carson stopped by earlier."

"Did he?" Nora paused, then shrugged her shoulders. "Didn't hear his buggy. I thought he wasn't due to check Michael's leg till next week. Funny, Michael didn't mention anything about seeing Dr. Carson this morning."

"He didn't," JoHannah corrected as she carried two bowls to the stove and held them while Nora filled them with ladles of chunky potatoes, carrots, turnips, and beef, all swimming in thin gravy. Steam rose up between the two women, and JoHannah escaped to put the bowls on the table and bring the third back to the stove.

"Just a social call?" Nora's expression turned stern. "Or did he want your advice again? I hope you told him—"

"He came to apologize, again, and he . . . he brought a replacement for my cape."

Nora put an extra serving of gravy on top of the stew in the bowl and put a lid on the pot. "And?"

JoHannah took a deep breath. "And he invited me to ride with him a bit on his way to check on Genevieve."

Nora wiped her hands on her apron. When she looked up at JoHannah, her tiny black eyes sparkled with censure. "You drove to Dolan and Genevieve's with Dr. Carson? In this weather?"

"I didn't ride that far, and the sun is out," JoHannah protested as she carried the bowl to Michael's place at the table. "I'll call for Michael."

"No need to call. I'm here. Where were you?" he commented dryly as he leaned on his crutches just inside the doorway. He looked at her oddly, then smiled as he stared at her hair. "Where's your cap?"

Nora butted in before JoHannah could answer. "She went for a ride with Dr. Carson." Her brows furrowed as she looked about the room. "Now where's that medicine? I must have left it upstairs. I'll be just a minute. You two get started without me."

Surprised by Nora's hasty retreat, JoHannah made her way to the table.

His eyes followed her. "You went for a ride in that downpour?"

"It wasn't raining when we left," JoHannah argued, taking her seat to put something solid, like an oak table, between them. The hard glint in his eyes told her he would not be happy to learn what had happened on her way back, but she did not intend to lie or make excuses for her excursion. "Dr. Carson wanted to tell me more about the O'Neals, and I rode with him because he had patients to see. I needed some fresh air, too."

Michael scowled and started toward the table. "I think I know all I need to about Brady O'Neal."

"Did you know he's just renting the farm? He moved his family here after he . . . well, he used to have a general store in Cresham, but—"

Michael startled her when he plopped down hard into his seat. "But he drank more than just the profits and lost it."

Surprised even more by the rancor in Michael's voice, JoHannah resisted the urge to come back at him in kind. "No. His store burned to the ground. They lost everything they owned," she said quietly. "After coming up with a year's rent money, he barely had enough for seed and a few supplies."

The wind apparently knocked out of the sail of his misjudgment, Michael sagged against the back of his chair. "Dr. Carson told you this?"

She nodded. "I was hoping I could visit Tess, but—"

"How can you even think about going back there? After what that man did to you—"

"He didn't mean it," JoHannah gushed. "He was just out of his mind with despair and grief. He's . . . he's apologized, and I think he deserves—"

"He . . . he what?" Michael roared and stared at her with gray eyes spewing steel daggers. "When? When did you see Brady O'Neal? So help me, if the man put a foot in my house . . ."

JoHannah squared her shoulders. "He apologized today when I met him."

Michael leaned forward and gripped the edge of the table. "You went to that cabin to talk with him?"

Heart pounding, she clenched her hands into fists. "I was

taking the shortcut home when I met him. It happened quite by chance.''

Michael gritted his teeth so hard JoHannah could hear them gnash together. "You walked home along the path? Alone? Do you have any idea of the dangers along the way?''

"I do now," she admitted. She tried to smile, but her best effort resulted in a weak grin. "There was this bull moose. . . . I was frightened out of my wits. Then Brady came along and helped me.''

"A bull moose?" Michael raked one of his fingers through his hair, inadvertently loosening a strand of silver. "You could have been killed.''

"Well, I wasn't," she huffed.

"No, you weren't," he admitted, but his tone was hard. "And at the moment, I'd wager that your guardian angel is probably too exhausted to ask for another assignment, but he will—if he's got any sense at all. You mean to tell me you walked home alone in a downpour, encountered a wild beast strong enough to break your neck with one swipe of his head, met a man who nearly killed you. . . ." He threw up his hands. "Are you daft or just too darn simple-minded to be left on your own?''

JoHannah flinched. "I wasn't aware that I had to account to you or to anyone else for my time as long as I fulfilled my duties. I managed well enough.''

"You were damn fortunate. What if O'Neal hadn't come along? What if you'd been hurt?''

Stung by his strong language, she stiffened her spine. "There's no need to swear.''

"No, there's not," he admitted, his voice still stern. "I apologize, but you need to learn a few more things about the world before you go traipsing off on your own. From now on, you're not to go anywhere without checking with me first.''

Michael sounded very much like her guardian when he had told her she had to submit to his authority. She was accustomed to following the rules set down by her Elder and Eldress, but she was not used to being ordered about so coldly. Michael's marriage proposal and vow to court her properly, with or without her consent, came hurtling into her mind. If this domineering attitude was anywhere close to his true nature, there was not a chance that she would even consider spending the rest of the meal with him, let alone a lifetime.

She took a deep breath and rose from her seat. "I'm not very hungry. If you'll excuse me, I'd like to check to see if my cap is dry. Then I'm going for a walk."

"Sit down. I'm not finished just yet," he argued.

"Yes, I think you are, Michael," she breathed softly and left him sitting at the table alone as she slipped on her attic coat, stepped outside, and closed the door quietly behind her.

Chapter 17

"Wait!" Michael called out as the kitchen door closed. He stared at the door while holding his breath, but no matter how much he willed it to happen, he knew JoHannah would not open the door and come back inside. Not just yet. She needed some time alone to sort out her thoughts.

He did, too.

He slammed his fist on the table. Angry at himself for being an obnoxious lout, he grabbed his crutches and beat a hasty retreat to the parlor before Nora came back downstairs. He was in no mood to answer questions about why JoHannah had left the table. One innocent question from Nora, and he would yell at her, further compounding his sins and his well-earned guilt.

The sound of his crutches as the tips hit the bare floor and echoed in the hall reminded him of JoHannah. As his nurse and healer, she deserved fairer treatment. As the woman he planned to marry, she deserved respect.

He had given her neither.

He had questioned and bullied her exactly the same way he had kept his officers and crew in line. But he was not aboard his ship and JoHannah was not a member of his crew, as Nora had so aptly pointed out just the other day. He was the master of Lawne Haven now. He should have acted like it. Instead, he played the role of a belligerent, domineering, arrogant . . .

He walked into the parlor and leaned on his crutches as he stared out the window. His eyes focused only on the future instead of the trees that lined the main road. If he truly meant to convince JoHannah that they belonged together as man and wife here at Lawne Haven, if he had any hope of ever returning to sea, he had made a terrible blunder after scoring a point in his favor by surprising her with the lilac-scented bath.

He took full responsibility for their argument today and realized that he had dug the new gulf between them all by himself. He could easily rationalize his behavior because he was upset that she had been in danger and that she had encountered the man who had tried to hurt her when she had no one to protect her, even if everything had ultimately turned out well.

Truth be told, he had stepped way beyond his intentions, and in the process, he may have destroyed whatever chance he had for winning JoHannah's hand. The real reason for his blatantly bad behavior was clear—if only to himself.

Lust.

Or his failure to curb it.

He should have found a way to control his ever-growing attraction to JoHannah and to spend time with her. Instead, he had taken the coward's way out. By using physical distance in lieu of self-control to ease the desire that surged through his body whenever JoHannah was near and to avoid the awesome temptation to kiss her into submission to his will, he had given no thought to what she might be thinking or feeling about the frightening and sad events surrounding Leah's death.

Lust.

It had taken over his every waking, breathing moment. It had snaked its way into his dreams. He barely could be in the same room with her without having his heart begin to pound and his fingers tingle with the overwhelming desire to touch her.

He physically ached for her, and the only way he had found to control his baser instinct was to closet himself in his room for the past few days with a set of account books he could have mastered in a matter of hours. He should have found a way to spend time with JoHannah, even if it meant he had to endure the suffering of having to wait until they were properly wed to share the pleasures of the marriage bed with her.

To be fair, he had never paid court to a woman before and had never really had to think about anything more than satisfying his needs. All of the women he had known intimately were more than willing bedmates who had either been well paid for their services or were unconstrained by any moral virtue. Courtship and marriage, on the other hand, demanded honorable behavior, but to have the woman he wanted to marry living in his house with her bedroom just across the hall from his would test the honor of a eunuch!

If he respected her, however, he should be able to control his desires and be satisfied to wait until they were married to explore all the physical delights that had turned his dreams of JoHannah into visions of endless seduction.

The cross of the flesh.

Isn't that what JoHannah called physical attraction and sexual temptation? He shook his head. How quick he had been to dismiss the metaphor as sanctimonious Shaker babble meant to keep followers on the path of righteousness by making them feel guilty for what was a naturally ordained instinct.

The cross of the flesh.

Indeed, he carried it now, too, and understood how difficult it must have been for JoHannah to carry it alone. Physical attraction and sexual desire were sins that shook the very foundation of her world of faith, however bizarre he judged that tenet to be.

His world—the one he wanted to share with JoHannah—surely would crumble in her eyes if he could not share the weight of the cross with her, instead of making her carry it alone. By controlling his own passion until she took his name and wore a wedding ring symbolizing their commitment to one another, he would earn the right to resurrect even more glorious delights of physical intimacy and passion than he ever had hoped to discover.

If he felt somewhat overawed by the depth of self-control that postponing these physical pleasures would require, he knew he had no other choice. He was inspired by the memory of how easily they had been able to talk things through on their way home from the O'Neals', at least until he had ruined it all by proposing marriage before she was really ready to entertain the thought. Squaring his shoulders, he almost felt the cross slip across his back. He vowed to spend time with JoHannah, even if it meant he had to take a dip in the creek to cool his ardor.

Carrying the cross of the flesh for a while suddenly appeared much easier to bear when he compared it to the crucible of regret that would dog him the rest of his life . . . if he failed.

After checking her cap and finding it still too wet to wear, JoHannah wandered about the yard and walked past the barn, too upset to care overmuch where she went—as long as she could be alone and away from Michael.

Spirit weary, she eventually paused to look up at her surroundings. She recognized the path she was on as the shortcut she had used earlier today, shrugged off Michael's earlier reprimand, and continued to walk until she found her way blocked by a puddle. Too wide to jump over, it was definitely too deep to walk through. Moss-covered rocks lined either side of the path, and she realized she had little choice but to turn around and go back the way she had come.

Reluctant to return to the house just yet, she looked around, alert to the possibility of meeting another bull moose. When the way seemed safe, she cut through the underbrush to reach a small clearing at the edge of a creek. Several large, flat boulders made for dry seating along the creek. She sat down, folded her legs to the side, and hugged her attic coat close around her. She rested the side of her face against the smooth surface of a large rock that formed a low wall beside her.

Warmed by the sun, she closed her eyes and pressed the palms of her hands against the rock. Solid and steady despite nature's harshest weather, the rock remained steadfast in its place in the World, here at the edge of a creek in a clearing protected by sentinel trees.

If only she could find her own place in the World, one as serene and safe as the one surrounding her at this moment.

Collier.

Like a child mourning the loss of innocence, JoHannah yearned for the past and wondered if she would ever truly be able to go home. By some miracle, if the court ruled in her favor, would she ever be able to go back and pick up the mantle of her faith? And if she did, would she do so because she was chosen and gifted with true faith, or would she be running away from the challenges of living in the World, challenges she was not strong enough to meet and if not overcome, to accept?

Michael.

His proposal had shocked her. His determination to win her as his wife still troubled her—almost as much as the thought of marriage had started to appeal to her mind and it tempted her traitorous body. His overbearing order today, however, dismayed her. Was she strong enough to meet his determination with her own? Was she strong enough to stand firm and forge a partnership with him in the World, or was she too weak to counter his powerful nature?

"But I am strong enough," she whispered out loud. "I want to be strong enough."

Strength, however, could not be found in self-righteousness. She realized that she had acted brashly this morning, although she did not deserve to be questioned like a heretic being cross-examined during the Inquisition. She should have admitted it was wrong to leave the house without telling anyone where she was going and when she would return. Common and mutual respect for one another demanded it.

She also realized that although Michael had chosen a domineering way of demonstrating it, he had been concerned about her well-being. At the same time, he also understood that she had been isolated from the dangers of the World for most of her life so that she could unwittingly put herself at risk.

To her discredit, she had not been strong enough to stay any longer to discuss her morning adventure with Michael. She had taken a defensive stand, unwilling to admit her own lack of responsibility to anyone other than herself—a World vice that she most definitely did not want to cultivate.

If she also felt weak in the knees whenever Michael was near, she knew now that she would never give in to the ultimate sin and share the intimacies of the marriage bed with Michael unless and until she decided to become his wife.

Was she strong enough to apologize and ask Michael to begin again? Only if he understood that they had to face temptation and overcome it or recognize problems and find solutions to them, together, before mutual misunderstandings resulted in permanent estrangement.

Sharing. Cooperation. Union. Weren't they some of the earliest lessons she had learned in communal living—ones that she had so quickly forgotten in the World? If she did decide to remain in the World with Michael as his wife, those lessons would have to be guiding lights along her journey in the World to prevent her from stumbling again.

She sat up straight and dipped the hem of her apron into the cold waters of the creek. After she wiped her face and hands, she stood up and straightened her skirts. Whether she had been blessed or cursed with any number of life paths now instead of one was irrelevant. They were there, and she would compare her travel on each one with an open mind until she knew which one God truly intended for her to follow.

She would begin by finding Michael to apologize for her irresponsible behavior and somehow make him understand that he had no right to treat her with any less respect than he had for himself. She would try, as well, to discover and explore the world of courtship Michael demanded—on her own terms.

Making her way through the clearing and back to the path, she emerged on the wrong side of the puddle from the way home. As she stood at the edge of the forest, she heard the muffled sound of someone approaching and moments later, Michael came into view.

Sunlight bathed his ebony hair with midnight blue highlights and shot through the silver strands at his temple like lightning bolting through a stormy sky. His eyes were set in a grim, determined line as he scanned both sides of the path. A canvas bag dangled from the top of one of his crutches.

"Michael?"

She called his name and before the echo of her voice came back to her, he turned in her direction. A dazzling smile softened his expression and added an extra beat to her pulse.

"I was hoping I'd find you." He practically sprinted toward her, maneuvering his crutches with abandon to the point that she was afraid he would slip and fall in the damp earth. When he reached the other side of the puddle, he stopped, took a long look at the puddle, and grinned. "If I had two good legs, I'd play the gallant and carry you across. As it is . . ." He lifted one crutch and shook his head. "How much longer do I have to play the four-legged wonder?"

She giggled. "Three or four more weeks. *If* you do your exercises. Then you can be promoted to a cane."

He grimaced. "And then I'll be a three-legged wonder."

"Just not as clumsy," she teased as one of his crutches started to slip in the soft earth at the edge of the puddle.

The canvas bag swung forward, but he caught his balance and laughed. "Nora would tie me to a chair in the kitchen if she had any inkling I was out here risking life and limb to find you." His gaze held her immobile. "Are you ready to have something to eat?"

"No. Not really."

His smile faded. "It's not very safe for you to wander about all alone. I thought we might have something to eat together. I packed a few things in here." He reached around and tugged at the canvas bag as he balanced himself on the crutch that carried the weight of his good leg; the other crutch simply leaned against him. It fell away as the bag swung forward out of his hand, pitching him off balance. He grabbed for the bag while struggling to stay upright.

The bag hurled through the air and landed with a monstrous splash—right in the middle of the puddle—and just inches in front of JoHannah, who had leaped forward to catch it. Without thinking beyond trying to salvage the picnic lunch he had brought, JoHannah grabbed the drawstring at the top of the bag and yanked it out of the mud, setting off a huge back wave of mud water that splashed onto Michael's chest.

"Oh! Oh, no. I'm sorry!" she gushed, absolutely mortified when she saw what she had done.

He made one long, leisurely inspection of his once immaculate coat and looked up at her. Eyes dancing, he broke into a fit of laughter and pointed at her feet which were planted smack in the middle of a mud puddle with water that reached her ankles. Muddied water dripped from the bag onto her skirts. "I don't believe I actually did that . . . or this," she moaned as she stared at her feet.

She eased her way out of the puddle to stand next to him, nearly losing one of her shoes in the process. "I'm so sorry. I've really made a mess . . . of everything."

He chuckled and wiped a speck of mud off the tip of her nose. "I'm afraid I muddied the waters first." He paused as though there was a great deal more he wanted to say before he looked at the dripping bag. He shook his head. "Maybe it's a good thing you aren't hungry after all."

Opening the drawstring, she peered inside. "Maybe it's not ruined." Her faced skewed into disappointment. A heavy stoneware jug, still intact, rested on top of a small basket covered by a towel. She lifted the towel and immediately grinned. "The bread is smashed down to the size of a biscuit, but it's not wet. Neither is the cheese." She closed the bag and held it out away from her skirts. "Would you like to sit and talk . . . while we eat? There's a clearing not far from the path and some smooth boulders to sit on,'' she suggested. ''I'll show you.''

She led the way to the clearing, determined to forge a new beginning with the one man who promised a life in the World for her that she might one day share with a willing heart.

Chapter 18

M ichael stretched out on a flat boulder near the creek and leaned back against a wall of rock, trying to understand how a morning that had begun so badly had been followed by an afternoon that had been one of the most pleasant he had ever enjoyed.

JoHannah sat next to him and although they were close together, their bodies did not touch. Sunshine dappled the creek with reflections of the ground cover and low shrubbery that lined the banks. Rushing creek water, powered by the heavy rainfall, carried light debris, but several small pools of water near the boulders lay silent and still and reflected the image of a blue spring sky.

With the salvaged picnic spent, general conversation fell into an awkward lull. He did not have to worry about controlling his baser instinct at the moment; it was buried deep beneath apprehension. He did not want to take JoHannah home until he had apologized and asked for her forgiveness, but it was difficult to know where to begin. As he tried to think of a way to broach the topic of their earlier disagreement that his arrogant attitude had caused, he attempted to skip a pebble across the creek. The small stone sank as soon as it hit the water. "I'm really not good at this," he said quietly as he tossed another pebble that sank just as quickly as the first.

"I am," she gushed as she leaned over the edge of the rock and picked up a pebble. "Hold it like this." She demonstrated briefly, threw the stone, and smiled when it skipped across the top of the water four times before sinking.

He cleared his throat and stared out at the creek, ignoring the tempting idea to keep conversation limited to a discussion of how to skip pebbles across the creek's surface. "I haven't been much company for you for the past few days. I'm sorry. I shouldn't have left you alone so much."

"You don't need to apologize for meeting your responsibilities," she said softly. "I know your accident has held you back, and you need to get caught up with your duties. It only stands to reason that now that you're nearly recovered you would use your time to work on the account books. There's really no need to—"

"It had nothing whatsoever to do with the account books."

He turned toward her and gazed into her eyes, fully intending to explain that he had avoided her because every day she continued to live in his house, he was tormented by the urge to touch her, to hold her in his arms and satisfy his driving need to seduce her and lay claim to her feminine charms. Because every night she followed him into his dreams. Because she was not the only one who carried the cross of the flesh. Because . . .

Sparkling violet eyes stared back at him, and all conscious thought and good intentions slipped out of his mind. Wisps of auburn curls that had escaped her knot framed her face, and he was filled with a heartfelt longing to unpin her hair and trail its silken beauty through his fingertips. At the base of her slender white throat, he could see her pulse beat a little faster . . . in rhythm with his own. Shallow breathing quickened the rise and fall of her breasts, and he wanted desperately to cup their magnificence with his hands.

Her lips parted slightly in what he hoped was an invitation, and he dipped his head as he leaned closer. Just a little closer, until he could feel her breath, feather soft, on his face. His lips tingled with the delicious anticipation of tasting her sweetness, and his heart began to beat a little faster, erasing his experience with other women from his mind and unlocking the deepest part of his soul that had been waiting for this one special moment.

The cross of the flesh he had promised himself to carry with her suddenly seemed impossibly heavy for any man to carry, especially with such sweet and innocent temptation so close and so very real. Torn between need and honor, he tossed the cross aside, just long enough to savor just one kiss before he would reposition the cross on his shoulders. Just one kiss. One that would help to sustain him until she accepted his proposal and became his wife, and he had the right to claim all of her beautiful body.

Mindful of his frequent lapses of judgment where Jo-Hannah was concerned, he paused and searched her eyes to be very sure that she felt the same desire as he did—desire without guilt and desire conceived in overwhelming, mutual attraction. Could she set aside his abominable behavior earlier and trust him not to hurt her again? If she could, did she know how hard it would be to stop . . . after just one kiss?

The whole world seemed to stand still.

JoHannah could not find the strength to take more than shallow breaths of air. Michael was so close . . . so very close that she could almost see her own reflection in his aqueous gray eyes. Mesmerized by the powerful longing and affection that came from deep within his heart and churned in the glorious gray mirrors of his soul, she felt

her heart begin to beat so fast she grew faint. Her limbs
were weak and heavy. Her lips tingled in anticipation of
her first kiss.

Michael's kiss.

She dared not move for fear he would misunderstand her
shyness and turn away from her. Her eyes misted with the
need to let him know that she wanted to touch her lips to
his, and her chest tightened with a yearning she did not
completely understand. Guilt tugged gently at her conscience as warnings of the dangers of the temptations of
the flesh flashed through her mind, but she did not yield to
its power to darken the wonder and joy that lit her spirit.
When his eyes flashed the question of whether or not she
truly welcomed his kiss and gave her the opportunity to
stop him, her heart leaped in her chest.

The overwhelming splendor of this enchanting moment
erased all the shame and doubt she had suffered during
those long days and nights when thoughts of Michael had
seemed sinful and wrong. How could these marvelous feelings that surged through her body be sinful? How could
the growing affection she felt for this man be wrong when
it felt so right to be near him and to want to touch him so
intimately? She closed her eyes and leaned toward him to
risk just one kiss so she would know for sure that the feelings she had for Michael were more than just sinful lust
and were truly based on an affection that was deepened and
honored with the promise of lifelong commitment.

Soft and ever so gentle, his lips caressed hers and sweet
sensation flowed through her body. Unlike the kiss of
friendship between sisters or long-ago kisses from her parents, Michael's kiss was totally different. It lit a fire in her
heart, touched the core of her soul, and held the magnificent
promise of a love that would be as enduring as the boulder
of rock beneath her—if she chose to embrace that love.

Just one kiss. Tender and precious.

She trembled, awash with joyous wonder.

Just one kiss. Sweet and innocent.

She felt him tremble, too.

Michael's lips lingered with hers for only a heartbeat longer before he ended their kiss. She kept her eyes closed, savoring the lingering feel of his lips pressed gently against her own. Reluctant to have the ecstasy of the moment end, she opened the window to her heart and slipped the magical enchantment inside to keep it from forever fading from her memory.

Trembling with unabashed desire for another kiss, she felt his lips press against the soft flesh of her eyelids. His hands cupped the sides of her face, and she slowly opened her eyes. She met his gaze and held it, looking very closely for any hint of regret or disappointment to darken the gray wonder that she had seen shimmering earlier in the depths of his eyes.

Amazed to see the same emotions in his eyes as she felt in the depths of her soul, she moistened her lips. More touched by their kiss than she ever could have imagined, she wondered if her amazing reaction to his kiss was normal. Unsure of what to say or do, she pressed him with one of the questions that rose from the level of conscious thought to her lips. "Is this . . . is this always part of courting?" she asked, wondering if by sharing this kiss with him, she had accepted him as her suitor.

"Not always," he whispered, sounding as moved by their first kiss as she had been.

Afraid that she had shamed herself by stepping beyond the bounds of World propriety, she tried to pull away from him.

He held her close. "The awe and the wonder I think we both experienced is not always part of courting," he murmured. "Not every man or woman is as blessed with mutual attraction as we are. But a kiss? Yes, that's part of courting.''

Relieved that she had not acted the part of a brazen woman, she exhaled slowly. Captivated by his sensitivity to her concerns as well as her inexperience, she turned her face into the palm of his hand and sighed contentedly.

He shook his head and looked at her with amazement. ''Why would you let me kiss you after I treated you so badly this morning?''

''We both made mistakes today,'' she whispered. ''I—I was wrong to have acted so thoughtlessly. I shouldn't have left the house without telling someone where I was going.'' She closed her eyes and swallowed hard, praying that he would accept her open admission of fault.

JoHannah touched her lips to his palm, and Michael's heart began to pound in his chest. He had shared his body with more women than he cared to remember, but he had never once experienced the tender emotions that wrapped around his heart—emotions that threatened to engulf him after only one taste of her sweet lips. Stunned by the power of her trusting innocence, he knew she deserved an apology for his abominable behavior earlier, and he would have to be as quick to admit fault as she had been.

''I was wrong to act like your keeper instead of your . . .'' He paused, reluctant to say betrothed or beloved when in fact, he was neither. He had never given JoHannah the chance to agree to this courtship at all and had teased her glibly about forcing her to accept his proposal. He took a deep breath, unwilling to consider the notion that anything more than powerful attraction had turned their first kiss into a searing kiss that scorched his soul. ''I've learned something important to both of us today.''

She cocked her head, and puzzlement filled her expression.

''Actually, two things.'' He chuckled as he sat back and

relaxed against the rock—until she moved closer to him. "First, I'm not going to hide in my room and stare at rows of figures in account books because I can't seem to control my thoughts or my body when I'm with you."

Her eyes widened. "And the second?" she breathed.

Was her thigh really pressed against his? When she took a breath, did her breast really touch his arm? His heartbeat accelerated, and he inched himself away. "Maybe I've learned three," he grumbled to himself. One kiss. Just one kiss and the woman practically dropped every barrier that had held him at bay.

"What did you say?"

He swallowed the lump in his throat. "I said . . . I said, that from now on, we're going to talk problems through so we have don't have any more misunderstandings."

She took his hand. "I'd like that."

"Good. Then everything is settled," he said after he cleared his throat.

"May I ask you something?" she said shyly as one finger brushed against the hairs on the back of his hand.

He nodded stiffly. "Such as?"

She shrugged her shoulders. "Such as . . . how often . . . I mean, if we . . . do couples kiss often when they court?"

She could have asked him if he would take her to the moon. He could not have been more surprised. She could have asked him about the state of his injury or . . . tarnation! Kissing? She wanted to discuss kissing? "Discussions are over for today," he grumbled as he edged toward the side of the rock and reached for his crutches. In the recesses of his mind, a stored thought about the poor soul who had to unravel her notions of marriage came back to haunt him. So did the unbelievable notion that with just one kiss, she had let him know that she was willing to let him court her.

May the good Lord have mercy on his soul.

He picked himself up and got his balance before he

helped her down from the rock. He decided to leave the cross behind because it would not be long before he claimed JoHannah's hand and he made her his wife. He could manage until then on his own, couldn't he?

He turned to leave and paused to look back to where they had just shared a kiss that still tingled on his lips, still not quite sure if he could believe what had just happened between them. If that one kiss was any indication of what lay ahead, he might need that cross after all, especially if she seemed as inquisitive about this whole darn courtship ritual as she led him to believe she was. That meant kisses. Lots of kisses. On second thought . . .

She tugged on his hand. "Did you forget something?"

He shook his head. "Just my cross. It's probably safer if I hold onto it."

Her eyes widened as though he had told her he had forgotten his head. "Your . . . your *cross*?"

"I'll explain while we walk back." He laughed, certain that by the end of this courtship, the cross of the flesh would be so heavy he would need Dolan's help to toss it aside . . . once and for all.

Chapter 19

If lilacs surrounded the gates of hell, precious innocence lined the road that led straight to an inferno hotter than any fire and brimstone sermon could forewarn. Or had that one sweet kiss a month ago, one he dared never to repeat until they were married, unleashed a temptress?

Michael's gaze locked with JoHannah's sparkling violet eyes. He clenched his jaw so hard his teeth ached. One cheek twitched. With the next pound of his heart, he lowered his gaze, and the Shaker ban on making eye contact with a person of the opposite gender, which JoHannah had totally abandoned after their first kiss, suddenly shifted from being a strict oddity to supreme wisdom.

"You're sure? It's not too . . . too sheer?" she repeated, turning about to apparently give him a full view of the cap Nora had fashioned from a mantilla found in one of the trunks in the attic.

Delicate Italian lace kissed her hair with dozens of tiny white snowflakes. He gulped down the lump in his throat. "No," he croaked, wondering why the crack in his voice had been resurrected from his adolescence to embarrass him as an adult. Thanks to JoHannah's forage in the attic, the old-fashioned knee breeches he still wore to accommodate his splint even made him look like a schoolboy.

The feelings he had, however, were most definitely adult. They were real. They were frustrating, and his manhood bulged beneath his breeches.

Trying to avoid looking at her face or the top of her head as well as his own breeches, he stared at the hem of her skirt. As she turned around, the bottom of her gown swirled just high enough to give him a peek at trim ankles and just a hint of shapely—damn!

He grabbed his hat and picked up the cane he used now that his leg was nearly healed and the splint was almost history. Limping to the door, he opened it and stepped back to let JoHannah go by.

Clear May skies and brilliant sunshine warmed the afternoon breeze, and he knew it would not be too long before a load of tight-budded blossoms covered the lilac bushes that grew wild and free at Lawne Haven. In the month of June . . . he shook his head, refusing to even consider how he would manage to tolerate the week or two when the scent of lilac hung heavy in the air renewing memories of the lilac bath he had prepared for JoHannah— memories he tried to forget.

"You're sure you have everything you need?" he inquired, hoping she might have to go back into the house and he would have a few minutes to recover.

"When Dolan took Nora over to see his new son this morning, she took everything for supper with her except for the cakes. Do you think they'll travel all right?" She leaned over the back of the wagon, and her shoulder kerchief slipped to the side. The sight of the soft swelling of her ample bosom sent his heart racing, and he moved to the front of the wagon.

"They're fine. If we don't get moving, Dolan and Genevieve will polish off supper before we get there."

She took a fingertip of frosting and plopped it into her

mouth before joining him. "I love frosting when it's still soft and warm, don't you?"

"Sure," he grumbled as he held her hand while she climbed into the wagon. Her face dipped so close to his he could see a thin line of frosting caught in the corners of her lips. His mouth watered, and he was tempted to kiss it away—if only to prove how much he loved the taste of warm frosted lips!

Apparently oblivious to the growing physical desire that shortened his temper and turned this ridiculous courting ritual into an endurance test, she settled herself on the seat. When he joined her, she took his cane, another attic treasure, and laid it across her lap.

He shifted the cross that bit into his shoulder, released the hand brake, and clicked the reins. Her leg pressed against his as the wagon rolled into motion, and he groaned out loud.

"What's the matter? Did you bump your leg?"

He glared at her. "Could you move over a bit?"

She blushed and scooted over to give him more room. As they rode, her fingers trailed the length of the black hickory cane he used as though studying every knob and twist. "Do you really think it's true?"

He frowned and kept his eyes on the road ahead. "What's true?"

"The story about your Uncle Silas. Do you really believe he used this cane to measure off the site for the house?"

Her curiosity about his family never ceased to amaze Michael. The swaying motion of the wagon and the scenic woods along the road to Dolan's soothed his earlier frustration, and he smiled. "According to family legend, Uncle Silas was one of the first settlers in New Hampshire. He cut the walking stick from a branch of an old hickory tree that eventually shaded the kitchen and used it to march off the perimeter of the house. As he cleared the land, he used the rocks he dug up to outline the shape he had drawn. He kept the cane as a reminder of Lawne Haven's birth.''

''It must have been a grand house for its day.''

He laughed. ''As grand as a one-room, dirt-floored cabin can be.''

She squinted her eyes. ''One room?''

''Originally the house had a single room with a loft for sleeping. It burned down twice. After a third fire nearly killed some of my ancestors in their beds, my great-grandfather decided to build the house that's standing now.''

She sighed her understanding. ''That's why it's stone.''

''And every one came from our land.'' He paused and tilted the brim of his hat forward to block the sun's glare. ''I suppose if you compare my home to your parents' house, there's quite a difference,'' he prompted in hope she would tell him more about the estate she would inherit on her next birthday.

Convinced that the estate her guardian managed on her behalf held one of the keys that might unlock the mystery of why he insisted she marry rather than live the rest of her life as a Believer, Michael tried to encourage her to tell him what she knew.

''More than I care to think about,'' she murmured. Her eyes darkened to deep purple, and he resisted the urge to prompt her further. As free as he had been in sharing his family stories, she had shut the door on her birth family and her former home as though it had never existed. She was just as closed about her guardian, and all Michael knew about him he had gleaned from her the night Leah O'Neal had died.

When the wagon rounded a bend and Dolan's farmhouse came into view, he tensed. The birth of Dolan's son triggered sad memories of Avery's losses and the three small wooden crosses that marked their graves. If only one of

Avery's sons had survived, Avery would never have left Lawne Haven, and Michael would have been free to follow his heart and spend the rest of his life at sea.

Awed again by the power of Fate to alter his life and just as determined to return to sea one day, Michael looked over to JoHannah and noted how her fingers wrapped tighter around the cane. "Jittery?" he said quietly when he finally brought the horses to a halt in front of the house. He put his hand on top of hers.

She nodded and took a deep breath. "I'm not quite sure what to expect."

He took one of her hands, held it, and rubbed his thumb over the palm. "They tell me babies have their own special magic. Just relax." After locking the brake and securing the reins, he helped her down from the wagon. She bowed her head when he handed her one of the cakes.

"What if . . . what if Genevieve wants me to hold him? I don't know the first thing to do. None of the children who came to Collier were babies. I've never even seen an infant."

He tilted her chin up so their gazes met. It seemed impossible to him there was another woman her age on earth who had never seen a baby, and he was reminded again of how very unique JoHannah was. "Women have a natural instinct about those things. Don't worry."

Her eyes grew darker in color, changing from soft violet to royal purple. He recognized the danger signal at once. Each time he thought he had won the courtship battle and had her on the verge of accepting his proposal, she retreated and reminded him he had yet to win her away from the faith that stood between them.

Dolan opened the door and stepped outside, breaking the barrier of silence that hung between them. " 'Bout time you two got here. Nora's fussing up a storm."

Michael laughed. "Grab a couple of cakes from the back

of the wagon, will you? I can't carry more than one. Be careful. If you drop one in the dirt, Nora will probably make you eat it anyway.''

Grinning, Dolan nodded toward the door. ''Go on inside, JoHannah. Me and Michael will get the rest. Nora's in the kitchen.'' He walked over to the wagon, retrieved three cakes, and handed one to Michael. ''Picked up the post yesterday. Got yours while I was at it. Remind me to give you the tin of cocoa, too. Stopped at the general store for you, just like you asked.''

Michael groaned. ''The cocoa was a surprise, Dolan.''

JoHannah giggled as she took a cake of her own to carry inside.

''Not anymore, but I appreciate the thought,'' Michael moaned.

She entered the house ahead of the men and noted the new wood that framed the door. Her mind awash with curiosity as well as apprehension, she looked around the large sitting room. Plainly furnished with several chairs arranged together in front of a hearth and gingham curtains on the windows, the room was homey and inviting. A sampler on the wall above the mantel was the only decoration. To her left, a wide archway gave entrance to the kitchen, and the smell of pot roast made her mouth water. She waited for Michael and followed close behind him as he carried his cake into the kitchen.

''I was afraid you both decided to stay home,'' Nora admonished as she turned from the stove to greet them. She pointed to an oak sideboard. ''Put the cakes over there. Supper is almost ready.''

Michael looked around the room. ''Where's Genevieve?''

''Tending to little Thompson. JoHannah, why don't you go on back and tell her you're finally here and we're ready to eat? Here, I'll take that cake for you,'' she offered as she walked over and took the cake out of JoHannah's hands. She looked up and smiled. "Go on, dear. Back through the sitting room to your right."

JoHannah looked at Michael, and he nodded reassuringly. She turned and made her way back the way she had come. When she reached the bedroom door, she knocked lightly. "Genevieve? It's JoHannah."

"Come on in. I'm almost done."

Not quite sure what to expect on the other side of the door, JoHannah slowly opened the door and stepped inside. The bedroom seemed quite small compared to the one she had at Lawne Haven. Given the size of the massive bed that filled the room, she decided at once that perhaps it was nearly as large but not nearly as well furnished.

Genevieve was bending over the bed tending to her newborn son and blocked any view of the week-old infant. She turned her head and smiled. "Wait till you see this handsome little boy. He'll melt your heart."

JoHannah swallowed hard and took small steps forward, surprised to see Genevieve on her feet so soon after giving birth. From what she had overheard about childbirth, it was a difficult and painful ordeal, but Genevieve looked strikingly well and healthy. In fact, she looked almost exactly the same as the first day JoHannah had met her. She also doubted very much that any child who had Dolan and Genevieve as parents would be little.

Since marriage for Believers was forbidden, no children had ever been born at Collier. Of all the World converts who had come to the Shaker village with their families, none had had a child smaller than a toddler, and JoHannah had had no experience with babies to prepare her for seeing this newborn. The moment she peered around Genevieve's round frame, she could not help but gasp in astonishment. "He's . . . he's so tiny!"

Tightly wrapped in the green knit blanket Nora had

stitched, the baby was completely bundled except for his little face. Wide-set, deep blue eyes set beneath a single shock of wispy brown hair growing right in the middle of his head stared back at her.

Genevieve beamed. She lifted him up and cradled him in her arms. "Cute little thing, isn't he? Would you like to hold him while I fix my hair?"

Gulping hard, JoHannah took a step back. "I'm not sure. He's awfully small. What if—"

Genevieve's laughter was gentle. "After all he's been through to get into this world, there's not much worse you can do to him. Sit over there," she said, motioning with her arm toward a rocking chair twice the size of Nora's.

When JoHannah had barely taken her seat, Genevieve plopped the baby onto JoHannah's lap. She went to the other side of the room and started to brush her long curls into order and left JoHannah to her own devices. Following Genevieve's earlier example, JoHannah nestled the baby in the crook of her arm. He stared back at her, and she put her other hand beneath his head.

Wonderment filled her spirit as she gazed down at his face. Beautifully formed, he was nothing less than a living, breathing miracle. Every little detail was perfect, from the shape of his lips and the curve of his button nose to the tiny folds in his ears.

"He's beautiful," she whispered, awed by this tiniest of human beings. Soft as an angel's, one of his cheeks pressed against the palm of her hand; the other nestled against the side of her breast. His lips moved ever so slightly, and he turned toward her breast to nuzzle at her gown. JoHannah was not quite sure what to do, but Genevieve's laughter brought a blush to JoHannah's cheeks.

"Greedy little mite! I just fed him. Try putting him over your shoulder."

JoHannah froze. Move him to her shoulder? He looked

and felt delicate enough to snap in two if she was not careful. After two tries, she finally had him settled with his little face resting on her shoulder just inches from her face. She held his back, and one tiny fist slipped out of the blanket and gripped the end of her shoulder kerchief.

As she began to rock, his eyelids began to droop. She could feel his heart beating strong, and all of the warnings about the evils of marriage and the sin of physical intimacy between a man and a woman once again seemed very misguided. How could this little miracle of life, in all his innocence, be the result of sin? If God created life to bring Him joy, what would happen if every man and woman followed the Shaker way? There would be no new life and no miracle of creation to add to God's glory on earth.

If the Shaker faith was truly given to only the chosen, did that mean all others who married and had children were sinners? Or was every child born in the World living proof of God's love and His blessing on the married state, as JoHannah suspected?

She did not have the answers to her many questions, but she knew in her heart that Michael was right. Her journey in the World was helping her to see and learn much more about life than if she had stayed at Collier. If she did decide to return to spend the rest of her days as a Believer, she would carry with her a deeper understanding of the World she had left behind as a child and a far greater appreciation of the sacrifice required to give up children of her own to love and cherish.

"There! I'm done."

Genevieve's announcement grabbed JoHannah's attention, and she handed the infant to his mother. Reluctantly.

"That wasn't so hard, was it now? Thompson took to you right away, didn't you, darlin'? Yes, you're Mama's precious little boy," she cooed as she carried him with her to the door. "Time to meet Mr. Lawne, and you best keep a dry bottom, young man."

Genevieve giggled as she opened the door. She turned to JoHannah. "Ready?"

JoHannah followed Genevieve back into the sitting room, but they had barely stepped through the doorway when Genevieve stopped abruptly. JoHannah sidestepped quickly to avoid walking into Genevieve and glanced around the room. With the next breath, her heart began to pound with worry.

Michael, his face pale and drawn, stood staring out the window. Nora, weeping quietly, sat on a chair with Dolan by her side. His expression was grim, but Michael looked forlorn . . . even defeated. Chills raced up JoHannah's spine. "Michael? Nora? What's wrong?"

Michael turned to her. Sorrow filled his eyes, and his fist tightened around a letter of some sort he had in his hand. Was it the post Dolan had picked up for Michael? Did it contain news from his uncle? The blood drained from her face. Despite his uncle's promise to stall any more suits, had the court ruled against her brethren in favor of her guardian?

She stared at Michael, and she could barely believe her eyes. Where was the proud and confident man who vowed to marry her even if her guardian won the court battle? "Please. Tell me what's happened."

He swallowed hard. "My brother died two weeks ago," he whispered hoarsely. He swallowed hard as though fighting to hold back tears of grief.

Relief that the news did not concern her quickly turned to horror. "Oh, no. Oh, Michael, I'm so sorry."

Michael shook his head. "I can't believe this is real. According to the post, Avery was driving the supply wagon at the rear of the group traveling to Kentucky. The axle broke, and the wagon went careening out of control. Instead of jumping out, Avery . . . Avery stayed with the wagon to try to save the supplies.'' He paused, took a long deep breath and sighed. ''Poor Avery. Always so worried about doing his best.''

Death, an omnipresent part of life in any world, cast a dark shadow of grief that had quickly consumed the joy of welcoming baby Thompson into the World, and JoHannah knew that life at Lawne Haven undoubtedly would be affected, too. Tears would wash away laughter, and hushed conversations would replace gentle banter as Michael came to terms with his brother's passing and Nora grieved for her son-by-affection.

JoHannah bowed her head and closed her eyes. She sent a silent prayer to heaven for Brother Avery, a Believer who had been in the faith for such a short time, and quickly added one for Michael and Nora. As JoHannah prayed, she thought of two little girls, now young orphans, who would be as confused as she had been when her parents died. She sighed, knowing that the good sisters and brethren who traveled with them would be loving and kind. God, in His infinite wisdom, had provided for Abigail and Jane well, even if He had called their father home to be with Him.

Chapter 20

"I want Abigail and Jane to come home. Uncle George has papers for me to sign for the agent we've hired to go to Kentucky to petition the court and bring the girls back to Lawne Haven. I wanted to tell you this before I left."

Michael's startling announcement, only two weeks after he had received news of his brother's untimely death, caught JoHannah totally off guard. Seated hand in hand with Michael on the flat boulder at the edge of the creek, she reacted instinctively as the terror of her own forced return to the World sent chills racing up and down her spine.

"No. Please don't do this," she pleaded. "This is wrong. So very wrong." She locked her fingers with his, searching for the words to convince him to listen to her. Fighting and winning the moral battle against the sin of anger, she unsuccessfully groped with profound disappointment that eclipsed the joy that had filled her heart this morning when he had invited her to take a walk after breakfast. The reasons why Michael had spent hours alone writing letters and reviewing estate matters for the past two weeks suddenly became clear, and like trees felled by lightning, they crashed across one of her life's paths.

"I thought you would understand," he whispered as he

squeezed her fingers gently. "Abigail and Jane belong here at Lawne Haven."

She pulled her hand away from him. "No," she gushed, trying to think clearly in spite of the loud pounding of her heart. "They belong where their father decided he wanted them to be. You don't have the right to interfere and take them away from their new home! They're happy there."

He turned toward her, and his eyes softened from cold slate to warm gray. "You don't know that, and neither do I."

"They were happy and well at Collier. There's no reason to think—"

"There's one very compelling reason to be concerned. Their father is gone now, and they're all alone."

She could not bear to look at Michael and stared out at the creek. Low from lack of rain, the current ran gently and for a moment, it soothed the troubled waters of her spirit. Michael had to understand the terror she had experienced when her guardian had pulled her from one world and dragged her back into another. Didn't Michael realize he was making the same mistake? Didn't he know how badly he would hurt the girls he claimed to love?

If possible, her heart began to beat a little faster. "They're not alone. They have caretakers who are good and kind," she argued. The anguished faces of Elder Calvin and Eldress Regina that awful day in the dining hall when they were unable to stop JoHannah's guardian from taking her away flashed in front of her mind's eye. "I know their caretakers will help them to deal with their loss. They're not alone, and they are very much loved . . . as I was."

"I love them," he argued. "Nora loves them, too. The girls belong with us. Their caretakers are basically strangers. Even if they are good people," he admitted, "they're not family."

JoHannah quieted the heartfelt urge to get up and run

away, to find a place where she could be alone and try to pretend Michael did not want to do this dreadful thing. But he did, and her mind overruled her quaking heart. She had to be calm enough to stay right where she was and some- how convince him that his decision to do the very thing to Abigail and Jane that JoHannah's guardian had done to her was unforgivable. Was he so blinded by his own sense of duty that he would be cruel—even unintentionally?

JoHannah shivered at the thought. "You'll frighten the girls if you do this. You'll confuse them even more. Please, don't let your own needs or sense of duty rule your mind as well as your heart."

"*My* needs? I'm only thinking—"

"About yourself." She swallowed hard and turned to face him again so that he could see how deeply he hurt her and that she could not support his decision. "You're blinded by your uncommon dedication to your family and its traditions. You aren't giving any thought to what the children might need or want, or what your brother wanted for them."

Michael's expression hardened and sent her heart into sharp palpitations. "My brother didn't know what he was doing. He wasn't . . ."

When he paused, seemingly at a loss for words, she felt her soul begin to tremble. "In his right mind? Is that what you want to say . . . but can't?" Tears filled her eyes, but she blinked them away. She knew Michael had tried to understand and to accept his brother's decision to become a Believer, but it was very clear to her now that he still considered her faith bizarre and her fellow Believers a band of distraught souls who did not have the courage to live in the real world and so escaped to find solace in an . . . in an illusion. Is that why Michael thought it would be so easy to win her away from her faith?

His eyes turned a sorrowful shade of gray. "I'm sorry.

I didn't mean that Avery didn't find contentment as a Believer. He did.'' Michael raked his fingers through his hair. ''I only know that I intend to keep my promise to Avery.''

Hope cast light on her dark, despairing thoughts. ''Promise?''

The look in Michael's eyes grew distant, as though he was traveling many miles away and several months back in time. ''Avery wanted me to keep Lawne Haven and make it prosper so that one day, when the girls had to decide whether or not to commit their lives to their new faith, they could choose to stay . . . or they could come home. I promised I would.''

JoHannah reached out and grabbed onto the one part of Michael's promise to his brother that flawed his thinking. ''You can keep your promise to your brother without bringing the girls home now. Don't you see? They're only children. They can't sign the covenant to become formal Believers until they're twenty-one. That's when your brother meant to have a home waiting for them. Not now.''

Michael stared at JoHannah. Long and hard. Her eyes flashed with desperation, and an agitated blush stained her cheeks. He swallowed the words that threatened to tumble out and resisted the urge to throttle her into thinking clearly. When he knew the time had come to tell JoHannah what he had planned to do, he had not thought it would be easy.

She proved him right.

Apparently frustrated and angry, she closed her mind and physically turned her back to him.

Damn it all! He was tempted to let her suffer with her own thoughts, except that they were dead wrong and so was she. No matter how he tried today to explain to her his decision, he knew she immediately compared him to her guardian and what he had done to her. If Michael had any hope of winning her over to his side, he had to make her remember other events from her past—events that probably still would be painful after all these years.

She would need time to come to terms with what had happened to her after her parents died. She needed to see that the only valid comparison to be made between what he was doing now for Abigail and Jane and what had happened to JoHannah was that it was something she would have wanted someone to do for her when she had been orphaned.

Unfortunately, she had had no relatives who could have claimed her and made her part of their family. Her guardian had failed her as well. Instead of keeping JoHannah at her birth home where she would have been surrounded by loving memories and the familiar comfort of home, he had sent her away.

Greedy, cold-hearted bastard.

According to what JoHannah had told Michael, Bathrick had wasted no time after her parents died. He installed his own family in JoHannah's home, took her to the Shaker village, and then returned to her parents' home, where he had lived for the past fourteen years. He had kept JoHannah hidden away until he was forced to meet the terms of her father's will and arrange for her marriage.

Just exactly how this whole scenario fit her father's will remained to be seen. How Bathrick might turn JoHannah's twenty-first birthday to his own advantage, Michael was not sure, but he was cynical enough to know her guardian had something in mind. Just what it was stymied Michael's imagination and made him even more determined than ever to marry JoHannah as quickly as possible after her birthday when she would no longer be under Bathrick's control and subject to whatever grand scheme he had had fourteen years to plan.

Michael turned her around and gripped one of her hands with both of his own. "Don't turn away from me. Not now," he urged when she tried to give him her back again.

"I want you to listen to me and really hear me before I have to leave."

She blinked hard and stiffened her spine. "I listened very carefully," she said, her voice tinged with indignation. "I heard your every word. You're bringing Abigail and Jane home to Lawne Haven, and I'm quite certain there's little I can say or do to change your mind, is there?"

"No," he said firmly. "You can't change my mind, but you can—"

She broke away and climbed down from the boulder. She walked over and stood at the edge of the creek and stared out at the water, shoulders set, her hands clenched into fists. Head bowed, she held absolutely still.

Michael had abandoned his cane almost a week ago, and his leg was nearly back to normal. After sitting for so long, however, the muscles in his leg had tightened. He eased himself down from the boulder and limped to her side. Only yesterday she might have welcomed his arms, but her stance today sent the clear message that she did not want him to touch her. His heart ached with what he knew he had to do now, but he took a deep breath and a giant leap of faith. If JoHannah could face the truth, she would eventually forgive him. If she did not, he had nothing to lose . . . except his ability to claim her as his wife.

He stepped beside her, close enough to be able to watch her downcast face and see the color of her eyes, but far enough away that she would not find him threatening. "I want you to understand that what I'm doing is the right thing. For me. And for the girls. In your heart, you know that's true," he murmured, hoping she would have the courage to face the past with honesty.

He had seen her wavering in her faith and dared to hope she would embrace life at Lawne Haven, but she had yet to accept his proposal. Had he destroyed any chance that she would?

Her bottom lip quivered. She caught it still.

"I still intend to marry you," he whispered.

She shook her head. "I never promised—"

"No. You were always very forthright, and even though I learned to respect your right to choose the world you want, I never gave up hope you would choose mine. I still believe—"

"Don't," she whispered. "Please don't say any more. I think you've said enough today to make my decision very easy . . . and very clear to me."

"No. I can't accept that," he argued. Too firmly, judging by how quickly she turned and started to walk away. He reached out, grabbed her hand, and led her back to the edge of the creek. "Before you walk away from me, I want you to see something." He knelt down and tugged on her hand until she was on her knees beside him. "Look in the water," he urged. "Tell me what you see."

Stone-faced, she stared straight ahead, her eyes focused on the opposite bank. Just as strong willed, he held still and watched her. He counted the seconds with his heartbeat as they passed into long, silent minutes. Still, he waited. Patiently. Quietly. Listening to the sound of her breathing and watching her eyes darken to troubled violet. "Please," he whispered and let go of her hand.

Her lips trembled. "I—I can't," she pleaded. "My faith—"

"For me. Just this once. Please. For me."

She swallowed hard and dropped her gaze. Blinking back tears, she stared at their reflections in the water. He watched her through her reflection. "Tell me what you see," he said gently.

"I see you. I . . . I see myself. I see . . ." Her voice dropped off as she looked at her own reflection. He studied her as she looked at her own image for the first time since she had been a child. Curiosity. Surprise. Wonder. They flashed through her eyes before she sighed, dropped her gaze again and grew silent.

"Is that all you see? I'm disappointed," he said, pleased when her eyes snapped up to meet his in their reflections. "Go on. Take a second look, but this time, let me tell you what I see."

He caught her gaze with his when their eyes finally met in their reflected images. He began slowly, trying to rebuild a foundation of trust and affection that his decision to bring the girls home could not destroy. "When I look at you, I see God," he murmured.

"That's blasphemy . . . or idolatry," she blurted. Her eyes widened, and the color drained from her face.

He smiled. "I don't mean that you are God or a goddess. I mean that I see His goodness and His love . . . whenever I look at you."

She blushed—even in her reflection.

"It's true," he whispered. "I see so much more than just the beauty of your face or the auburn highlights in the hair that slips out from beneath your cap by the end of the day. I see your gentle spirit and your uncommon heart. That is why I want you to be my wife and the mother of my children. However I feel about your faith or the people who raised you, I know they have a way of life and a faith that helped you to become the very special woman you are today."

She closed her eyes briefly, and he wondered what she was thinking. Before he lost her to her own thoughts, however, he started to talk to her again. "When you looked at my reflection in the water, did you see me or did you see your guardian's face?"

She sighed. "You look nothing like him, so I would never confuse you with him."

"Wouldn't you? I wonder."

Before she could respond, he pressed her with another

question. "When you saw yourself, did you see an adult or a child?"

Her eyes blinked open, and she stared at him in his reflection like he had been overtouched by the sun. "I see an adult. Of course."

He held her gaze. "I'll be home in three or four days, but after I've gone, I want you to look again. There's something I want you to think about when you do."

She bowed her head. "I don't need to look again or think about anything more—"

"Yes, you do. While I'm away, I want you to think back and remember when you were a child. Remember how you felt when your parents died. And try to imagine, if you can, what it might have been like if you knew you had someone you loved—an aunt or uncle, maybe even an older brother or sister—someone who could have come for you at the Shaker village and did not."

Her eyes started to fill with tears. "That's pointless. I had no one."

"I know," he said as he wiped away the single tear that trickled down one of her cheeks. "But Abigail and Jane do have someone. They have me. Don't you think they would want me to come for them?"

She looked away from him. "I think you should go now. In fact, I think if you feel so strongly that you're doing the right thing, you should go to Kentucky yourself."

He gave her a smile even though he knew she could not see it. "It could take months just to get a court decision, and I don't want to leave you for that long, even though I know Dolan is nearby if you need anything. Not now. Not when there's so little time left before . . ." His chest tightened with the mere thought of losing the battle to win her hand.

"Please don't send someone else on my account," she muttered.

''You really can't stop me,'' he warned as he turned her around to face him. ''Please think about what I said, and we can talk it over when I get back.'' He pressed a kiss to her forehead. When he felt her body stiffen, he pulled away from her with a heavy heart. ''Promise me,'' he whispered, searching her eyes for an answer before it touched her lips.

His heart stood still. He waited for her to agree, to give him some hope that beneath her disappointment and pain, there was still some chance she would consider his proposal. Or had he lost her already?

The words he longed to hear never came.

Her eyes closed as she bowed her head, and for the first time in months, he saw one slender hand open and start to shake toward the ground.

Chapter 21

As the forest swallowed up the sound of Michael's re-treating footsteps, JoHannah stared at the creek. Every slow and deliberate beat of her heart echoed the final challenge in his request to think about everything he had said: *Promise me. Promise me.*

Shocked by his intention to bring Abigail and Jane back to Lawne Haven, JoHannah had no defense against the hot flames of disappointment that seared her spirit and left her feeling very vulnerable. Very much like a ship whose anchor had been cut, set adrift to be claimed by the sea, she floundered, realizing there was no place left for her to go but to the depths of her own heart to find the answers to Michael's questions.

Remember when.

Stored deep, memories of her early days at Collier floated to the surface of her mind and carried with them all of the feelings that had accompanied them. Once more a child in her heart and mind, she felt the utter desolation and cold loneliness she had experienced after her parents died. Death was a concept she could not grasp at the tender age of seven, and the terror of being taken away from home and abandoned with strangers swept through her body.

Trembling, her fingers moved as if to grip the worn little travel bag she had packed only days after she had arrived, determined to find her way home. Caught by Sister Lucy and Eldress Regina, she had agreed to stay the night and hung on to the promise of going home the next day.

With childlike innocence, she had watched as one tomorrow had stretched into another, and only now when Michael challenged her adult recollections of that sorrowful time in her childhood did she remember the terrifying nightmares that had awakened her in the middle of the night or the desperation that had driven her to study every human face she had encountered.

As days stretched into weeks and months, she had prayed even harder and had patiently waited for someone—anyone—who would take her home. Every visitor, every new coach or wagon that pulled into the Shaker village, had filled her heart with hope that some kind soul had finally come to take her home. But as time passed, she had accepted the cruel reality that no one, other than her cold-hearted guardian, could have rescued her, and he was the very man who had sent her to Collier.

Rescue. Escape. Those were the thoughts that had dominated her young mind when grief and confusion ruled her heart. As she had grown older and time had helped to heal her broken heart, her nightmares had ended and dreams of one day going home had faded into the nearly forgotten past.

The love of the sisters and brethren had soothed the ache in her heart. The gift of devout faith eventually had given her new dreams, and she had come to love her new home at Collier—one she had been determined that no one would ever take away from her. Her guardian had shattered her hopes and dreams several months ago. For the second time in her life, she had faced the terror of losing all that she had held dear to her heart.

Did little Abigail and Jane have those same dreams? Or did they wake up in the middle of the night, their sleep broken by the nightmare of losing both parents, one at a time, and of being surrounded by men and women they barely knew? Did they pray that their Uncle Michael would come and take them home? Did they cry out for Nora, a woman who had loved them and cared for them since the day they were born?

Tears flowed freely when the answer came whispering into JoHannah's heart, and she dropped to her knees, crying until her tears were spent and her face was flushed. After untying her shoulder kerchief, she dipped one end into the cold creek water and wiped her face. Tentatively, she stared at her reflection and searched her own eyes to see the truth and acknowledge it.

To her adult mind, growing up in the Shaker village had become a blessed journey into a new world of faith. To her child's mind, however, she knew it had been a bittersweet journey from the past to the present where every day she had lived in present moments that had been wrought with memories of the parents she had loved and lost and the home she had once had with them.

Michael.

Even if he had been driven to his decision because of his new role as the master of Lawne Haven as well as his position as the girls' uncle, JoHannah knew in her heart that for Abigail and Jane, he was doing the right thing.

"I've been in the World too long," she whispered to her reflection. If she were true to her faith, she would resent Michael's decision and grieve for the loss of two precious children who might someday have joined the community of true Believers. But her faith had weakened and her heart had softened to the World, and she could only pray that when the girls reached maturity, they would have only fond memories of their short time with the Shakers. With God's blessing, they would be called back to their true home and live the rest of their lives in a community of faith. Only then would Michael be forced to keep his promise to his brother to let the girls go.

JoHannah trailed the end of her kerchief in the water and watched the ripples distort her image before she stood up and shook the dirt from her skirts. She turned and walked back through the clearing to the path that would take her back to the house. She knew her way now almost without thinking, and as she walked, she realized that of all the life paths that stretched before her, the one that led to Michael and Lawne Haven was beckoning to her more strongly than the one that led back to Collier. If only she could be sure which path to take. If only she knew the truest yearnings of her own heart and discovered where God wanted her to be.

As the sound of her steady footsteps echoed in the silence of the forest, she knew one path, beset with obstacles too terrifying to consider, was one she had barricaded in her mind: the path chosen for her by her guardian.

In spite of the heat, she shivered away the thought that he might win the court battle being waged on her behalf and hurried on her way back to the house to see Nora.

Certain that Nora's rheumatism was flaring up again, JoHannah ignored the housekeeper's protests to the contrary. She walked over to the cupboard, but the bottle of medicine Michael had brought home from the infirmary at Collier was not in its usual place. "Where's your medicine?" she asked as she turned around.

In spite of JoHannah's suggestion to let the dishes air dry for once, Nora was drying the dinner dishes JoHannah had just washed. "I don't need it anymore," the housekeeper mumbled. "I told you I'm feeling fine."

"You're foolish and unusually stubborn today," Jo-

Hannah admonished gently. "I don't understand why you won't take a good dose of medicine and let yourself rest for the afternoon."

Nora's back stiffened. "I'm not ailing. Not that badly."

Unconvinced, JoHannah pressed her case. "Is that why you insisted on washing the bed sheets and hanging them out to dry? When I got back from my walk, I saw you hobbling back and forth from the basket to the clothesline. Why didn't you wait and let me do it?"

"You and Michael had a lot to discuss before he left, and I didn't want to miss half a day of sun."

Relieved that during dinner she and Nora had openly discussed the purpose behind Michael's trip to Hillsboro and JoHannah's belated support for his decision, JoHannah still felt guilty for leaving Nora with strenuous work. "Please tell me where you put your medicine."

"It's gone," Nora announced. "I used the last of it a week ago."

Astonished to think Nora had endured needless suffering, JoHannah walked over to the housekeeper. "Why didn't you tell Michael? He would have ridden to Collier—"

"He had enough on his mind. I didn't want to bother him. When he gets back . . ."

"You shouldn't have to wait that long," JoHannah insisted as she led Nora over to her rocking chair.

Nora eased herself down and set the chair in motion. "I did without it for a long while before Avery sent it home with Michael. I can wait."

After all Nora had done to help JoHannah find her way in the World, she did not waste a moment's hesitation to think beyond Nora's needs. She removed her apron and hung it on a peg on the wall near the sink. "Do you know the way to Collier?" she asked as she filled a jug with water.

Nora's chair halted midrock. "Of course I do, but I sure

don't like the path your thoughts have taken. Michael won't like it, and neither will the court, for that matter," she warned in a tone of voice she usually reserved for Michael.

Undeterred, JoHannah smiled. "Michael will be gone for at least four days, and I'll be back long before he is. I'll tell him all about it when he gets home. As far as the court is concerned, you need your medicine and I'm the only one here who can get it for you."

Reluctant to leave the security of Lawne Haven to travel alone in the World she found so confusing, JoHannah shook away frightening memories of Brady O'Neal's reaction to seeing her. The fact of the matter was that Nora needed her medicine. Despite the possibility that she would encounter a World person who judged her harshly, Jo-Hannah simply would have to pray that the Heavenly Father would protect her on her mission of mercy.

Nora stood up and put her hands on her hips. "You can't be traveling alone. What if something happens along the road—"

"It won't. If I hurry, I can be back by supper."

Nora took off her own apron and put it next to Jo-Hannah's. She lifted the stoneware jug out of JoHannah's hands and nodded toward the door. "You go hitch up the wagon while I—"

"You can't travel," JoHannah gasped.

"Well, I most certainly can't sit home in my rocking chair while you go traipsing back home to Collier all alone. I'd be sick with worry. It isn't proper in the first place, and in the second, Michael would never forgive me if I let you travel that far without someone along."

Home.

The judge's order and the echo of his warning not to run back to Collier without the court's permission almost chased away the delightful visions of Collier that danced through JoHannah's head.

JoHannah pressed her lips together. She was not a child, and she was not going to let anyone or anything, especially a World court, keep her from helping Nora. At the same time, mixed emotions troubled her heart when she thought about seeing Collier again. Would she be able to visit, even briefly, and leave again, knowing she might never go back? Had she been so tainted by the World that Collier would look different somehow? She closed her eyes, savoring the blessed memories of her Shaker village—memories that were too precious to risk losing.

A short visit to Collier, however, would be just what she needed to help her make up her mind about which world she wanted to claim for the rest of her life.

While Nora locked up the house, JoHannah hitched up the horses and brought the wagon to the kitchen door. With the jug of water stored under the driver's seat, she had no sooner pulled up when Nora struggled out the door with two travel bags. Thoroughly befuddled, JoHannah climbed down from the wagon and took the bags out of Nora's hands. "What on earth are you—"

Nora's eyes twinkled. "Thought about the trip and decided we should stay at the village for a few days. These old bones might not be able to take the round trip in one day. We'll just stop a moment to ask Genevieve to take care of my goats." She nudged JoHannah to put the travel bags in the back of the wagon. "You could probably use a few days at home, too."

When JoHannah looked down into the housekeeper's face, her dark black eyes were shining. "You can't go back in time and change the past, but you can take a good look at all of your choices before you decide which future you want to claim—assuming George can help your cause and delay any court interference before your birthday."

JoHannah's chest tightened with affection for the tiny woman who had become such a good friend. "Have you always been this persuasive and strong-willed?'' She chuckled softly.

''Always,'' Nora answered as she settled herself on the wooden seat.

JoHannah climbed aboard and picked up the reins before she released the brake. As the wagon rolled forward and JoHannah guided the horses to the main road, she looked sideways at Nora. Seated primly, her hands were braced on the seat on either side of her and a broad grin covered her face.

Chuckling, JoHannah let her spirit soar. She was going home where she would be able to pray with her sisters and brethren once more. Home . . . where she could find peace and tranquillity instead of confusion and constant challenges to her faith. Home . . . to Zion, if only to have time to strengthen her faith just enough to help her make the right choice about her future.

Lilacs. Their sweet, heavy scent laced the air as Michael rode north. Clouds of lilac blossoms, deep violet and pale purple, lined the roadway and reminded him of the precious woman he had just left behind. He urged his horse into a canter. Even with the best of luck, he had two days travel to Hillsboro and back, but every hour he was away from Lawne Haven he would be tortured by his last vision of JoHannah, standing forlorn and all alone at the edge of the creek.

He hoped that with a little time to herself, she would understand why he was fighting to bring Abigail and Jane home. Nora would help JoHannah to sort out her feelings and thoughts, but in the end, he knew that JoHannah had to accept his decision and embrace it with her whole heart if there was any hope that she would agree to marry him.

Michael also needed time away from Lawne Haven. As JoHannah's birthday approached, he knew he faced more than one skirmish in the war he waged to claim JoHannah as his wife. He had been winning the battle for her hand, at least until today, and he prayed JoHannah would eventually agree with his decision.

Yet another battle loomed ahead with her guardian, Eleazar Bathrick. With each day that passed, Michael grew more concerned that her guardian had some ulterior motive for forcing JoHannah into marriage, and while Michael was visiting his uncle, he had every intention of doing a little scouting into Bathrick's past and his handling of JoHannah's parents' estate. Bathrick would not be the first executor who had mishandled funds entrusted to his care. As a guardian who indentured his ward, he certainly was not unique, except that JoHannah apparently was not destitute or in need of a trade to support herself.

Dusty from half a day's travel and perspiring in the late afternoon sun, Michael stopped at the edge of a stream to water his horse and refill his canteen. As he knelt down to wash his face, he paused when he caught a glimpse of his own reflection. Reminded of his unanswered plea to JoHannah for her to think about her childhood at Collier, he closed his eyes and took a deep breath.

JoHannah.

Had his plea for her to face the truth about her past done nothing more than place yet another obstacle between them? Was she as understanding of herself as she was with others so she could see that she had not always been the devout Believer she had grown to be? Was there any hope left she would accept his proposal?

He bowed his head and prayed there was.

JoHannah halted the horses at the bottom of the hill and let them water at the marble trough Brother Thomas had carved years ago. Collier rose just ahead on the hill, an oasis in the barren desert of her mind. "Home," she murmured, and her face broke into a smile that started in her heart and rose to her lips. On the left, a stand of white birch trees shaded the trustees' building. Directly across the road, a symmetrical double line of heavy-limbed maple trees guarded the entry to the meeting house. The village lay just beyond.

Nora edged closer to JoHannah and shielded her eyes with one of her hands against the glare of the sun. "Are you sure they won't mind if I stay? I mean . . . Michael never said he had a problem, but he was visiting his brother."

"You're my guest. You'll be most welcome," JoHannah insisted, surprised by Nora's last-minute reticence.

Nora nodded. "Well, we'll be together, and you can—"

"Not exactly," JoHannah said quickly. "According to our custom, I'll have to be alone for twenty-four hours."

"Why on earth—"

JoHannah dipped her head. "Believers who go out into the World are . . . are contaminated. When we return, we must spend a full day in prayer before we can rejoin the community."

She heard Nora sigh and turned to look at her. "I'll ask Sister Evelyn to visit with you. Eldress Regina will most likely want to see you, and she'll probably let Sister Lucy come with her. Are you sure—"

"I'll be fine. I just want you to remember one thing."

JoHannah grinned. "Only one?"

"All that matters is what you feel in your heart, and if you've been contaminated by anything at Lawne Haven, I hope it's been love."

Tears misted JoHannah's eyes, and she nodded slowly. "I have," she whispered. She wrapped her arms around Nora's shoulders and hugged her close. "Thank you."

Nora returned JoHannah's embrace and took a deep breath. "Let's go, young lady. It's time you went home."

As the wagon rolled forward, JoHannah could feel anticipation build into excitement. Her heart started to beat faster, and her palms grew sweaty as she guided the wagon up the drive to the trustees' office to request permission to return for a short visit with Nora as her guest.

For the next few days, at least, she would simply be Sister JoHannah again. The very thought gave her a burst of energy, and within moments, Nora was settled on a wooden bench in the foyer. JoHannah followed Brother William into a small office to see Brother Edward, one of two trustees who handled business affairs between the village and the World.

Overly anxious to plead her case as quickly as possible so she could start her full day of isolation and be reunited with her family in faith, she took a seat in front of his desk. Careful to maintain proper order, she kept her gaze low and her voice soft as she followed custom and requested permission to visit with Nora as her guest. "Nora has been suffering without her medicine," she concluded.

"Suffering is to be expected in the World and endured as punishment for sin. As much as I would like to give you permission to visit, you simply cannot stay."

His abrupt and unexpected refusal sent her mind reeling. She bowed her head, but understanding could not break through the profound disappointment that laced her chest so tightly she could scarcely breathe. It had never occurred to her that she would not be welcomed home, and she tried to hide her embarrassment from him. "Forgive me," she murmured as she tried to fight the feeling that she was being treated like a wayward child instead of an adult. "I was only hoping to stay for a few days."

"The court's directive was very clear," he admonished. "If your guardian or anyone associated with the court discovered your willful violation, our suit on your behalf would be irreparably harmed." He stood up and walked around his desk to stand next to her. "World opinion about our faith is often harsh, and your actions today invite further censure and misunderstanding. The good of the community is far more important than any single Believer."

He paused to clear his throat. "The World has taken our children away for too long. Instead of meekly allowing that to occur, as we have in the past, the Elders have decided to aggressively pursue the issue in World courts. That's one of the reasons why our suit on your behalf is so important. You must have faith and pray harder for obedience and patience. The sin of selfishness and impetuousness must be cleansed from your spirit."

Chastised severely, she locked her gaze on his shadow which splayed on the floor at her feet. "May I at least have medicine for Nora?"

"I'll send Brother William to the infirmary. Is there anything more I can do for you before you leave?"

She wanted to cry out and ask him to open his heart and understand that she only wanted to see her home again. She never meant to risk the reputation of her community, and she could not help but wonder why he responded as coldly as he did to the urgent need she knew had been evident in her voice.

She took a deep breath and squared her shoulders. "We'll just be on our way. I'm sorry to have troubled you," she offered as she rose and followed him out the door. She sat with Nora while Brother William secured the medicine from the infirmary. Very quietly, she explained that they had to return to Lawne Haven immediately.

"I'm so sorry," Nora whispered. "I shouldn't have suggested—"

"It's not your fault. I thought it was a good idea at the time, remember?" She smiled and rested her hand on top of Nora's. "At least you'll have your medicine, and there's still plenty of daylight left so we can be back at Lawne Haven before dark.''

As she sat next to Nora, JoHannah realized that the thought of going back to Lawne Haven right away did not make her as unhappy as she should have been. The only thing her heart regretted, much to her added surprise, was that Michael would not be there waiting for her.

Chapter 22

Seated on the side porch of his uncle's cedar shingle bungalow after supper, Michael studied the last of the documents copied from official court records. Delayed in Hillsboro four days longer than he had expected to be, Michael was far from satisfied with the information the documents contained about JoHannah's parents and her guardian, Eleazar Bathrick. "You're right," he admitted as he looked up at his uncle. "There's nothing unusual or illegal here."

Taking a long pull on his pipe that momentarily turned the embers in the bowl golden red, George Weldon nodded. "Thomas Sims' will was probated and followed to the letter. The executor's reports Bathrick has filed with the court are responsibly detailed."

Michael put the documents down on a wicker table at his side and stretched out his legs. He leaned back in his chair and took a deep breath of rose-scented air tinged with the pungent aroma of tobacco. "I was certain Bathrick had embezzled funds or done something illegal."

"Why? Because the man put his ward out to indenture or decided to bring her home a few months before it expired? That might prove him to be coldhearted or motivated by his own self-interest, since he had the gall to install his own family on the Sims' estate, but that doesn't mean the man's a criminal. He's shrewd and legally well versed. He stepped just to the boundary between legal and unethical, but he never stepped over the line.''

Shaking his head, Michael could not explain the gnawing feeling that he and his uncle had missed something important. ''I was certain there would be something in the will or executor's reports that would explain why he forced JoHannah to leave Collier when she clearly wanted to stay.''

His uncle exhaled a long trail of smoke that swirled in the damp summer air. Without a hint of a breeze to carry it away, it hung overhead like a cloud dropped to earth. ''He didn't know that when he decided to bring her home, did he?''

Thinking back to the incident in the dining hall at Collier that JoHannah had described, Michael paused and carefully tried to review what she had said. ''No,'' he admitted. ''From what JoHannah told me, he seemed rather surprised that she wanted to stay at the village, although he never relented. He still forced her to leave.''

''Be fair, Michael. Would you expect the girl to choose otherwise? She couldn't very well turn against the people who had raised her when they were all around her. Think about it. The girl hadn't even seen her parents' home for nearly fourteen years. Why would she even want to go back?''

''Better argued,'' Michael suggested, ''is why Bathrick would care where she went. As soon as she turns twenty-one, she inherits everything from her parents and Bathrick's duty is done. It shouldn't matter to him whether she signs her inheritance over to her community or to her husband.''

His uncle chuckled. ''It's no small pittance that's involved here, in case you failed to read the documents closely. JoHannah Sims is exceedingly wealthy, or at least she will be next month. Bathrick has supervised the family estate as well as a number of import businesses and land in Georgia that her mother inherited and brought to the marriage. If Bathrick allows JoHannah to donate the entire part and parcel of her inheritance to a faith that most people consider bizarre and on the fringe of lunacy, he just might be held accountable by the court."

Frustrated, Michael raked his fingers through his hair. "JoHannah is an adult. She can make her own decisions." His chest tightened with the thought that she had decided not to accept his proposal because she did not understand why he was so insistent on bringing Abigail and Jane home to Lawne Haven instead of leaving them in Kentucky with the Shakers. Had she stayed by the creek and found the courage to face the sad and frightening moments after her parents died to understand what Michael had done, or had she retreated behind the rigid wall of her faith?

"She's an innocent." The old judge leaned forward in his chair and turned toward Michael. "You know that better than anyone. She's very vulnerable, and with her wealth, I don't blame her guardian for wanting to secure an acceptable match for her. There are many unscrupulous men who prey on unsuspecting wealthy women and marry them to gain title to their fortunes. I know times are different now, and young people seem to know their own minds when it comes to courting and selecting their marriage partners, but in my day, parents and even guardians had much more say about the matter. Didn't you say Bathrick was about my age?"

Michael nodded his agreement. "On the near side of sixty, I'd venture. His wife, apparently, is much younger."

"What you probably have here, if you'll forgive my saying so, is just a difference between the generations. I'm sure if you and JoHannah want to be married, her uncle will have no objections. Your family name is well known and respected, and although you have little hard coin, you have Lawne Haven. I'm sure Bathrick won't be adverse to your suit."

Swallowing hard, Michael stared at his uncle. "I want JoHannah for my wife. I was attracted to her from the first moment I saw her. Until I saw her father's will, I had no idea—"

"I know. I know," his uncle said quietly. "Has she accepted your proposal?"

Has she? The same question swirled through Michael's mind and pounded incessantly in his head with every beat of his heart. "I'm—I'm not sure. I hope when I get back, she'll have made up her mind. I wanted to thank you for stalling Bathrick's suit for as long as you have."

His uncle slapped Michael's knee. "You're more than welcome. There's nothing more to be done here now. I think it's time you went back to Lawne Haven. You're seeing John Newland off on the stage in the morning?"

The reference to the agent who was traveling to Kentucky on Michael's behalf brought some relief to the frustration of wasting four days to get documents that proved Bathrick to be an ethical guardian. At least Michael had managed to implement his plan to bring his nieces home. "At five. I wanted to thank you for taking care of his fee. I had no idea it would be so costly. Dolan will be working with me to fell timber, and as soon as I can . . ."

The sound of the grandfather clock in the hall striking midnight carried through the open door. Standing, his uncle stretched his back and nodded toward the house. "I told you to consider it a gift or an advance on your own inheritance. What else would I do with my money? It brings me great pleasure knowing that Abigail and Jane will soon be home where they belong.''

Michael stood and offered his hand to his uncle. ''I still intend to repay you.''

''As stubborn as your mother,'' his uncle noted as he gripped Michael's hand and shook it. ''A lot less finicky, though. How about we go inside and have a glass of port before bed? Might even let you try of bit of tobacco. . . .''

Laughing, Michael followed his uncle into the house. ''No sir. I paid a pretty good price for that once before. I'll join you in some port, though.''

Several hours later, Michael was in his room where he packed his saddlebag and stored the documents he had collected between the folds of one of his shirts. He buckled the bag closed, and on impulse, opened the other side of the bag and pulled out a small square box. He carried it with him as he walked to the open window that overlooked the side gardens.

Caught by the heavy scent of roses, he stared down at the garden his bachelor uncle cultivated with all the care most men reserved for wives and children. Multilayered rows of rose bushes surrounded an old-fashioned sundial in the center of a large oval garden. By the light of a full moon, he could even make out the wide spectrum of colors in the rose blossoms that ranged from white and palest yellow to dusky pink and deep scarlet.

The one set of rose blossoms he searched for, however, were on the bush closest to the sundial. Pale, pale lavender, they had reminded him of JoHannah the moment he had seen them shortly after he had arrived. He took a deep whiff of the fragrant air and closed his eyes as his hand tightened around the box.

''JoHannah.''

Just whispering her name made his heart swell with emotion, and the image of her face took shape in his mind. His sweet JoHannah, with her shimmering violet eyes and shining auburn hair . . . she was everything he had hoped for in a wife who would be mistress of Lawne Haven. The memory of their first kiss set his pulse racing, and his body ached with the need to satisfy the ever-growing passion that flared between them.

He opened his eyes and stared up at the sky. A host of dazzling stars met his gaze, and he searched them for the answers to the questions that plagued his mind. Would she accept his proposal? Did she know that the world he offered to her at Lawne Haven would be far better than the one at Collier? Had she forgiven him for making her remember the past? Did she understand why he had to make sure that Abigail and Jane came home to Lawne Haven?

With trembling fingers, he untied the string around the box and opened it. Counting on the answer he had so often seen in her eyes but had yet to hear her express with words, he had purchased a ring for her to wear the day she became his bride. Forgoing plans made long ago to gift his future wife with the ring his father had given to his mother on their wedding day, Michael knew that his mother's wide, heavy ring did not suit JoHannah. She would probably never wear ornate jewelry as a matter of faith or her own taste, and he had deliberately selected a very narrow but distinctive band of braided gold and silver for the very unique woman she was.

He lifted the ring out of the box and held it up to the moonlight. It was elegant in its simplicity, and the blending of precious metals was symbolic, indeed. If JoHannah agreed to be his wife, they would forge a new world together at Lawne Haven—one that would continue his family's traditions and merge them with ones she brought with her. Only then would he be free, one day, to return to the one true love of his life: the sea.

As the grandfather clock in the hall began to strike the first hour of the new day, he secured the ring back in its box and tucked it into his saddlebag. In a matter of hours, he would see John Newland off to Kentucky and start the journey home. With his mind totally consumed with thoughts of JoHannah, however, Michael had little hope of getting any sleep tonight. The only consolation he took to his bed was that with any sort of luck at all, he would not be sleeping alone for very much longer.

With Michael overdue by several days, JoHannah started her day the same way she had started every day for the past week. After finishing the outside chores, which included milking the ever-sensitive goats and sharing a light breakfast with Nora, JoHannah tidied her own room before dusting and sweeping Michael's room just across the hall.

Worried that something had gone awry with his carefully made plans to send someone to Kentucky for Abigail and Jane, she paused in her work. Still clutching the broom with both hands, she studied the painting over his bed. Dramatically caught by the artist, the *Illusion* still rode high on the seas, forever en route to adventures along the way to some distant shore. Or was the ship returning to home port, just as Michael had returned to Lawne Haven?

An illusion—that's what Michael had called her life at Collier. After her unsettling experience last week at the village, JoHannah had done a lot of soul searching. She eventually understood and accepted Brother Edward's refusal to let her visit for a few days. She also came to the new realization that however fulfilling her life would be at Collier if she returned, there were limitations inherent in communal living that now bothered her.

The individual needs of Believers were always superseded by the interests of the community, and the elders and eldresses held tremendous authority over them in the same way that parents held authority over their children. If the gift of true faith was given to all Believers, why did they need someone in authority to tell them what to do?

Now that she had been in the World, she liked being treated like an adult instead of a child. Maybe that's why she resented the interference of her guardian so much, even before she had learned to think with her own mind instead of letting fear speak for her. More importantly, she had come to realize that one of the reasons she enjoyed being with Michael was that he treated her as a person with thoughts and feelings that were as important as his own. She was honest enough to admit that they both had stumbled their way to this mutual respect, but it was there. And she liked it.

The longer she stayed with Michael at Lawne Haven, the more Collier paled in her mind as the only way to spend the rest of her life. Her faith in the Heavenly Father and Holy Mother Wisdom was stronger than ever, but the strict regulation of daily life at Collier now seemed to stifle challenges that, once met and overcome, strengthened her understanding of God instead of binding it in a rigid mold.

Was the freedom she had found in the World truly threatening to her salvation as she had been taught, or was the freedom to make her own decisions only a danger to the authority the elders and eldresses wielded?

Michael.

She stepped closer to the painting and tried to imagine him at the helm of his ship, shouting orders to his crew and winning his battle against the elements. He was strong willed and compelling. He exuded power and authority— the ideal of a man who captained a ship and had responsibility for the lives of his crew.

He still pursued her with such fervor, he nearly took her breath away and sent her mind whirling in such a tizzy she could hardly think straight. Confident and single-minded, he was also sensitive, compassionate, and caring. Rather than simply announcing his decision to bring Abigail and Jane home and expecting her to abide by it, he had tried very hard so JoHannah would understand and accept his reasoning. After much soul-searching at the creek, she had accepted his decision. And in the process, she realized how much his need to have her as his partner in life instead of his subordinate meant to her.

Michael.

He was more handsome than a man had a right to be. He was broad shouldered and powerfully built, with gorgeous gray eyes and a smile that lit a fire in her heart. His touch was tender and gentle, and the memory of their first kiss still made her lips tingle and her heartbeat stutter. He told her that he was attracted to her and that he wanted her for his wife—not just with his words, but with every look, every gesture, every touch. He made her feel precious in a way so different from anything she had ever felt before.

Did she love him?

With every beat of her heart and every breath she took.

Should she marry him and live in his world, forsaking life within her community of faith? Or should she embrace the world he offered, cherish it, and then return to life as Sister JoHannah, knowing the full measure of the sacrifice she would be making as a Believer?

As rapidly and quietly as a hummingbird, her answer had flown back and forth these past few days, hovering at both options and feasting on the sweet nectar of each one while she prayed for guidance and searched her heart. Today, with the first rays of light peeping over the horizon, she finally had reached a decision that made her heart sing with joy.

When Michael returned from Hillsboro, she would give him the long and patiently awaited answer to the proposal he had so confidently predicted she would accept the first night he had held her in his arms.

She would marry Michael Lawne, carry his name, bear his children, and serve the Heavenly Father in the wondrous and challenging world He had created. She would be surrounded in this world by many good people: Nora, Dolan and his family, and Dr. Carson. But most of all, life in the World meant loving Michael and being loved—completely and uniquely—by a most incredible man.

It occurred to her that he had never declared his love for her, but she knew in her heart Michael was a proud man. Perhaps he held back his own declaration of love until she accepted his proposal. Or perhaps he did not want to admit that the attraction that had drawn them together had grown into a much more powerful emotion—one he had tried to deny to himself as a way of softening her refusal if she decided to return to Collier.

Humming softly to herself, she started sweeping the room and tried to think of a special way to tell Michael that she wanted to marry him. She had never dared to mouth the words he longed to hear for fear of giving him false hope, but now . . . "I want to be your wife, Michael," she whispered out loud.

It sounded so wonderful, she said it again. "I want to be your wife, Michael. I want to marry you." Joy bubbled in her chest, and she started to giggle. She wanted to climb to the highest mountain and listen to her echo! If Michael did not come home soon, she knew she would never be able to hide her happiness from Nora. Michael certainly deserved to hear her answer first, and she could barely stand the wait.

When a man's voice carried up the stairs, she cocked an ear and dropped her broom. Michael must be home! She hurried from his room and practically flew down the stairs.

When she reached the bottom step, she gripped the banister
for support and blinked her eyes to make sure she was not
mistaken. Just in front of her in the opened front doorway
stood her guardian, Eleazar Bathrick.

Chapter 23

"There's no need to have a long discussion. The Shakers have decided to drop their lawsuit. You're coming home with me," Bathrick said calmly. Seated on the sofa, he looked around the small parlor with disdain.

Shocked by his statement, JoHannah was also relieved that Nora had agreed to let JoHannah speak privately with her guardian. The sneer on his face told JoHannah he thought the parlor woefully inelegant compared to the drawing room of her birth home. Ignoring his poor manners, JoHannah tried to calm her racing heartbeat and to think through his startling announcement.

Was it true? Had her community dropped its lawsuit? It hardly seemed possible, considering what she had learned on her visit to Collier last week.

Once she had made her decision earlier this morning not to return to Collier, her one regret was that her community had wasted needed funds on her behalf. Brother Edward's words once again rang loud and clear in her mind. If the Shakers had decided to withdraw a suit meant to test the power of the World against them, why had they changed their minds? Had her aborted visit prompted them to rethink their decision, or more likely, had her guardian found a way past the stumbling block Michael's uncle had placed in Bathrick's way?

"I don't believe you," she responded. Standing next to the hearth with her back to the window, she held her head high and met his gaze. "There's been no word from the court—"

With a wave of his pudgy hand, Bathrick halted her words. "There will be. Elder Calvin wrote the court just this morning after my visit." His eyes narrowed and flashed with mocking self-satisfaction. "The attempts to stall the suit were quite ingenious. It's too bad Mr. Lawne isn't back from Hillsboro yet. I would have enjoyed telling him that his uncle's efforts failed in the end."

JoHannah swallowed hard. "You knew?"

He smiled and shook his head. "I've been practicing law for many years. When my suit got caught in a legal quagmire, I didn't have to look far for the reason why. Once I made the connection between the judge and the man you were sent to nurse, it wasn't difficult to make a reasonable conjecture. Apparently misguided out of some sense of gratitude, I simply presumed that Mr. Lawne spoke on your behalf to his uncle who arranged for the files to mysteriously disappear. All of which is rather irrelevant now."

He leaned against the back of the sofa and rested his folded hands on the mound of his stomach that stretched the seams of his waistcoat. "I'd like to get in a full day's travel, so if there's anything you need to tell the servant, you're advised to be quick."

"Nora is my friend," JoHannah said quietly, relieved once again she had insisted on speaking to her guardian alone. Unlike the day in the dining hall when she had let surprise and fear rule her heart and mind, JoHannah held firm against her guardian. "I don't intend to leave Lawne Haven without proof. If what you say is true, then—"

He snorted. "As your guardian—"

"You have every right to protect my interests. I understand that," she argued. "I'm no longer a child you can toss aside or order about. I'm old enough to make up my own mind about the way I want to live my life." Reluctant to inform him just yet that she did not want to return to Collier, she was just as reticent to tell him that she had chosen the man she wanted to marry. Her guardian had made it very clear that he intended to choose an appropriate husband for her. Unless she stood up to him now and demanded to know the reasons behind her community's surprising reversal, she would not be able to convince Bathrick to accept her choice of a marriage partner.

She stepped forward a few steps and looked down at him. "How did you convince Elder Calvin to drop the suit?"

"Expense. Futility. All the obvious reasons," he responded in a brusque tone of voice.

She noted how he avoided looking directly at her and knew at once he was not telling her the whole truth. "I went to Collier last week and talked to Brother Edward. My family in faith had no intention of dropping the suit."

Bathrick rose to his feet so quickly she rocked back on her heels. "You violated the order of the court?"

"Nora needed medicine, and there was no one else to send."

"How convenient for you," he mumbled irritably. His chest shook as he took several deep breaths of air. "You've become rather independent and willful since you've been here. Not an attractive quality, my dear, especially when you must soon learn to bend to the will of your husband."

"No. I've learned to be an adult and to speak my mind," she countered, refusing to take a step back from him and give him any inkling that he intimidated her. In truth, her knees were shaking, and her heart literally skipped a beat. "The truth. I simply want the truth of what you said to Elder Calvin to make him change his mind."

His eyes darted from side to side before they settled into a glare that several months ago would have reduced her to tears. "The only issue you need to be concerned with now is whether or not you will accept my authority as your guardian. I've gone to a great deal of trouble these past fourteen years to administer your parents' estate on your behalf. Once I've chosen a proper husband for you—"

She arched her back and threw back her shoulders. "I'm old enough to make that choice for myself."

Disbelief and rage distorted his features, and his lips pumped futilely for several seconds. "You . . . you decided not to return to Collier?"

Breaking the promise she made to herself to tell Michael her decision to accept his proposal before anyone else, she nodded. "I've done a great deal of soul searching about where I want to spend the rest of my life. I—I want to stay here with Michael."

Bathrick clenched his jaw, and the tiny hairs on the mole on his cheek stood out straight like pins on a pin cushion. "Licentious bastard! He's got quite a reputation with women who are certainly well below your station. I should have known! Even half dead the mongrel still managed to turn your head. Do you really think I'd let you spend the rest of your life with him? The man doesn't have one hard coin to rub against another. He's not a tenth of the man you deserve, unless . . ."

His eyes narrowed and gleamed with such hatred that JoHannah's entire body went cold. "Are you still pure, or did that whoremonger—"

"M-Michael would never . . ." Unable to even give voice to the horrid accusation her guardian made, tears pricked her eyelids. "Michael has always been honorable and forthright in his intentions. He has asked me to marry him, and I . . . I intend to accept," she said firmly. "I know that you believe you have my best interests at heart, but you don't know Michael. He's a good man. I hope we'll have your blessing, but if not—''

"No. You most certainly do not. It's a good thing the fortune-hunting worm isn't here, or I'd squash him like the vermin he is.''

Chills raced up and down JoHannah's spine. "Michael doesn't need my wealth, if indeed I have it. He has his own land and a way to support me that suits me well.''

Bathrick rolled his eyes. "You stupid, naive girl. His uncle probably sent him an accounting of your holdings, and he can tell you the value of every one of them. If I didn't know better, I'd be tempted to think they planned the whole scenario. The sooner I get you out of here, the better.''

He grabbed her arm, but JoHannah pulled out of his hold. "No. I'm simply not going to leave without seeing Michael. He's due back any day—''

"You have no choice. You're coming with me.''

She tilted her chin and braced her legs. Her guardian's accusations against Michael were so ludicrous, she gave them as much credence as she gave thought to drawing a breath of air. "Not until I see Michael. If he still wants to marry me, I'm sure we can find a minister or a justice of the peace to perform the ceremony with or without your permission. I'm not a child, and you don't have a sheriff with you this time to intimidate me into leaving. If you try, Nora will send for Dolan. He'll stop you from taking me away against my will.''

She looked down at her guardian and detected new and troubling emotions in his eyes. She saw fear . . . and guilt, as though there was much more at stake if she married Michael than just the choice of a proper husband or her guardian's reputation as the executor of her father's will. "Why are you so insistent on choosing a husband for me? What could you possibly hope to gain by refusing to let me marry Michael?'' she breathed.

Bathrick's cheeks turned scarlet, and his lips turned white with rage. "How dare you!"

His heated response only fueled her suspicions, but before she could even contemplate a guess as to his real motives, he pulled a document from his pocket and shoved it in her face. "You'll leave. And once you read this, you'll do exactly what you're told and marry whomever I decide."

JoHannah turned her face away from him.

"Elder Calvin certainly thought twice about challenging me," her guardian taunted. "Take a look. If you still want to defy me, then so be it. But rest assured, I have no qualms about using this affidavit to destroy you and everyone else who stands in my way."

JoHannah refused to look at him. She simply reached out and took the document into her hand. She carried it with her as she walked to the window, her steps slow and deliberate in spite of the trembling in her legs that made it almost impossible for her to keep her balance. She sank into the chair and laid the affidavit on her lap. Bowing her head, she prayed for divine help before lifting the papers up close to read them.

Shock. Horror. Outrage. They screamed through her mind as she quickly read her guardian's first allegation, and her gaze rested on a series of dates that spanned the past fourteen years. The paragraphs directly below made her tremble:

It is the plaintiff's position that on the above mentioned dates, the Elders at the village of Collier, New Hampshire, with malice and forethought, deliberately prevented Miss Sims' legal guardian from visiting with his ward for the express purpose of keeping said minor child under their direct control so that she would reach her majority and elect to remain as a formal member of their faith and sign over her considerable inheritance to them.

As further attested by Miss Sims in precise detail on an attached deposition, this is a wicked practice used by the Shakers to prevent all contact between other indentured children at Collier and their legal guardians for financial gain.

Her eyes stung with tears, and her vision blurred. Her hands shook so badly it took several attempts to get past the first page to the rest of the document. Skimming quickly over the words that filled six pages of text, her heart splintered as a crueler and more dangerous accusation stared back at her.

Motivated by determination to expose the Shakers as a threat to society, Bathrick had launched an extensive investigation and allegedly discovered that they had illegally obtained the land where their village was situated. He had researched the deed to Collier that had been filed nearly thirty years ago and contacted the surviving brother of one Augustus McKinney. Bathrick provided evidence that the Shakers had orchestrated an elaborate scheme which included falsifying McKinney's signature on the land transfer. He offered a recently located letter allegedly written by McKinney himself in which he pleaded with his brother to help him to escape from the religious sect and denied any intention of signing his land over to the Shakers.

Thwarted by a limited mental capacity, McKinney's brother was unaware of the true meaning of his brother's words and had taken no action, even after his brother's sudden death at the age of thirty-seven. It was only Bathrick's interest that resurrected evidence of the crime, and he was acting now on behalf of Herbert McKinney who was aged, infirm, and still quite incapable of understanding what had happened to his brother.

JoHannah's alleged signature to a statement that she had been told by Elder Calvin that Bathrick's allegations were true took her breath away. Unable to continue beyond the third page, she closed her eyes and gulped back the lump that had lodged like a nettle in her throat. Pain knifed through her chest, and she took small shallow breaths of air to keep from fainting. If Bathrick filed this affidavit with the courts, her family in faith would be forced to give up their village—even though she was certain that the letter Bathrick produced from McKinney was pure fabrication.

"This is a vile assortment of lies," she whispered, overwhelmed by the depth of her guardian's evil deviousness. "I never attested to any of this, and I can't believe that—"

"You most certainly did," he argued. "Take a look at the last page. There's a sworn deposition with your signature to prove it."

"A forgery," she responded, voicing her belief out loud. "As fake as McKinney's letter and the entire affidavit."

"Look more closely," he urged as he took the document out of her hands and turned to the very last page. He poked it angrily with his finger. "There. That's your signature, isn't it?"

In spite of her determination to reject any explanation he might give to prove his point, she glanced down at the page he held in front of her face. Staring back at her, in the precise script she had practiced in the very Shaker community maligned in the affidavit, was her signature that attested to her alleged sworn statement.

She gasped. "I would never, ever sign my name to anything like this." In the back of her mind, a fleeting memory of the day she had arrived back at her birth home filtered through a maze of pain and disappointment that crowded her mind.

After a long journey back to the home where she had

been born and viewing the portraits of herself and her parents, she vaguely remembered going into the study and signing a number of documents her guardian had insisted were quite routine. Dazed and devastated at the time, she had signed them without giving a second thought to what they were or caring what they contained.

She had blindly trusted her guardian, and he had knowingly and deliberately misled her. Too late, she realized that he was a man who had done more than act in his own self-interest. He had taken advantage of her naiveté and innocence, precisely what he accused Michael of doing.

"Well? Are you convinced?" he sneered as he pulled the affidavit out of her hands and put it back into his pocket. "Elder Calvin found your deposition most disturbing . . . and most convincing. The evidence from McKinney's brother is irrefutable. If necessary, I can show you a copy of your Elder's letter to the court. He was most agreeable to dropping the suit to have you restored to the Shakers, once I assured him that I had every intention of filing this affidavit with the courts unless he cooperated."

Shaken to the very lining of her soul, JoHannah prayed that Elder Calvin would know that she had never written the ugly lies contained in the affidavit. She prayed he would forgive the role her trusting ignorance had played in contributing to the validation of the affidavit as a true account of practices at Collier.

Her whole body trembled.

It was one thing to decide against living the rest of her life as a formal Believer; it was quite another to deliberately destroy the lives of innocent men and women who devoted their entire lives to serving the Heavenly Father by thinking only of herself and standing by as they were forced from land they acquired legally, despite any alleged evidence Bathrick offered to the contrary. Images of her sisters and brethren in faith crowded her mind, and her heart swelled with memories of the love they had shared with her. She could never destroy their simple lives of faith by allowing anyone to force them from their land in a scheme her guardian had concocted in an effort to force JoHannah to bend to his will.

Michael.

She loved him with every breath she took. She also knew that it was only by God's grace that she had never accepted his proposal. The ever-faithful spirit of Holy Mother Wisdom had judiciously prevented JoHannah from accepting Michael's proposal because JoHannah knew he would have moved heaven and earth to claim her if she had.

Faced now with her guardian's ultimatum, there was only one choice left to her: She would have to marry another man.

By leaving now before Michael returned, she could spare him the anguish of knowing that as much as she wanted to be his wife and share his world, she could not marry him. If Michael even guessed that she loved him, he would try to convince her to marry him in spite of her uncle's threat to destroy the reputation of the Shakers. Recalling the threat of violence that had flashed in his eyes and molded his body the night he had held his crutch to Brady O'Neal's throat, she shuddered. To prevent Michael from exploding into murderous anger he would direct at her guardian, it would be safer to make him believe that she had decided to rejoin her community of faith and that her guardian had agreed to let her go back to Collier to resume her life as Sister JoHannah.

Michael.

The pain of living without him and not sharing her life with him sliced deep into the shattered remnants of her heart. To sacrifice the love they could have shared would be the hardest thing she had ever done in her life. She remembered the conversation she had had with Nora so many weeks ago when the housekeeper so wisely told her that to sacrifice something that was close to your heart was a far greater sacrifice than if you gave up something you had never known.

Life without Michael would never have any meaning, and life without his love would be a very sad and lonely life indeed. She faced a bleak and empty future where she would be forced to share her mind, her body, and her reputed fortune with a man who would never be able to claim her heart because she had already given it away . . . to Michael.

She rose from her seat. "It would be better for all concerned if . . . if Michael and Nora thought I was returning to Collier," she said quietly, determined to fight her guardian if he denied her this one request.

When he nodded his agreement, she sighed with relief. "I—I just want to say good-bye to Nora," she murmured, praying for the strength to lie convincingly to her friend to make her believe that it was JoHannah's guardian who had changed his mind, dropped his lawsuit, and agreed to take her back to Collier.

Michael had promised to respect her decision if she wanted to remain a Believer, and lying was the only way open to her. Given time, he would eventually accept being second to her faith as the choice of her heart, but he would never accept losing her to another man without becoming embittered. She had no doubt Michael would some day marry to beget a male heir for Lawne Haven, but she knew he would close his heart to loving another woman and being loved by her in return—a fate too cruel for such a good man.

She walked woodenly from the room, mounted the stairs, and paused just outside of Michael's room. Pulled inside by the desperate need to be near him one last time, she stepped inside and looked around. Michael's irreverent prayers that she would lose her cap brought a tremulous smile to her lips, and she removed her cap. She folded it into a small square and placed it on his pillow as a way of saying good-bye to the man she loved and would never see again. She knew Leila would probably burn every piece of Shaker clothing, and JoHannah could not bear to see flames destroy the delicate lace cap. It would be much more fitting to direct that fate to the poor-fitting, makeshift cap she had stitched with her own hands.

With tear-filled eyes, she stared at the painting over his bed one last time. The joy she had felt just hours ago when she had whispered out loud for the first time that she loved Michael and wanted to spend the rest of her life with him at Lawne Haven suddenly appeared to be nothing more than a promising illusion that had been destroyed before it had had a chance to sharpen into reality.

That's what life would be without him, she decided as she made her way to Nora's room. An illusion. And with every beat of her heart, she hoped to find a way to escape into that illusionary world—just once in a while in her sleep. Perhaps then he would find her the way he had done for ever so long . . . in her dreams.

Chapter 24

Frustrated to the breaking point, Michael finally arrived home at Lawne Haven the last week in July. Only hours after leaving Hillsboro, his mount had pulled up lame, and he had spent a hellishly long week in the small hamlet of Birchville while he waited for his horse to mend. Once he reached Lawne Haven, he unsaddled his horse and turned it loose in the corral next to the barn. He tore past the laundry drying on the line in the hot, midday sun and entered the kitchen with his saddlebags slung over his shoulder.

In the heat of summer, the hearth was unlit, but a small pot of soup filled the room with aromas that made his stomach growl. Far more anxious to assuage his need to see JoHannah than to worry about satisfying his hunger, he walked stealthily through the hall to the parlor, intending to surprise her since she obviously had not heard him arrive.

Finding the front room also empty, he took the stairs two at a time and went directly to her room. Heart pounding, he stepped through the open door and rocked back on his heels. All trace of JoHannah was gone. The door to the empty wardrobe hung open, the bed had been stripped down to the mattress, and the drape over the mirror had been removed. There was no sign of her trunk, and the curtains she had removed now covered the windows.

Catching a side glimpse of his startled expression in the mirror as he spun around, a score of reasonable explanations for JoHannah's absence each clamored for priority as he stumbled across the hall to his room. With one step inside, his gaze locked on the small square of lace resting on top of his pillow. Blinking back the twin swells of disbelief and disappointment that stung his eyes, he dropped his saddlebags to the floor and made his way to the bed as one impossible notion gripped his soul.

Gone. She was truly gone.

"JoHannah." He whispered her name, and the pain of losing her sliced through all his pretentious claims that he wanted to marry her to satisfy the fateful attraction that surged between them the first time they had met and touched and gazed into one another's eyes, or because she would be the perfect mistress for Lawne Haven and the mother of his children. He now knew, in the depths of excruciating loss that claimed his very breath, that he wanted to marry her for only one reason: He loved her. He loved her! Craved her. And needed her to make his life complete.

"JoHannah!"

His hoarse cry echoed in the room like the wailing of a shrill wind.

With her gentle spirit and precious, most uncommon heart, she had unleashed deeper, more compelling emotions than he had ever known—emotions that had transcended extraordinary, passionate attraction and developed into a love so pure and so true that his heart had been locked with hers forever.

The powerful truth of his feelings for JoHannah made his heart and body tremble. He loved her. And he knew now how very hard he would have to fight to keep her in his arms, in his heart . . . and in his world.

He picked up the sheer lace cap she had worn and opened it so it fit over his hand. Sweet memories caught in his throat when he recalled the day she had asked him if he liked the new cap Nora had made for her out of one of the treasures she had found in the attic. How could he have misjudged his feelings for this magnificent woman? Had he been so obsessed with his own need to meet his responsibilities at Lawne Haven so he could satisfy his thirst for adventure at sea that he had been blinded to Fate's most precious gift of all: true love?

Had he pushed JoHannah so hard that she had fled back to the safety of her old world when he had tried to convince her that bringing Abigail and Jane back home was the right thing to do? Or had his uncle's efforts to stall her guardian's suit failed, allowing Bathrick to come for her and force her to leave?

He turned around, intending to find Nora to get an explanation before he jumped to the heartbreaking conclusion that JoHannah had simply rejected his proposal because he had never told her how much he truly loved her.

Standing in the hall just outside his door, Nora caught his gaze, and her face lit with surprise. "Michael!"

Swallowing hard, he attempted a smile that fell woefully short. "Where is she?" he managed, his voice cracking with deep emotions he did not need to hide from the woman who probably already knew how much he loved JoHannah, even if he had tried to deny it to himself. "Where's JoHannah?"

Her eyes brimming with tears, Nora moistened her lips and twisted her hands in front of her. "She's . . . she's back at Collier," she whispered in a voice laced with the same pain he had heard when Avery had gone away. "She left over a week ago with her guardian."

Two of Nora's words, *Collier* and *guardian*, seemed as unlikely to belong together as purity and sin, and Michael sidestepped the saddlebags on the floor and walked out into the hall. "Tell me what happened," he urged as he put his arm around the housekeeper. "Every detail," he added as he led her down the stairs to get away from the agonizing sight of JoHannah's empty room.

To think that Bathrick had given up his lawsuit and had abandoned his plans for an arranged marriage for JoHannah did not sit well with Michael's perception of the man. If Michael had any hope of unraveling the reasons for Jo-Hannah's departure, he had to set aside the pain of rejection that twisted like a double-edged sword in his chest. He had to keep an open mind and listen carefully to Nora's tale. Although his uncle's reasoning had made perfectly good sense in light of the documents Michael had examined, in-stinctively, he did not accept a generational difference in custom as the motive for Bathrick's actions. Neither did Michael believe for one shaky heartbeat that Bathrick had allowed JoHannah to return to Collier, not after hearing about the man's insensitivity when JoHannah had begged not to leave in the first place.

Michael led Nora downstairs to the kitchen and over a light dinner, she told him exactly what had transpired when JoHannah's guardian had arrived so unexpectedly. Cha-grined to learn Nora had not been present during the man's conversation with JoHannah, Michael counted on Nora's friendship with the woman he loved above all others and No-ra's uncanny ability to assess a person's character to surmise the truth about what really had happened. When she finished telling him all she knew, he sat back and rubbed his fingers along his jawline. "You're certain she told you Bathrick withdrew his suit so she could go back to Collier?"

"Absolutely. JoHannah would never lie to me or anyone else, although I found it hard to believe at the time. She was quite persuasive," Nora insisted, but her eyes seemed troubled.

He narrowed his gaze. "Hard? Why? What made you think—"

She scowled. "He was boorishly arrogant and rude when I told him he couldn't see JoHannah. He barged right past me into the house, and he sure didn't seem in a kindly mood."

Nodding, Michael again recalled JoHannah's description of Bathrick's strikingly similar demeanor the day JoHannah had been forced to leave Collier. "What about when they left together?"

"A real change. Almost like the man had been doused with honey. Thanked me for taking good care of JoHannah and said he was sorry you weren't here so he could express his gratitude to you in person. Made my skin crawl when he took hold of JoHannah and led her to his coach."

As he mulled over Nora's astute observations, Michael took a long breath and held it before exhaling slowly. The only reason for Bathrick's odd reversal in attitude could be that he had convinced JoHannah to do something that perhaps he had intended to do all along: secure JoHannah's inheritance for himself.

Greed was a powerful vice, and it was entirely plausible to assume Bathrick had grown accustomed to living the life of a country gentleman. After fourteen years of receiving hefty fees for administering JoHannah's inheritance and living on an estate that was beyond any means he could hope to legitimately earn for himself, he had been faced with making his own fortune. Bathrick must have been totally appalled to think that everything he coveted would be signed over to the Shakers—if JoHannah was allowed to sign the covenant.

Purely caught up in his own conjecture, Michael knew that Bathrick had somehow convinced JoHannah to sign over the bulk of her wealth to him and make a token donation to the Shakers.

Poor little saint.

Even if he assumed she had been on the verge of accepting his proposal, she had been forced to choose between life in the World with a total stranger as her husband, or life back at Collier—on Bathrick's terms. Michael had not an iota of doubt about what she would have chosen.

It did not ease his troubled heart to learn that JoHannah had reached some level of understanding that Michael was doing the right thing by fighting for his nieces' custody. Or had she lied about that to Nora as he suspected she had done about returning to Collier? If she had, Michael looked at himself through her eyes and saw a man who had disappointed her to the point of unforgiveness. Her guardian's proposition would have seemed like divine intervention and had spared her the pain of refusing Michael's proposal in person.

He loved JoHannah for many reasons, but most of all, for her uncommon heart—a heart that was gentle and forgiving—and he knew in the depths of his soul that something was very, very wrong.

He rose from his seat and checked his pocket watch. ''Don't wait up for me,'' he said as he kissed Nora on the forehead.

''Why? Where are you going now? You just got back—''

''I have to see her. I have to hear her tell me with her own words that she truly wants to live at Collier. If she does,'' he said softly, ''I'll spend the rest of my life reliving and regretting every mistake I made with her. If she doesn't,'' he added forcefully, hoping with every beat of his heart for a way to get to the truth behind JoHannah's departure, ''I intend to bring her home.''

Nora stood up and gripped both of his hands with hers.

Her wrinkled face trembled. "It—it won't do any good. They won't let you see her."

He squeezed her hands gently. "They let me see Avery."

"He was your brother, and Avery must have told them he was agreeable to your visits. I wasn't going to tell you—"

"Tell me what?" he interrupted, his pulse beginning to accelerate again.

"Dolan took me to the village the day before yesterday. I haven't been able to sleep much since JoHannah left. I just wanted to be sure. . . . They turned me away. They wouldn't let me see her." Sniffling back tears, she rested her head against Michael's shoulder. "I'm sorry, Michael. If only you had been here—"

"Shhh. It's not your fault," he crooned as he wrapped her in his arms. "I'll find a way to see her. I promise. You just set your worries to rest."

She looked up at him, her eyes streaked with red. "Are you sure you can get past the trustees? Even Dolan couldn't bluster my way in for me."

He tipped her chin up. "Didn't you used to tell me I was the most devious little rascal you'd ever met?"

She chuckled in spite of her tears. "Yes, but—"

"Accepting failure is not in my nature. I intend to see JoHannah, and no one—not even an army of saints—will hold me back."

Michael immediately took his leave, knowing that his pledge to Nora was not the whole truth of the matter. A few simple words from one sweet little saint would be enough to stop him dead in his tracks.

A preponderance of lilac bushes along the road to Collier made Michael's ride even more difficult than it should have been. Bush after bush, every heart-shaped leaf on the branches reminded him of JoHannah's sweet face. To keep his own sanity, he kept his head down and glued his vision to the center of the road.

Determined to get access to the village and search it building by building and room by room if he had to, he knew there was only one way to guarantee success. Borrowing a page from Bathrick's personal diary, he stopped in the town closest to Collier and tied his horse outside of the sheriff's office.

Except for the sound of raucous laughter and loud piano music emanating from a saloonery down the street, the town was quietly at supper. Most businesses had closed down for the night, and there were only a few people hurrying down the bricked sidewalks.

As soon as he opened the door and stepped inside, he approached the sheriff who was at his desk with a supper tray. After removing his hat, Michael extended his hand and introduced himself. "Michael Lawne. Sorry to interrupt your meal," he said, fighting back the anguish that twisted his gut with what he had to do to make very sure he could see JoHannah.

Pushing aside his tray, Lunden rose and shook Michael's hand. "Lunden. Peter Lunden. What can I do for you?"

Michael looked at the sheriff's half-eaten meal and grinned. "For now, sit down and finish your meal. I can talk while you eat."

Eyes twinkling, Lunden sat down and picked up a leg of boiled chicken and proceeded with his supper. "Can't waste the missus's cookin'. She'd be sure to have both our heads," he said between bites.

"I understand the Shaker village falls within your jurisdiction," Michael began, choosing every word carefully. If his plan to see JoHannah was going to work, he needed Lunden's cooperation.

His mouth full, the sheriff nodded, but his face darkened with concern.

Taking a deep breath, Michael explained the purpose behind his interest in the village. Lunden listened carefully, and his good-natured expression gradually disintegrated into disbelief and disappointment. Clearly reluctant at first, he finally agreed to Michael's request.

Within half an hour, Michael and the sheriff left for Collier. The sun had already started its descent, and golden streaks of light sputtered the day's waning glory. By the time they reached the village, the trustee's office had been locked up tight.

Undaunted, Michael pounded on the door until he heard the sound of footsteps descending the inside stairway. A bolt on the other side of the door slid free, and within moments, the door swung open. A full-bearded Shaker stared at him.

Michael stepped back to let the sheriff handle the matter at this point. Lunden spoke quietly to the man, and for several tense moments, Michael wondered if his plan to see JoHannah was a bit too dramatic. As the verbal stand-off continued, he carefully observed each man, praying that it would not be necessary for Lunden to use the trump card Michael had given the sheriff to play—if necessary.

When Lunden took the document Michael had signed less than an hour ago out of his pocket, the trustee read it quickly and paled. Visibly shaking, he handed the paper back to the sheriff and ushered both World visitors into a small office before scurrying away.

Pulling on his chin, Lunden had a grim expression on his face as he sat next to Michael. "Sorry. Unless I showed Brother Edward your written complaint, he wouldn't budge. He won't give either of us any information about JoHannah Sims or allow any visitors. He went to get Elder Calvin."

Michael stared at the paper Lunden had put on the desk, hoping and praying JoHannah would forgive him. If she had really returned to her community of faith of her own accord and had signed over her entire inheritance to the Shakers, Michael believed she would forgive him—eventually. If Bathrick had swindled a fortune for himself, she might even agree the false charge against her was well worth the opportunity to get her community its due. Whether or not Michael could convince her to change her mind about marrying him was something he did not dare to even think about . . . not when he was not even sure he would be allowed to see her.

Just when Michael was wondering if Brother Edward had gone to the opposite end of the earth in search of Elder Calvin, both men walked into the room. Brother Edward remained just inside the door while Elder Calvin took a seat behind the desk. He said nary a word, but picked up the document and read it silently to himself.

When he finished reading, he handed it back to the sheriff. "I understand JoHannah Sims is about to inherit a fortune in her own right," he said softly. He turned and glared at Michael. "The charges you have filed against her are hardly believable and very serious."

"Stealing always is," he answered solemnly. "The missing jewels belonged to my late mother. They have a great deal of sentimental value, and I want them back. If I could see JoHannah alone, I'm sure I could convince her to return them to me. At that point, I would be more than willing to withdraw my complaint. If I'm wrong, I'll apologize."

Michael studied the man's eyes. They flashed briefly before they shuttered any and all emotion from view. "JoHannah is clearly a troubled young woman," he murmured. "Unfortunately, I can't help you."

Confused by the Elder's comment about JoHannah, Michael was consumed with guilt for unjustly branding the woman he loved as a thief. At that moment, he could not think past the idea that the Elder refused to let him see her, even with the sheriff at his side. His blood began to boil, and he started to stand up as he turned toward Lunden. "Sheriff, if you would kindly inform this man—"

"Please. Sit down," the Elder said gently. "There's nothing the sheriff can do to force me to let you speak to JoHannah."

Before Michael could bolt to his feet, the Elder held up one hand in protest. "JoHannah is no longer a Believer. She's not here."

Every muscle in Michael's body tightened into rigid coils, and he gripped the side of his chair. His pulse pounded in his head, and he glared at the Elder. "If this is some kind of foolery—"

"I'm afraid not. Our dear Sister JoHannah has been claimed by the World, may the Heavenly Father have mercy on her soul." His eyes clouded with deep pain. "You should be able to find her at her birth home with her guardian."

Rendered totally speechless, Michael grabbed the complaint off the desk and tore it into shreds. "I'm sorry. You're right. Obviously JoHannah would have no need to steal from me. I was misinformed," he grumbled by way of explanation to the two startled men who regarded him as nothing less than an escaped lunatic.

Michael stormed past Brother Edward and out the door, mounted his horse, and rode away in a gallop, hell-bent on one destination: JoHannah's home.

Chapter 25

The final triumph of evil over good in the World fulfilled every faith-inspired prophecy JoHannah's elders and eldresses had made. Gripped by suffocating pain and grief, the only solace she had found since returning to her birth home had been prayer, and through endless hours of meditation came one glorious gift of inspiration that finally had snapped her out of a paralyzing depression. As the month of July drew to a close, JoHannah rose from her bed just before dawn and climbed up the winding stairs to the observatory.

Her heart beat wildly with anticipation as she pressed her hands against the wall of glass and stared toward the eastern horizon. When the first streaks of daylight finally appeared in the distance, she watched with bated breath as the eternal power of dawn gently triumphed over the overwhelming darkness of night.

A brilliant summer sun emerged in the sky and eclipsed the light of the moon. With the promise and glory of the World spread before her eyes, she saw incredible beauty that had been crafted by the hand of God. Mountains, tall and majestic, reached toward heaven, their summits no longer encrusted with snow. Trees, lush and green, fulfilled nature's spring promise after standing thin and barren in winter. Summer flowers covered rolling hills with carpets of pink and yellow and white.

She closed her eyes, leaned her forehead against the warm glass and thought of Michael. Her heart swelled with the memory of the image of his face and the feel of his lips when he had kissed her. She loved him, desperately and completely, and she had betrayed his love by wallowing in heartbreak for the past ten days and praying desperately that he would keep his promise to rescue her one day. She could not imagine anything more threatening than her guardian's wicked plan, and wondered if somehow, there would be one shining moment when Michael would appear and carry her back to Lawne Haven even though he believed she had returned to Collier.

Being dependent on others was a lifelong weakness disguised as faith, and she faced it square in the eye today and rejected it. When she had lost her parents and her guardian had sent her to Collier, she had waited for endless days and nights for someone to come for her. In total honesty, she could forgive herself because at the time, she had been a small child.

Now that she had reached maturity, however, she fared no better. When her guardian had forced her to leave her village last February, she had once again waited for someone—her Elders and their lawyers or the courts—to determine her fate until Michael challenged her with his love and Nora befriended her. When JoHannah's guardian had forced her back to her birth home for the second time, she had retreated into self-pity, expecting the Heavenly Father to work a miracle on her behalf.

Not any longer.

Through prayer, she realized that God had created her with a good, logical mind, a strong will, and a deep and abiding love for Him. He would guide her and protect her—if she had the courage to fight for her heart's desire.

Buoyed by determination to control her own fate and find her way back into Michael's arms, she paced around the observatory. There was only one way to stop Bathrick from forcing her into marriage to a total stranger. Somehow she had to find that vile affidavit and destroy it.

She was absolutely certain he kept it with him on the estate so he would be able to flaunt it in her face if she even intimated she would try to defy him by refusing to marry the man he had chosen for her. Obviously, she could not find the affidavit by remaining closeted in her room, which is where she had kept herself from the minute she had arrived. There were seventeen days left until her birthday, and she would use each and every hour they contained to search for the affidavit, find it, and destroy it.

Unwilling to waste another precious moment, she hurried back to her room and dressed as quickly as her trembling hands would permit. As expected, Leila had ordered all of JoHannah's clothing from Collier to be burned, and this time, she had watched the servants feed every item into the fire built for that very purpose in the hearth in JoHannah's room.

Before JoHannah went downstairs, she walked over to her bed and pulled out a small bit of cloth, tied closed with a ribbon, that she had hidden beneath her mattress. She carried her little relic containing the ashes of her cap and gowns to the open window, untied the ribbon, and watched as a light summer breeze lifted the ashes and carried them away.

If she found the affidavit in time, she knew exactly what she would do with it. She would burn it, one page at a time, until every pernicious lie had been reduced to ashes.

Her plan now set, she left her room and made her way quietly down the stairs. While the rest of the household slept, she would begin her search of the house. With God's love to guide her and Michael's love to sustain her, she pressed forward.

By the following afternoon, JoHannah was worried that Bathrick had not hidden the affidavit anywhere in the house. She had searched nearly every room, certain he would never keep it in any of the Bathricks' private sleeping rooms where a servant might find it. That left the most obvious room: her guardian's study. Locked to most of the servants, the study was the one room she would not be able to search without finding someone other than Bathrick who might have a key. By carefully disguising her interest to the servants as purely proprietary now that she was about to assume her duties as the mistress of the estate, JoHannah had learned that none of them had been entrusted with a key to the study.

She moved on to the next plausible possibility—that either Leila or Cassandra had a key. In an attempt to learn if that might be the case, she rejoined them for meals. Tolerating her guardian's sneers, Leila's rudeness, and Cassandra's taunts, JoHannah listened to them carefully as they talked to one another. She learned little except they were leaving soon, exactly as she had surmised. Unfortunately, the topic of the study or the existence of duplicate keys had never come up.

In early afternoon of the second day of her plan, she followed the sound of Cassandra's voice and found the girl in the foyer just outside the front sitting room.

Gleefully flitting along five opened trunks, Cassandra directed two maids to put clothing they held in their arms into different trunks. "No. The silk ball gown goes in the first trunk," she whined. She took the gown out of the middle trunk and packed it correctly herself.

As shocked by the abundant display of ostentatious clothing as she was by seeing Cassandra's trunks being packed, JoHannah felt her pulse begin to race. "Are . . . are you leaving already?" she asked quietly as she approached.

Cassandra's face lit with a smile. "Mama and I are leaving on the hour. Just thinking about our trip makes me giddy." Her eyes began to dance. "It's too bad you can't join us. If you're a good little wife, maybe your husband will decide to take you on a trip, too."

How odd, JoHannah thought. Leila and Cassandra were taking a trip? JoHannah had never given that possibility a thought. She had expected them to be resettling into a new home. Nevertheless, no matter where they were going for a holiday, they would have to settle down at some point. Was her guardian staying behind to find a new home, or had he already done so? Noting Cassandra's unusual friendliness, JoHannah tried to engage her in further conversation in hopes of learning whether or not the girl had a key to the study. "I think I've done enough traveling. I'm anxious to settle in one place and stay there."

Bubbling with excitement, Cassandra shooed the servants back upstairs for more apparel and turned toward JoHannah. "Aren't you going to ask me where we're going?"

Caught off guard, JoHannah fidgeted with her skirts. "I . . . I didn't think it was any of my concern. I didn't want to seem impertinent."

"Still the same meek little Shaker." Cassandra giggled, and her curls shook like tiny springs as she looked over JoHannah's shoulder. She bent closer to JoHannah, a conspiratorial gleam of delight in her eyes. "Promise you won't tell Papa if I share something with you? I'll simply burst if I don't tell someone."

Nodding, JoHannah held her breath and wondered why Cassandra would confide in her at all.

Cassandra paused as if she was about to change her mind. In the next heartbeat, she grinned. "We're going to

Europe! Papa and Mama are taking me on a grand tour. London. Paris. Rome. Can you imagine?'' She swirled around, caught up in her own excitement. ''There will be balls and soirees, the theater, and dozens of titled bachelors. Mama has written to her cousin Maude, and she's promised to introduce me to earls and dukes, and there's even an Italian prince with his very own castle!''

She looked at JoHannah and sighed dramatically. ''But I know none of this interests you, especially now that you're almost a married woman. I can hardly wait to see how many offers Papa gets for my hand.''

Blinking back her surprise, JoHannah stifled a gasp. ''You're . . . you're going to Europe with your mother to find a husband?''

Cassandra looked at JoHannah like she had been born without a brain. ''Papa is going with us,'' the girl insisted. ''We're leaving for Boston today to secure our passage. As soon as you're married, Papa will join us, and we'll all sail to London together.''

She narrowed her gaze and stared at JoHannah, who had been rendered speechless. ''You don't expect me to marry anyone around here, do you? Mama said European noblemen simply adore beautiful American women, and I intend to marry the richest man I meet. I'll be a lady or a duchess or even a princess, and poor Papa won't ever have to work for anyone else again. We'll all live in luxury in Europe while you . . .''

Cassandra lowered her voice. ''You aren't too jealous, are you? Jealousy and envy are sins, I think. Tsk. Tsk. I'd hate to think you were going to lock yourself back in your room and flog yourself because you wish you could marry into nobility like me.''

Understanding that Cassandra's apparent openness was just another ploy to poke fun at her, JoHannah smiled sadly. ''I feel so sorry for you.''

Cassandra's face contorted into a scowl. "*You* feel sorry for *me*?" Her laugh was brittle. "At least I'll be able to choose the man I marry instead of being auctioned off like a prize breeding mare!"

Too shocked to draw a breath, JoHannah felt faint. "Auctioned?" she whispered as her entire body went cold. "What are you talking about?"

Grabbing JoHannah's arm, Cassandra pulled her into the sitting room and pointed at the wall over the mantel. "You remember that portrait, don't you?"

JoHannah's gaze locked on the portrait that hung on the wall. Expecting to see the painting of her with her parents, she was totally unprepared to find the portrait Richard had painted of her last winter. Dressed in the vulgar and decadent lavender gown, her own image stared back at her. She pulled away from Cassandra and turned to leave the room.

Cassandra blocked her way. "You'll be there to watch it all, you know. Papa sent the portrait on tour up and down the East Coast. Only the wealthiest men have been invited to attend the auction. The highest bidder for your portrait gains far more than an ordinary painting," she spewed. Her eyes narrowed with wicked pleasuere. "He wins the right to marry you and control your fortune, and Papa gets to keep the bid. He'll have enough funds to keep us in grand style in Europe to attract the attention of titled men, any one of whom I'll choose to marry."

Trembling so hard her teeth chattered, JoHannah's mind refused to function beyond outrage. Now she completely understood why Bathrick had refused to let her marry Michael and had written the affidavit. Even if she had decided last February to accept her guardian's plans for her to marry, she would never have submitted to being auctioned off to the highest bidder! He had had the affidavit prepared to guarantee she would not be able to run away and disappear.

Evil and sin had taken many forms during JoHannah's stay in the World, but she had never fully understood the depths of her guardian's wickedness or Cassandra's depravity until this very moment. Cassandra was more than a vain and self-centered young woman. She was as twisted and demented as her father, and JoHannah knew immediately that Bathrick would never have trusted Cassandra with a key to the study.

By telling JoHannah about the auction more than two weeks ahead of time, Cassandra guaranteed JoHannah far more anguish than Bathrick had intended by hiding his horrid little finale to his scheme. JoHannah would have been better off staying in her room, the weak side of her chastised, but her ever-faithful heart encouraged her to be undaunted and unafraid.

She had faced the lion of her heart and tamed him. Could she slay the dragon that breathed fire into her dreams and turned them into ashes? Or was she as easily frightened as Nora's silly goats?

Refusing to be baited or harassed further, she stepped around Cassandra and slowly walked back to the observatory to plan her next move. Now doubtful that Bathrick would have given his wife a key either, JoHannah reluctantly admitted to herself that her guardian held the only key to the study. She had to get that key!

Not such a large feat, she thought, compared to the miracle it would take to survive being auctioned off to the highest bidder—if she failed.

She focused all of her thoughts on Michael to give her courage and dismissed the threat of the impending auction as a nightmare too awful to even consider. If she could spend a little time alone in the observatory, maybe she could think of a way past Bathrick and the servants, pick open the lock to his study, and find the affidavit—without getting caught.

The opportunity to have time to safely pick the lock to Bathrick's study came later that very afternoon. With an unobscured view of the estate from the observatory, including the winding road that led from a gate in the wrought-iron fence that surrounded the property, JoHannah watched the coach carrying Leila and Cassandra to Boston leave shortly after four o'clock. A wagon carrying a host of trunks followed behind. With the window curtains in the coach pulled back to let in air, their forms were clearly visible—and so was her guardian.

Evidently, Leila and Cassandra were going to travel by stagecoach to Boston, and Bathrick was escorting them to town. JoHannah watched the coach and wagon as they stopped at the main gate, and a servant stationed there opened it to let the small caravan pass through. Once they disappeared from view, she hurried down the winding staircase, rushed through the sewing room to her own room, checking her hair while she ran. Satisfied that the hairpins were still in place, she used the front staircase to make her way to Bathrick's study on the first floor.

The servants were nowhere to be seen or heard, and JoHannah assumed they were also taking advantage of the Bathricks' departure. Slipping a pin out of her hair, she poked one end into the keyhole and jiggled it. Nervous perspiration dotted her upper lip as she worked the pin in and out then side to side with one hand while she twisted the door knob with the other without success.

The sound of approaching voices sent her scurrying past a long table and back to the staircase where she stood at the bottom landing and fussed with her skirts. Out of their direct line of vision, JoHannah listened to them without fear of being seen. She recognized the voice of a downstairs maid, Anne, arguing with another servant, Ralph, who apparently had just returned from town with the day's post.

"I have to give 'em right to Mr. Bathrick. He'll fire me sure as Sunday is comin' if I leave 'em in the hall," he snapped.

"He won't be back till after supper," Anne taunted, her voice harsh. "What are you going to do? Stand here and hold them? Put them in his study."

"I can't," he answered testily. "The door's locked, and the man wouldn't trust me with the key."

JoHannah held very still and listened hard. Anne and Ralph, however, lowered their voices, and all JoHannah could now make out were an occasional few words that did not help her cause. Eventually, she heard their footsteps as they walked back the same way they had come. JoHannah slipped back up the stairs, her disappointment echoing in her slow footsteps.

It was clear to her now that any attempt to pick the lock was doomed to failure. There were simply too many servants about to give her enough time to work at the lock without being discovered. Once Bathrick returned, it would be virtually impossible to escape his notice.

Retreating to the privacy of her room, she closed the door and threw the bolt. She walked over to the window and dropped to her knees. Bowing her head in prayer, warm sunshine bathed her with evidence of God's love.

Long after the sun had traveled on its path to light the other side of the world, she was still on her knees, praying for inspiration to find a way into the study.

Inspiration, sadly, that never came.

Chapter 26

From the other side of the room, Michael stared at JoHannah's portrait. Seething in a haze of hot red fury, he resisted the powerful urge to strangle Bathrick and watch his eyes bulge as he struggled for his last breath. The sorry excuse for a man deserved to die very, very slowly and infinitely more painfully, he decided without a qualm.

Drawing on his experiences at sea, Michael envisioned a number of horrible ends for Eleazer Bathrick, but even if Michael used every one simultaneously, the murderous thirst for vengeance that parched every pore of his body would not be quenched.

Calling on every square inch of self-control he possessed, he held himself in check. The muscles in his entire body tensed until he nearly lost all sense of feeling, and his hands clenched into fists of steel. His left leg ached so badly he could not avoid favoring it as he limped closer to the portrait of JoHannah that hung over the mantel.

Ignoring Bathrick, who wisely stepped to the side, Michael locked his gaze on her painted image. His heart nearly stopped beating. Captured for all the world to see, Jo-Hannah's beautiful shoulders and full, perfect breasts were bared by a revealing lavender gown that accentuated the striking color of her eyes. Her hair, totally exposed to view, was coiffed in the latest style, and it glistened with red highlights like it had been dipped in a sunset.

JoHannah.

Pain sliced through his chest, and he gulped down a lump of misery that made it impossible to take a deep breath. He felt the humiliation and the shame that must have made her spirit cry out for mercy while she had been forced to sit for endless hours as a man painted her image. For a woman who had been strictly raised to view her body as a vessel of sexual temptation and sinfulness, he did not know how she had survived the experience. His regret deepened when he thought about all the times he had teased her with compliments.

He narrowed his gaze and studied her eyes. The artist had captured the essence of her soul in miraculous eyes the color of spring lilacs. Deep in their depths, he saw that faraway look he recognized immediately as the one she had used when she retreated from the world she found so confusing and escaped back to Collier—if only in her mind.

To imagine that Bathrick actually had put JoHannah's portrait on display in exhibitions along the eastern seaboard as part of his nefarious scheme turned Michael's heart to stone. To think Bathrick had the unmitigated gall to conduct an auction where the highest bidder took possession of JoHannah as well as her portrait brought bile to the back of Michael's throat.

He turned away from the portrait and glared at Bathrick. "I'll rot in hell before I let you get away with this," he snarled.

Bathrick smiled benevolently. "An interesting thought. Predicated on a number of false assumptions," he said calmly as he took a seat and steepled his hands as his elbows braced on the side of the chair.

Surprised by the man's arrogance, Michael nodded stiffly. "Such as?"

"First, that I give your threat any credence. Second, there's nothing you can do to stop the auction. You're welcome to participate, of course. Guests are invited to arrive at ten o'clock on the eve of JoHannah's birthday, August fourteenth. The auction begins at eleven thirty. I'm expecting a starting bid of five thousand dollars, although I daresay that's a mere pittance. Verbal response to invitations has been very positive, and indications are that the bidding will go much higher."

He flashed Michael a deprecating smile. "A bit too costly for you, I fear. It's my understanding the only asset you claim is your land. Quite desirable acreage, though. It would fetch a handsome price rather easily."

Gritting his teeth, Michael snorted, furious that his holdings had been investigated. "Lawne Haven has been in my family for generations. If you think for one minute—"

"I don't have to think about it at all," Bathrick retorted. "I only have to accept the highest offer and award the delectable prize. Quite simply, Mr. Lawne, there's nothing you can do to stop me. If you're set on marrying the girl, put the title to your land in as a bid. If it's the highest offer, you have my word as a man of—"

"Your word?" Michael spat. "There's no guarantee you won't reject any offer you deem unacceptable. You're a veritable monster disguised as a man."

Bathrick glowered. "Gordon Shipley, the manager of the bank that holds JoHannah's funds, will be here to open the bids and certify the highest bid as the winner, just to assure all participants that the auction will be valid. The minister will conduct the ceremony at precisely midnight. It may gall your soul, Lawne, but as you can see, I am the man in charge, aren't I?"

"Not for long," Michael said icily. "I'm going to tear

this house down, brick by brick and timber by timber if I have to, but I'm going to find JoHannah and take her home with me. Your bloody auction be damned!'' He spun on his heels and stormed toward the door.

''She won't go.''

''Like hell she won't,'' Michael growled without missing a step. He was nearly out into the foyer when the sound of Bathrick's snickering laughter brought him to a stunned halt. He swirled around and saw Bathrick still sitting calmly in his seat. ''What have you done with her?'' he demanded as a fearsome wave of nausea rumbled in his stomach. ''Where is she? I swear on my mother's grave, if you've done anything to her—''

''You really must harness your temper and your vivid imagination,'' Bathrick cautioned.

Michael wanted to rip the man's tongue out of his mouth and feed it back to him.

''Sit down. I wouldn't be stupid enough to damage my grand prize now, would I?''

On second thought, castration appealed to Michael's more vindictive side. Just raising his voice had sent many a burly seasoned seaman scampering for safety, but Bathrick had not even flinched during the whole ugly match of wills. Pausing to study the man closer, Michael realized that JoHannah's guardian was overly confident and decidedly unruffled.

A sense of overwhelming dread doused the fire burning in Michael's mind, and he waited until cool reason prevailed. Bathrick obviously had anticipated any and all complications, and Michael was more than obsessed to find out what nefarious plan Bathrick had devised to stop anyone— even JoHannah—from spoiling his grand scheme.

With the exception of the one storm that had almost cost him his ship, Michael had battled nature often enough to be able to second-guess and outwit most men. Stonewalled at the moment, he called Bathrick's bluff. "You have one minute. Talk."

Shrugging, Bathrick pulled a document of some sort out of his pocket and held it out to Michael. "I'm a patient and generous man. Take all the time you need."

Michael walked over and grabbed the papers out of Bathrick's hand. It took less than thirty seconds before he realized he had underestimated Bathrick's depravity. Michael's heart pounded into a deafening roar in his ears, and he forced himself to slow down and read every despicable word.

Learning of the auction had engulfed him with a haze of red fury. The affidavit, obviously a copy, threatened the very existence of the village where JoHannah had grown up, and he knew she would never allow anything to jeopardize her former home. His fury turned white, hot enough to melt diamonds or incinerate hell itself.

He tore the affidavit into shreds and threw them to the floor. "Bastard," he hissed, and his eyes narrowed into slits of hatred so intense it burned straight through to his soul. Bathrick had fashioned the only weapon that would have left JoHannah no choice but to agree to marry Satan himself to spare her former community. "I assume you have enough gall to file the original affidavit with the courts."

"Of course," Bathrick said quietly. "It's safely hidden, I assure you."

"Why don't you just take JoHannah's whole damned inheritance and leave her alone? Why go to all this bother?"

Bathrick looked stunned. "I would never cheat the girl. I have my reputation to uphold, and I certainly would have to explain to the court—"

"Reputation?" Michael shook his head, unable to follow the man's twisted logic. Outmaneuvered for the moment, but definitely not defeated, he squared his shoulders. "I'd like to see JoHannah."

"For a sweet farewell? How touching." Bathrick rose and straightened his wrinkled waistcoat. "I'm a determined man, but I'm not totally without a heart. I don't see any harm in a short visit, especially now that we understand one another. Chaperoned, of course. Wait here. I'll bring her downstairs."

Bathrick left the room, and Michael paced back and forth while he waited. He thought he understood now why JoHannah had lied to Nora about returning to Collier, but he still did not know for certain what JoHannah's answer to his proposal would have been. Even if that seemed a moot point, under the present circumstances, he needed to know. He needed to hear her tell him that she loved him and wanted to marry him, and then he would stop short of nothing less than murder to make her his wife.

Did that include giving up Lawne Haven? Did he love her enough to sacrifice land that had been in his family for more than two hundred years? Did he have the right to sell Lawne Haven when he had promised Avery that Abigail and Jane would be able to return home, and had even sent Newland to Kentucky to make sure they did?

Tragically torn between love and duty, Michael faced a dilemma so rife with inequity his heart literally stopped beating in his chest.

Feeling guilty for his selfish concerns, he turned his thoughts to JoHannah. What if she had decided to return to Collier instead of marrying him? If he truly loved her, would he have found the strength to let her go? He braced to a halt and raked his hand through his hair. If JoHannah did not want to marry him, how could she survive marriage to a perfect stranger? Would he still fight Bathrick to see her free to live her life as a Believer?

It was one thing to consider abandoning his dedication

to preserving family traditions for the sake of marrying the woman he loved. It was quite another matter to give up everything he had ever dreamed of having and sacrifice it all for the sake of a woman who did not return his love.

No matter how he tried to examine the situation, he could not think beyond losing JoHannah. When he heard the swish of skirts and soft footsteps, he turned around to face the doorway.

JoHannah walked ahead of her guardian to meet the mysterious caller who waited for her in the sitting room. Her thoughts tumbling with trepidation and curiosity, she took one step into the room, and her mind walked straight into total shock. "Michael!"

Standing tall and rigid, he held unearthly still. She recognized controlled anger in the jut of his chin and the hard line of his jaw. She saw frustration in his tightly clenched fists. The bleak expression in his eyes told her he knew about the auction. She dropped her gaze, saw small shreds of paper on the floor at his feet, and her heartbeat slowed to the sad rhythm of a dirge.

She lifted her gaze and searched Michael's face, trying to decide what to do or say to him that would ease his pain. She wanted to run into his arms, hold him and tell him about Bathrick's bluff—one she hoped to call by finding and destroying the wicked document, a copy of which her guardian must have shown to Michael. With Bathrick in the room, however, Michael might be so angry that the slim thread checking his self-control might snap.

She could deny her heart's desire and tell Michael she did not love him. She could try to assure him that she had agreed to an arranged marriage of her own free will, but she loved him too much to be able to hide it from him.

She could lie and tell him she wanted to go back to Collier, accepting her fate as penance for succumbing to the temptations of the flesh and failing God's divine test of her faith. She would never be able to convince him.

Her heart began to pound as the love in her heart for Michael grew into longing that wrapped around her soul. This might be the last time she ever saw the man who had captured her heart, and it was too precious a moment to waste.

Ever so slowly, she started to walk forward.

So did he.

When he opened his arms, she slid into his embrace. "Michael," she whispered as their heads leaned together and her lips brushed against his hair.

He held her tight. "JoHannah. My precious JoHannah," he groaned as he molded her body against his powerful frame as though trying to capture a fleeting mirage. "I can't believe—"

"Hush," she murmured. "It's not done yet. Just hold me a little while," she pleaded, treasuring the unexpected gift of feeling his heart beating against her own.

"I can't let this happen to you," he whispered. He pressed a kiss to her temple before resting his cheek against her own. In the next heartbeat, he tensed, lifted his head, and gently set her away from him.

Confused, she turned her head and followed the hard line of his gaze. Realizing her guardian was standing in the hallway observing them, a wicked voyeur cloaked in the guise of propriety, she sighed as she turned around to face him.

Michael stepped alongside her and reached out to take her hand. Bathrick cocked his head and looked directly at Michael. "As you can see, the girl is perfectly unharmed. I'd like to invite you to stay for some refreshment, but I'm reluctant to give you any advantage over the other bidders." His gaze switched to JoHannah. "You may go back to your room now."

She laced her fingers with Michael's and tilted her chin

up ever so slightly. "Michael and I have a lot to discuss."

Bathrick shook his head. "Some sort of desperate escape plan? Don't waste your time—or mine. Go to your room."

Michael pulled at her hand. "I'll be back," he reassured her. "We'll talk—"

"No." She started walking toward the door and tugged Michael along with her. She stopped in front of her guardian and took a deep breathe. "Michael and I are going to spend some time together. Alone. You have one very good reason to make you confident I would no sooner run away to foil your scheme than practice Satanic rituals. I want to speak to Michael, and considering the few demands I've made on you, I expect you to agree. If not, file the affidavit if you dare. I'm sure any one of the bidders would be fascinated to learn his future wife was about to become embroiled in a scandalous court battle."

Bathrick paled, and the mole on his cheek started to twitch. "Ten minutes," he grumbled.

She smiled and looked at Michael, noting a look of surprise at her audacity. There was only one place she wanted to be with Michael. It defied World convention for an unmarried woman to be with a male caller beyond the public rooms on the first floor, in direct opposition to Shaker tradition where men and woman lived and worked together, restrained from sin by their faith. "I'd like to show you something," she murmured and led him from the room.

Holding hands with JoHannah in the observatory, Michael stared out at the vast expanse of fenced property JoHannah would soon inherit. Her future husband would command more wealth than some European monarchs, Michael realized as the list of her parents' holdings ran through his mind. He had no doubt that her wealth alone would attract a fair number of bidders to the auction.

For JoHannah to marry him meant she would have to

leave this estate for a house at Lawne Haven that would easily fit inside the glass-topped mansion, because he would never live anywhere but Lawne Haven. While her wealth could provide servants to spare her chores of any kind, life at Lawne Haven would be irrevocably changed.

He looked at JoHannah and studied her as she stood in the observatory. Perched high on the roof in a glass cage, she was like an exotic bird who survived captivity by living with the illusion of freedom.

Yet hadn't he survived—for years—the same way? It suddenly occurred to him that his obsession with the sea and his thirst for a life of adventure at the helm of his ship had been nothing more than an illusion, a rather ironic thought when he recalled how glibly he had told JoHannah that her life at Collier had been an illusion.

He put his arm around her shoulders, wishing he could fly away with her and disappear behind the billowing white clouds that dotted the brilliant blue sky.

Caught up in emotions that swirled around them, neither of them had spoken yet, and he was reluctant to say anything that would break the sheer miracle of being with her again. However surprisingly assertive she had been with her guardian, Michael knew that their time together was not unlimited. "Tell me what you're thinking about," he urged, giving her the opportunity to speak about what was troubling her most.

"You," she whispered as she laid her head on his shoulder. "I was thinking about you. We never really had a chance to say good-bye."

He swallowed hard. "My horse pulled up lame after an unexpected delay in Hillsboro. I went to Collier looking for you," he murmured, regretting the false charges he had filed against her more than ever. Just the thought of what he had done put him in a category so close to Bathrick that shudders ripped through his heart.

"You promised to let me go," she said softly.

"No, I promised to court you until you agreed to marry me," he countered, reluctant to press her further and dreading to hear the words that had haunted his nightmares. He had to know if she wanted to marry him because if she did, he would find a way—legal or illegal—to stop Bathrick.

She pulled from his embrace and stood in front of him, blocking any view but of her. She put her hands on the sides of his face. "Go back to Lawne Haven, Michael. You are a good man who will give Abigail and Jane a good home at Lawne Haven . . . where they belong."

Hope sprang in his heart. "Where do you belong, Jo-Hannah?"

Her eyes filled with tears. "It doesn't matter now."

"It does to me. Just say the words I've been waiting to hear for months, and I'll—"

She touched her lips to his. "Just one kiss," she whispered as she brushed her lips tenderly across his bottom lip. "Just once kiss before you leave."

He pulled her into his arms and captured her lips. He teased their full perfection with his lips as she melted in his arms. Soft and full, her breasts pressed against his chest, and his heart began to beat so fast he thought it would take wing.

Tenderly. Sweetly. He courted her lips until they parted. Hungrily, he devoured the sweet recesses of her mouth until his body tingled with longing . . . such powerful longing he could hardly breathe. Desire, pure and raw, claimed his body. The rapturous joy of love filled his soul.

Breathing hard, he ended their kiss and gazed into her passion-filled eyes. "Tell me, JoHannah. Tell me you want to marry me."

JoHannah dropped her gaze and listened to the sound of her own heartbeat. She loved Michael, and she knew him well enough to be very certain that if she whispered the words he longed to hear, he would never find a moment's peace until he had done everything in his power to free her from Bathrick's control. When he failed—or committed a crime which would land him in prison—he would hear the echo of her words every minute of every day of his life. He would suffer the added anguish of knowing that she carried another man's name, warmed his bed, and birthed his children.

Love, true and abiding love, meant sacrifice.

Unless she was able to find the awful affidavit, her guardian would proceed with the auction, and Michael would be forced to participate. She loved Michael enough to want to spare him the anguish of having to choose between Lawne Haven and her—an impossible dilemma no man should ever have to face.

She turned from him and stared out the wall of glass. "I'm sorry. You should go, Michael."

He turned her around and tilted her chin up to stare into her eyes. "I love you. I'll always love you. Only you," he whispered.

The declaration she had yearned to hear was bittersweet balm for her wounded heart. "God will guide me along the path I must take. Trust in His wisdom," she pleaded, torn between giving Michael any hope that they would someday be together and facing the rest of her life without him if she failed to find the affidavit.

His eyes churned with agonizing pain. "I love you. And until I hear you tell me you feel otherwise—"

She closed her eyes and caught a cry in her throat before it escaped. "Please go."

He kissed her forehead, his lips lingering against her flesh. "I still intend to keep my promise," he whispered.

Puzzled, she looked into his eyes.

"To come twice to the rescue," he said gently.

She dropped her gaze as a single tear trickled down her

face and doubts about her ability to find and destroy the affidavit filled her mind. If she failed, there would be no shining moment when he could save her without sacrificing everything he owned, and she could not live with him for the rest of her life knowing the price their love had cost him. Eventually the love he had for her would harden into resentment, and she could not bear to see their love destroyed.

The sound of his retreating footsteps faded into a silent echo she heard only in her heart, and with every breath she took, she vowed to find the affidavit and destroy it. In the light of the fire that burned them into ashes, she would have her shining moment—one that would guide her along the path that led straight back to Michael's arms.

Chapter 27

*S*now-dusted trees surrounded Michael. Through stark bare limbs, he could see straight through the trees into the depths of the monochrome forest with the only splash of color in occasional clumps of evergreens. In the silence of nature entombed in winter, he listened to the dull thud of his own heartbeat.

Cold in body and spirit, he plunged ahead. His gaze methodically scoured the barren landscape for a hint of her presence. A swish of movement. A footprint in the snow. Something. Anything.

"JoHannah!"

His voice carried his cry in the frigid wind, and the echo of his desperation shouted back at him.

"JoHannah." Tossing and turning, Michael whispered her name and slipped his hand beneath his pillow. He wrapped his fingers around the lace cap she had left behind and clutched it in his fist as the nightmare receded. Cold reality drenched his sweat-covered body, and he shivered as he sat up in bed.

Long days of felling timber that had left him physically exhausted had failed to ease his bitter disappointment and angry frustration. Nightmares replaced the dreams that had given him hope that JoHannah would someday be by his side.

He threw back the covers and dressed for another day. He carefully folded the lace cap and put it into his pocket, looking forward to felling another series of trees, each symbolizing the bastard who had come between JoHannah and himself. With each swing, as his ax hit the mark, he could almost hear Bathrick groaning in agony. He envisioned the lumber that would be milled from the timber as the narrow planks of Bathrick's coffin.

He did not know when it would happen or how he would do it, but someday he would destroy Bathrick for what he had done. If symbolic vengeance temporarily satisfied his lust for retribution, he knew nothing would ever ease the ache in his heart for the woman he loved. Sweet, gentle JoHannah. Memories of their last meeting sharpened into focus, and he was amazed again by her transformation. Docile and submissive to the point of sainthood when he had first met her, she had learned to share her thoughts and speak her mind with him. But he had never seen her as assertive as she had been when she stood her ground against her guardian and insisted on speaking to Michael alone.

"It isn't done yet."

He repeated her words out loud. Was her newfound sense of self a desperate defense against the inevitable moment when she would have to capitulate to her guardian? Or was she trying to tell Michael she had discovered a flaw in Bathrick's plan—one she intended to unravel herself?

"There is no flaw," he gritted as he made his way downstairs in the gentle light of dawn. Unless he was willing to go to the auction and bid the title to his land, JoHannah would marry another man. She knew how devoted Michael was to Lawne Haven because he had told her more about himself than he had ever shared with anyone.

Yet even when she knew in her heart there was no hope

that he would be able to bid for her hand, she had thought
of him—only him. She refused to utter the words he longed
to hear: I love you. The three simple words would have
been branded in his heart, binding him to her forever and
forcing him to choose between his land and his heart.

But she did not know he had seen her love for him shining like a distant star in the galaxy of her soul when he
gazed into the depths of her violet eyes. He had tasted love
on her lips and felt it when her heart beat against his when
he held her in his arms.

She loved him.

And the only thing standing between them was Lawne
Haven. For a man who had fought to claim her as his wife,
the most bitter irony of all was that unless he had the courage to turn his back on traditions that had anchored his very
existence, he would be the one to turn away from his own
proposal.

No key. No affidavit. No Michael. Only three days remained before the eve of her birthday when the auction
would take place. Recognizing desperation as a useful emotion, JoHannah garnered her courage and slipped outside.

Cloaked in darkness and dressed in a pair of men's trousers and shirt she had snatched furtively from the drying
line, she inched her way across the veranda and down the
steps. Sin is often disguised as good intentions, her conscience warned. She had been deceitful, defiant, and had
resorted to thievery.

She shoved aside any guilt and moved forward. She had
planned every move down to the last detail, but she had
not imagined her heart would be beating so fast, her limbs
would be shaking so hard, or her stockinged footsteps
would sound so loud.

She paused to rest a moment and leaned against the far
side of a tree, out of sight in case anyone should look out

a window. At two o'clock in the morning? The servants were long abed, and Bathrick slept at the other end of the house.

She put her hand into a trouser pocket. Satisfied her small tools were still there, she worked her way down the path that ran along the side of the house. She stopped at the double windows to Bathrick's study and prayed the Heavenly Father would understand her motives. She stepped from the path and edged between two rose bushes. Thorns pricked her thighs, but she bit her lips into silence until she was beyond them.

Hugging the side of the house, she made her way to a thick bush, grabbed the stool she had hidden behind it, and carried it back to the window. With her feet planted on the stool, she pressed her body against the window whose lower edge was now just below her waist. The interior of the study was hidden from her view by heavy drawn drapes.

After slipping her hand into a glove, she took a jagged rock from her pocket, praying that the drape would help to muffle the sound of breaking glass. Even if it did not, she had every hope that by the time one of the servants alerted Bathrick and he stumbled downstairs with the key to the study, she would have had enough time to search the room, find the affidavit, and rip the pages up before the door swung open. She was not quite sure what Bathrick would do to her, but with the servants as witnesses, he would be constrained from hurting her . . . at least long enough for her to find a way to escape.

Before fear changed her only recourse, she tapped the windowpane closest to the bolt that locked the two windows closed together. A spider web of cracks mottled the glass. She tapped again until it shattered into a small hole with noise that sounded like a crack of heavy thunder to her ears.

With her gloved hand, she worked shards of broken glass

free and used the rock to encourage more stubborn pieces away. When the hole was large enough for her hand, she reached inside and slid the bolt free. Heart pounding with success, she leaned to the side, swung one window open, and crawled inside.

Too late, she realized she should have brought a candle. The room was pitched in total darkness. She turned to the side, pulled the drapes back, and surveyed the room as well as she could in the meager light from the moon.

Bathrick must have denied the servants entrance to clean. A pile of correspondence littered the top of an ornate wood desk to her left, but the candle she needed was there as well. A stack of periodicals and newspapers sat on the floor in front of a wall of books. A tray with a half-empty decanter of hard liquor and several used glasses rested on a table next to an upholstered chair in front of a hearth still dirtied with ashes.

She cocked an ear, dismayed by the sound of distant whispers and running footsteps. Without wasting another precious second, she managed to light the candle, and with shaking hands, she started to rummage through the drawers of the desk. No affidavit. She sorted through the correspondence, her heart beginning to race with failure. No affidavit.

Refusing to admit defeat, even when she heard the sound of footsteps outside the window and in the hall just on the other side of the door, she started pulling books from the shelves on the wall, quickly searching each one to see if Bathrick had hidden the affidavit there.

She worked frantically, tossing aside volume after volume until tears of frustration blurred her vision. She paused to wipe them away. The fateful turn of a key in the locked door sounded like a death knell, and she froze in place as the door swung open and light poured into the room.

"Trying to find something interesting to read?"

The sound of her guardian's sneering voice sent chills down her spine. Fear dripped from her heart and pooled in her feet. As she turned around, she caught her guardian's image in a gilt-framed mirror and saw the affidavit clutched in one of his fists. A shroud of hopelessness descended slowly over her heart and soul.

She had failed.

Oh, Michael!

The only shining moment now would come on the day of her final judgment when the divine light of heaven shined on her face and fulfilled the promise of an eternity filled with joy after a lifetime of abject loneliness that would have marked all the days of her life in the world . . . without Michael.

Michael reached the landing at the end of the skid road and walked past logs stacked and ready to be skidded to the sawmill. He and Dolan had worked from sunup to sundown for the past week. Yet another day of hard physical work that would tax his body lay ahead, but he was consumed with grief for the empty years that stretched before him without JoHannah by his side.

All for the sake of the land that surrounded him—land that now seemed desolate even though it was covered with thick forest abounding with wildlife. Try as he might, he could find no way to thwart Bathrick without giving up title to this land, and even then there was no guarantee Michael's bid would be the highest one. His promise to JoHannah to come twice to her rescue was like a crown of thorns that pierced his heart. He had never imagined the price to keep his promise would be one he could not afford to pay.

He followed the sound of an ax hitting wood, turning east to look for Dolan who had already started the day's work by making an undercut on a tree they would fell together. The dull grating sound of a saw cutting through timber quickened his steps. The double-handled saw required two men, and even with Dolan's size and girth, Michael knew it was impossible for Dolan to use the saw alone.

Michael finally caught sight of Dolan and stared hard at the man on the other end of the saw. As he approached, keeping a steady gaze on Brady O'Neal, Michael glared at Dolan. "Hired yourself a new helper?" he asked coldly, dismissing the scowl on Dolan's face and turning to glare at O'Neal.

"If you're gonna make up for lost time, you need to fell a lot more timber than you and me can saw in a day. Figured you could do the undercuttin'. O'Neal and me can fell the timber, and while we move on to the next one, you can skid it to the landing."

O'Neal wiped the sweat from his brow. "I'd appreciate the work, but if you'd rather . . . I'll just head on home."

Images of the children's piqued faces swam before Michael's eyes, and he remembered JoHannah's defense of the man Michael had nearly killed in a fit of rage. She had accepted O'Neal's apology. Could he do anything less than help the man feed his family? "I can't pay wages until I get a settlement from the sawmill," he said firmly.

O'Neal's face broke into a grin. "I can wait."

Michael turned his gaze to the trunk of the cedar tree and walked to the other side to check the undercut that would direct the tree's fall once Dolan and Brady sawed through. Michael squatted down, studied the angle and height of the undercut, and scanned the surrounding area to gauge where the tree would fall.

He saw immediately that the men were going to have to saw through a large knot that size alone told him would cause problems. He stood up and pointed to the knot. "Got a slight problem here, Dolan. Take a look," he suggested, careful to avoid hurting Dolan's feelings.

Dolan held one end of the saw while stepping closer to Michael. "Trunk's got a knot. We'll cut through it."

"Maybe. It's a lot faster and a whole lot easier to move the undercut," Michael said as he heard the echo of his father's voice teaching him the rudiments of lumbering.

Dolan scowled. "I've got twice your strength. No knot is gonna slow me down. I'm goin' right through it."

Michael chuckled. "Do it your way, then. You always do like to charge right through something instead of working your way around it. Replaced any door frames lately?"

Dolan's face reddened. "Just yesterday. Thought little Thompson had sapped Genny's spirit, but she's finally back in form. That woman's got the most beautiful temper I ever saw," he boasted before nodding to O'Neal and setting back to the task at hand.

Michael stepped back as the men began to work the saw. True to his word, Dolan flexed his muscles and almost single-handedly forged right through the knot like he was sliding a hot knife through cold butter.

"Timber!"

With a creaking shudder, the massive tree fell to earth and the ground literally shook beneath Michael's feet. If only he could fell Bathrick's scheme as easily, he mused as his gaze narrowed, and he found himself lost in thought. He brought JoHannah's image to mind, and he suddenly realized that he had wasted all his time searching for a way around Bathrick instead of facing him head-on—which was exactly the way Michael reacted whenever he was faced with a problem.

He had spent most of his life dodging his own demons where Lawne Haven was concerned. He had spent years at sea studying the skies and anticipating the weather to avoid nature's pitfalls. When JoHannah had first come to Lawne Haven, he had tried to force her to leave to avoid facing the truth: He had fallen in love with her. And when Bathrick devised an impenetrable scheme, Michael had wasted precious days and nights trying to find a way around it.

Torn between his devotion to family tradition and the woman he loved, he knew Bathrick had given Michael no choice but to forsake his land if he wanted to follow his heart and make JoHannah his wife.

A glimmer of hope began to flicker in his soul as Bathrick's words detailing the auction echoed in his mind. A plan, outrageously rudimentary, started to take form in his mind. He had no right to Lawne Haven, and he did not deserve JoHannah's love if he let Bathrick devise a scheme and write all the rules in his own favor.

If what Michael had in mind actually worked, he could keep his land and claim JoHannah as his wife. As his mind literally raced with a thousand details he had yet to consider, he grabbed Dolan's arm. "We're done for the day." He nodded to O'Neal. "Get Dr. Carson and meet us back at Lawne Haven. Dolan, head on home, get Genevieve and the baby, and bring them with you to my house." Grinning, he slapped Dolan on the back. "There's one helluva tree that needs felling, and I'll need your help."

By midday, everyone was seated around the round kitchen table at Lawne Haven. Michael stood behind Nora, his hands planted on her shoulders. She was the only one he had taken into his confidence when he had returned from seeing JoHannah, and she had silently simmered for days at Bathrick's interference in JoHannah's life.

Step by step, he explained to the gathered group Bathrick's perverted scheme down to the last nefarious detail. He answered every question with total honesty and found their affection for JoHannah a balm for his aching heart.

"You're giving up your land?" Dolan's final question brought a hush to the room.

"Not if I can help it," Michael responded. "Not if I can count on your help. All of you," he cautioned. "I intend to beat Bathrick at his own game, but I can't do it alone." He gazed at the faces around the table. "JoHannah's birthday is the fourteenth. The auction will be held two nights from now at her parents' estate which is a full two-day journey. We'd have to leave at first light, and even then, I'm not sure there's enough time."

Dolan stood up and put his hand on his wife's shoulder. "We'll help any way we can."

O'Neal pulled on the end of his scraggly beard. "Can't see how I can help," he said as he got to his feet. "Can't say no, neither."

Michael's gaze rested on the physician.

Dr. Carson stood up and squared shoulders bent with age. "I doubt there's much I can do, but I'll try."

Michael swallowed hard and battled for breath when a lump of gratitude swelled in his throat.

Nora patted his hand. "Tell us what you want us to do."

For the next half hour, Michael hashed out his plan with everyone contributing some helpful idea that had not occurred to him in his rush to action. After agreeing to meet again at dawn, the impromptu meeting ended and his neighbors and friends left for their own homes. He mounted the stairs with Nora, saw her to her room, and stepped inside his own, closing the door behind him.

He packed quickly and stored the ring he had bought for JoHannah inside her cap, which he kept in his trouser pocket. He put the title to Lawne Haven into his travel bag, just in case his plan failed. When he was certain that everything he needed was in the bag, he snapped it closed and set it by the door.

Too pent up with emotion to sleep, he stood at the window and stared out into the night as his promise to rescue JoHannah echoed in his mind. ''One shining moment,'' he whispered, vowing with every beat of his heart that he would keep his promise to rescue her.

Chapter 28

Confined to her room since her attempt to find the affidavit had resulted in an abysmal failure, JoHannah refused to waste the last few hours before the auction in a stupor of despair. She had done her best to stop Bathrick, unaware that he had carried the affidavit on his person to make sure that neither she nor Michael interfered with his scheme. Instead, she took great comfort in knowing that Michael would not be attending the auction because she had denied him the words that would have forced him to choose between his duty to family tradition and his heart: I love you.

Although she believed with all her heart that the Heavenly Father would guide her through tonight's events and give her the courage to face a future without Michael, she was still subject to her own humanity. Her nerves were on edge, her eyes were still a bit puffy from a bout of tears, and a profound sense of loss filled her spirit.

Unable to postpone the inevitable any longer, she knew it was time to prepare for her grand entrance at the auction just before midnight. She stared at the bed where the lavender and lace gown lay neatly pressed to perfection for her appearance tonight, and the shame and humiliation she

had felt when she had posed for her portrait washed over
her again. She wondered what kind of men had been inspired to bid for her portrait and the right to claim her hand
in marriage. Were they libertines captivated by the sinful
display of her body, or were they fortune hunters who
lusted after her inheritance? Would a good and virtuous
man ever bid for a wife he would love and cherish in the
same way he offered for livestock?

Unable to fathom the nature of her future husband without trembling, she turned away and walked toward the bath
Sally had prepared for her. Tears stung her eyes as she
stared at the small lavender petals floating in the water and
inhaled the sweet smell of lilacs that permeated the room.
Unwilling to spoil Sally's excitement earlier when she had
brought the lilac-scented bath scents to JoHannah in an attempt to ease her distress, she had hidden her true reaction
with a tremulous smile.

She untied her silk robe and let it drop to the floor. As
she slid beneath the warm water, poignant and bittersweet
memories of the bath Michael had surprised her with after
returning from the O'Neals' swept over her. As the warm
water lapped at her breasts and caressed her body, she knew
she would never discover the joy of physical intimacy with
the man she loved. Huge tears fell and dropped into the
water. She watched as her teardrops rippled the water and
distorted her reflection, evoking memories of the day at the
creek when she had seen her own reflection next to Michael's.

Would any man be as sensitive or as caring as Michael?
Would any man be as patient with her as she coped with
her fears of the World and showed her the joys of his?
Would any man make her heart beat faster and her body
tingle . . . with just one look? She wiped away her tears and
took a deep breath. Daydreaming about the kind of man
who would be her husband instead of Michael—in a matter

of hours—only made matters worse.

No man would ever be able to take Michael's place in her heart, and if she had any hope of surviving tonight, she had to accept her fate and hope that the Heavenly Father would help her to survive a life without Michael's loving presence.

She began washing her body and concentrated on one task at a time. She would finish her bath and let Sally dry and style her hair before leaving to join the other servants, most of whom had been given the night off. And finally, JoHannah would don the lavender and lace gown she would wear to the auction.

If Bathrick expected her to simper and beg him to reconsider or intended to humiliate her tonight as a final form of punishment for her attempt to find and destroy the affidavit, she had a surprise in store for him. If the men who had come to bid for her portrait thought to sample any of her charms before submitting their bid or to treat her with less respect than she deserved, she would shame them with her stoic behavior.

She had no intention of debasing herself. She would bear the pain of her own loss privately and with dignity. She would hold her head high and conduct herself with stoic self-respect.

For herself.

For Michael.

To prove that her love for him transcended the World, and to prove that she was a woman who was worthy of his love. When the clock struck midnight, she would be forced to step into a new World where she would carry another man's name, but he would never claim her heart . . . because she had already given it to Michael.

Like a band of roving gypsies, Michael and his companions had made a second camp just a few miles from JoHannah's home. More than satisfied that the first phase of his plan had been implemented more easily than any of them had imagined, Michael had declined dinner and had headed off to be alone as the crucial hour of the auction drew near.

From his secluded spot, he could hear the voices of his friends and neighbors as they rehearsed their roles after finishing their meal. Too tied up in knots to sit any longer, he began to pace beneath the shade of a stand of white birch trees as he mentally reviewed every step in the remainder of his plan, looking for possible miscalculations or weak points. Reminded of nights when he used to pace the deck of the *Illusion*, when he could hear the voices of his crew planning ways to spend their first night at port while he carried the responsibility for a successful voyage on his shoulders, he knew that success or failure tonight rested with him.

Risk.

Everything came down to one last calculated risk to win the right to claim JoHannah as his wife.

He almost had lost his mind when he had returned from Hillsboro to find JoHannah gone. It was then that he knew it had been only an illusion to think that his feelings for her were based simply on attraction or respect. He loved her to the depths of his soul, and in the blinding aura of that love, he understood the difference between all-encompassing, soul-searing love and mere obsession.

For the very first time, he had realized that his life at sea had only been a life-filling obsession that was a pale illusion of the fulfillment of true love—love he had found with JoHannah. His plans to marry her, hatched in the haze of mutual attraction and respect for her abilities to be a capable mistress for Lawne Haven and the mother of his children so that he could return to his adventurous life at sea, now seemed hopelessly naive and selfish.

How quick he had been to tell her that her life at Collier

was only a poor imitation of life in the World. All along, he had been the one clinging to the falsest illusion of all: that the sea could ever give him a life as full and meaningful as the one he would find in the arms of the woman he loved with all his heart.

Fate, it seemed, had designed an ingenious maze, hurling him down one wrong path and then another as he searched for his place in the World. Yet, until he had opened his heart to JoHannah and acknowledged his love for her, he had never truly known where he belonged—at Lawne Haven with JoHannah by his side.

Did he have the courage and strength to conquer the final obstacle that Fate had put in their way as a final test of his love?

The deed to Lawne Haven was in his vest pocket, and he was fully prepared to submit title to his land in the bidding war—if all else failed. Beads of perspiration lined his forehead and upper lip, and he wiped them away with the back of his hand. Even in the shade, the August heat was stifling. He hoped the last waning rays of sunset would signal the beginning of a cooler night, although his body was more likely responding to the tension of trying to outmaneuver and outthink opposing bidders he did not know.

The sound of approaching footsteps caused him to stop and turn around. His face broke into a smile. "Nora! I thought you might be resting."

Hobbling a bit, she scowled as she approached him. "Can't do much more than stand in this fancy gown. I'll never understand why some females submit to such torture."

He held his hands out and steadied her. "You didn't have to come. You should have stayed—"

She glanced up at him with the same feisty look that always swallowed up the last half of his reprimands, however gentle they always were. Looking regal in the soft black gown spun with silver threads, she had been trans-formed from an elderly housekeeper to the wealthy widow she was supposed to be. "You look lovely," he murmured.

She actually blushed, a female reaction he thought long relegated to her youth. "I thought we might talk a spell," she murmured. Her dark eyes held his gaze. "There's something I want you to consider before . . ."

He swallowed hard. "I know what I'm doing is right."

"Do you?"

He nodded, knowing how disappointed she must be to know that if all else failed, he was willing to turn his back on his duty as the last surviving Lawne and relinquish Lawne Haven. It seemed to fulfill her suspicions that he was not ready to meet his responsibilities after Avery deeded the family land to him, and he relived the same sense of failure he had felt when he had been unable to force Avery to come home.

"I love JoHannah," he whispered, hoping to convince Nora that he did not betray his responsibilities for any friv-olous reason. "I need her, and I want her by my side." His voice choked with emotion, and he paused to clear his throat. "If I have to, I'm willing to—"

"I know what you're going to do . . . if you must," she said as her gaze softened. "I understand how much you love her, and if JoHannah wants to share her life with you . . . then I approve of what you're doing. That's why I'm here. To give both of you my support. If JoHannah truly—"

"Of course she does," he countered as his pulse began to accelerate.

"I know in my heart she loves you, but did she actually tell you she wanted to marry you?"

He looked away, unwilling to lie but unable to look at the woman who had devoted her life to him and to his family. "Not exactly," he gritted. "She thinks I will have to bid my land to marry her, and she only wants to spare me from making the choice between Lawne Haven and . . . and her.''

Nora's voice softened. "What will happen to Abigail and Jane?''

''I'll keep my promise to Avery and make a home for them . . . and for you, wherever JoHannah and I live.''

''I see.''

He spun back to face Nora and found her smiling. "I just wanted to be sure you both wanted the same thing. I know you'll do what's right.'' She rose on her tiptoes to kiss his cheek. "I think I'll go back to the others. Are you ready to join us?''

Shaking his head, he smiled. "I just need to be alone a while longer.'' He watched Nora as she made her way back to the camp, his mind swirling with doubts he thought he had already resolved.

In light of Nora's question, his chest tightened when he thought of the last time he had seen JoHannah. He had been so angry with Bathrick and frustrated by any chance of rescuing her that day, Michael had had little room in his mind for anything beyond his own feeling of powerlessness. Obsessed and driven by his love for JoHannah, was it possible that he had seen only a reflection of his own heart and soul in her eyes?

In view of Bathrick's near-perfect scheme, if JoHannah had to choose between marrying a perfect stranger and Michael, he knew as sure as his heart was beating she would choose him. But what if she loved him and yet still wanted to return to her old world, sacrificing the love she felt for Michael?

Bathrick denied JoHannah's right to choose the way she would spend her life, but was Michael any better? If he stood before her at midnight, triumphant in his bid for her hand with or without losing title to Lawne Haven, would she marry him out of a sense of obligation? Would he win the right to have her by his side, but lose in the end because her heart and spirit truly longed for the harmonious world she had left behind at Collier?

Comparing himself to Bathrick again made him shudder. He glanced at his pocket watch and realized that it was time to leave, and there was precious little time left before the auction. He hurried back to the camp, determined more than ever to win the most important battle of his life.

After double checking to make sure both service gates were still chained and locked, Michael rode back to the main gate where Nora's coach was still waiting just out of the light cast by torches burning at the main gate that lit the entrance.

It was one hour before midnight, and Michael judged that by now, Bathrick would be in a profound state of apoplexy. "The best is yet to come," he swore under his breath as he dismounted. O'Neal promptly opened the gate. "Don't disturb the sign," Michael warned as he led his mount through and waved Nora's driver to bring the coach inside exactly as he had been instructed to do earlier.

"Tied it real good, just like you said. Workin' like a charm, too," O'Neal whispered. "Not too many folks are willin' to break a quarantine for scarlet fever. Drivers on all four coaches turned tail, even when I tried to tell 'em the auction would be held next month."

Rigid with a combination of anticipation and determination, Michael allowed a small sense of satisfaction to soften his posture. With the servant who normally guarded the gate safely out of the way, he was counting on O'Neal not to let any prospective bidders enter the estate—even if they were fool enough to challenge the quarantine as legitimate. "Did the minister and the banker arrive?"

"Right on cue. Got 'em both inside and had time to put up the sign before anyone else came."

Michael led his horse behind the small guard post and tethered him to a tree. O'Neal followed along. "Any other problems?" Michael asked tersely.

"Nope. Dr. Carson and Dolan went up 'bout half an hour ago. Guess it's time," he noted with a nervous catch in his voice. "Good luck to you, Mr. Lawne."

Michael shook O'Neal's hand and left him at his post. He walked over to Nora's coach, opened the door, and climbed inside. In the shadow of light cast by the torches behind them, he could see her face, and her lips were twitching nervously. "Ready?" he asked as he gripped her hands. Normally cold with age, they felt frozen.

"I've never been this nervous my whole life," she admitted as she dropped the black veil on her bonnet that would hide her identity from Bathrick.

"You'll do just fine. Stay close to Dr. Carson and Dolan. They're not going to let anything happen to you."

"I just hope . . . well, it's all gonna end soon enough. One way or another—"

"We don't have any time to waste," he rasped as he pulled a sealed envelope containing the deed to Lawne Haven out of his pocket. He held a lifetime of hopes and traditions and memories in his hand. Narrowing his eyes, he briefly envisioned the woman of his dreams. He handed the deed to Nora. "I want you . . . I want you to use this for me if our plan fails."

She gasped. "Why? Aren't you—"

"I'm not going inside," he said hurriedly, giving in to the instinct that had made him successful at sea—until the one time he had ignored it and paid with his ship. "I'll send O'Neal up in a few minutes. I'll stay outside until the auction is almost over just in case a bidder arrives at the last minute." He pressed Nora's hand around the envelope with the deed. "I don't trust Bathrick, either. With everyone inside the room with him, there's no telling what unexpected stunt he might pull. I'll make sure I can see and hear what's going on inside while still keeping watch for late arrivals."

He lifted her veil, kissed her forehead, and made a hasty retreat from the coach. He signaled the driver to leave, and as the coach disappeared around a bend in the winding road that led to the mansion, his heart went with it.

He turned and strode toward the guardhouse to tell O'Neal about the late change in plans. Buoyed by his decision to guard JoHannah himself, he felt the same energy surge through his body that he had felt just before a storm at sea. Unlike the last time, when he had been caught unprepared, he was absolutely certain now that he had thought of every possible contingency to guarantee his success.

Hell, he had even had proxy marriage papers for JoHannah and himself drawn up just in case something bizarre happened, like falling and reinjuring his leg which would have left him unable to travel in time for the auction. "Talk about ridiculous," he grumbled as he made a mental note to get the papers back from Nora once he exchanged vows with JoHannah in front of the minister.

The papers would make an interesting memento, he noted, not that he did not plan to make the night absolutely unforgettable when he took JoHannah to the marriage bed and introduced her to delights that would singe her soul.

And his.

Chapter 29

G ordon Shipley, manager of the bank handling Jo-
Hannah's inheritance, stood beneath the candle-lit
mantel and clapped his hands together to silence the si-
multaneous conversations in the room. "Ladies and gentlemen, it's time to begin the auction."

Facing Shipley, Bathrick held JoHannah's arm in a gentle grip. He leaned toward her, and the hairs from his mole
scratched her jaw. "I'd hoped for a bigger showing of bidders, but the ones who came appear to be well established,"
he whispered nervously.

She pulled her face away and tried to appear calm, but
her heart was beating so fast she could barely think straight.
Well established? If her guardian knew the truth, he would
probably burst a blood vessel! She stared at the banker and
tried to keep from laughing out loud.

Whatever JoHannah might have imagined about the bidders who would attend the auction, nothing could have prepared her for the shock when one by one, the people she
had grown to know or love at Lawne Haven had entered
the room, dressed as grand as if they were attending court.
Bathrick, of course, did not know any of them, except for
Nora, and she had cleverly hidden her face behind a veil.

Unfortunately, Bathrick had never left JoHannah's side, and she had been unable to ask any of the questions that cried out for answers as persistently as the hooting of an owl echoing in the distance.

Besides the fact that Dolan and Brady were already married, none of them could possibly hope to outbid the offers her guardian had received in the post and perversely showed to JoHannah, along with proxy marriage papers, just before she came downstairs. One, from a man in New York City, was for six thousand dollars; the second bid of eight thousand dollars came from South Carolina.

Still, she was touched beyond measure by the presence of her friends. Even though they could not stop her guardian from achieving his goals, she loved them all the more for trying to help her.

The only person missing was Michael, and for the last half hour, her gaze had been riveted on the doorway, waiting for him to arrive. Had she truly convinced him that she did not love him, or had he decided after much soul-searching that he could not part with Lawne Haven, no matter how much he loved her?

Michael. Why aren't you here?

"I can almost feel your presence," she whispered softly to herself as her body began to tingle with the same wondrous sensations she had felt the very first day she had seen him at Collier and her cheeks warmed with a blush. Dismissing her body's reaction as resulting from nothing more than wishful thinking, she sighed and turned her attention to the dreaded auction.

More than curious as to why no legitimate bidders had shown up, she wondered if Michael had tried to rig the auction. If so, why hadn't he come? Was he convinced his scheme would work, unaware that her guardian had received bids by post, replete with proxy marriage papers?

Dr. Carson and Nora walked over to stand beside her while Dolan and Brady took places next to her guardian. When the banker took the first bid from Dolan, there was no time to ponder the answers to any of the questions that left her mind numb with misery. She stood up straight and held very still as she waited to hear the announcement of Dolan's bid.

"The first bid is from Mr. Dolan Tucker," the banker proclaimed as he opened the envelope.

Beaming, Dolan leaned in front of Bathrick and winked at JoHannah.

"That will be enough, Mr. Tucker," Bathrick grumbled.

Her nerves stretched to the limit, JoHannah chewed on her lower lip to keep from giggling out loud. If Bathrick knew that Dolan had a wife who would be able to squash her guardian to death by merely sitting on him, he would not have that outrageous smirk on his face. She sobered immediately when she thought about Dolan and how badly he would feel to know that his efforts would be in vain.

The banker opened the bid, blinked several times, and brought the paper closer to his face.

"Read the bid, Mr. Shipley," Bathrick barked, clearly impatient.

"Oh, the bid. Yes, well, the bid is . . . ten dollars."

Bathrick's mouth dropped open, and his face turned crimson. "You must have misread the bid. Do you normally wear spectacles?"

"Certainly not. My eyesight is nearly perfect. The bid reads ten dollars."

Dolan bobbed his head. "Yes sir, that's absolutely right, and the portrait's worth every penny."

Bathrick glared at Dolan as though he had the brain of a peacock. He turned back to the banker and scowled. "The next bid, please."

Shipley took an envelope from Brady, broke the seal and

pulled out the bid. "From a Mr. Brady O'Neal. The bid is . . ." He paused to mop his brow. "Five dollars."

Brady's face was somber, but Dolan whooped for joy. "I knew I'd have a high bid!"

Trembling as a mottled angry blush rose up his neck and stained his face, Bathrick ignored both of them. "Kindly continue, Mr. Shipley, if you will. I apologize to those of you who are *serious* bidders for allowing these supposed gentlemen to waste our time."

Dr. Carson's bid of fifty dollars brought tears to Jo-Hannah's eyes and a slump to Dolan's shoulders, but sent Bathrick into a sputtering rage. "Th-this is outrageous. I— I can't believe . . . the audacity—"

"It seems to be high bid at the moment," the physician said calmly as he gave JoHannah a smile that melted her heart. "I wish it could have been more. Quite a bit more."

Visibly shaking, the banker looked at the assemblage and shook his head. "I believe that's the last bid," he croaked. "The winner of the portrait—"

Nora's hands rose in a flutter. "What about my bid?" she asked as she rushed forward and pressed an envelope into the banker's hands. "My son will never forgive me if I return home to Philadelphia unsuccessful. He is totally smitten with the lovely young girl in the portrait, but his health is poor, and he couldn't travel all this way. You will accept the bid from me on his behalf, won't you? My husband left me a considerable estate made in manufacturing, and I assure you—"

The banker raised a brow. "All bidders were required to be present since the winner will be marrying—"

"But I have proxy papers," she said as she rummaged through her reticule. "The lawyer assured me—"

Bathrick waved his hand magnanimously as the clock chimed the three-quarter hour. "I have no objection to taking her bid on behalf of her son."

He studied Nora intently, and JoHannah held her breath to the point she grew light headed. If Bathrick recognized Nora now, the entire scam her friends worked would unfold. Even though JoHannah knew that Nora's bid would not top the ones Bathrick had secreted in his pocket, she was afraid he would lose his temper and there was no telling what he might do to the tiny housekeeper in a fit of rage.

"I trust a woman of your obvious background," Bathrick intoned in a decided affront to the others. "Rest assured, madam, if your son has the highest bid, the portrait and JoHannah will be his. Go on, Mr. Shipley. Read the bid so we can be done with the business at hand."

"The bid is from Mr. George Bancroft in the amount of two hundred dollars."

From a safe vantage point just outside the window where he was hidden in night's shadows, Michael watched with bemused satisfaction as the auction reached the conclusion he had planned. While Bathrick ranted inside about the ridiculous bid from Nora's "son," Michael started walking around the side of the house to get to the front door. He had stepped onto the veranda when the sound of a horse galloping in the distance sent chills up his spine.

Jumping off the porch into the shadows, he raced down the winding road. Heart pounding, he stopped at the bend, stepped into the center, and braced both feet—directly in front of a rider. The horse reared and whinnied as the rider pulled hard on the reins.

"Are you crazy or addled?" the rider spat as Michael grabbed hold of the horse's bridle and walked up to the rider who was dressed in formal attire.

"That seems to be a question you might want to ask yourself," Michael said coldly. "Didn't you see the quarantine sign?"

"Hah! I saw it. Stupid coach driver. He wouldn't believe

me that some clever bastard tried to rig the auction in his favor. Cost me precious time to go all the way back to town and rent this bedraggled nag, but I—''

''Your driver had more sense than you do,'' Michael commented. ''Now you're in for forty days.''

Even in the moonlight, Michael could see the man pale.

''Forty days? Are you serious? The quarantine is real?'' He swayed in the saddle and started to dismount. ''You wouldn't be trying to—''

With one solid punch, Michael rendered the man unconscious. He dragged him to the side of the road and tethered the horse to a tree. Michael's hands shook as he rifled through the man's pockets. He froze in place when he read the man's bid which was for twice the value of Lawne Haven. Given the choice, he would have liked to bound and gagged the man, but there was no time to waste. He ripped the document into shreds and tossed them aside.

JoHannah.

The last thing he had seen was the announcement of Nora's bid on behalf of her ''son.'' Had Bathrick discovered that the proxy papers which would bind JoHannah to a nonexistent man were phony? Or had he reneged on his vow to accept the highest bid, and despite Dolan's imposing presence, found a way to keep JoHannah under his authority? Frightening scenarios swam through Michael's mind as he ran back to the house. Winded, he reached the veranda as the sound of the clock striking midnight echoed from inside. He was nearly to the door when it burst open, and Dolan came barreling full speed outside.

''I've waited long enough. I don't care what Nora says, I think you should get inside. Fast. JoHannah—''

Michael ripped past his friend and bolted into the house without waiting to hear anything beyond JoHannah's name. He tore through the foyer and flew into the sitting room where the auction had been held. O'Neal and Dr. Carson were standing alongside Nora who had removed her veiled bonnet and was wiping tears from her face. He scanned the room, and his heart leaped into a furious series of poundings that ripped through his chest. Bathrick was nowhere to be seen; neither was the banker or the minister.

The one person he longed to see more than any other was JoHannah, but she too was gone. The love of his life and the keeper of his dreams was gone. Even her portrait had been removed from its place over the mantel.

"JoHannah," he cried and felt his blood turn to ice. Instinctively, he put his hand into his pocket and caressed the dainty lace cap that held JoHannah's wedding ring, now as worthless as the future he faced without her.

Seated behind her guardian's desk in the study, JoHannah held the pen in her hand as she was about to sign the proxy marriage papers in the presence of her guardian and the banker, the minister having been dismissed just moments earlier. She paused, thought for a moment, and put the pen down. She looked up at her guardian who stood in front of the bolted door as though he expected her to try to flee. "The affidavit. I want the affidavit before I sign the papers," she insisted, refusing to look away when he glared at her. "There isn't a reason on God's good earth why I should trust you to give it to me later," she commented. "You have my word I'll sign the papers, and I've never broken my word to you or to anyone."

He finally shrugged his shoulders and pulled the affidavit from inside his waistcoat and held it out to her. "I really wouldn't have used it. I only wanted to be sure—"

She counted the papers quickly. "There are only five pages here. There's one missing."

He paled, and the hairs on his mole twitched. "I think you're mistaken."

She squared her shoulders. "No. I counted them twice. You got far more than you deserved from the auction, and I won't marry anyone unless you give up the missing page."

"I only wanted to make sure—"

She clutched the affidavit in her hand so hard her fingers went numb. "I want the missing page with my sworn statement," she boldly demanded, trying to make up for failing to find the affidavit when she broke into the study.

Sweating profusely, he turned and walked over to the bookcase that lined the opposite wall. He removed several books, and her eyes widened when she saw the door to a safe in the wall. Moments later, he tossed her sworn statement onto the desk. "That's all of it now," he grumbled. "Let's get on with it."

Ignoring his order, and equally disregarding the banker who sat nervously in a chair across the room, she perused the document again to make absolutely sure no other pages were missing. Satisfied that she had every page of the vile affidavit, she picked up the candle that lit the room and carried it to the unlit hearth along with the affidavit. She bent down, put the document in the hearth, and touched the candle's flame to the corners of the pile.

Golden blue flames caught the edges and curled them inward as the fire caught. She watched as the flames joined forces and erupted into one huge burst of fire that quickly rendered the affidavit into ashes. After waiting a few minutes for them to cool, she scooped them up with one hand. Still warm, they were as light as the petals of a flower as she carried them to the open window and watched them flutter into the night like silver and black moths taking wing.

The clock chimed the quarter hour after midnight as she

took her seat at the desk. "It's my birthday," she murmured. "I'm twenty-one."

"Yes. Yes. Now sign the papers," Bathrick ordered.

JoHannah picked up the pen again, poised it over the paper, and looked up at the banker who was sitting on the edge of his seat. "Is it true that once I'm married, I won't have control of my inheritance? That my husband—"

He nodded. "Quite the rule of law," he agreed. "It's usually for the best. Most women don't understand the world of business—"

"But I'm not married yet, am I?" Her eyes began to twinkle. From the ideas that had been percolating in her mind ever since the dramatic end to the auction, she had finally extracted a solid plan of her own, and this time she did not intend to fail—or miss any important details.

Her guardian bolted toward her. "You gave your word you would sign the papers!"

She smiled. "And I will. I have others, however, that I intend to sign first." She stood up to gain a height advantage over her shorter guardian and locked gazes with her banker. "I assume you have an accounting of my inheritance."

He nodded, loosening his cravat. "At the bank."

"But you have an idea of the extent of my holdings, don't you?" she asked as her heart began to beat faster.

"Certainly, but—"

Bathrick swirled to face Shipley. "You were given your instructions, and I expect you to follow them."

"Your instructions," the banker said primly, "are no longer valid. Miss Sims is in control of her inheritance now, and your role as guardian is quite finished."

"She wouldn't be in that position if you hadn't—"

"Sit down. Both of you," she said quietly. "There's much I need to do, and it will only prolong the night if you continue to argue." She held her breath until her guardian took the chair in front of the desk and the banker pulled his chair closer to her.

"This is what I want you to do," she began as she passed Shipley pen and paper and prayed that Michael would someday accept what she was about to do.

Chapter 30

Michael stared at the empty wall over the mantel where JoHannah's portrait had hung. No outside bidders had been present at the auction, and he could only assume that somehow he had overlooked the possibility that someone had had the foresight to bid for JoHannah by post and submitted proxy marriage papers as well—a bid that had been higher than Lawne Haven. Why else would both JoHannah and the portrait be gone? Why else would Nora be crying?

Utter disappointment crashed into devastation so profound he could only survive by retreating into reckless anger. Despite his plans and his bid of Lawne Haven, he had failed unforgivably to stop Bathrick from forcing JoHannah into a mockery of a marriage that would make the rest of her life a living hell on earth.

"Not while I live and breathe," he swore, unwilling to let a code of honor prevent him from stopping such an injustice. He turned on his heels and met Dolan in the foyer. "Where did the bastard take JoHannah?" he spat as his muscles tightened with anticipation.

"Did you talk to Nora?"

Michael glared at his friend. "I don't have time to rehash

every sordid detail of what happened. Tell me where she is.''

Dolan pointed behind Michael. "Straight ahead. First door. They're all in the study, but I think you'd better—"

Michael sprinted to the door and pounded on it with both fists. "JoHannah? Bathrick, open this door! Now!"

No response.

He pounded again, his fists smarting as they hit solid oak with every ounce of his strength. "So help me, Bathrick, I'll kill you twice if you don't open this door!" he shouted.

Not a sound.

Michael braced his feet and lowered his shoulder as he charged the door. It held fast, and bright lights danced in front of his eyes as pain shot through his upper body. Grimacing, he backed away from the door. "Dolan. Get over here now," he ordered. "Dammit, hurry up!"

Dolan ran as fast as his tree-trunk legs allowed. He looked at Michael like he had mush for brains. "Are you sick in the head? What are you—"

"Break it down," he heaved as he held his shoulder and took deep breaths to ease the pain.

"I can't do that," Dolan argued as he ran his hand over the finely polished wood. "Besides, it's really not necessary—"

"So help me, Dolan, if you don't break down that door, I'll burn every piece of lumber you've stockpiled to build Genny's porch. And I'll tell her—"

"Oh, hang it! If you're gonna get me into trouble with Genevieve just because you—"

"Dolan!"

Before the next blink of an eye, Dolan crashed open the door, and Michael stormed past the splintered frame. His heart pounding, his hands clenched into fists, but he rocked to a halt the moment his gaze locked on JoHannah's form as she sat behind the desk, her eyes wide.

"Michael! What's wrong? You . . . you frightened me."

Blinding fury evaporated into abject concern. "Are you all right?" he rasped as his chest tightened. If her image in the portrait, which was now leaning against the wall, was captivating, her actual form dressed in the lavender and lace gown was astonishingly beautiful. She took his breath away—what was left of it.

"I'm . . . I'm fine. It's over now," she murmured, gazing at him with such tender affection in her eyes he had to gulp down a lump in his throat. He loved her so much his heart ached with real pain, and he turned toward Bathrick with every intention of grabbing him by the throat and physically forcing him to free JoHannah from whatever arrangements had been made for her at the conclusion of the auction. It was no consolation now that Michael had thwarted a last-minute bid by the man who was still lying by the side of the road. It also mattered nothing that Michael still had title to Lawne Haven.

He had lost the woman he loved.

Cold determination to wreak revenge fueled his walk as he started toward Bathrick, who stepped behind a chair. Michael snorted derisively. "Nothing is going to protect you from me now, Bathrick."

JoHannah's voice whispered a plea that wrapped around his heart. "He's just leaving. He has a ship to board in Boston. Please, Michael, you don't understand—"

"I understand perfectly," he spat. "And he's not going anywhere. Not until—"

"Please, Michael. Let him go."

He swirled around, unable to fathom why she would be willing to let Bathrick leave unscathed after what he had done to her. Mesmerized by the tears glistening in her eyes like the morning dew caught on spring lilacs, he shook his head as his love for her doused the fires of his wrath. "He deserves—"

"To leave unharmed," she pleaded.

She held Michael's gaze, and his sense of failure was so deep, he knew he could deny her nothing, not even this uncommon mercy for her tormentor. He nodded stiffly to Bathrick. "Get out. Before I come to my senses."

Bathrick skirted past Michael and stayed just out of reach. He paused just outside the door to the hall where Dolan stood and turned around. "I'm sorry. I'm truly sorry. Thank you," he sputtered to JoHannah before he walked out of view.

Shipley edged closer to the door, his eyes darting from JoHannah to Michael. "If there's nothing further . . ."

"No. Thank you. I appreciate everything you've done to help me," JoHannah answered.

Extending his hand to Michael, the banker visibly trembled. "I'm sorry, Mr. Lawne. I tried to—"

"You did everything possible to help me," JoHannah interjected before the banker revealed what she had done without giving her a chance to explain everything to Michael herself.

Battling the urge to throttle Shipley for aiding and abetting Bathrick's scheme, Michael allowed that the man must have redeemed himself, at least in JoHannah's view. He shook Shipley's hand and kept his gaze on JoHannah as the man beat a hasty retreat.

He heard the creak of the nearly unhinged door as it closed behind the banker, grateful to Dolan for giving Michael a private moment with JoHannah. Facing the unbearable moment when he would have to say good-bye and see the disappointment in her eyes that reflected his own dismal sense of failure, he felt his pulse slow to a dull thud and his stomach churned.

How could he bid farewell to the woman who had intrigued him from the very first moment he had seen her? One long, lingering look, and he had been captivated. One gentle touch, and he had lost his heart. Just one kiss, sweet and innocent, and he had lost his soul to the woman of his dreams.

"JoHannah," he whispered. His eyes filled with tears, and the one shining moment he had promised her faded into a midnight despair that would darken his spirit for the rest of his days.

Too overcome with emotion to stand, JoHannah gazed at Michael, and the intensity of the love shining in his eyes took her breath away. The proud and courageous man who had risked his life to lay claim to traditions that gave his life meaning stared at her, his image stripped of any pretense. The fierce lion that had nipped at her heart, the cunning fox who had tried to outwit her, and the serpent who had tempted her had, in truth, long since been tamed. The arrogantly confident man who had predicted he would make her fall in love with him had grown into a man of great sensitivity who had opened his heart and soul to love her completely and without reservation.

Given his rather dramatic and forceful entrance, she assumed he had discovered that his attempt to stock the room with bidders and force Bathrick to accept a high bid of two hundred dollars had failed. Had Nora told Michael that Bathrick accepted Lawne Haven as the high bid, and Michael was outraged to have lost his land? Or did he think Bathrick had rejected Michael's bid of Lawne Haven in an effort to punish him for trying to undermine the auction and accepted one of two bids he had received by post—a threat Bathrick had made at the conclusion of the auction?

She could not bear to see the devastation in Michael's eyes, but she had to explain very carefully what had actually happened or lose hope of ever reconciling Michael to what she had been forced to do.

She stood up and walked very slowly to stand before him. He tensed, as if it were difficult to have her so near.

Taking a deep breath for courage, she took his hand and led him to stand in front of a gilt-framed mirror that hung on the wall near the door. Side by side, their faces were muted reflections in the softly lit room. Their eyes met in their reflections, and she saw deep pain flash through his eyes.

"Don't," he rasped as he turned his head away.

"For me. Just this once. Please. For me," she said softly, using the very words he had whispered long ago to cajole her to look at her reflection in the creek.

He inhaled sharply and turned back to stare at her in her reflection.

"Tell me what you see," she prompted.

His eyes widened. "I see you. I see me."

"Is that all? I'm disappointed," she said quietly. "Look again, and let me tell you what I see."

"JoHannah, I can't," he murmured as he turned to face her. "This is hard enough—"

She stepped close enough to feel the heat of his body and cupped his cheek with her hand to gaze deep into his eyes. He shuddered as his eyes grew troubled and darkened to the color of rain clouds.

"I see God whenever I see you. I see His goodness and His strength, His courage and His joy in the world He created." A swell of emotion brought tears to her eyes. "I see the man I love with all my heart." Her voice cracked, and she paused to blink back tears. "I love you."

"Not now," he pleaded as he stiffened. "Don't say—"

"I must," she insisted. "I love you, and I did what I had to do, what I needed to do. . . . If we are to spend the rest of our lives together, I need to know—"

His eyes widened with disbelief, and his hands wrapped around her upper arms. "The rest of our lives? What are you trying to say? That Bathrick—"

"He insisted that unless Nora gave him the proxy marriage papers that you had signed, he would take a lower bid. I—I couldn't let that happen,'' she gushed. ''I'm sorry. I know I should have waited for you, but there didn't seem to be a choice. Either I married you . . . or another. I wanted to marry you, Michael. Only you.''

He shook his head and pulled her into his arms where he held her so tightly she could barely breathe. His heart pounded against her own. ''No wonder Dolan tried to stop me from breaking down the door. You mean, it's done? You signed our proxy marriage papers?''

She pressed her cheek against his face. ''Only after I forced him to give me the affidavit.''

His face lit with wonder and awe. ''Then you could have chosen to go back to Collier?''

She shook her head and smiled. ''I couldn't leave you. I love you, and I intend to spend the rest of my life with you. But I couldn't let you sacrifice Lawne Haven for me.''

His smile dazzled her. ''I'd give my life for you,'' he whispered. ''We'll forge a new world. Together. Wherever—''

''But we can stay at Lawne Haven,'' she blurted.

Shock filled his eyes. ''What? I thought you said—''

A blush rose to her cheeks. ''I told my guardian I would sign the proxy papers after he gave me the affidavit, but . . . but I didn't. I made the banker prepare other papers that I signed first.''

He took a deep breath. ''Other papers? What kind of papers?''

She took a similarly deep breath. Michael was a proud man, and she only prayed he would accept what she had done as a measure of the love she had for him. She walked back to the desk and lifted up a paper with notes she had taken as the banker had written out more detailed documents she had had to sign. She held it out to Michael. ''I think this describes them all.''

He took the paper and began to read. He stopped less than thirty seconds later and cocked his head. "You gave away your fortune?"

She grinned. "Almost all of it. That's why the banker was so apologetic to you when he left. He thought you would be upset."

He started to smile. "What did you think?"

"I never believed you were interested in my fortune, but I wasn't sure what you would say," she admitted as her heart began to pound. "I didn't think you'd disapprove of most of what I did. The community at Collier is growing, and they need help. I wanted to give that to them."

He nodded approvingly, but when he studied the note again, his lips dropped into a frown. "Why is Bathrick's name here?"

"Well, I . . . I wanted to be sure he would take his family to Europe and stay there for a good long while."

Michael snorted. "I should say he will. Between what he got from you and what he'll reap after selling Lawne Haven—"

"That's what I've been trying to tell you. He can't sell Lawne Haven," she gushed as the moment she had dreaded was finally at hand. "He doesn't own it. You do," she said as she picked up the title to Lawne Haven and walked it to him. She put it into his hand and wrapped his fingers around it. "I never wanted you to have to choose between your land and . . . please, don't be upset with me for buying Lawne Haven back for you. I know what it means to you, and I know how hard it would be for you to live anywhere else. I want Abigail and Jane to be able to come back to the home they remember. Don't let your pride . . ."

He swept her into his arms and kissed her soundly. When she felt she was about to faint, he ended his kiss and tilted her chin up to face him. "My pride at the moment is for a woman who managed to almost single-handedly undo a very nefarious scheme, and I can hardly believe that this particular woman, who just might be getting a bit too bold for her own good, is my wife.''

Her smile was shy. ''You don't mind that we married in a very unusual way? I didn't know if you would be upset that we didn't say our vows in front of a minister.''

He pulled her into his arms and kissed her again. ''I have a most beautiful wife with a precious, most uncommon heart,'' he whispered as he brushed his lips against hers and dangerous sensations began to race through her body. ''It doesn't matter to me whether we said our vows together in front of a minister or our names were signed to a piece of paper. We're duly married,'' he said, his voice full of wonder.

He put his hand into his pocket and took out the lace cap she had left for him on his pillow. Her eyes filled with tears. ''You saved my cap.''

He smiled gently. ''It kept you close to me,'' he whispered as he unfolded the cap and, from its lacy depths, pulled out a beautiful ring of silver and gold. He paused and locked her gaze with his. ''I'll love you all the days of my life,'' he pledged as he slipped it onto her finger. ''I will cherish you and protect you, honor and respect you above all others.'' Tears ran down her cheeks as he raised her hand to his lips and kissed her ring.

''I'll love you all the days of my life,'' she repeated, and echoed the rest of his vows in a tremulous voice.

''My beloved. My wife,'' he said with such awe in his eyes he took her breath away. Glorious passion glazed his eyes, and he scooped her into his arms. He opened the unhinged door carefully and swept her down the hall, ignoring Dolan's astonished look as they passed him.

''Michael! What are—''

''You may have handled the actual marriage ceremony and settled your business affairs, Mrs. Lawne, but there's one very important detail I claim the right to orchestrate,'' he crooned as he carried her up the stairs.

"Detail?'' she repeated, awash with the wonder of being held in her husband's arms.

"Oh, yes, one very important detail. According to tradition,'' he vowed as he carried her into the first bedroom he found, "our time together as man and wife should most commonly begin here.'' He closed the door with a shove of his shoulder and carried her to the bed. "But I promise you, sweet JoHannah, that the joys and pleasures I have waited so long to share with you will be most uncommon indeed.''

"I love you,'' she whispered as she kissed him again, and she knew with every beat of her heart that the one shining moment Michael had promised her was now at hand, filling her heart and soul with the joy of promises kept, love fulfilled, and destinies met.

Epilogue

Five years later

Even before he had the fieldstone house in view, Michael could hear the sound of children's laughter. He hurried his steps and emerged from the shade-dappled path into warm and brilliant June sunshine that mirrored the glow in his heart.

The heavy scent of lilacs laced the air, and as he passed the tool shed, he stopped and picked a sprig of deep purple blossoms.

"Uncle Michael!"

Jane and Abigail raced toward him with his four-year-old son, Avery, in tow. "We're going on a picnic!" they trilled, their faces flushed with excitement.

Avery grinned. "Picnic, Papa," he panted, his legs covered with dust from being half dragged across the yard.

"Was this your idea or your mama's?" Michael asked as he swept his son up into his arms.

He chuckled as the raven-haired little boy struggled to get down. Deep violet eyes twinkled back at him. "Mama said—"

"To meet you and tell you she's waiting for you at the

clearing,'' Jane announced with ten-year-old authority.

''We're to mind Avery while . . . go on, Uncle Michael,'' Abigail urged as she lifted Avery out of Michael's arms. ''Nora is just packing the picnic basket, and we'll put it in the wagon so we can leave as soon as you get back.''

Michael cocked his head. ''Where's Joseph?'' he asked, wondering about his second son who was only two years old but already the mirror image of his mother.

Jane rolled her eyes. ''He's in his chair making an unholy mess of the last bit of frosting for the cake.''

Michael laughed out loud and tousled Avery's hair. ''What else have you planned for the day?''

''Nothing,'' the girls chimed.

A little too quickly.

He narrowed his gaze and studied their faces. Eyes sparkling and cheeks rosy, there were no signs of the trauma that had marked the early years of their lives. They had arrived back at Lawne Haven several months after he and JoHannah had married. While being home with Nora helped to ease the pain of their confusion and loss, it was JoHannah's gentleness and kindness that had gradually molded them back into a family. He broke the sprig of lilac into two pieces and gave one to each of the girls.

''Tell Nora we won't be long,'' he murmured as a swell of emotion caught in his throat. No man had a right to life this full and this good, and the only thoughts he ever had of the sea since his marriage to JoHannah centered on finding a way—someday—to take her to sea with him on an extended, passion-filled holiday.

He made his way to the clearing to meet the uncommon woman who had made all of his dreams come true, wondering what had lit the glint of guilt in Abigail and Jane's eyes.

When he turned off the path and walked through the forest to get to the clearing, he caught a flash of color through the trees. *JoHannah*. His heart started to race, and he sprinted forward to close the distance between them.

As he emerged into the clearing, she looked up and ran toward him. Arms open wide, she broke into a smile as they met and embraced. He molded their bodies together and lowered his lips to hers. Tasting. Nibbling. Teasing. *Lord, may the magic never end!*

Giggling, she broke their kiss and stepped back from him. Her cheeks flushed prettily, and her eyes sparkled with wonder as she touched her lips. "You still make me tremble," she whispered.

He reached out to pull her back into his arms, but she swirled out of reach and started to run away. "Oh no you don't," he chuckled as he took off after her. Flashes of the dream that had sustained him through a long painful illness and taunted him as he had courted JoHannah merged with reality.

He ran faster and caught her about the waist when they were in the middle of the clearing. He pulled her back against his chest. Breathing heavily, he nibbled at her ear and saw her pulse pounding at the base of her throat while her breasts heaved against his arm. "I've finally got you," he rasped, fulfilling the quest that had eluded him in his dreams.

JoHannah arched her back, offering him the full column of her throat. "I—have—a—surprise—for—you," she panted as she tried to fight the pleasure and desire that nearly distracted her from her plan to surprise Michael.

"*Mmm,*" he murmured as he cupped her breasts with his hands and teased her nipples into hardness through the folds of her gown. "Tell me more."

"Michael!" she gasped as pleasure ignited into a fire raging through her blood. "Michael, stop."

"In a hundred years," he teased as his hands fanned along her waist to her hips.

She pulled away and tugged at his hand. "My surprise—"

"Is delightful." He grinned and reached out to pluck the pins from her hair. A mass of auburn waves fell to her shoulders, and he caught his breath, the very same way he had when he had unpinned her hair for the first time.

She pursed her lips.

He smiled. "I waited ever so long to do that. I simply can't help myself."

"Michael Lawne, if you don't stop this instant—"

"Oh, I don't intend to stop," he warned, his eyes simmering with passion that took her breath away. "I'll never stop loving you. Ever."

The smile that rose to her lips came from the depths of her soul. "And your sons?" she asked sweetly as she led him to the two trees they had planted together after each of their sons' births.

Michael looked at the saplings and nodded solemnly. "You have given me the greatest gift—"

"Look again, Michael," she urged and turned him to his left.

In the center of a small mound of freshly dug earth stood a small seedling, its bed rimmed with small stones. He gulped hard and turned to face her. "JoHannah?"

Her heart overflowed with joy and the blessed wonder of the new life within her. "In early winter. I—I didn't want to wait to plant the—"

He pulled her into his arms, and she could feel him tremble. "I love you," she whispered, just before he claimed her lips in a kiss that seared her—body and soul.

He locked his gaze with hers, and she trembled anew with the love that churned in the fathomless depths of his gray eyes. "You have made every dream come true for me," he rasped as he curled a lock of her hair around his finger.

Deliriously happy and feeling uncommonly bold, she undid the lacings on his shirt.

"Wanton woman," he groaned as he planted his hands around her waist.

She grinned and snuggled close. " 'Tis a cross you will have to bear."

"Not a cross," he countered as he stroked her cheek with the back of his hand. "A wondrous gift. One we share with one another," he said softly as he proceeded to unwrap the precious wrapper of love that was his wife. "I love you," he whispered.

"Beyond eternity," she responded, knowing that even when they had passed to the next realm, they would carry the gift of their love with them . . . along with memories of the wondrous world they had created on God's precious earth.

Together.

Against the backdrop of an elegant Cornwall mansion before World War II and a vast continent-spanning canvas during the turbulent war years, Rosamunde Pilcher's most eagerly-awaited novel is the story of an extraordinary young woman's coming of age, coming to grips with love and sadness, and in every sense of the term, coming home...

Rosamunde Pilcher

The #1 *New York Times* Bestselling Author of *The Shell Seekers* and *September*

COMING HOME

"Rosamunde Pilcher's most satisfying story since *The Shell Seekers*."

—*Chicago Tribune*

"Captivating...The best sort of book to come home to...Readers will undoubtedly hope Pilcher comes home to the typewriter again soon."

—*New York Daily News*

COMING HOME
Rosamunde Pilcher
_____ 95812-9 $7.99 U.S./$9.99 CAN.

Royd Camden is a prisoner of his own "respectability." But when he sees beautiful Moriah Lane—condemned by society and sentenced to prison for a crime she didn't commit—he cannot ignore her innocence that shines through dark despair. He swears to reach the woman behind the haunted eyes, never dreaming that his vow will launch them both on a perilous journey that will test her faith and shake his carefully-wrought world to its foundation. But can they free each other from their pasts and trust their hearts to love?

by Delia Parr

"A UNIQUELY FRESH BOOK WITH ENGAGINGLY HONEST CHARACTERS WHO WILL STEAL THEIR WAY INTO YOUR HEART."
–PATRICIA POTTER

For years John Logan had searched for the infant
daughter his wife had taken from him. The trail leads
to Autumn Welles, an artist who paints tinware for a
living and who is posing as the mother of his child.
John knows that Autumn's world is built on the shift-
ing sands of deceit and he plans to use all means necessary to reclaim his child.

Luring her into a tangled web, John leads them across
three states, from Connecticut to Ohio, bound to each
other by a marriage that is supposed to be a charade.
But as the awakening fires begin to touch their souls,
they find in each other a love born in secrets and
deception, and a love that may not survive the changing seasons of their hearts.

The Fire in
❧ Autumn ❧

Delia Parr

No one believes in ghosts anymore, not even in Salem, Massachusetts. And especially not sensible Helen Evett, a widow who lives for her two teenaged kids and who runs the best preschool in town. But when little Katie Byrne enters her school, strange things begin to happen. Katie's widowed father, Nat, begins to awaken feelings in Helen that she had counted as dead. But why does Helen get the feeling that Linda, Katie's mother, is reaching beyond the grave to tell her something?

As Helen and Nat each explore the pain of their losses and the joy of their newfound love, Linda Byrne's ghost plays a bold hand, beseeching Helen to uncover the mystery of her death. But what Helen finds could make her the target of a jealous killer and a modern Salem witch-hunt that threatens her, her family...and the magical second-time-around love that's taking her and Nat by storm.

BESTSELLING, AWARD-WINNING AUTHOR

ANTOINETTE STOCKENBERG

Beyond Midnight